A TOM MARLOWE THRILLER

BROAD
SWORD

NEW YORK TIMES #1 BESTSELLER **TONY LEE** WRITING AS
JACK GATLAND

Hooded Man MEDIA
INNOVATION • PRODUCTION • PUBLICATION

Published by Hooded Man Media.

Cover design by L1graphics

First Edition: May 2024

PRAISE FOR JACK GATLAND

'Fast-paced and action packed, Jack Gatland's thrillers always deliver a punch.'

'This is one of those books that will keep you up past your bedtime, as each chapter lures you into reading just one more.'

'This book was excellent! A great plot which kept you guessing until the end.'

'Couldn't put it down, fast paced with twists and turns.'

'The story was captivating, good plot, twists you never saw and really likeable characters. Can't wait for the next one!'

'Totally addictive. Thoroughly recommend.'

'Moves at a fast pace and carries you along with it.'

'Just couldn't put this book down, from the first page to the last one it kept you wondering what would happen next.'

There's a new Detective Inspector in town...

Before Tom Marlowe had his own series, he was a recurring character in the DI Declan Walsh books!

LIQUIDATE THE PROFITS

An EXCLUSIVE PREQUEL, completely free to anyone who joins the Jack Gatland Reader's Club!

Join at bit.ly/jackgatlandVIP

Also by Jack Gatland

DI DECLAN WALSH BOOKS

LETTER FROM THE DEAD

MURDER OF ANGELS

HUNTER HUNTED

WHISPER FOR THE REAPER

TO HUNT A MAGPIE

A RITUAL FOR THE DYING

KILLING THE MUSIC

A DINNER TO DIE FOR

BEHIND THE WIRE

HEAVY IS THE CROWN

STALKING THE RIPPER

A QUIVER OF SORROWS

MURDER BY MISTLETOE

BENEATH THE BODIES

KILL YOUR DARLINGS

KISSING A KILLER

PRETEND TO BE DEAD

HARVEST FOR THE REAPER

CROOKED WAS HIS CANE

TOM MARLOWE BOOKS

SLEEPING SOLDIERS

TARGET LOCKED

COVERT ACTION

COUNTER ATTACK

STEALTH STRIKE

BROAD SWORD

ROGUE SIGNAL

ELLIE RECKLESS BOOKS

PAINT THE DEAD

STEAL THE GOLD

HUNT THE PREY

FIND THE LADY

BURN THE DEBT

DAMIAN LUCAS BOOKS

THE LIONHEART CURSE

STANDALONE BOOKS

THE BOARDROOM

For Mum, who inspired me to write.

For Tracy, who inspires me to write.

For Alan, who read these until the end.

watching the Home Secretary shudder, and with good cause too. The last time Joanna Karolides had dealt with anything based on artificial intelligence, she found herself kidnapped, and involved in a gunfight on the A40. It was also the reason she'd borrowed one of the most security conscious, armour-plated vehicles the government owned, based on the request of her protection team, "just in case."

In the end, they'd learnt it had been nothing more than a plan by a secret organisation to gather information to sell to the highest bidder, a pepper's ghost, rather than actual phenomenon. But it was still enough to give Karolides goosebumps whenever she heard the name *Fractal Destiny*, and force a twitch when artificial intelligence was mentioned.

'Great,' Karolides sighed, leaning back onto the seat as the car continued to drive through the base. 'So, now we'll have planes that fly with AI. What could possibly go wrong?'

'I think it's more of an enhancement from what I can work out,' Deborah read through the notes. 'The pilot still does everything. The AI just assists. Although I'd like to state loudly that I'm fully supportive of it.'

She winked.

'You know, so if they're listening, and when the robot revolution comes, they'll know I'm one of the friendly meat-suits,' she stage whispered with mock seriousness.

'You're a fan of AI?' Karolides asked. 'You're not worried it'll take your job?'

'I won't be replaced by AI,' Deborah replied with a knowing wink. 'I'll be replaced by a human *using* AI.'

'Well, this will be fun,' Joanna Karolides forced a smile, no longer in the mood for jokes.

The car pulled up, and a tall, slim man in his forties,

wearing the uniform of an RAF Wing Commander walked over, opening the door.

'Home Secretary,' he smiled as he held a hand out for her. 'Welcome to RAF Lossiemouth. I'm Wing Commander Thomas Dovale, Sixth Squadron. I'm afraid the Group Captain is off base today, so I'll be walking you through the testing phase.'

Karolides took the proffered hand, about to emerge from the car.

'He's sick?'

'No, Ma'am, he broke his leg yesterday while rock climbing. He's currently having it looked at,' Dovale replied, peering past her into the car, as if expecting someone to be hiding within. 'I was under the assumption the new Defence Secretary would be attending?'

'Gippy tum, suggested we stop this until he was feeling better, but we in the Home Office felt the test was too far down the line to delay for him,' Karolides replied. 'And I think I'm important enough to attend in his place.'

She winked.

'Although between us, he probably didn't want to be near me.'

Dovale went to reply, curious, but Karolides beat him to it.

'Because they keep dying around me,' she finished.

It was stated so deadpan that Dovale couldn't be sure if it was a jibe or not, and so he weakly smiled back. Karolides wasn't wrong; when Kate Maybury had attempted to steal government data, two Defence Secretaries had died – firstly, Harriet Turnbull, had been shot on stage during a veteran's ball, and then her replacement, Peter Fraser had been shot in the central offices of Whitehall.

Government job security had really plummeted over the last year.

As for the current Minister for Defence, Russell Robertson's food poisoning excuse was probably just that – an excuse not to be anywhere near the cursed Karolides in case someone else was likely to die. Which, considering there was AI everywhere, made a lot more sense.

'So, what's the plan?' she asked, attempting to change the subject, and was surprised to see Wing Commander Dovale climb into the front passenger seat, passing directions to the driver.

'Change of location,' he said as the car turned, slowly returning out of the base now. 'We'd arranged it with the Minister for Defence.'

'Of course you did,' Karolides glanced at her aide. 'I'm guessing he neglected to mention we weren't coming here?'

'No, ma'am,' Deborah replied. 'Probably slipped his mind.'

'Or he wanted to bugger me about,' Karolides muttered. 'So, what's the location, and why do we need to be there, rather than here?'

'We need to be on the cliffs to see the test,' Dovale replied almost apologetically, 'and, well, there's a golf course between us and them.'

'We're playing golf?'

'No, but we have a setup in Burghead, a few miles west of here,' Dovale explained as they continued down the narrow country roads. 'It's a Pictish fort, but nobody visits this time of year, so we have a deal with the council, and a setup we can use when needed.'

'Burghead,' Deborah had pulled up the Wikipedia page. 'A small town in Moray, mainly built on a peninsula that projects north-westward into the Moray Firth, surrounding it by water on three sides.'

She looked up.

'People from Burghead are called Brochers,' she added. 'But there's around two thousand inhabitants there right now. Isn't that a little public for a stealth demonstration?'

'It'll be over the sea, and they're used to that sort of thing,' Dovale replied tersely.

'And there's nowhere more secluded?' Karolides was surprised.

Wing Commander Dovale turned in the passenger seat to face them in the back.

'The north of Moray is filled with holiday homes, golf clubs, holiday camps and more golf clubs,' he explained. 'Better we have a village that knows us, rather than transitory tourists who want to film everything and stick it on TikTok, Ma'am.'

Karolides was tiring of the conversation and so nodded as they drove down the narrow, grey, Burghead streets, where, in the distance she saw some RAF guards at the end of the tarmac.

'Private party,' Wing Commander Dovale said with a wry smile as he saluted the guards, who quickly stepped aside, allowing the car through.

In the car park for the visitors' centre, they finally climbed out of the car, Karolides pausing as she saw the empty field looking over the North Sea.

Not quite the view you were hoping, eh? she thought to herself with a rueful smile.

Now in his element, Dovale stood confidently before Karolides and Jones, a dossier in his hand, having been passed to him as they walked past the visitors' centre.

'Now, you'll be aware that the aircraft you're about to see is not just any stealth fighter, it's been reconfigured with the latest advancement in artificial intelligence, codenamed "Broad Sword,"' he began, ensuring his tone was both informative and accessible. 'This AI doesn't replace the pilot, but works alongside them, enhancing decision-making and responsiveness in complex combat scenarios.'

He flipped open the dossier to a diagram of the aircraft, pointing to the integrated systems.

'Again, you'll be aware that—'

'Let's just assume I'm aware of nothing, and treat me like someone hearing it for the first time,' Karolides interrupted. 'It's been a long day and if you keep informing me how I'm aware of things, we'll be here even longer.'

Dovale took a breath and nodded.

'Broad Sword is designed to process vast amounts of data in real-time, from enemy positions to potential threats, and even calculate the most efficient attack routes,' he explained authoritatively. 'It can suggest manoeuvres, manage onboard systems to optimise stealth and performance, and even take control if the pilot is incapacitated.'

'But to be clear, the AI doesn't replace the pilot?' Karolides frowned.

'Essentially correct ma'am, but for short periods, and only in a life or death, last-case scenario, the AI will decide on one of two protocols,' Dovale replied. 'If there's an attack, it'll use what we call the *Pacifier* protocol, which is to remove the now incapacitated pilot from all danger by suppressing whatever forces are against them; its programming is to get the pilot out of harm's way, and in doing so take on any enemy, but only in defence, so responding to a missile rather than launching one deliberately.'

Karolides nodded. She understood this.

'And the other?'

Dovale shifted a little.

'It's called the *Devastator* protocol,' he continued. 'It'll decide the pilot's life must be protected at all costs. And will react with ruthless aggression, limiting the threat to life by taking out potential attackers.'

'That being?'

'Firing first - killing anything and everything it deems as a threat - and fulfilling mission parameters if the goal is bigger than the pilot's immediate safety,' Dovale said ominously. 'This way, a mission can still continue if the pilot is incapacitated.'

He then smiled, his face brightening.

'We won't be seeing that now, however, as today's demonstration will showcase Broad Sword's capabilities in a simulated combat environment.'

He paused, likely for some kind of dramatic intent, his eyes meeting the Home Secretary's, emphasising the significance.

'You'll witness its ability to seamlessly integrate with the pilot's commands, making split-second adjustments to flight path, targeting, and evasion tactics. This is a leap forward in our operational effectiveness, offering unparalleled support to our pilots and a significant edge in air superiority.'

He allowed the weight of his words to sink in.

'The integration of AI systems like Broad Sword into our defence arsenal represents the future of combat aviation. It's not just about having the most advanced aircrafts anymore, but about how we augment their capabilities with intelligent systems to protect our skies more effectively.'

He looked out onto the bay now, his eyes glazing slightly as if his mind was a thousand miles away.

'Seeing how drone warfare in Ukraine over the last few years has progressed immeasurably, shows us that the future of aviation would be both human centred *and* software centred warfare,' he continued. 'I was involved in the early trials of Broad Sword, and not only can it assist a pilot, but it can link via a hive-mind control collar to other fighters, drones, missiles – the list is endless. In a world where soverign states are more and more relying on drones to keep their skies safe, imagine an RAF fighter that could enter enemy airspace, and then *override* every drone fighter sent to nullify it? That could turn those enemy crafts into allies?'

'It's a sobering thought,' Karolides admitted.

As he concluded his explanation, Wing Commander Dovale offered a reassuring smile.

'I'm confident that what you're about to see will not only demonstrate the technological marvel that is Broad Sword but also reaffirm our commitment to maintaining a cutting-edge defence posture.'

There was a long, awkward silence, as Dovale seemed to be waiting again for some kind of applause. Karolides looked over at Deborah, wondering if she, too, was feeling the same uncertainty about the situation. It felt very much like this was a rehearsed speech for Robertson, which had been completely wasted on the two women standing in front of him.

Eventually, Dovale, realising there was no imminent emergence of applause, whoops or cheering for him, straightened, and almost with a saddened resignation, held his hand out to point towards a viewing platform created on what looked to be a children's play area, fifty yards to the right. It was a set of stairs that led to what looked to be effectively a grey-walled Portakabin, the roof seemingly covered with radio antennas.

'This is the viewing platform?' Deborah asked, surprised. 'I had expected—'

She didn't get a chance to finish as Dovale laughed.

'Were you expecting some kind of skybox?' he inquired, a little too patronisingly. 'Perhaps people serving you drinks as you watch the show? I'm afraid here at the RAF, we're a little more ready for action.'

He continued, not looking at Karolides as he spoke, but the words obviously meant for her.

'You might be our Home Secretary for the moment, but we've been here for decades and will be here for decades more, just as we are.'

Karolides bristled at the immediacy of his statement. It sounded very much like he was waiting for her to be replaced.

Maybe he was a voter for the other side, she thought to herself, as she gave him a warm and incredibly fake smile and started over towards the Portakabin.

At least it was moveable, she thought to herself. *The poor buggers of Burghead didn't have to look at it every day.*

'Can you remind us who'll be with us here today?' Deborah asked, trying to keep things civil. 'The advanced briefing material was a bit sketchy if I recall. Probably because it was meant for the Minister for Defence.'

Dovale checked his notes.

'We will be meeting members of the technical team most associated with Project Broad Sword here in the UK,' he read from the notes now. 'They will be available to answer any questions you may have at a more understandable level.'

For the second time in as many minutes, Karolides bristled; but then she realised the chances were the questions they would expect would be far more complicated than she could ask anyway, so the idea of having someone a bit more baseline was probably a good thing.

'Anybody from the team that created the AI?'

'No, Ma'am. Doctors Moritz and Eskildsen are in Spain, still working on the code.'

'But the device is here in Scotland?'

'They can link to the network, and remotely update the software if needed, over the MoD Skynet Communications satellite. Like when your phone gets a new Operating System update overnight.'

Deborah winced.

'Skynet and AI,' she muttered. 'What could possibly go wrong.'

Karolides understood the trepidation. The Skynet series of military communication satellites had been around since the sixties – but since the *Terminator* movies also used the name, the thought of rampaging AI-based kill machines connected to "Skynet" was never closer than right now.

'You said if needed,' Deborah frowned, changing the subject. 'Is it needed?'

Dovale didn't answer, looking back at the Portakabin.

'As you will also be aware, we also have some executives from the firm that created the new stealth fighter,' he tailed off. 'It's based on a Lockheed Martin F-35 Lightning II, the current F35 Stealth design, and it's powered by a Pratt & Whitney F135, who create the most powerful fighter engines in the world.'

He'd started recalling off facts as he walked, checking his

top notes, likely passed to him from the Base's Group Captain, as he did so.

'It produces over forty thousand pounds of thrust, and comprises a three-stage fan, a six-stage compressor, an annular combustor—'

'A what?'

Wing Commander Dovale sighed, probably a little louder than he had intended, and turned to face the Home Secretary.

'All right, let's boil it down to the essentials, since time is money, and I'm sure you have very important places to be,' he said. Karolides couldn't quite work out if he was being patronising or not, so deadpan was his expression. 'The annular combustion is basically the heart of a jet engine. Imagine a big metal doughnut – not the kind you eat, but one that's crucial for flying. In this metal doughnut, air and fuel meet, and this controlled inferno blasts the jet forward, turning expensive fuel into even more expensive travel experiences.'

Karolides gave a wide smile.

'Thank you for explaining,' she said in mock-innocence. 'Please continue.'

'Well, there's also a single-stage, high-pressure turbine, and a two-stage, low-pressure turbine,' Dovale replied, almost waiting for Karolides to ask again. 'Anyway, there's execs from both Pratt & Whitney and Lockheed in the viewing area. They were rather hoping to see the Defence Secretary.'

'I'm sure they were,' Karolides nodded, realising that it might not have been her that Robertson had been wanting to avoid. The chances were if Lockheed board members and experts sat waiting in the Portakabin, they'd be hoping to discuss research budgets to perfect this wonderful device.

Both Lockheed and Pratt & Whitney were likely incredibly keen to remain associated with the Broad Sword project, in the hope that a successful series of trials would prompt a deployment into RAF fighters – because then they'd have a chance to make the *big* sales.

'Look,' she said, calmly and coldly, 'I'm here to see a plane. I was asked to come along by the Prime Minister himself. The Minister for Defence can't make it, and I understand that you're very sad, and I'll do my best to keep in with your little boys' club. But know this now; once this is over, I will get in my big, black, armoured car and drive off out of this quaint little village. I will not be investing in small talk, or listening as you try to sell me the next big thing, especially as the people who created the AI couldn't even be bothered to turn up.'

Wing Commander Dovale straightened, turned and stared at her.

'The *aircraft* in its current state might not be RAF,' he replied, 'but some of the engineers connected to the AI are RAF, and the pilot *definitely* is RAF. I don't care what you do with the people in that room, Ma'am, but I would expect you to give the RAF the respect it deserves.'

'That's what she's saying,' Deborah quickly stepped in. 'She's here to see the RAF side, not the sales and marketing side. Aircraft manufacturers are one thing, but the AI is external to the suited men in that cabin. And I think you can agree, being blindsided and taken out of the base, driven over to a small town miles away, complete with board members of the companies that made the aircraft does sound a little like a corporate ambush – especially when the Group Captain isn't here, and you were part of the original plans and designs, so have a more than personal stake in the success of the project.'

Dovale softened slightly, nodding briskly as he motioned for them to follow him up the steps.

'For our records, can I confirm the name of the pilot?' Deborah asked. 'I'm guessing it's not you?'

'Squadron Leader Richard Mille,' Dovale replied.

'Like the watch?'

Dovale paused and stared back.

'Richard Mille,' Deborah continued. 'They make amazing watches.'

'I don't think this is the same man,' Wing Commander Dovale forced a smile, obviously tiring of the conversation as, opening the door, he ushered the two women into the room.

KAROLIDES WAS NOT SURPRISED TO SEE THAT THEY WERE THE *only* two women in the room not in uniform. In fact, the levels of alpha-male testosterone that now wafted across to her could have been found in any sports club locker room. Still, she smiled, stepped forward, and shook hands with all the proffered gold-watch-adorned boardroom palms that were held out to her.

'Squadron Leader Mille is already in the air,' Wing Commander Dovale said, pointing out at the large window in front of them that looked out across the North Sea. 'We've provided a few tactical tests for him to run through, and the AI device will learn as it goes along.'

He pointed to a bank of computer monitors at the side; a member of the air control team, the stripes of a Flight Lieutenant on her shoulder, and the only other woman in the Portakabin, currently working the console.

'This is a recreation of a rival country's radar and anti-aircraft awareness unit, connected to RAF Lossiemouth, and run by Flight Lieutenant Rutter, who has been involved in Broad Sword since the start of this phase of testing,' he added. 'As you can see here, Squadron Leader Mille has not appeared, therefore he is not around us.'

Dovale stopped, looking around the room, almost torn, before turning back to Karolides.

'Are you absolutely sure the Minister for Defence—'

'He's not coming, and even if he was, he'd never bloody find us here,' Karolides replied tartly. 'Just start the sodding test.'

There was a nod, a reluctant sigh, and Dovale turned to Rutter, waiting for his response. A second, more curt nod to her, and she started whispering into the radio.

'As you can see, Broad Sword is still not within our radar range,' he said. 'Our stealth jet has a maximum speed of Mach one-point-six, which is one-point-six times the speed of sound. In layman's terms, that's over a thousand miles an hour—'

As he said this, there was a low rumble, and a whoosh of displaced air as an aircraft flew over the top of the Portakabin at speed. It was the stealth fighter, black and sleek, and half of the old, rich, suited men, who a moment earlier had been giving their strongest alpha-male handshake, stumbled to their knees as if expecting the aircraft to crash through the top of the Portakabin, or for the roof itself to fall in, which, as Karolides had surmised, was possibly something that could have happened, given the state of the place.

Wing Commander Dovale smiled, looking around, one of the few people who hadn't ducked – mainly as he'd expected it.

'My apologies,' he said. 'It looks like our enemy's radar did *not* pick up Broad Sword.'

At this, Karolides grinned. She was also one of the few that hadn't ducked, expecting such a stunt. She might not have liked Wing Commander Dovale that much; he seemed stuffy and very much a jobsworth, but that he too had taken great delight in annoying the suits made him, in part, tolerable.

'Greyhound to Broad Sword, Greyhound to Broad Sword,' Flight Lieutenant Rutter spoke into the microphone.

'*This is Broad Sword,*' the voice of Squadron Leader Mille spoke through the speakers.

'Are you ready to begin task one?'

'*I am,*' Squadron Leader Mille replied. '*But I—*'

There was a pause, and static.

'*I'm sorry,*' Squadron Leader Mille's voice came through once more, slightly more stressed, '*I have an issue, please wait.*'

The radio turned off and, as they watched, they saw Broad Sword lazily turning over the Moray Firth. Karolides glanced at Dovale, who seemed rather perturbed at the shortness of the conversation. It didn't feel like he was annoyed that a Squadron Leader had spoken to him and ordered him to wait; it felt more like a worry that something wasn't going to plan.

The radio screeched as the connection restarted.

'*Greyhound, this is Broad Sword, Greyhound, this is Broad Sword, we have a problem.*'

Dovale, seeing the concerned expressions on the surrounding suits, walked over to the bank of computer screens, leaning past the Flight Lieutenant, tapping and leaning closer to the microphone.

'Repeat again, repeat again, what seems to be the problem?' he hissed.

'Greyhound, Broad Sword is not responding,' Mille's voice was calm, but Karolides could hear the stress within it. *'It's trying to do things that it shouldn't be doing, and it's trying to take control of the stealth fighter. I'm forcing myself to stay calm because it's reading my heart rate, and if ...'*

He faded away as the static overtook his voice.

'What's going on?' Deborah asked.

Dovale looked back, and Karolides could see this was definitely not one of the stunts. He was genuinely concerned here.

'Broad Sword can check every bio-based data stream of the pilot's wellbeing,' he said. 'Heart rate, stress levels, heat, the lot – it's a smart-ring on steroids. The problem is, if Squadron Leader Mille starts to get stressed, Broad Sword's AI might think there's something *more* going on ...'

'And it might think he's under attack, and move into *Pacifier*, or *Devastator* protocol,' Karolides finished the sentence the reluctant Wing Commander was delaying in speaking. 'Is it armed?'

'If you're enquiring whether the aircraft is armed, then yes,' Wing Commander Dovale looked around. 'I'm sure it's just a glitch—'

'Mayday, mayday, mayday, it's—it's—no, wait, don't—Christ no! Wait—'

That was all Squadron Leader Mille could say before there was an explosion out over the sea. As the crowd now turned in shock and awe to observe it, they saw the pilot eject from the aircraft, the parachute opening as Broad Sword and millions of pounds of expensive stealth fighter lazily spun in a slow circle, and crashed into the Moray Firth.

Karolides looked over at Flight Lieutenant Rutter, now frantically pressing buttons, flicking switches, and typing on her keyboard.

'Is he okay?'

'It looks so,' Rutter looked back over to Wing Commander Dovale. 'He ejected from the fighter before it crashed and the parachute will bring him down two miles northeast from here.'

'Probably in the middle of a bloody golf course. Get a helicopter out there now,' Dovale grumbled irritably as he looked over at Karolides.

'I am so sorry about this,' his attention turned back to the Flight Lieutenant as he continued. 'We thought it was ready.'

'It was ready, sir,' Rutter replied, turning and rising from her seat to stand at attention, literally forcing herself to push any anger from her tone. 'We'd worked for weeks to get it ready, and Doctor Moritz herself examined the code after I set it.'

'It's fine,' Karolides gave a smile. 'I'm sure you'll be able to get the aircraft out of the sea. We'll fix whatever it is, and next time the Minister for Defence can come.'

She turned to the other men in the Portakabin, probably all seeing their end-of-year bonuses go up in smoke matching the plume now rising from the water, gave them a nod and without saying anything else, left them to their own conversations.

Nobody went to shake her hand this time.

———

As they walked down the steps, she turned to Deborah, giving a faint smile.

'Let's just get back to London, where things work properly,' she said before pausing, staring out across the Moray Firth, and past it to the North Sea, where the plume of smoke still rose above the water.

There was something off here, but she couldn't say what. Dovale had been unnaturally desperate for Robertson to be there – why? It wasn't the first time a Home Secretary had replaced a Minister for Defence. Was it because of his Group Captain's accident? Or was there something more going on here? Backhanders, perhaps? Robertson was a sneaky, untrustworthy bastard at the best of times.

She chuckled.

'Bloody AI,' she said as she climbed into the Ministerial car. 'Bane of my life. Can we stop on the way back? I think I saw a fish and chip shop down the road.'

1

THE WAKE

Tom Marlowe utterly *detested* funerals.

He'd been an attendant at too many in his time, and recently the death toll had been rising more rapidly than he cared for. He'd only been back in London for three days before he heard the news; Monty Barnes had passed away. If he was being honest, it hadn't surprised him much. The man was in his nineties, and had recently been the victim of a rather traumatic experience involving a beating by a gang of teenage louts, led by a wannabe Essex gangster.

Marlowe had gained revenge for Monty's attack, but he was aware it hadn't been enough. However, he'd foolishly thought he'd fixed what needed to be done. Monty's great-grandson Sammy was now free of a life of crime he had accidentally found himself in, a bad apple had been sent packing, and Marlowe had left for Las Vegas, hoping that Monty and his great-grandson could reconnect, spend some time together – some *quality* time before Monty eventually shuffled off this mortal coil.

Of course, that hadn't been expected to be for quite a while. Even though Monty was nine decades old, he was fitter than half the people Marlowe knew. If anybody was going to live to get a letter from Buckingham Palace when they hit a hundred, Monty was top of Marlowe's list.

But now he was dead.

He had been found on the hallway carpet of his apartment. There were no wounds, no injuries, no sign of any kind of fight on his body. Things had been too much for him.

The apartment, however, was a different story.

The wooden door to the apartment had been shattered into pieces, some kind of controlled and shaped explosion blasting it inwards. The police, hearing about the recent connection between Monty and an armed Essex gang, had now launched an investigation with Raymond Gibson, known as "Razor" to his friends, as the prime suspect. Perhaps the shock of the explosion had killed Monty, and Razor had run from the scene of the crime? There was nothing missing, and if Razor had entered and found Monty, there was no way in hell he'd have left without leaving a single mark on the old man's face.

The explosives on the door could have been a message for me, Marlowe surmised. *After all, I had used explosives on the door of the Robin Hood pub. Could this have been Razor returning the favour?*

Whatever it was, Marlowe would be looking into it himself. He had a pretty good idea where Razor and his goons would have run to after their confrontation. Before Marlowe had stopped him, he'd been cozying up to Arun Nadal, a serious and vicious player from West London. Arun and his gang were scumbags of the highest order, but Nadal was young, ambitious, and dangerous to know. Just the type of person Razor would offer his services to. Marlowe intended to have a chat with Nadal as soon as he could find him.

There was the sound of an organ starting, and the hymn "Jerusalem" being, well, attempted more than played, and this brought Marlowe back to the present. The church, although small, was filled, which was good to see. Monty had always been a popular person, loved by the people who worked with him and his friends alike. And Marlowe wasn't surprised to see a few familiar faces in the congregation. To the side, sitting at the front, were Marshall Kirk and his daughter Tessa, as Marshall had trained under Monty back in the day, and they'd kept in touch ever since. Emilia Wintergreen, one of the main desks of MI5 now, but also the onetime head of Section D – Marlowe's old unit – sat across the pews from him. She had avoided his gaze throughout the entire funeral.

Marlowe assumed that once more he was in the doghouse.

He'd also been surprised to see Alexander Curtis at the funeral. It had been a few months since he'd last seen the man, shot in the line of duty; a vicious chest wound that almost cost him his life. Slim, and in his fifties, Curtis had stepped down on leave while he recovered, but it seemed that now he was preparing to come back.

That, or he was about to fight Emilia Wintergreen for the role of London Section Chief of MI5.

Marlowe actually didn't know which of them would win that. Wintergreen was a stone-cold bitch, but Curtis had literally been shot in the heart, or as near as dammit, and come back for more.

Marlowe looked away before he caught Curtis's eye, but paused as he scanned the church once more. There, two rows in front and to the side of him, Marlowe could see Sir Walter McKellan. Old-school British spy through and through; lean, vicious-looking and in his sixties, McKellan had been Deputy Director of MI6 but had almost lost everything when Kate Maybury had made him the scapegoat of her plan to take Fractal Destiny, because of his clandestine role in the discredited Caliburn think-tank.

A plan that Marlowe had unwittingly helped in the process.

He'd also been there when McKellan was shot in the foot by Trix, so he guessed he wasn't high on McKellan's Christmas list these days.

Marlowe had arrived late, so sat near the back. He hadn't wanted to make a scene. He hadn't wanted to speak to anybody if he was being honest. There were too many questions being asked at the moment. Questions involving secret organisations named *Orchid*, and his loyalty, whether it was to King and country, or to something far darker.

The funeral service continued on as the congregation rose to sing the hymn, but Marlowe wasn't really listening as they finished, sitting back down as the priest at the front gave a eulogy. All he could think of was Monty's last time at his house.

He had arrived broken and bleeding, and Marlowe had actually believed, for a split second that Monty had done this to himself, purely to get information on Orchid. Marlowe had promised to fix things, and had done so, but he'd never had that conversation afterwards with Monty – the one where he finally knew for sure whether Monty had played him or not, or whether there was more to be said.

And now he wouldn't.

At the front, sitting with his family, was Sammy Barnes. He'd glanced back at Marlowe when he'd arrived in the middle of the service, even flashed him a smile and a nod. Marlowe had nodded back, sliding into a back pew, melding into the woodwork, using years of tradecraft skills to, well, hide from the rest of the mourners.

And then it was over.

The service was finished.

Now the body would be taken to be cremated, as per Monty's wishes.

Marlowe wasn't staying. He'd said enough goodbyes.

MARLOWE EMERGED FROM THE CREMATORIUM'S CHAPEL, walking back to his car, trying to get to the burgundy Jaguar XJ before anyone reached him. He hadn't wanted to speak to anybody. He wasn't in the mood.

But he should have guessed that wasn't going to happen today.

'Marlowe!'

After hearing his name called, he paused, turning back to see Marshall Kirk, standing, watching him from the chapel's entrance.

'You okay?'

Marlowe shrugged, then, deciding to be honest, shook his head.

'I know what you mean – I can't believe the old bugger's dead,' Marshall walked over, shaking his own head as he did so. 'That guy was going to outlive all of us. You know I started my fitness regime purely so I could reach the same age as he was? You look at Monty Barnes, you immediately realise that you could enjoy a long and healthy retirement, you know?'

'I don't think any of us in this business have long and happy anythings, Marshall,' Marlowe made an attempt at a smile, but his attention was diverted by Emilia Wintergreen emerging from the chapel.

'Going to speak to your old boss?' Marshall enquired, a little too innocently.

Marlowe smiled and shook his head.

'I'm not here looking for a job,' he said.

'Well, of course not. You don't need one anymore, do you?' Marshall raised an eyebrow. 'You have *your* own job.'

Marlowe said nothing in return, but the message was clear. Marshall Kirk had been in Vegas and knew the situation that Marlowe was currently in. Whether he had told anybody else was up for debate, but Marlowe hoped he hadn't. Marshall was a good man, and Marlowe would have hated to feel that he had misjudged him. Also, there was the point that Marlowe would probably require the man's help down the line, as he took on the mission he'd given himself.

Once he worked out what the mission was, exactly.

'You in town long?' Marshall asked, knocking him out of his thoughts.

Marlowe shrugged.

'In and out, I think,' he said. 'I need to start—'

'You don't need to tell me what you need to do,' Marshall shook his head. 'If anything, I'd rather not know. Plausible deniability and all that, yeah? But know when you need me, I'm just a phone call away. Okay?'

Marlowe nodded, shaking Marshall's hand. Marshall looked back into the church.

'Tessa's in there,' he added. 'You could go say hi.'

'I'm not really in a small talk mood right now,' Marlowe shook his head. 'Tell her I said hi, and I promise I'll contact her soon.'

Reluctantly Marshall nodded and once more they shook hands. But, as Marlowe turned to leave, he saw across the crematorium a figure watching from the far edge of the car park, in a long black coat, buttoned up to the neck, his hands in his pockets.

Frank Maguire.

Frank had been the gangland boss who had originally employed Razor, who had, in turn, employed Sammy. When Marlowe, under his alias of Irish bomb-maker Kieran Lachlan had asked for Sammy to be released from this, and for Razor to be punished for his actions towards Monty, Frank had used this to his own advantage and asked Marlowe to remove Razor from his employ by any means necessary, in the process allowing Sammy his freedom, while removing a traitorous problem in his side, now aware Razor had been meeting with Nadal.

He'd also known about the attack on Monty, so this could have been nothing more than Frank Maguire paying his respects, but seeing Marlowe there was not a good sign. He didn't know Marlowe; he knew *Lachlan*, and that's how Marlowe wanted to keep it.

Marlowe turned and walked away, hoping that Frank hadn't really paid attention to the people walking out. However, once more, before he could reach his car and escape, Marlowe was stopped again; this time it was Alexander Curtis. He no longer had his arm in a sling, but he carried himself with a stiffness at the shoulder that someone with a recent gunshot wound to the upper chest would do. Marlowe recognised it, as he had his own stiffness there.

'I was hoping you'd be here,' Curtis said, as Marlowe sighed and turned to face him, a resigned expression on his face. 'I need to have a word.'

'Curtis, I don't work for MI5 anymore, haven't you heard?' Marlowe smiled. 'It seems I'm a bit of a hot commodity at the moment.'

He narrowed his eyes.

'Or are you thinking of turning me into an *asset?*'

Curtis shook his head.

'I know nothing about that,' he replied, and for a moment Marlowe actually believed him. 'Look, I'm not on active duty yet, but I *am* warming my seat back up. I had a phone call last night. Joanna Karolides.'

'The Home Secretary?' Marlowe frowned. 'What's so surprising about that? You were London desk. You will be again once you're back on active duty. Of course she's going to go to you; she hates Wintergreen.'

'She wasn't contacting me as MI5,' Curtis continued, almost apologetically. 'She was contacting me because she knew I'd be seeing you today.'

'Me?'

'She needs a favour. And she was hoping you could help.'

Marlowe hadn't meant to make such an audible groan at this, and Curtis laughed.

'Yeah, I'm not the biggest fan either, but she was stressed. Wouldn't even tell me. Only reason she did, is because I'm not on active duty right now. Which to me, makes me think—'

'She doesn't trust MI5 right now,' Marlowe finished the sentence. 'Did she say where and when?'

Curtis looked around, unconsciously checking for eavesdroppers, before leaning in.

'*Westminster Arms*, back room, noon, tomorrow.'

Marlowe didn't need to ask the address; there was only one pub with that name they'd both know.

'She said you owed her, but if you went, she'd owe you,' Curtis continued. 'Go alone, though.'

Marlowe knew what Curtis was insinuating.

Don't take Trix.

'Hey, on that note,' Marlowe replied, now back into "normal conversation" mode, whatever the hell that was. 'When you take over MI5 again, are you going to un-suspend Trix Preston?'

At this, Curtis raised his eyebrows in surprise.

'I can't,' he said. 'I thought you knew?'

'Knew what?'

Curtis adjusted his stance, and Marlowe wondered whether this was purely to give him time to consider the answer.

'Trix quit a week ago,' he said. 'When she got back from whatever happened in Vegas. She's working her notice out while suspended, but she won't be coming back.'

Marlowe wanted to shout, to swear, to punch something. Last he'd seen her, she'd taken a share of the Vegas takings, but also agreed to assist Marlowe in stopping a civil war within Orchid, in the process taking down St John Steele, before he returned the favour. Marlowe had been considering this as more a "contract" role for her, while she waited out her suspension.

But apparently she'd decided to go full time.

'Thanks,' Marlowe shook Curtis's hand. 'I hope things work out for you.'

'You act like we'll never see each other again,' Curtis

laughed. 'Come on, Marlowe. Whatever sneaky shit you're about to drag Trix Preston into, you know we'll end up getting involved.'

Marlowe tried not to smile in return, mainly as Curtis didn't know how true that was. His own agent, Vikram Saeed, was an Orchid asset, as were many others in the Security Service.

'Speak soon, then,' he said, nodding briefly as he saw Sammy, emerging from the chapel and looking around, he turned and walked swiftly over to his car, finally climbing in and driving off before anyone else could stop him.

THE MAN BY THE GRAVESTONES WATCHED THE CAR DRIVE OFF, following it with his eyes as long as he could, before he shook off the cold, straightening, and pulling the lapels of his pea coat up. He wasn't dressed for a funeral; he was tall and slim, with a black sweater under the coat and red chinos over Timberland boots. He had a blue, tweed "baker's boy" cap on that covered most of his brown and silver peppered short hair. His face was pockmarked and scarred down the left-hand side, but it didn't seem to bother him.

'You here for the funeral?' a voice asked, and the man turned to see Frank Maguire, also standing, looking over at him.

'No, not really,' the man replied casually. 'You?'

'Mourning a veteran, whose death was indirectly caused by my actions,' Maguire replied, looking back at the car park. 'Although I think I just saw a familiar face.'

'You see a lot of them at funerals, I've been told.'

'So, why you here, then?' Maguire asked, turning to fully face him.

The man grinned.

'I'm just the gravedigger,' he said with a tip of the cap, before walking off. 'I'm waiting for my next job.'

———

Best not to think about such things.

Joanna Karolides nodded as Marlowe entered, waving him to the seat opposite. Marlowe did as asked, sitting down, folding his arms and leaning back as he stared at her.

'I must admit, this is quite a public place,' he said. 'People would have seen me walking in. They would have seen you walking in.'

Karolides shrugged dismissively.

'Let them see me,' she said. 'I'm not doing anything suspicious or secretive. I'm meeting a onetime MI5 agent to discuss an old project, something the Home Secretary might do all over the place. Perhaps I'm meeting you off the record to gather opinions on an asset that I'm looking to gain.'

'Or you need my help,' Marlowe replied, looking at the assistant. 'Have we met before?'

'In passing,' the assistant replied. 'Although we never spoke. I'm Deborah Jones, chief aide to the Home Secretary. It was in Whitehall, when you placed the Home Secretary's life in danger with your foolish stunts and naivety.'

Marlowe held the smile on his face, even though he didn't really want to give anything more to this woman. She had a point, after all.

'And are you a Deborah or a Debbie?' he smiled wider. 'You seem like a Debbie.'

'Deborah is fine, even Ms Jones would be preferable, Mister Marlowe.'

Marlowe nodded, sat back in the chair, and looked at Karolides.

'So, why exactly am I here?' he asked. 'I'm guessing you need my help.'

Karolides didn't reply, but her body language shifted subtly. She was irritated, he could tell.

'I have a problem,' she said. 'Something I was hoping you could fix for me.'

'I'm afraid I don't work for MI5 anymore,' Marlowe replied. 'Perhaps it's something that one of your *actual* civil servant employees could sort out?'

'Only if they had the same skill set you do.'

Marlowe chuckled.

'Ma'am, you own MI5 and MI6. I think there's many people there with the same skills I have.'

Karolides considered this and then shrugged.

'Well then, let's class this as a debt you owe me,' she said. 'I need someone to go in off-record on my behalf and find out something.'

Marlowe leant forward, placing his elbows on the table.

'Buy me a drink and I'll listen,' he said.

'If I buy you a drink, I'll have to claim it,' Karolides smiled, 'and we're not having this meeting. We're in a pub. You're giving me a report, nothing more.'

Marlowe sighed, looking around the room.

'So, what trouble has the government got itself into this time?' he asked.

'Actually, it's not the government.' Karolides pushed a file across the table. Marlowe took it, opening it up.

'Project Broad Sword?' he asked, looking back at her.

'Stealth fighter based on the Lockheed F-35.' Karolides looked over at Deborah, indicating for her to continue. Deborah stared back at her boss and then reluctantly opened up her notebook, theatrically sighing as she did so.

'The stealth fighter in question has an AI device known as Broad Sword built into it,' she explained. 'It's not there to replace the pilot, but assist him, and it's a Defence Department situation.'

'Then why are you looking into it?' Marlowe asked. 'Surely this is MI6 and the Ministry of Defence's issue?'

'Your guess is as good as mine,' Deborah sighed.

'Because I went to Scotland to watch it fly,' Karolides replied, ignoring her aide, 'and instead, I watched it crash into the water. The pilot was able to eject safely, but the plane was lost in the Moray Firth.'

'Apparently not deep enough,' Deborah returned to the conversation now, looking back at Marlowe. 'Within hours of the crash, the Royal Navy sent in some divers looking for it. We were hoping it wasn't so deep that we couldn't retrieve it. And as it was, they found it was easily reachable. They're still removing the aircraft from the water right now. However ...'

She trailed off, as if unsure of what to say.

'However, the AI device is missing.'

Marlowe considered the statement.

'Do you mean destroyed?' he asked. 'Maybe it exploded, and that's what caused the crash?'

'No, it was in a literal black box, the kind that flight recorders go into,' Deborah replied. Marlowe noted that it wasn't a snarky-style response. She had fallen into a professional mode now.

Someone had gone in and taken it out.

Marlowe examined the file once more.

'It says here that during the test, the pilot ... Mille?' he looked up.

Karolides nodded, and Marlowe continued.

'This pilot was complaining about the AI before the crash. So, I'm guessing someone must have got in there between the moment the aircraft hit the water and you guys arrived to take it back. How long was the opening?'

Karolides pursed her lips as she considered the question.

'Not more than a matter of hours,' she said. 'The RAF and Royal Navy were quick to move to retrieve it. I think they had people in the water later that same day, definitely before I arrived back at Whitehall, and government jets are fast.'

'So, whoever did this expected the accident,' Marlowe examined the file further as he spoke. 'This is the only way they could have got in there quickly. They must have had the equipment ready. They might even have been in the water waiting as the aircraft crashed. Did Mille aim the aircraft at the water to save lives, or did he eject out before the aircraft made its final trajectory?'

'He didn't eject himself,' Deborah replied. 'He was literally evicted from the seat before the aircraft turned and crashed into the water.'

Marlowe nodded at this.

'So, basically, someone hacked the AI, or the AI itself decided it would remove him, jettisoned him from the aircraft, and then targeted the crashing fighter into a place where they could get to. Was it armed?'

'The AI?' Karolides frowned.

'The stealth fighter,' Marlowe looked up. 'Did it have missiles? Things that could also be taken?'

Understanding now, Karolides shook her head.

'We weren't informed that anything else had been removed,' she replied. 'Just that when they got to the aircraft and immediately went for the black box, they found it was gone.'

Marlowe flicked through the paperwork.

'There's nothing mentioned about armaments being taken,' he said. 'Can you check for me? Speak to someone there?'

'Actually, that's why we're speaking to you now,' Karolides lowered her voice now, and Marlowe realised *this* was the part she didn't want others to know. 'I'd like you to go up to Scotland and investigate this on my behalf. You can take Trix Preston with you as well. I've already vouched for her with Charles Baker. It didn't take much time, as he was the one who originally placed her in MI5.'

Marlowe frowned at this.

'Ma'am, I'm not in MI5 anymore,' he repeated. 'There are plenty of better people that you could speak to who could do this for you ...'

His voice trailed off as he watched Karolides' expression.

'You don't know who to trust, do you?'

'The last time I was involved in anything like this, I learned that people I thought were loyal to the government, MI5 and MI6 agents, were actually part of a secret cabal aimed at bringing down the government. I know there's still members in MI5, hiding in the shadows, and yes, I don't know who I can trust.'

Marlowe accepted this and flicked his attention between Karolides and Deborah as he considered his next move.

Karolides smiled, already anticipating his next comment.

'Yes, I know. I've already been informed about your father and your "funeral gift", she added. 'I also know that the last two times you faced Orchid, you've given them bloody noses and taken out rabid dogs with issues that needed to be removed. If anything, I would say that you're trying to turn Orchid into a force for good rather than the slightly right-wing terrorist organisation everyone believes it is.'

Marlowe said nothing to this. Not because he didn't know what to say, but because the line had brought back a moment from Vegas. A video of his late father staring down from a giant screen.

'*You are your mother's son more than mine, and that has made you strong, stubborn, bloody-minded. And those character aspects are what will get you through this. I hope, in the same way that my son will be taking my company and making the best of it and turning it into something light rather than dark, you can take what I give you and do the same.*'

Marlowe had wondered from that point on whether Taylor Coleman, facing his own mortality, had decided that he would rather Marlowe cleaned up Orchid than allow his other son, Byron, to go down that route and turn it into something worse.

It was irrelevant now, though; Byron was dead, murdered by St John Steele.

'I also thought your connections to Orchid might assist you in this,' Karolides continued. 'After all, if it *was* somebody within their ranks, then you'd be the best person to find out.'

'You mean the best person to throw in the way and see what happens,' Marlowe smiled. 'Don't play me for a fool, Home Secretary. I've had that done to me too many times.'

'And yet you're so good at it,' Deborah replied mockingly, apparently returning to her original attitude. 'Just one look at your résumé shows the amount of times you followed the wrong person or believed in the wrong cause—'

'A second look at my résumé would show you the number of times I've saved the country, the Prime Minister, the Houses of Parliament, and the world,' Marlowe snapped back angrily. 'Don't for one second think you know me.'

'*That's* the Marlowe I want,' Karolides smiled darkly, nodding at Deborah, and again Marlowe realised he was being played, led by the nose. 'You might have left MI5. You might have left the service of King and country. But the service of King and country has not left *you*. I know you'll do what needs to be done.'

'Even if it involves something terrible?'

'These things always involve something terrible, Mister Marlowe,' Karolides said with a sigh. 'All I hope is that the bloodstains don't lead to me.'

Marlowe watched the Home Secretary for a long, quiet moment. Eventually, he straightened, picked up the file, and closed it, holding it in his hand.

'I do this for you,' he said, 'what do I get in return? As opposed to saving the free world as we know it. King and country and all that. Come on, even James Bond got a salary.'

'From what I hear, you don't need one,' Deborah replied, and Marlowe felt that the snark he had heard at the start was definitely returning to her tone. 'If what happened in Vegas is true ...'

'Oh, you know the old adage,' Marlowe grinned .'What happens in Vegas stays in Vegas.'

He glanced back at Karolides.

'If you want me to look into this on your behalf, then I *am* doing it on your behalf, not from the shadows,' he said. 'I want top access, clearance above where I would usually be. If I need to go to somebody high on the food chain, I need to be able to rattle their cage without them getting stressed or kicking me out. You want this solved, you give me the access I need.'

'And if I don't?' Karolides raised an eyebrow.

'Then I'll get Trix Preston to hack into your servers and get it for me,' Marlowe replied, casually leaning back on the chair. 'She has a very good acrylic eye made of your retina.

It'll open the doors we need. But I'd rather it was done officially.'

At this, Joanna Karolides laughed.

'I've heard about the eye, and Preston's offered to make me a copy of Baker's,' she eventually said. 'There are a lot of people hunting for this device and if it gets onto the black market, whoever's got it will make billions if they work out its dirty little secret, and create one of the most dangerous weapons in the world – the *Pacifier* and *Devastator* protocols alone could kill thousands.'

Marlowe shook his head here.

'What's the dirty little secret?' he asked. 'There's nothing in the report.'

'Because it's apparently the next wave of the device,' Karolides leant closer. 'The AI can currently control the fighter, look after the pilot, defend him at all cost. But the software has coding that means down the line it can cold-hack any drone or missile attacking it, taking it over, making it an ally.'

Marlowe nodded, understanding. The AI of a stealth fighter was nice to have; the AI of a stealth fighter that could, down the line take over all over weaponry in the ware became very interesting.

'You could hack a missile, send it to a destination of your choice, and they'd never know it wasn't missile error,' he replied cautiously. 'Terrorists could detonate in cities and nobody would ever be able to link it to them.'

'And the rest,' Karolides replied. 'Imagine if it was used to detonate a nuclear reactor? Sure, it's not possible yet, but down the line...'

'This isn't another Fractal Destiny,' Deborah added, leaning closer. 'This is a real device, something that could actually hurt someone rather than some bollocks Trojan horse purely aimed at gaining money.'

Marlowe had taken enough from this woman, so he straightened, turning to face her.

'When I assisted Kate Maybury,' he said, 'it was because I believed I was doing the right thing, and you might call me naïve for that. But by doing that, you underestimate the abilities of the people she brought in. She didn't only con me; she conned *everybody*. And yes, I helped her. But in the end, I was the one who stopped her when nobody else could. I was the one who stopped a bombing at the Houses of Parliament when nobody else could. I stopped the assassination of President Anton McKay when nobody else could. And I recently took down one of the major financiers of Orchid when no one else could.'

Deborah didn't reply, just a subtle nod to acknowledge that he had spoken to her.

'And that isn't even including the various Czech mercenaries, international assassins, and billionaires he's taken out along the way,' Karolides added to Deborah with a smile. 'You don't need to prove to me that you're one of the good guys, Marlowe. The fact that MI5 doesn't want you in their offices means there's something going on.'

She patted him on the shoulder in a kind of "mates" way and gave him a theatrical wink.

'Besides, if we lose the next election, I might need friends in high places, and I understand you're doing quite well in that respect,' she added, rising from the chair.

Marlowe rose to face her.

'When can I expect—'

He paused as Karolides nodded to Deborah, who pulled a

plastic box from her bag. It was narrow and secure, the type IDs and disks might be held in.

'Oh, it's all in there,' Karolides nodded to the box. 'All the codes you need to enter the highest levels of Whitehall's networks, legitimately. There's even a couple of IDs for you and Miss Preston to use. Real ones, for a change.'

She glanced quickly at Deborah before continuing.

'I knew you'd be accepting, and I wanted to make sure this went quickly. I have plane tickets for you. Government expense, I'm afraid, so it won't be the business class you're more used to. Maybe you can upgrade with Avios or something. Although I'm afraid you won't be able to keep those, either.'

Marlowe chuckled at this.

'Thank you, ma'am,' he said. 'When does the plane leave?'

'You're already running late,' Karolides replied, turning and walking past him. 'Keep me updated, Marlowe.'

'Yes, Home Secretary.'

Marlowe smiled at Deborah as she walked past. She, in return, gave him nothing, which was expected if he was being brutally honest.

WALKING BACK OUT INTO THE MAIN BAR, HE WASN'T SURPRISED to find Trix Preston waiting for him, nursing a pint of cider.

'He wouldn't let me in,' she grumbled, nodding at the barman. 'I'm guessing you've got some kind of stupid mission that you're going to need help on.'

'Actually,' Marlowe flicked through the plastic box,

finding the ID for Trix Preston, 'we're *both* on some kind of stupid mission. Welcome back to MI5.'

Trix looked down at her ID, her eyes widening.

'This is the same clearance as Wintergreen,' she said. 'I won't need to use the 3D ocular printer to fake any eyes this time.'

Marlowe nodded.

'It's going to be a very interesting week,' he said. 'Go pack. We're pretty much leaving immediately.'

3

INVESTORS MEETING

Spencer Neville the Third was his own man, prepared to forge his own identity, destiny, and make his fortune.

At twenty-four years of age, he intended to become one of the youngest billionaires on the Forbes list. Of course, technically he was already a billionaire, thanks to his father, but he wanted to make his *own* billion, to prove he could do it, and silence the rumours, show he wasn't the "nepo baby" people seemed to think he was.

He was an entrepreneur, a go-getter.

The only thing he had going against him was his name.

If he had been simply Spencer Neville, then things would have been easier. He would have still had the Neville name, after all, his father and his grandfather were all Nevilles as well. But he would have had his own concurrent identity.

But he wasn't Spencer Neville. He was Spencer Neville *the Third.* His father was Spencer Neville Junior. His grandfather was Spencer Neville the First, although you never said "the first" unless you had two or three people following you with your name. It was a tradition that many old money families kept; the firstborn child always kept the name. Spencer knew that it was expected of him to have a son and do the same: Spencer Neville the Fourth, the Fifth, the Sixth. It was the American upper class's way of sounding as if they were royalty.

Spencer Neville the Third hated it. It wasn't that he hated the Neville name. It was the fact that the simple line "the Third" made it sound like he was already reaping the harvest his father and grandfather had sowed. That no matter what he did with his life, he would never move from their shadows. He was aware this was something that many people in his position would have felt. It didn't mean he had to be happy with it. His father didn't even use the name himself, often being called by his middle name, "Buck", to disassociate him from his own father. Which made the whole "keep the same name" idea utterly pointless.

So, over the years, Spencer had tried to find ways to move out of his father's shadow. His grandfather had made the Neville fortune in banking, back at a time when banks were trusted, and people would happily put their money into them. "Buck" Neville, the second of the name, had never claimed to be a genius when it came to business. If anything, he'd been lucky, coming in at the start of a global recession and credit crisis, where financial institutions that had been around for centuries crumbled in the space of hours. When he started creating his FinTech empire, it had been out of desperation, looking for a way to latch onto something that he knew would only be around for a short, incredibly profitable amount of time before somebody else cleaned up. He didn't care about research; he didn't care about technology. All he cared about was taking the banking billions that his father had left him and moving it into something that could make trillions.

It was a noble gesture, and an encouraging ambition, but it would never happen. There was always a limit on what could be achieved in such a restricted space. But Spencer the Third, now he was clever. He didn't want to work a day in his life, but he understood how to make others do it for him. He had invested heavily in blockchain, web3, AI – things his father didn't care for, but things that had already made him, percentage-wise, far more of a gross product than his father had at his age.

Most fathers would be proud of their sons for doing this. Spencer had quickly realised that Buck hated his son.

How dare he show up his father, regardless of the fact he was doing exactly what he had done to his own?

Sure, sons were supposed to succeed and build upon what their fathers had left them, but Spencer's father hadn't moved on yet, and as such hadn't left him anything.

Spencer knew how to make money, and from the start knew that to do this, he had to do something extravagant, something grand, something unforgettable. This was why he decided to pick up the slack where Lucien Delacroix had failed, investing in next-gen AI, purely to gain lucrative military contracts.

The software development lab at La Escuela Superior de Ingeniería in Spain was quite sparse for the amount of money paid into it, with only a small server wall and a couple of laptops on the benches, intermingled with parts of what looked to be drone technology – Spencer didn't know if they were, as he'd never really looked into it that much. But this was a testament to show how much of the money was put straight into the research and development of artificial intelligence. Spencer appreciated that. He might have had billions to spare and an expense account that gave him whatever he wanted, whenever he wanted it, but he understood how driven people worked, as he entered the door to the department and walked through it.

He didn't look like a student; Spencer Neville the Third was young and blond, with piercing blue eyes, wearing a white shirt with his collar open, which in turn was under a navy-blue, tailored suit, white leather sneakers finishing this ensemble.

He looked like *money*, though. *Old* money.

At the end of the office, strangely empty of technicians and scientists, was a door. On it had two names:

DOCTOR NORA ESKILDSEN
DOCTOR LINA MORITZ

Spencer went to open the door to walk through, but then paused, and took a moment. This was his first time meeting them properly. Walking through the door without announcing his presence gave a sense of ownership. He didn't expect to knock because he didn't feel he needed to. This would *not* go down well at the first meeting, and so he reined back his ego, knocked three times, and then opened the door; the concession made to at least *pretend* that he cared about their feelings.

In the room were two women, both in their late fifties. One was a harsh-faced, slim woman with short, gunmetal-grey hair in a pixie cut, while the other was more Scandinavian in looks, with long, blonde hair pulled back into a pony-tail. The blonde looked up, frowning.

'Can I help you?' she asked, her voice still holding a tinge of a Scandinavian accent, mixed with what sounded to be crisp British middle-class, probably picked up from her time working in software labs across London.

'I'm Spencer Neville the Third, owner of NevTech,' he said, smiling. 'I'm the guy keeping the lights on right now.'

At the name, both women broke into smiles, and the Scandinavian, Nora Eskildsen, rose from her chair, walking over and shaking Spencer's hand warmly.

'If I'd have known you were turning up, I would have brought cakes and wine,' she said. Spencer gave a small, warm smile. The wines he usually drank were worth more than her yearly salary per bottle. Whatever she would have provided, no matter how much it cost, would have been nothing more than vinegary swill. But he played the part, nevertheless.

'I wanted to make sure everything was going okay,' he said. 'I understand there's been a problem.'

At this, Eskildsen and Moritz – he decided to call them by their surnames mentally, rather than give them the rights of their positions – looked at each other nervously.

'You've heard?'

'Of course I've damn well heard,' Spencer snapped, the smile now gone. 'I've pumped millions into your funding. You think I wouldn't hear if your pilot shit the bed and dumped it in the ocean?'

At this, the two women didn't seem to know what to say. So Spencer carried on, filling the space with his own information.

'Look,' he said, 'I know this was Lucien Delacroix's baby, and I know you've been working with a variety of different governments since he died to keep this going, under names like Charlemagne and all that, but when you said you needed investors to help keep the British Government interested, I came in open-eyed. My brokers gave me the information, and I knew this was something that would help mankind.'

'I thought you came in because you heard your father was about to boost investment, had arranged the assistance of an RAF base, complete with stealth fighter for the next stage of testing, and you wanted to beat him?' Eskildsen raised an eyebrow in amusement.

'Well, there is that,' Spencer conceded. 'But now I'm hearing the pilot had the AI go against him, had to dump the whole thing, including the AI into the ocean. And I've also heard that the Flight Lieutenant, Rutter? She's dead. Killed herself or something.'

At that news, the two women seemed surprised, and Spencer realised that the information he'd paid for was way better than whatever they had been getting.

'Lisa's dead?' Moritz whispered. 'She's been here – *had* been here – since Dovale was. Before Richard Mille, even.'

'Well, either way, that's nothing to the main news. I'm hearing that Broad Sword is missing,' Spencer waved away the concern. 'How much of a problem is this?'

'How much of a problem?' Moritz glanced nervously back at Eskildsen before replying. 'Mister Neville—'

'My *father* is Mister Neville,' Spencer snapped quickly. 'Just call me Spencer.'

'Spencer,' Moritz nodded in acceptance. 'When we created this device for testing stages, we were aware that if it was stolen, it could fall into the wrong hands. We knew people like your father were building their own versions, and to steal our work would bypass years of research and design. Because of that, we put in fail-safes, retinal scans that only the lead design team and the operators could use. There were only five retinal scans that were connected to the system: myself and my partner here, Flight Lieutenant Rutter as she installed the technology into the jet itself, and Squadron Leader Mille, as he needed to be able to access code if needed and refined the war game data that went inside.'

'You said there were five. You've just given me four.'

'The base's Wing Commander, Dovale, was the last one, as he'd been the original pilot before he was promoted, and we never removed him from the access logs when Mille replaced him. It seemed logical to keep him on, while he was still on the base and could oversee the project...'

'Nobody from Lockheed, or the others connected to the aircraft?'

The two women considered this.

'Nobody else has the retinal scan,' Eskildsen answered. 'The aircraft manufacturers created the avionics and comms package the AI was installed in, but not the AI itself. They had no need to be involved, apart from an advisory capacity.'

'If the eye is damaged, the retinal scan does not work,' Moritz continued. 'If someone has taken the device, without the retinal scan to enter the AI's brain, it is nothing but useless hardware. The brain itself would not work.'

Spencer nodded, starting to pace as he considered the outcomes.

'Do you have any idea who could have stolen it?' he asked.

Moritz and Eskildsen shook their heads.

'Well then, let's hope that somebody finds it soon,' he smiled, back to being warm again. 'Is there anything I can do for you in the meantime? Are you working from backups, for example?'

'There are no backups as such, we were working on the

original source code, nothing more,' Moritz admitted ruefully. 'All the data we had was passed across to the RAF base when the testing started. Rutter was the only one who knew where it was, as she would have been in control of the war gaming data, held on software data servers and backup up inside the Ministry of Defence itself, but we never had access to any of that—'

'And now she's dead,' Spencer interrupted angrily, clarifying the fact once more. 'Mille? Dovale?'

'She may have told them, for sure,' Eskildsen nodded. 'But until we know, we'll not be able to gain the demo copy for the trial back.'

'But if you had Broad Sword, you could gain that information back?'

'Yes,' Moritz nodded. 'The entirety of the data is within the brain. Both the AI itself, and the data it works from.'

Spencer sighed, nodding to the two ladies. 'I'm sorry to be the bearer of bad news, in relation to Flight Lieutenant Rutter. I didn't know how important she was to the project.'

He started for the door now, leaving the two ladies alone.

'When I came to you, it was because I was in Spain, and bored,' he finished. 'I took the funding on as a distraction, and yes, to piss off my father, but I now know how important to the world it is. I know the authorities will work this out before something terrible happens. All the best, ladies, and Godspeed.'

'What about the investment?' Moritz asked. 'Are you still behind this?'

'Let's wait until the AI is found before returning to that, yeah?' Spencer smiled as he left the office.

ALREADY STRIDING DOWN THE CORRIDOR, HE HEARD THE DOOR open and shut behind him, and realised that Nora Eskildsen had followed him out.

'What the hell was that?' she snapped as she grabbed him by the arm. 'You *know* not to turn up, you were never supposed to show your face to her.'

Spencer turned and eyed Eskildsen up and down.

'What's the matter, Doctor?' he said almost mockingly. 'Scared your girlfriend might decide to play for the other team? She's not my type, and she's old enough to be my mom for a start.'

'From what I've heard, that's just your type,' Eskildsen muttered. 'I don't know what your plan is, Spencer, but this isn't what we arranged.'

'You think I did this?' Spencer raised an eyebrow at the accusation. 'Sorry to burst your bubble, but this wasn't me.'

He leant in closer.

'When we discussed this, I told you I was unhappy with the deal the British government had given you,' he continued. 'Lucien had his own plans with the French, and your woman in there is still following those. We're not playing with Orchid anymore. We're not playing with the French anymore. We're not playing with governments anymore.'

He paused. He'd almost told her his true plans for the device, how he wanted to use it to ensure that NevTech was the dominant force in Silicon Valley; but that would come later.

'Do you know who stole it?' Eskildsen asked.

Spencer laughed as he looked at her.

'Of course I damn well know,' he said. 'It was my father, trying to take it from me, after I swooped in and took it from him.'

'Your father?'

Spencer nodded, glancing back at the door, making sure that Doctor Moritz couldn't hear.

'He was working with Lucien,' he said. 'When I took this over, I'd overstepped him. Now he wants it back for his new friends.'

He didn't give the name of whoever the new friends were, simply turning and leaving Eskildsen alone in the hallway.

'Go tell your masters in Whitehall that,' he shouted as he walked out of the main door. 'And don't think for one moment I don't know who you really work for, Nora.'

4

PACKING

MARLOWE HAD RETURNED TO HIS DECONSECRATED ONE-TIME-church apartment, unsure of what exactly to pack for the mission. Typically, as an MI5 agent going undercover, he would take minimal items, but recently, he had been travelling with just a go-bag, some gold coins, various denominations of money, and a couple of fake passports in case things got complicated.

This time, however, he was going officially, which felt odd.

He wasn't sure if he liked it.

Trix hadn't been that bothered. But then, Trix was more accustomed to sitting in the back rooms and working on computers. She had only recently acquired her first fake-named passport, whereas Marlowe had been using them for years.

Upon returning to his apartment, he quickly moved down the faux staircase, traversing through the decoy cupboard that led to his underground vault. This vault had been meticulously constructed within the deconsecrated church's crypt over months, with each construction team being replaced by another before they could deduce the true purpose of their work. The upstairs apartment was for show, allowing anyone entry – a fact proven by St John Steele and others since Marlowe had properly moved in –which was pretty much the whole point. The surveillance cameras he had installed allowed him to monitor everything, while he remained concealed in the church's crypt, now his personal "Batcave".

It was also in this crypt that he gathered his armoury. Knowing the ID given to him by Karolides was gold-level and government-issued, meant he could carry weapons officially, a change from having to conceal them.

Also, he was eager to try out a new gun.

The CZ 75BD was the same size and weight as the SIG Sauer P226; a de-cocker, just like the SIG, it had a double-action first round, a single-action follow up, and the magazine capacity could take up to nineteen rounds. It was the same model Ryan Marks had bought for him in Las Vegas; in fact, it was Marks who had sourced this one, too. Despite his preference for the SIG Sauer, the CZ 75 fitted better in his hand and offered more comfort. Its uniqueness also meant he was less likely to be implicated in any future murders, although there was still the issue of Byron Coleman's murder in Las Vegas, committed with a CZ then in his possession, later taken by St John Steele and used against him.

Marlowe mused that *this* was a debt for another time.

He'd hoped Orchid wouldn't be involved in this mission, but simple tasks had a way of becoming complex. Marlowe had contacted Ryan Marks the day he'd departed Vegas. Marks had a friend who was a talented gunsmith, working out of a custom shop in Mesa, Arizona. He'd taken the already decent CZ trigger and given it a seven-pound double-action pull and three-point-five-pound single, with reduced reach and shorter reset. It was as smooth as butter, and Marlowe had approached Marks directly this time, requesting a new, similar weapon.

He was surprised when the weapon and a half dozen 18 round magazines arrived through a US-led diplomatic post just two days later, suggesting the customised pistol perhaps had come from a request made earlier, most likely by Marshall Kirk, who was aware of Marlowe's weapon loss.

He was almost chuckling to himself about this as he gathered his items. This was effectively detective work, a domain his uncle was more likely to know what to do with. Or even Wintergreen herself, who had worked for the Metropolitan Police before she left it to work for MI5. Perhaps he should have taken Wintergreen with him; that would have been amusing, as she was once a DI in a Metropolitan police force. After all, he was now the same MI5 grade as her, according to the documentation Karolides had given him.

There wasn't much else to take if he was being brutally honest. The weapon was there as a backup, but the main bulk of his equipment comprised a suit, a voice recorder, and a few other minor items. Almost by habit, he'd picked up a couple of bullion coins, each worth a couple of grand, a change of clothes and a fake ID, as well as a handful of credit cards for use if needed.

It seemed you could take the spy out of the game, but you couldn't take the game out of the spy.

Once his bag was packed, he made his way out of the crypt, back up the stairs and into the main apartment. The flight was in two hours, and it would take him another thirty minutes to get to the airport, plenty of time to get through security. He wasn't worried about being late; it was only a trip to Scotland, and therefore not international. As long as he made the boarding gate before it closed, he was fine.

Rifling through his passports to ensure he now had the correct one to match his shiny new Security Service ID, he accidentally dropped it onto the floor as he stood in the main part of the church, within what was once the nave, and under the one remaining stained-glass window. Annoyed, he bent down to grab it and flinched as one piece of the stained-glass window popped, a small pane of glass crashing down to the wooden floor as the sniper's bullet hammered into the sofa behind him.

Marlowe dived to the floor, glancing around. From the angle, the sniper had to be high up on the building next door, looking down at the church.

He looked up at the stained-glass window, while moving to a better position. The church was old, and the window itself was grimy and dirt-covered, as Marlowe had preferred this to one that gave full view of everything inside. There was no way the shooter could have seen him within the apartment, which meant they had to be using thermal imaging.

At the moment the wall blocked him. If he walked into view of the window, however, the assassin could try again.

That wasn't his biggest fear, though; he'd been downstairs in the crypt for a good half hour and had come up through the secret entrance. If they were using thermal scopes, then the assassin might not have seen him until his heat signature suddenly appeared. This meant any assassin watching could possibly learn about the secret room, as people appearing out of nowhere wasn't that common an occurrence. There was nothing he could do, however, so after a moment's waiting, he took a deep breath and ran for the kitchen, sliding along the now tiled floor, and hiding behind the counter. It was metal, with a marble work surface and aluminium corners on the sides, which, with luck, would have shielded his heat signature as much as the crypt would have. Marlowe hoped that by doing this, anyone still watching might have seen his heat signature dip in and out, thus making it more believable that something else on the ground floor had hidden him before the shot was taken.

There were no follow-up shots, even though he was probably briefly in the sniper's sight, so he paused for a breath. He had a backup gun in the kitchen, but next to it, in a drawer he could reach up for was a DRAGON-S in-line, thermal sniper sight. A friend in the Special Reconnaissance Regiment had lent him one a few months earlier, and it'd fallen into the drawer, mainly as he'd simply forgotten about it. A compact, matte-black device with a cylindrical shape, it had a thermal imaging sensor at the front, a digital display eyepiece at the back, and adjustment knobs on the top. There were tactical mounting rails to allow for easy attachment to rifles, but Marlowe didn't have one to hand as, grabbing it, he looked up himself, trying to see through the glass. According to his friend, the scope could detect a figure over a mile away so the building next door should be a breeze.

Seeing nothing through the window, he took a breath and quickly moved before anybody could shoot again, running up the steps to the mezzanine level where the bedroom was situated. There was a smaller window on the east side, nothing more than a circle, but it was clear, and high enough for him to move up to, using the scope to observe the roof of the building next door as he reached it.

There was nobody there.

That meant somebody could have been on their way to the apartment itself.

Marlowe prepared himself, CZ in hand, as he ran to the back entrance, leading out into the churchyard. Once in the open, he checked his surroundings before heading north, following the edge of the church around in an anti-clock-wise direction until he was just slightly east of the property he needed. There was a fire escape to the side, a long ladder built into the brickwork of the building; it was likely where the assassin had climbed, and Marlowe followed his lead, climbing quickly onto the roof, the CZ leading his view.

He needn't have worried, though, because when he arrived, there was nobody there.

Shit.

However, as he crouched low, heading towards the only spot at the edge of the building that someone could have taken the shot, looking down onto the church, he found, on the floor, a single spent rifle cartridge. Using a pen from his pocket, Marlowe picked the cartridge up, rummaging around in his pockets and eventually placing it in a tiny plastic bag, sealing it up. It had held one of the bullion coins; it was big enough for the cartridge, but also meant the fingerprints, if there were any, wouldn't be smudged. Then, carefully, he placed it into his jacket pocket. He knew somebody who could check it for fingerprints, although it'd have to be dropped off quickly, as he was already running later than expected for the flight.

He *would* drop it off before he flew, however; he wanted to know who was taking a shot at him.

Now, with the thermal imaging scope, he peered down at the church itself, looking for any signs of thermal movement, in case the assassin had decided to swap places with him, or worse still, head to his crypt base.

There wasn't any. Whoever the assassin had been, he was long gone.

Or they were already in the crypt. No, don't think that way.

Marlowe wondered idly if this was the same person who had taken out Monty Barnes, but the one thing that annoyed him the most was that they'd attacked him at his church. The apartment was always supposed to be just that, a cover for anybody to come and visit. But now he wasn't sure whether his *other* secret had been revealed as well.

Which concerned him.

Climbing down the stairs, returning to the apartment the same way he had exited, he rummaged around the kitchen area, still keeping alert, before finding some cardboard. Climbing up and taping it to the small hole in his stained-glass window, he sealed the hole for the moment. He planned to fix it when he returned, but right now, he had other things to do.

Before he left, however, he provided one last gift for anybody who came to visit while he was away. After he closed up the secret wall that led to the staircase down to the crypt, he attached a thin wire; a tripwire boobytrap, connected to a claymore, which in turn was aimed at a small collection of C4 bricks.

If anybody turned up and went looking in his crypt, they wouldn't last long enough to talk about it.

This done, and bag in his hand, Marlowe exited the deconsecrated church-turned-apartment, locked the door behind him and, keeping a weather eye on all the surrounding roofs, he climbed into his car and headed off towards Central London and a police divisional surgeon who owed him a favour, to drop off the cartridge before continuing on to City Airport, and his flight to Scotland.

In a way, flying up north seemed to be the safest thing he could do right now. Which, considering he was hunting someone mad enough to down a prototype fighter to steal AI tech from the military, was saying something.

AS THE BURGUNDY JAGUAR DROVE OFF DOWN THE WEST London street, the Gravedigger emerged from the shadows, watching after him. He'd not expected to hit the target; he'd meant the shot as a warning.

He looked up at the building to his right; he'd placed the cartridge there deliberately, and he did hope Marlowe had taken the time to examine it. He really wanted the message to be crystal clear.

He'd taken the Gravedigger's name in vain, and now it was time to pay the price.

He wasn't sure where Marlowe was off to now, but it didn't matter. The man was easy to follow for a spy.

They just didn't make them like they used to, he thought to himself as he walked over to his rental BMW and, starting the engine, followed the target.

5

HIGHLANDER

IN ALL HIS YEARS IN THE MILITARY AND SECRET SERVICES Marlowe had never needed to go to RAF Lossiemouth before.

It was a new experience, and once Trix and Marlowe had arrived in Scotland, passing through a special screening area in Inverness airport – one where explanations of firearms concealed under jackets weren't needed – they proceeded to head to the base itself, hiring a car at the airport and driving the thirty or so miles through Scottish countryside.

Marlowe had considered driving up to Scotland, but it was a six-hundred mile, ten-hour drive from London, and he didn't really want to add the mileage to his car. Then there was the fact he'd have to drive back, and currently, he wasn't sure if he'd even be doing that. If someone had stolen Broad Sword, there was every chance they were going to try to *sell* Broad Sword, and that wouldn't be happening in a small Scottish seaside town.

There might be more travelling ahead.

Trix had packed light for the trip, and by that Marlowe meant at least one bag was filled with laptops, monitors, and various items of technology he had no idea of the use for. He always found it was best not to ask Trix, and when they arrived at the main gate of RAF Lossiemouth, she'd already unpacked half of it onto her lap in the passenger seat as she logged in to a variety of networks, most likely drunk with the power her new ID access gave her.

Unsurprisingly, it seemed they'd been expected, as the RAF guards waved them through the main gate after the most cursory of ID examinations, pointing them off to the right, towards the visitors' car park, where another RAF officer arrived and almost covertly gave them visitor passes for the base. Marlowe had a moment where he felt he wasn't welcome, but then realised it wasn't paranoia; he probably wasn't. The last thing the RAF needed was someone shining a light on an incredibly embarrassing theft.

Now parked, Marlowe and Trix left their bags in the car and, with an aide leading the way, they headed towards the officers' building of Sixth Squadron and where their contact, a Wing Commander Dovale, was waiting for them.

On entering the office, Wing Commander Dovale looked as happy to see them as they probably were to be there, rising from his chair and nodding to Marlowe and Trix as they entered.

'Mister Marlowe,' he said, not extending a hand, just simply nodding once more as a greeting. 'I understand you've been sent by the Home Secretary, yet another in a long line of suits who've been sent from Westminster, it seems.'

'We have,' Marlowe replied, ignoring the barbed comment. He'd expected others to have visited before him. 'This is Trix Preston, my technical expert. She'll be looking around as well. I expected Group Captain McKean to be here?'

'He's on medical leave, bad break to the right femur, they're deciding if it needs corrective surgery or not. Until he returns, I'm acting Group Captain. I understand you're armed.' Dovale stated it as a matter of fact rather than a question.

Marlowe pulled aside his jacket to reveal the holster.

'If it's a problem, you can let me know now,' he said. 'I don't want to ruffle feathers, but let's be honest, there's been a theft and the culprits might not be happy about me being here. It's more for personal defence than anything else.'

Dovale shrugged.

'If you started anything, we'd just take you down quite quickly, Royal Marines Commando or not.'

Marlowe nodded. *Wing Commander Dovale had done his homework.*

Dovale, meanwhile, had turned to face Trix.

'Are you armed?'

'I don't need a gun to destroy your day,' Trix gave a small smile. 'Never really been one for weapons.'

'She did shoot a high-ranking MI6 member in the foot once, though,' Marlowe added. 'We feel it's probably best not to give her a gun.'

Dovale wasn't sure if this was a joke or not, and so simply pursed his lips for a moment, considered this and then nodded, walking away from his desk and heading towards the door, indicating for them to follow.

'You have full access to the base and its personnel,' he said as they started across the tarmac outside. 'Although I'm not sure what you'll find. We'll be as transparent as we possibly can, as there are areas that your clearance does not give you access to.'

At this, Marlowe raised an eyebrow.

'I was under the assumption we were given all-areas access?'

'Even the Prime Minister doesn't get all-areas access,' Dovale replied, leading them along the walkway. 'I mean, he probably thinks he does, but some things are best left to trained experts, not transitional MPs who haven't read the notes they're given. You understand?'

Marlowe understood better than Dovale probably knew, and he smiled.

'Preaching to the choir, Wing Commander,' he said. 'Although it does sound a bit like holding secrets from everyone.'

'Sometimes it's "everyone" who can't be trusted,' Dovale didn't look back as he spoke, and Marlowe assumed he and Trix were being lumped within these ranks. 'But, don't worry, none of that would apply to this. As well as being an operational RAF base, Lossiemouth used to be a research and design centre for many things, as well as pilot training simulation. We even dabble with drones here. As you can understand, we try to keep it compartmentalised.'

'Squadron Leader Mille,' Marlowe asked as they walked, deciding to move on, changing the subject. 'I understand he had to eject into the sea. Is he okay now?'

'Shaken, but back at work,' Dovale replied. 'He landed on the seventh green of the Moray Hope Golf Club. By the time our helicopters got to him, he was already in the "nineteenth hole", downing a brandy.'

Marlowe smiled at this. The legends of the RAF were filled with fighter pilots crash-landing or ejecting from their crafts and finding places where they could grab a drink while waiting to be rescued.

'Can we speak to him?'

'I'm having him made available,' Dovale nodded. 'He's still very shaken.'

Marlowe frowned.

'It's been almost a week,' he said.

'Unfortunately, this has been the case for the last few days, as the story has been changing constantly.' Dovale walked out into the parade square, crossing it as he headed for some single-level buildings.

'I was under the assumption the story was the same from the start?' Trix now asked. 'That the AI had gone rogue, ejected Squadron Leader Mille, and then crashed into the sea?'

Wing Commander Dovale paused, looking around, then turning to face Marlowe and Trix as he moved closer.

For the first time, Marlowe saw doubt cross the man's face.

'We all know, Mister Marlowe, Miss Preston, that this is not the case,' he spoke softly now. 'If we're being frank about this, the AI could have taken control, could have ejected Squadron Leader Mille, and could have crashed into the sea. But what it *couldn't* have done is disappear into thin air. Which is exactly what it did.'

He glanced about, as if expecting to be watched.

'I'm afraid this was a set-up, plain and simple. And if someone was here to do that, then they were most likely the people who made sure the software wasn't working right.'

Marlowe nodded as they now continued across the parade ground.

'Have you found any sign of tampering?' he asked.

'Tampering?' Dovale reddened. 'We have the finest security here! Nobody would get near the aircraft without—'

'What my colleague means to say is, have you found

evidence of anyone hacking into the system?' Trix quickly added. 'Are you available to be reached from the outside? Could somebody have hacked into the radio frequencies or even got to the aircraft before it started?'

'That is where the story changing happens,' calming, Dovale nodded. 'We did have to use frequencies to connect, as we had an outpost a few miles northeast of the base. Which meant we could have been attacked without knowing, although I highly doubt it.'

He sighed.

'We'll never know, though,' he finished.

'Why?'

'The communications operator on the day, Flight Lieutenant Lisa Rutter, was also one of the key team members working on the installation of the AI software into the avionics package, harmonising the AI with the jet's flight services. Because of that, she was at the control centre managing the telemetry and comms systems,' he explained. 'She didn't turn up for work two days ago. When we went looking for her, we found her in her quarters.'

His face darkened.

'She'd hanged herself. There was no note, no reasoning. But she'd been the person working on the aircraft directly beforehand, and was one of the five people who had full access to the system. This was as much her baby as any others.'

He looked out across the parade ground, deep in thought, as he continued.

'Now, there's every chance that she was embarrassed of what had happened, felt this was her fault, as she'd also been on ops during the test, and the guilt had caused her to commit suicide. However ...'

He didn't need to continue, trailing off, as Marlowe nodded.

'However, she could have been the person who helped steal it, and was left as a loose end,' he said. 'I get that. We'll need information on Miss Rutter—'

'*Flight Lieutenant* Rutter,' Dovale snapped.

'Flight Lieutenant Rutter,' Marlowe repeated, holding a hand up in apology. 'We'll check into it, Wing Commander, and we'll find out what happened.'

'*We* will be checking into it. And *we* will find out.' The attitude had definitely become more icy, as Dovale spoke.

Marlowe stared at the Wing Commander for a long moment.

'Did you know Flight Lieutenant Rutter?'

Dovale went to answer, to snap back some kind of terse reply, and then softened, nodding.

'We were close,' he said.

And that was all Marlowe needed to know.

He reached up, placing a hand on Dovale's shoulder, something the Wing Commander hadn't expected, and who flinched slightly at the touch.

'We'll find them,' he said. 'And I swear to you, I'll gain retribution for what's been done.'

'I've read your reports,' Dovale straightened. 'I saw what happened at Westminster, what you did on the A40. I believe you.'

He waved at a building in front of them.

'Shall we continue?'

SQUADRON LEADER MILLE SAT ON HIS BED AND HELD HIS HEAD in his hands.

They got to Lisa. He'd be next.

He hadn't said anything, but he knew his time was running out. He'd heard there were new government suits on the base now, likely to dump him into a black site.

It wasn't his fault.

He started to half scream, half whimper in impotent fury, pulling at his hair and when he straightened, he found a clump in his hand from where he'd torn it out of his scalp.

Stupid. Stupid. Keep calm. They can't prove anything.

His phone buzzed; not his personal one, but the burner he'd been given back when this all started. It was small and hidden inside his pillowcase. Pulling it out, he read the message.

> We need you to get off the base and come to us. We need you in Punta Cana.

Mille almost laughed at this. They honestly believed he could walk out of RAF Lossiemouth without raising any alarm bells.

They were idiots.

He went to type a message back, but paused as he heard steps outside his door. Quickly placing the phone away, hoping it wouldn't buzz again, he rose as the door opened, and Tom Dovale stood there.

'Karolides has sent a couple of dogs into camp,' Dovale said matter-of-factly as he stood in the doorway. 'They'll find out what happened, Richard. So, if there's something you want to tell me ...'

The sentence was left hanging, and Mille knew this was

deliberate; Dovale was giving him an opportunity to get ahead of this.

'No sir,' he replied coldly, keeping his emotions in check. 'I've told the main investigation team everything.'

'Did you mention how you met with Garner in the golf club after you landed on the seventh green?' Dovale straightened as he spoke. 'Because they'll find out. There's something about this new guy, something different to the jobsworths that came before. He'll learn about Garner, some way. And he'll speak with him, too.'

Mille knew Dovale was fishing here, as Garner wouldn't have said anything.

'Thank you, sir, for your concern, but nothing happened,' he repeated.

'And Lisa?'

'Lisa couldn't handle the pressure—'

'For *Christ's sake,* Richard!' Dovale snapped, finally angry. 'It's Lisa! How can you be so bloody cold about it! We both know why she did it, the debts ... the guilt ...'

'With all due respect, Tom, we both know if she had guilt and wanted to repent, it was more likely to be about the affair she had with you,' Mille spoke softly, his voice ice-cold. 'So, next time you come into my personal space and start throwing accusations, remember what the *facts* are.'

There was a long, uncomfortable pause in the room, the atmosphere thickening. Dovale stared at Mille, his eyes cold and narrow, before continuing.

'You're restricted to base until further notice,' Dovale hissed. 'You'll be talking to the Minister's dogs tomorrow, not beforehand. And you'll be surrendering your personal phone.'

He held out his hand, and reluctantly, Mille pulled his smartphone from a jacket, passing it over.

'I'll know if you go through it, sir,' he said softly, as he stepped back to attention. 'Anything else?'

Dovale went to speak, thought better of it, and then left the room, the door remaining open. Mille walked over and closed it, before returning to the bed and removing the burner phone.

He was near the end. He knew it.

Typing a message into the phone he blinked back tears – whether of sadness, rage or impotence, he didn't know.

> I won't be able to go. I don't think I'll be around much longer. Honour your part of the deal no matter what, and I'll make sure I can't give you up.

The message sent, he walked over to the locker at the side of the room, reaching in and pulling out a hidden Glock 17. He wasn't supposed to have something like this on the base, but he'd been prepared for this for a while now. He quickly checked that the magazine was full and a round was chambered.

There was a buzz, a new message. Mille quickly checked the phone.

> The money will be wired three months from now to stop any suspicion. Now you must make sure nothing comes back to us – by any means necessary - if you cannot get out of this.

Tears in his eyes, Richard Mille took a deep breath, holstered his Glock, and then took apart the burner phone, snapping the SIM card and breaking the pieces up before throwing them into the bin.

Tomorrow, then.

6

THE CHEF COOKED IT

IF HE WAS BEING HONEST, MARLOWE WOULD HAVE ADMITTED that the entire day had been a waste of time. Wing Commander Dovale wanted nothing to do with the government agents sent on the Home Secretary's behalf, and cast a lot of the blame onto the mechanics and engineers who had worked on the more corporate side of the aircraft, rather than the smaller team that created Broad Sword. He argued that Lockheed and the development companies that had collaborated with them were more likely to have caused the issues than the RAF. Marlowe had agreed, nodded patiently, and smiled, knowing there was nothing that could be done to change Dovale's mind.

As he walked around the base with Dovale, discussing the "beyond reproach" airmen and engineers, he wondered whether the RAF truly was involved in whatever had happened. Dovale might have been a jobsworth, but Marlowe recognised talent where it was due. From what Marlowe could work out, he couldn't see anyone who could have done this, let alone would have wanted to. Squadron Leader Mille was almost killed in the process, and from what Marlowe could deduce, people he'd spoken to about Mille on the base all seemed to like him.

Trix, meanwhile, had found a corner in the officers' mess to sit, and had been going through the mountain of digital documents and files at her disposal. She was more interested in who was making money from the device than what happened to it. A military contract was a lucrative one, and her first impressions had been that the jet's brains were taken, not because it was faulty, but because, like Fractal Destiny, it didn't work, and somebody had wanted to remove it to save their share prices.

Marlowe hadn't really placed much stock in this theory, though. As a jet manufacturer, Lockheed was second to none. Their fighters were all over the world. And it would take more than one dodgy test to cause an issue.

No, he was pretty sure this was a theft for the AI within it.

The problem he had though was who it could have been, and how they did it.

———

THEY'D RETURNED TO THEIR GUEST HOUSE THAT NIGHT, learning they'd missed dinner, but could still order hot drinks. Marlowe had laid out his notes on the table while the server grabbed them two coffees, Marlowe staring down at the notes and frowning as he did so.

'I don't get it,' he muttered to himself. 'There has to have been easier ways to get hold of this.'

Trix, having been looking at her own set of notes, nodded.

'Hypothetical,' she said. 'You're given the opportunity to sell an expensive AI weapon. Do you take it before the mission, during, or after?'

Marlowe leant back.

'Are you asking me what I would have done if I were in the same situation?'

Trix shrugged, placing her hands behind her head as she leant back in the chair, mimicking Marlowe.

'Sure, why not,' she smiled. 'What I'm trying to say is that up to this demonstration, from what I can work out from these notes, the Broad Sword AI was untested. Sure, it had theoretical tests, and they'd extrapolated some war games data, apparently moved through several previous iterations, starting with drones before the RAF moved to stealth fighters, but nobody had flown it.'

'They went straight to live demo?'

'Christ, no. They trained the AI in smaller, uncrewed planes first and worked upwards,' Trix shook her head. 'Probably where the drones came in. Squadron Leader Mille was the first, as he'd been working with it since he replaced Dovale, but nobody else had taken it out. Maybe it was a dud? I mean, if you're going on them *not* classing the AI taking over the aircraft as a win...'

Marlowe considered this.

'If it was a dud, then there'd be millions of pounds wasted.'

'Exactly,' Trix replied. 'Look, the only AI we've got experience with was Fractal Destiny, and that turned out to not be AI. But maybe this is the same. Some kind of fake device, but not deliberate. Maybe they thought it would work and it didn't once they moved from drones, and they've been skimming money, trying to get it to work. Now it's hit the point where government suits are looking, and the board members have arrived. Someone somewhere has decided to remove it as quickly as possible.'

'Possible,' Marlowe nodded, accepting the situation. 'So you're saying that somebody's pulled it out of the aircraft and then thrown it somewhere else in the sea, hoping no one will ever see it again?'

'I don't know,' Trix shook her head. 'We're not that lucky. But if you were going to take this device and sell it, surely you'd wait until the first mission was done. Proof of a successful mission has to up the price.'

'Maybe,' Marlowe looked down at his notes, flicking through them. There was something missing. Some part of the jigsaw he hadn't seen yet. He'd never wanted to be a detective, that was more Alex Monroe, his uncle's world. And although he'd assisted him on many occasions, he never wanted to be an actual police officer.

The guest house's only server walked over, refilling their mugs.

'Would you like something to eat with that?' she asked, seeing the paperwork and estimating a long night was on the cards.

'I thought your kitchen was closed?' Marlowe frowned as he looked up. 'The chef's gone home or something; that's what we were told on reception when we arrived.'

'Oh yeah, he's gone,' the server grinned. 'But it's not like we can't whip something up. Most of the things he creates for dinner, he leaves a few extras, you know? All we do is stick them in the microwave and heat them up for you. We might not be a chef, but we can still do what he needs us to do. And you, you still get some food. Would you like to see a makeshift menu?'

Marlowe grinned.

'That would be lovely,' he said.

As the server walked off to find out what could be microwaved, Marlowe returned to the matter at hand.

'Have they given a report on the aircraft?' he asked.

Trix scrolled through a couple of documents, opening up a new folder.

'When they found the AI device was missing,' she read from the screen, 'the black box had been pulled out. But the wires weren't broken. It had been carefully removed.'

She watched Marlowe.

'You're making a face,' she said. 'Why are you making a face?'

Marlowe hadn't realised he had been, but he had been considering this issue.

'There's no way they could have done that, underwater, in the timescale they had,' he replied. 'Absolutely no way.'

Marlowe picked up his freshly filled mug of coffee and took a long draught. He knew it was going to be a long night.

'You crash an aircraft into the North Sea, or the Moray Strait, or wherever the aircraft went down, you've got a team ready,' he mused. 'Water's cold as hell. You want to be in and out as quickly as possible because you don't want to freeze. But if you're telling me they had to take their time to do this, then that goes against what the data says.'

'How so?'

'The RAF could have a helicopter over the crash site within minutes,' Marlowe continued. 'You've got no confirmation where Squadron Leader Mille would have parachuted. If the wind had taken him in another direction, he could have been directly over the aircraft – and therefore the people stealing from it. You want to make sure that you can get into that aircraft fast, remove Broad Sword quickly and get out.'

He looked at a printout of the northern coast.

'There's plenty of opportunities to get into the sea around there,' he said. 'But nearly all of them are public. Whether it's the Scottish towns we went through like this one here. Or, there's a golf club or two, a couple of holiday camps … too many witnesses, even at this time of year.'

He shook his head.

'Maybe they travelled south from the Tarbat Peninsula?' Trix suggested.

'If it was night, then sure. But we're talking middle of the day, maybe late afternoon. Still light, still bright. If there's a boat on that water, there's no way Squadron Leader Mille didn't see it. To be honest, there's no way that the RAF didn't see it. They would have checked for boats before they even started the test.'

'What are you saying?' Trix asked.

Marlowe rubbed at the back of his neck, trying to ignore the tightness growing there.

'This woman, Rutter, the one who hanged herself. What have you found out so far?'

'I'm checking into it, but it's not exactly the easiest of things to do,' Trix replied carefully. 'You think she was involved?'

'Makes sense,' Marlowe replied. 'But at the same time, it doesn't. She was the software integration lead, linking the jet's avionics and comms into the AI package – so why help screw the test up?'

Placing his mug down a little heavier than he expected,

the resounding solid clunk of the metal cup hit the wooden table, alerting the surrounding people.

'Look,' he replied, a little more quietly now. 'The only way they could have got that device out as calmly and neatly as you reckon they did had to be before the flight. But we know that isn't the case, because of the transcript.'

He tapped the piece of paper on the table.

'The AI was fighting him,' Trix agreed. 'So, the AI was definitely in while Mille was flying.'

They paused as the server wandered back with a menu.

'You can have any of the first four mains,' she said with a smile before walking off.

Trix stared at Marlowe as he held the menu, looking down at it.

'Any time you want to pass it over ...' she muttered. 'Marlowe?'

Marlowe dropped the menu to the table, looking up.

'The chef cooked the meals.'

'Yes. I know. I was here when she said it.'

'No. I mean the chef cooked the meal, and then later someone with less skill heats it up.'

Trix narrowed her eyes.

'Okay ...' she replied, confused as Marlowe started tapping the notes, excitedly.

'What if the AI wasn't in it? What if he flew the fighter pretending the AI was in it?' Marlowe leant forward, scribbling now on a fresh piece of paper. 'Think of it. Rutter's been working on this since the beginning, but so has Mille. Rutter is the person who likely positioned Broad Sword's AI into the aircraft. She could have taken it out. Christ, Squadron Leader Mille himself could have taken it out, or disconnected it at the start of the flight. He was up in the air for quite a while before they started the test.'

He started flicking through the papers.

'As he's flying, he says there are problems. But Rutter doesn't see any. Sure, she makes out there are, but there's no data to say that there was anything wrong, as the telemetry data is corrupted.'

He looked up at Trix.

'Rutter removes the AI, or at least disconnects it. That should leave a trace in the telemetry record monitoring the health of the AI, but there's nothing there. Maybe she's the one who fakes up a dummy AI to provide fake telemetry data? That's what they're following, not Mille? Then Squadron Leader Mille takes the test flight, and while in the air, he removes the device itself.'

'The chef cooked the meal, he's just finishing it.' Trix smiled, understanding now.

'So now we have Squadron Leader Mille claiming he's being kicked out by the AI,' Marlowe continued. 'Jettisons his own escape chute. Floats down to a nearby golf club, where he hides the device somewhere in the rough. Nobody's going to find it for a while. By the time the RAF finds him, he's at the nineteenth hole, remember? Some passing golfers had seen him and run over. What if he passed it on to them? A contact, playing golf with his friends?'

He flipped through some more papers, finding schematics of the Broad Sword AI. It was a box, tubular, about the size of a A2 poster tube.

'You could place that easily in a golf bag,' he said.

'Jesus,' Trix shook her head, disbelieving. 'In the space of five minutes, you've gone from underwater theft into creating a conspiracy involving a dead Flight Lieutenant and an RAF pilot ejected from his own aircraft.'

'What's the alternative?' Marlowe asked. He sighed, rubbing at the back of his neck.

'I think tomorrow we need to speak to Squadron Leader Mille,' he said. 'There's more to this than we realise.'

'And now?'

'Now we order dinner,' Marlowe smiled. 'After all, the chef cooked it.'

7

DORM ROOMS

MARLOWE STARTED THE SECOND DAY ON BASE BY CHECKING Flight Lieutenant Rutter's quarters.

Dovale hadn't been happy about this, but understood there was a very strong chance she was involved, considering she had taken her own life shortly afterwards. While he did this, Trix made a point of checking all records from that day, returning to the officers' mess, where she'd decamped the previous day, and setting up her workstation once more in a corner – probably for the unlimited mugs of coffee she'd be able to beg from the kitchen staff. Surprisingly, even though they had a high level of clearance, she found many of the files were still out of her reach, something that both annoyed and intrigued her.

Flight Lieutenant Lisa Rutter had lived in a room on the RAF base, and when Marlowe entered it, he experienced a surge of remembrance from his younger days. It reminded him of his quarters when he was in the Royal Marines, with a small single bed, desk, and wardrobe setup; designed more for space-saving than privacy. The likelihood was that the enlisted men and women were in dormitories, or at least shared rooms, whereas Rutter, being a Flight Lieutenant, had the luxury of privacy.

The building was old, not centuries, but old enough to eschew the prefab style that many of the base's buildings had adopted. And because of this, he could see a heavy metal bar running along the top. It was likely some kind of support for the upper levels, but this would have been what Flight Lieutenant Rutter had used to secure the rope that ended her life.

After looking around there wasn't much he could find. Flight Lieutenant Rutter was unsurprisingly neat and organised in her belongings, so after a couple of minutes of fruitlessly wandering around the room, he decided to call it a day.

However, as he was leaving, another RAF Officer poked his head through the door.

'Sorry,' he said quickly. 'I saw the door was open and wondered who it was.'

It was a man, in his twenties, with short ginger hair and freckles across his forehead. Marlowe looked up.

'Did you know Flight Lieutenant Rutter, Mister ...' he asked by way of introduction, waiting for the new arrival to identify himself. The new officer, wearing the stripes of a fellow Flight Lieutenant, nodded.

'Wilson, sir,' he said, instantly assuming Marlowe was of higher rank by his presence in the room. 'We came up together through training. Neither of us were in the ranks, if you know what I mean.'

Marlowe did. He'd gained the rank of Corporal before he'd left. But he had his fair share of training group arrivals, officers from other areas of the military who were supposed to lead their troops, yet had never embarked on a single actual mission. It wasn't the same as during the Napoleonic

Wars, when any wealthy son of a Duke or Lord could simply buy a commission in the army. This practice persisted almost up to the First World War, with untrained aristocrats believing they knew best – but it wasn't that far away, sometimes. And nine times out of ten, when they came to train with the Royal Marines, they were identified pretty quickly.

Marlowe almost chuckled as he realised that most of *those* individuals had now just moved into intelligence and security services, but he simply nodded and looked back at the room.

'Was she depressed?' he asked.

'Lisa?' Wilson shook his head. 'Not really, sir. She was stressed, sure, I mean she had a big job, and then there was all the hoo-ha, but ...'

'What do you mean by hoo-ha?' Marlowe paused, looking back at the RAF officer.

'I don't want to say, sir.'

Marlowe played a hunch.

'Was this because of her and Dovale?' he asked, allowing a small smile to cross his face to show the officer this was more scuttlebutt than actual data gathering.

Wilson looked unsure.

'Sir, I don't think I should be ...'

'Flight Lieutenant, right?' Marlowe asked, stepping forward, showing the ID Karolides had provided him. 'Do you understand what this is?'

'Yes, sir.' Wilson's face darkened now. 'It means you're not a member of this base.'

'That's true,' Marlowe replied. 'I'm not. But I'm not a pencil pusher either. I've served. I've done my years.'

'Air Force?'

'Royal Marines,' Marlowe smiled. 'So, I hung around with a lot of you folks.'

'Yes, sir.' Wilson smiled weakly. 'We were probably your chauffeurs, I'm guessing.'

'No, actually, you were the guys who got us out of the shit more times than I care to remember. I have a lot of respect for the RAF, Wilson, and anyone who joined to serve in it. For Rutter to take her own life meant something bad happened. I was wondering if it was because of Dovale and Mille.'

'No, sir, she was on top of all that,' Wilson said, and Marlowe internally smiled. Wilson was already assuming Marlowe knew what he was about to say. 'Wing Commander Dovale and Lisa had been nothing more than a fling, a drunken kiss at a Christmas party. They knew it shouldn't have happened, especially as he's married, and it was against regulations. But Squadron Leader Mille, however ...'

Wilson paused, looking away.

'They'd known each other since before they came here,' he said. 'They were a handful of years apart, but they grew up in the same town. When Lisa arrived on base, Richard had been here a good year, knew the lay of the land by then. They had a friendship that bypassed everybody else, and ... well, of course, that was going to turn into you-know-what.'

Marlowe didn't reply, just simply nodding.

'But you don't think that would have affected what happened?'

'No, sir,' Wilson shook his head. 'Rutter was an outstanding officer. If whatever happened ...'

He trailed off, staring up at the middle of the room where the rope would have hung.

'What is it?' Marlowe asked.

'Sir, I saw her the day she died,' Wilson replied. 'She was fine, I swear to you. She wasn't stressed, she was talking about what she was going to eat in the mess later on that day. We were arranging to get some leave together, have a laugh in Glasgow. She was annoyed that—'

'That Broad Sword didn't work,' Marlowe finished for him. 'I know about it, carry on.'

'She was aggravated the test didn't work correctly, sir. But that wasn't her fault. It was something to do with the actual aircraft itself, and she knew she wouldn't get the blame for it. She wouldn't take her own life over that.'

Interesting, Marlowe thought to himself. *If she'd been involved, she wouldn't have been annoyed, unless this was part of an act.*

'No, she wouldn't,' he mused. 'Was there anybody else who ever came to see her, apart from Mille or Dovale?'

Wilson considered the question.

'There was a local,' he said. 'Owns one of the golf clubs in the area.'

Marlowe raised an eyebrow.

'Did she play golf?'

'She was considering it, apparently.' Wilson didn't seem convinced. 'She was probably looking for a sugar daddy to replace Mille and Dovale or ...'

He chuckled for the first time.

'Look, she wasn't that happy here. It's a long and stressful job, and she knew she was helping keep the world safe and all that, but she was spending a lot of her time with contractors and outside forces. She was being offered jobs left, right and centre. A lot more than she'd make here. She was coming up to the time to think about whether she stayed or moved on.'

He paused, as if worried he was saying too much, before continuing.

'The thing about being an RAF officer is you're always

moving forward, always showing your ambition. And if you don't move forward, then—'

'Then there's something wrong,' Marlowe nodded. 'And you probably get forgotten.'

'Or at least moved sideways into a less vital role,' Wilson argued. 'I think Lisa knew she was getting close to her time. Broad Sword was coming to an end, and she was looking to jump before she was pushed – especially after Dovale reckoned loudly to the higher ups that she was leading him on.'

Marlowe looked around the room. From what he understood, the abilities Flight Lieutenant Rutter possessed meant this room would have been the size of one of her walk-in wardrobes if she had gone into the private sector.

'Thank you,' he replied. 'If I have any more questions—'

'Sir, I hope you don't mind me saying, but I don't really want to be involved in this,' Wilson said. 'I was just checking to see who was in here. I don't want to talk about my friend's death.'

'I get that, and I won't trouble you again, unless it's vital,' Marlowe nodded. 'Do you remember the name of the man who owned the golf club?'

'Garner,' Wilson replied as he walked to the door. 'Charles Garner.'

'Thank you again.' Marlowe straightened as Wilson left the room, taking one last look around. There was more going on here than he could fathom. And now he had a possible lead. If Lisa Rutter was looking to leave, or was looking to layer a new nest egg, she'd need outside interest.

He needed to look into Charles Garner.

But that would be later, for now it was time to speak to the other person involved.

After he texted Trix, with an update of the base's love triangles, that was.

As it happened, it was Trix who found Squadron Leader Mille first.

He had headed into the officers' mess for his breakfast later than everybody else, and Trix, sitting in the corner, had spied him so she walked over.

'Squadron Leader Mille?' she asked.

Mille looked over at her, frowning.

'Have we met?'

'No, sir,' Trix forced a smile to try to relax the conversation a little. 'My name is Trix Preston. I was sent by Whitehall to investigate the Broad Sword test.'

Mille chewed his lip as he pondered the comment. He eyed Trix up and down, probably wondering how such a young woman was given such clearance, and then walked back to her table area, probably because it was less exposed and out of the way, motioning with his hand to the chair opposite her, subtly asking whether he could sit. Trix nodded, placing her laptop to the side so she could look across the table at him, as Mille sat down and then leant forward.

'I'll give you the report you want,' he said. 'That sodding AI tried to kill me. It buggered around with my settings, ejected me out of the cockpit, and luckily that was as far as it went, because if it had gone all *Devastator*, and managed to fire any of the weapons, we probably wouldn't have half the buildings on the Moray Firth.'

Trix had spent many years with people living double

lives. Most recently with MI5, but before that, she'd worked for Francine Pearce, who, with Pearce Associates, had spent many years blackmailing politicians and powerful people. Over that time, Trix had gained an idea of when somebody was avoiding the question.

Richard Mille was *definitely* avoiding the question. So, she decided to change her attack, leaning closer, staring in wonder at Mille's eyes.

'My God,' she whispered. 'You have the most beautiful central heterochromia iridum in your left eye. Have you ever been told that?'

'My what?' Mille frowned as Trix rummaged around in her bag.

'There are very faint spikes of different colours radiating from the pupil,' Trix triumphantly pulled a camera out of the bag, turning it on. 'It's beautiful. Do you mind?'

'Um, sure, I'd never seen it before ...'

Trix took a picture of Mille's face and then looked at the photo with a disappointed sigh.

'Oh, it doesn't photo well,' she muttered, placing the camera back into the bag. 'Oh well. Probably the lighting. Tell me about your relationship with Lisa Rutter.'

If Squadron Leader Mille, already thrown by Trix's photo antics had expected that question, he made a very good impression of someone stunned.

'I don't know what you mean,' he replied cautiously.

Trix looked across the officers' mess, seeing Marlowe entering through the door.

'I was under the assumption that you and Miss Rutter knew each other.'

'We ... yes, we lived on the same estate.' Mille was flustered, following a line of conversation he hadn't expected, and as he went to rise, he paused as Marlowe approached, now standing next to him.

'Squadron Leader Mille,' Marlowe held out a hand. 'I'm Thomas Marlowe. I'm with Trix Preston here, on behalf of Whitehall.'

'She just said – she just told me that,' Mille swallowed nervously as he nodded.

'I've been examining the situation,' Marlowe continued, watching the pilot in front of him. 'We understand the AI device was removed from the aircraft underwater, but looking at the schematics, it seems quite difficult to explain how such a thing could happen.'

'Basically, Squadron Leader Mille,' Trix continued, using his full title to give a sense of authority, 'the only way it could have been removed in the timescale it had was if it had been removed before you flew. And, when you ejected, you kept it with you, perhaps held on your person.'

'Are you saying I was involved?'

Marlowe shrugged.

'It's our job to look at all angles,' he said. 'So, because of that, one angle has to be one where you were involved.'

Mille couldn't fault this logic, and so sat still, unsure where the conversation was going now.

'Did you see Flight Lieutenant Rutter after the test, perhaps on the day she committed suicide?'

'What, now you're saying I killed Lisa Rutter?' At this, Mille rose, glaring. 'How dare you!'

'The golf course you landed on,' Marlowe continued, ignoring the outrage. 'Was it the Moray Hope golf course, a few miles west of here?'

'I think so, yes.' Mille was thrown, yet again, by another

change in conversation direction. 'I don't remember, it was a blur.'

'But you'd know if Charles Garner was, by chance, playing a game when you landed? Maybe he met with you, helped you out of the parachute?' Trix asked.

'Charles Garner, who also knew Flight Lieutenant Rutter?' Marlowe had thrown the last line in as a fishing exercise, hinting that there might be something more going on, trying quietly to open a door or two, loosen Mille's tongue.

What he didn't expect was for Squadron Leader Mille to grab Trix's laptop and throw it at him.

As Marlowe raised his arms to avoid being struck in the face by the flying laptop, Mille exploded from the seat, sprinting out of the mess hall.

Marlowe needed nothing else. With a shout for Trix to inform Wing Commander Dovale of this, he started running after the now fugitive Squadron Leader. He needn't have worried though, because as he arrived outside, he found Mille standing, lost, looking around for anything, *anyone* who could possibly help him.

'It's over, Richard,' Marlowe said, forcing his voice to stay calm. 'Whatever you did, whatever you provided, we'll find out. We're very good at it.'

Mille nodded. It wasn't an acceptance of the statement; it felt more an acceptance that Marlowe would fulfil any promise he made.

'I can believe that,' he said as, from behind his waist, he pulled a Glock 17.

'Now wait a moment,' Marlowe said, pulling out his own CZ expecting a gunfight. From the corner of his eye, he could see RAF guards running over, their assault rifles out. As far as they were concerned, the man from MI5 had turned up and pulled a gun on one of their own, and the "don't really keep weapons on us in the base" rule seemed to have been thrown out.

This was not going well.

'Don't do this,' he said. 'You don't need to—'

'You think I can carry on after this?' Mille laughed. 'After I killed Rutter, after they blackmailed me into doing what I had to do?'

'You killed Lisa Rutter?'

'I had to,' Mille shook his head, tears running down his face. 'She was going to out me, out us. Someone outside the group had funded her, she was going against her orders. I met with her, we fought ... it was self-defence.'

'You hanged her, man!'

'Only after, to hide what happened!'

'In that case, you deserve everything you get,' Marlowe snapped. 'But think about what you're doing, though. Help us and we can help you get out of this.'

'Oh, I am thinking how to get out of this,' Mille said sadly, as he raised the gun to the base of his chin. 'I have a debt. A big one. And if I go to prison... well, someone I love doesn't get the help they need. I'm kind of damned either way. So... tell my friends that ... well, tell them whatever makes me sound good, yeah?'

'Wait,' Marlowe held his hand up, noticing the guards still approaching, weapons hot but not aimed at them. 'At least tell me who did this to you. Allow me to get revenge for you.'

Squadron Leader Mille said one word before firing the trigger. His head snapped back as the round went through his brain, and his body fell backwards onto the parade ground floor, sprawled with the contents of his skull, splattered out on the tarmac behind him.

As the RAF guards now burst into action, screaming at Marlowe to drop his own weapon, Marlowe held his hand up, the gun now visible in the air and away from anyone. As the guards took the weapon, and as Marlowe saw Wing Commander Dovale running forward, his face pale as he saw what had happened, Marlowe wasn't really listening.

All he could think of was the one single word that Mille had said, the word that explained who it was that had done this to him.

Orchid.

8

NINETEENTH WHOLE

'ARE YOU ALL RIGHT?' MARLOWE GLANCED AT TRIX AS THEY drove along the road towards the Moray Hope Golf Club.

Quietly, Trix nodded.

'I'm not as used to death as you are,' she replied, her voice no louder than a whisper; an unusual status for Trix to be in.

'I don't think you can ever be used to death,' Marlowe replied, giving a small smile as reassurance.

It had taken an hour for the RAF guards to relax their stance on Marlowe. Finding a man with a gunshot in his head and another standing over him had caused them to immediately assess the situation incorrectly, assuming Marlowe had somehow forced Squadron Leader Mille to kill himself, having been close enough to see Mille shoot himself, but not hear the conversation that led to the act. Dovale had been furious, believing that Marlowe had been the cause of some overconfident, cack-handed detective work that had not only spurred Mille to run, but had caused his death in the process.

Marlowe understood the anger. The Wing Commander

was currently the de facto base commander while the Group Captain was away; he wasn't expecting to find bodies on his doorstep.

Marlowe and Trix had promised to keep the base updated on what they learned, but Marlowe had already decided that RAF Lossiemouth was a dead end. Whatever was happening with Broad Sword had now moved on elsewhere; the instigators just happened to be on the site. The stealth jet itself and the weapons within were still being examined, but they weren't the prize.

Anyone could buy a missile these days.

Trix, still shaken, glanced at her tablet. She'd been looking up Charles Garner. He was a London stockbroker made good, who a few years earlier had moved to the north of Scotland, creating several golf clubs in the process. Several American industrialists, including one that had recently run for president against Anton McKay, had invested in these clubs and even though they were at the far north end of Scotland, Trix saw a car park full to brimming as she and Marlowe arrived at the largest of these, the Open Championship course of Moray Hope.

Marlowe, meanwhile, was still considering the last word Mille had spoken before killing himself.

'*Orchid.*'

He had hoped he'd misheard. Or that maybe this was another rogue splinter group. This was weeks after the events at Las Vegas, maybe people hadn't received the memo that murderers like Delacroix and Rizzo weren't the best option for progress.

Either way, Marlowe was going to be having words.

As they arrived at the main reception of the golf club, a woman sitting behind the desk looked up, noted their suited appearance, frowned and pressed a button on the reception desk. Marlowe wondered what it was about them that had triggered some kind of alert.

Had she been part of this? Had she been warned by her boss to look out for strange, suited people who were likely authorities or worse?

'We'd like to speak to Charles Garner,' Marlowe said as he walked up to the counter, resting his elbow against it as he stood, flashing a winning smile at the woman. 'I understand he's expected to be here today.'

'Do you have an appointment with him? Mister Garner is a very busy man, and splits his time between three golf courses,' the woman replied, not looking Marlowe in the eye. 'I can check, but I'm not sure he's here today. Can I say who's calling?'

Marlowe said nothing. The woman looked up.

'I asked—'

'I know what you asked,' Marlowe said. 'But I'm not telling you my name until he arrives. Just say I have a coin that needs to be flipped.'

Trix frowned as he spoke this; she'd already reached into her pocket and probably had her MI5 ID ready to wave if needed. The woman, sensing this was something different to what she expected, nodded, tapped some buttons, then turned away, speaking softly into her headset. After a moment, she looked back at Marlowe, turned away and Marlowe heard the whispered word "beard", giving him the distinct impression she was describing the two people standing in front of her. And then her face setting into a fake, fixed smile, she turned to face them.

'Mister Garner will be here imminently,' she said.

Marlowe smiled and nodded.

'I expected nothing less,' he replied casually.

Trix was still frowning as Marlowe walked over to the chairs in the waiting area, plopping himself down on one.

'What do you know that I don't?' she asked.

'Orchid,' Marlowe replied. 'If Mille worked for Garner, and Orchid was the force behind it, then Garner knows, works for, or possibly even is a member of Orchid. So, a nameless man with arrogance to boot mentioning coins might make him more receptive to us.'

'More likely to reply to criminals than the government,' Trix nodded. 'I get that.'

After a couple of minutes of waiting, Marlowe spending them staring across the reception area at the receptionist, watching her become increasingly nervous the longer they waited, a man emerged from the back of the reception area through a door labelled "Employees Only". He was middle-aged, late forties, maybe early fifties, his hair brown without a trace of grey, possibly bottle-dyed, with a fat, jowly face, and one of those bodies that looked slim but seemed fat at the same time, a definite lack of muscle, possibly because of a sedentary job.

Marlowe was surprised by this; after all, playing golf should at least keep you fit.

The man wore a pair of cream chinos over white sneakers and a bright emerald-green polo shirt with the Moray Hope Golf Club's logo on the chest. It was definitely Garner; Marlowe was sure of it.

'So, what's all this about?' he asked, walking over to Marlowe and Trix, who, still sitting in the chairs, the coffee table in front of them, said nothing. 'My secretary mentioned coins. I'm an avid collector, you know. Perhaps you have one I can see?'

'Are you Charles Garner?' Marlowe asked, ignoring the request.

'Who's asking?'

'We're here in connection to Flight Lieutenant Mille of the RAF Lossiemouth base,' Marlowe continued. 'We understand you had quite a shock when he parachuted onto your golf course a few days ago.'

'Yeah, okay, I was there when it happened. So, are you here because of that?'

'In a manner of speaking,' Marlowe replied. 'We're looking for an AI device called Broad Sword.'

At the mention of the name, Garner seemed surprised; he probably wasn't used to authorities giving away such vital information. Even Trix seemed taken aback by Marlowe's revelation.

'Well, that's something you should take up with the Squadron Leader himself then,' Garner smiled. 'I never met him.'

'But you know of him?'

'Never heard the name before,' Garner shrugged. 'All I know is some RAF pilot landed, and we gave him a mug of tea, or a shot of brandy—'

'Yet you know his rank,' Marlowe interrupted. 'I said Flight Lieutenant, but you correctly identified him as a Squadron Leader.'

Garner flushed slightly, visibly unsettled.

'Look, if you don't mind, I'm very busy. I suggest you go speak to him and—'

'We would speak to him, but he's dead. Shot himself in the head earlier today,' Marlowe kept his voice calm and stated. 'So, now I'd like to speak to you.'

Charles Garner didn't move, staring directly at Marlowe.

'I'm sorry,' he said, cautiously, glancing around the reception area, 'I didn't exactly get your name. Would it be Marlowe, by chance? Thomas Marlowe?'

Marlowe reached into his pocket, but instead of bringing out his ID, he brought out a small, blackened coin. It glinted in the light as he placed it down on the coffee table.

He said nothing else.

To any normal person, this coin was nothing but a novelty keepsake, a strange item that a member of the public might ask, 'Why are you showing me this coin?'

Charles Garner, however, didn't ask. Instead, his face darkened as he recognised the blackened coin of the Orchid High Council. Marlowe had guessed this; if Garner had known his name as part of the investigative team, he'd have stated it earlier.

'Orchid has no place here,' he said. 'I told them that when I stepped away.'

Staring down at the coin once more, he nodded to himself.

'I knew I was right,' he said. 'I knew you from your description. You're Taylor Coleman's bastard, aren't you? The one who's been given the ticket.'

'The ticket?' Trix asked.

'Wonka's golden ticket. You think you're going to get the whole chocolate factory, don't you?' Garner shook his head as he looked back at Marlowe. 'I don't know what your plan is, mate, but Orchid has been around longer than you or your deadbeat dad were alive.'

Marlowe didn't say anything, allowing the quiet moment to stretch. There were two types of people: those who were comfortable in silence and those who needed to speak to fill the space.

Garner was obviously one of the latter.

After a moment, Garner couldn't help himself.

'If it is you, this isn't High Council business,' he continued nervously. 'Placing down that coin is nothing more than a pissing contest, or a fishing exercise.'

He considered his next words carefully.

'He didn't know that I was Orchid. Or, rather, he probably knew I was once Orchid, but not how high.'

He smiled, watching Marlowe now.

'You're thinking to yourself, was I in France when Delacroix died? Maybe I was. Was I in Vegas when Rizzo died? When your half-brother died? Again, maybe I was, maybe I wasn't.'

Marlowe shook his head.

'You know me from description, not by a physical presence, so I know we've never met. If you had been at either of those places, you'd definitely have remembered me,' he said. 'How long have you been Orchid?'

Garner quietly counted down on his fingers.

'About twelve years,' he said. 'But I stepped away when Delacroix died. Not my game anymore.'

Marlowe noted the comment. *Garner was likely an ally of Lucien Delacroix – which made him a threat.*

'But yet you still worked with Mille?'

'Favour to a friend, who was looking to move into the AI market,' Garner replied, and his expression showed this wasn't a favour he'd wanted to repay, as he looked over at Trix. 'I'm guessing you're not Orchid. You're not trying to show off with a shiny coin.'

'No,' Trix replied. 'I've never been one for joining.'

'Oh, if you want to be an Orchid, you definitely have to be

a joiner,' Garner laughed at this, glancing back at Marlowe. 'Lone wolves are definitely not appreciated.'

'Look, as exciting as this conversation is,' Marlowe interrupted. 'I'm not here to talk about the joys of membership.'

'No, you want to know about Broad Sword,' Garner leant closer. 'But the real question is whether you're here from Orchid or from Whitehall? Yeah, I heard that there are two suits at the RAF base. That you're sitting in front of me wearing one makes me think you're one of them.'

Marlowe nodded.

'We have been brought here by the Home Secretary, yes,' he said. 'But why we've been asked to turn up and why we're here are two different matters.'

He glanced quickly at Trix, mainly to make sure she was still on the same page as him.

'Let's just say, since Vegas, we've been a little more affluent than we used to be,' he continued.

Garner chuckled.

'I heard you had a bit of a win at Vegas,' he replied.

'Some people are lucky and some people aren't.' Marlowe simply smiled. 'But I am here on behalf of some interested parties who would like to make an offer for the device, though. If your friend, the one moving into AI, wants to make an offer, that is?'

Garner glanced around the room to make sure they weren't being listened to and steepled his hands together, placing his two index fingers against his chin as he contemplated the suggestion.

'Hypothetical situation,' he said.

Marlowe looked over at Trix and then grinned.

'Sure,' he replied. 'My last week seems to have been filled

with hypothetical situations. But before you give me yours, let me give you mine. An Orchid member, or someone connected to one, decides to steal a high-level AI device, one that can overwrite the coding of enemy drones, missiles, that sort of shit, and hive mind them together, but it's locked into a stealth fighter. He either blackmails or bribes two members of RAF Lossiemouth – the Flight Lieutenant who will be running ops and who is part of the team building the AI, and the Squadron Leader who'll be flying the aircraft – to take the device, claiming there was some kind of error during the test. The RAF and government authorities will believe that someone came in afterwards, deep in the water, and took the device out after the crash. But in reality, the Squadron Leader, upon landing on a golf course, passes the AI device, about the size of a poster tube, to a friendly face, one such as yours.'

'That's a nice hypothetical,' Garner nodded. 'Shame it can't be corroborated. I heard what happened at the base already. I have contacts who like to keep me informed. It's a sad thing to hear about Mille and Rutter, though.'

Marlowe's eyes narrowed.

'I can tell you're crushed by what happened,' he said dryly. 'So, tell me your hypothetical story.'

'Hypothetically, if someone was to gain such a device, whether by illegal means or purely by chance,' Garner now opened his arms out in a peaceful gesture. 'Hypothetically, that person would want to sell it. They would go to a broker.'

Marlowe nodded, leaning closer.

'If they went to a broker,' he said, 'then this isn't Orchid.'

'What do you mean?'

'If they were working for Orchid, they would have contacted the High Council and told them they had the item,'

Marlowe continued. 'But you haven't. Because if you had, I would have known.'

'What, do you think the High Council tells you everything?' Garner laughed at this. 'I don't want to piss on your parade, mate, but you're the bastard of Taylor Coleman, remember? None of them want you there. Especially after you killed your own brother.'

Marlowe didn't mean to, it was instinctive, but his hand shot out, grabbing Garner around the throat.

'I didn't kill Byron,' he hissed. 'St John Steele did.'

'Steele? Don't make me laugh,' Garner rubbed at his throat as Marlowe pulled away. 'I've known Steele for years. He's a sneaky bastard, but he's not a killer.'

Marlowe raised an eyebrow at this.

'Are you sure we're talking about the same man?'

Garner ignored him.

'Even if what you say is true,' he said, 'Steele's not stupid. There's no way you have proof of that. It's your word against his.'

'Actually, we do have proof,' Trix replied.

'If you did, you would have gone to the authorities, or at least placed it in front of the High Council.'

'Why?' Marlowe asked. 'It's an internal Orchid matter, and when I speak to Steele, we'll be discussing it.'

Garner stared from Marlowe to Trix, his face still creased into a smile, and then he continued to loudly laugh. It was a full-on belly laugh, as if he'd just been told the most amusing thing he'd ever heard.

'Mister Marlowe, I believe you,' he said. 'I believe that you genuinely want to speak to Steele, and I'd like to help you do that.'

'And why would you do that?' Marlowe asked innocently.

'Because I don't like you,' Garner replied. 'I mean, I *really* don't like you. I don't like what you stand for. You've walked into one of the top positions in an organisation you obviously don't like. You don't understand how we work, and you haven't treated me with the respect that someone of my level in the organisation should have.'

'I thought you'd left?'

'You never truly leave. You'll learn that when they come for you once more,' Garner shrugged.

Marlowe kept quiet again, allowing Garner to fill the empty space. Garner happily did so.

'You want Broad Sword? Go speak to The Broker.'

'Which broker?'

'*The* Broker,' Garner said. 'That's all I'm giving you. But you'd better hurry because it goes on auction tomorrow at midnight.'

'Where?'

'A resort ten miles south of Punta Cana, in the Dominican Republic.'

'And you're just giving me this for free?'

'You turn up there, they'll either be expecting you, or they'll kill you on sight,' Garner shrugged. 'I lose nothing either way. I might even get a finder's fee.'

He looked around the room, nodding over at the bar where a group of golfers had just arrived.

'That's the captain of my club. I'm afraid I need to go and speak to him. If you want St John Steele, you'll find him in the Dominican Republic, Mister Marlowe. As well as your AI device and any answers you require. The acquaintance I helped is looking for funding, and that's where you'll find everything you need.'

He waved to the apparent golf club captain, motioning for him to stay, that he was finishing up.

'I was just a middleman, working for somebody else,' he finished. 'But Orchid always gains from stuff like this.'

Marlowe rose.

'The deaths of Squadron Leader Mille and Flight Lieutenant Rutter are on your shoulders,' he stated matter-of-factly.

'Rutter never worked for me,' Garner admitted. 'I tried, but I could never turn her. Mille though? Yeah, he was all about the money. I'm middle managing an arrangement, covering some very large bills for his mother. She'll be dead in a year unless she gets some serious medical help. Six figures worth. He asked me to do it in a few months, so nothing landed on her. I'll still make sure it goes through, even though his death didn't really help me. But his death isn't on my shoulders. You did that, forcing his hand.'

Marlowe shook his head.

'There's a debt you owe. And believe me, once this is all done, you will pay.'

'Oh, how will I survive?' Garner replied in mock horror. He thought about it for a moment, and then his eyes widened as his face brightened.

'Oh, I know,' he said. 'I'll let them kill you, and then I'll sleep like a baby. Goodbye, Mister Marlowe. Have a nice flight.'

———

THEY'D LEFT THE GOLF CLUB AS SOMBRE AS THEY'D ARRIVED; they had more information, but Marlowe felt he was still as far away from the prize as he had been when they started.

'Did you gain anything from Garner in there? Maybe a tell, or a line he spoke?' Marlowe broke the silence.

'I did better than that,' Trix grinned widely. 'I force-connected and cloned his phone while you talked. I have all his WhatsApp messages. I reckon we'll get what we need by the time we arrive somewhere sunny and hot.'

Marlowe went to reply, but his phone beeped a new message. He pulled it out, checking the message. It was from a family friend, a divisional surgeon and forensic officer in London named Rosanna Marcos, who he'd sent the rifle cartridge to, the previous day.

> Watch your back, kid. Someone's screwing with you.

> Only one fingerprint on it. Montgomery Barnes.

Marlowe stared at the message, his eyes narrowing.

'Problem?' Trix, noting the expression, asked.

'Someone's playing games and I'm sick of it,' Marlowe showed her the message.

Trix shrugged, scrolling through her phone as she spoke.

'You're only pissed because they're changing the rules of the game and cheating,' she said. 'Start cheating back at them. You'll feel fine in no time.'

She held up her own phone triumphantly.

'Also, go book two tickets on the government dime,' she smiled. 'I know where we're going.'

9

VIVA THE REPUBLIC

'WELCOME TO THE ROYAL PLAZA.'

The Dominican receptionist smiled at Marlowe and Trix as they arrived through the main doors. It had been a long and irritating journey for Marlowe; ten hours in a cramped economy flight seat had left him tired and cranky. He'd also been told to leave his gun behind. However, after speaking to a couple of people, he'd found somebody in the Republic who could sort something out for him. The British Embassy wasn't just filled with civil servants, after all. It also helped to have the clearance level he currently had, and a Home Secretary who wanted this fixed at any cost.

As it was, the CIA had offered to help, with the assistance of an agent Marlowe had many prior contacts with.

The hotel was a few miles south of Punta Cana in La Romana, a bright and sunny area that had transitioned from a sugar cane hub to a location with luxury resorts along its coastline. These resorts all prided themselves on providing privacy, and catered to tourists and individuals needing discretion, so Marlowe knew he was in the right place. La

Romana's beaches were clean and quiet, and from the moment he arrived, Marlowe could see they were suitable for private conversations.

After Trix had rooted around the dark web and learnt the location of the auction by process of elimination and a few well positioned algorithms, the event hidden under a real, charity-based auction of luxury antiques, they'd booked a superior suite, effectively two rooms adjoining a central area. The auction would happen that very night at the Ocean's Palace resort, nestled a few miles down the road, and next to the cliffs by the ocean in Cap Cana, a stretch of pure white sand beach beneath it. Marlowe had only ever been to the Dominican Republic once, staying at an all-inclusive hotel by the sea, a far cheaper option than the one he was currently at. All he could remember was that the food was nice, the people were friendly, and the snorkelling was lacking slightly. This resort felt more *James Bond* than he'd ever felt before. All he needed was his own Felix Leiter to meet him with information on the upcoming mission.

Amusingly, this turned up in the form of Brad Haynes. He was waiting for Marlowe and Trix in the bar, positioned on the east side of an open area square, beside a small stage where each evening a performer would most likely provide entertainment. He was wearing chinos and a linen shirt over beach loafers, and grinned as Marlowe walked towards him.

'It's quicker for me to get here than you, I understand,' he smiled. 'Came down from Washington as soon as we heard.'

'We heard?' Marlowe glanced around. 'Sasha's here?'

'You should be so lucky,' Brad grinned. 'Although the last time I saw you, you were going off with someone else.'

Marlowe ignored the comment. Now wasn't the time to discuss pillow talk.

'I was just curious whether you were here alone, or with backup,' he asked.

'We're all here alone,' Brad replied. 'I'm simply representing an interested party who's looking to purchase Broad Sword.'

'The CIA want it?' Now it was Trix who asked.

'The CIA wants Orchid to believe they want it,' Brad grinned. 'So, I understand you guys are top-level code clearance right now?'

'Apparently so,' Marlowe nodded.

'Outstanding.' Brad pulled out a small piece of paper from his chinos pocket. 'I have a few questions I'd like you to check up for me. I've always had a concern about your royal family.'

Marlowe laughed.

'It isn't that kind of clearance,' he said.

Brad sighed theatrically.

'Worth a try,' he replied. 'Anyway, to work – I couldn't find any SIG Sauers for you, but I understand you like the CZ75.'

'*I* understand you might be able to sort something out.'

'Already done; in your room under your pillow ...' Brad frowned, again, over-egging the theatrics of the situation. 'Or it's under Trix's pillow. I'm not too sure which one of you wants which room. So, I picked the least pretty of the two. You're a gentleman, after all. I'm sure you'd give Miss Preston here a better view.'

'Damn right,' Trix nodded pointedly.

Marlowe hadn't really considered it. But the die was now cast, and no matter what, he was now in the less attractive of the two rooms.

They sat down, Trix ordering a Pina Colada without rum, and Marlowe choosing to drink a Virgin Mary – effectively, a spicy Bloody Mary without the vodka – as he needed to keep himself straight-headed this evening. The auction might not be until midnight, but he was still a wanted man in Orchid's eyes following the death of his brother.

That said, he still didn't know if this was an Orchid situation. Garner might have been an Orchid employee, but the impression Marlowe had gained while talking to him was that this had been done off his own back. Charles Garner might have been joining the ranks of Lucien Delacroix and Gabriel Rizzo, rogue agents of Orchid, doing things to push forward their own agendas.

Marlowe was starting to wonder whether Orchid was as unified as he believed.

'So, what's your plan?' Brad asked.

Marlowe shrugged.

'Playing it as I go along,' he said. 'I'll wave my coin, claim that as High Council I want to be more involved, but that the AI cannot and must not leave the Dominican Republic.'

'That might not be your say,' Brad replied ominously. 'And I don't mean that the CIA might want it. There's a lot of high hitters here. I've seen people from the Middle East, a couple of North Koreans I've tussled with in the past. This place, and the one in Cap Cana are safe ground. It's like a church in *Highlander*.'

'What's that supposed to mean?' Trix frowned.

'You know, like where the Kurgan and Macleod ...' Brad started, but then trailed off. 'You really don't know?'

'I try not to watch films that came out before I was born, unless they're really good,' Trix sniffed dismissively.

'*Highlander's* a masterpiece.' Brad looked at Marlowe for support. But Marlowe, having had many conversations like this in the past, simply smiled and leant back in the chair.

Brad, realising he was likely being played, sighed.

'Look, in *Highlander*, you've got these immortals, yeah? And they all want to kill each other. But if they meet in a church, they can't touch each other. It's Switzerland. It's no-man's-land. That's this hotel, and the Ocean's Palace, where the auction is. No one's going to take you out until after the auction. Once the item's sold, all bets are off.'

'And there can be only one,' Trix nodded with a grin.

Brad groaned, looking at Marlowe.

'How do you deal with her?'

'You get used to it,' Marlowe shrugged. 'Your mistake was letting her play you like a rookie, rather than assuming she'd not only seen it, but probably watched the show, too.'

'Every episode,' Trix said ominously. 'And the films, although the second is only good in the Renegade Cut.'

Marlowe decided it was time to change the topic.

'Do we have an estimated price?' he asked.

'Take your highest number and add a couple of zeroes to it,' Brad replied. 'The person placing this up for sale went against the RAF, effectively killed a pilot and a comms specialist involved, and took out one of the most dangerous technological pieces of equipment that you Brits have ever created.'

He shook his head.

'Only Brits would make a simple stealth jet computer out of something that could take over entire air forces at a whim. This isn't a small-time theft. This is your Fractal Destiny times a hundred.'

Marlowe grimaced at the name, but he knew what Brad meant.

Brad, however, leant closer.

'There are rumours, though,' he said. 'I'm hearing they

actually don't want to sell it. This is mainly a fishing exercise, gaining high bids, and then taking the top players to a private viewing, where they'll bid again. So, you're bidding to be invited to the bidding.'

'That'll piss people off,' Marlowe replied, surprised. 'If they think they've bought it, they'd want it.'

'I get the impression it's a case of see who's interested and then invite them to another event,' Brad nodded. 'One where the winner spends hundreds of billions to effectively hold the world to ransom. Maybe even franchise the code to their mates.'

Marlowe considered the news. It was bad enough when the fear was that one insane warlord would have the AI. Now, with multiple possibilities, the world became a little scarier.

'Come on, let's get you properly settled in,' Brad rose from the table. 'Besides, this cocktail's going right through me, so I need to use your bathroom.'

'Why not use yours?' Marlowe grumbled.

'Because I like my bathroom,' Brad winked, and Marlowe didn't want to continue the conversation as they headed to the rooms.

———

'DO WE KNOW WHO'S SELLING THE DEVICE?' MARLOWE ASKED, as they entered the suite.

Brad nodded.

'Apparently,' he began, reaching into his pocket and pulling out his phone, 'we're looking for a Doctor Lina Moritz. Parisian engineer, graduated from MIT in ninety-four. She's been working for NATO on a variety of different options over the years. She was involved in the Science and

Technology Organization, the NATO-Industry Forum, and the NATO Industrial Advisory Group.'

He scrolled up, showing an image of a woman. She was slim, in her mid-fifties, with short gunmetal hair, cut into a pixie cut. She had piercing green eyes and a hawkish nose, and Marlowe already felt intimidated by her, simply by looking at the photo.

'She was involved in Broad Sword from the start,' Brad continued. 'She worked with her partner, Nora Eskildsen for years on this, and then when the UK took over from France in the development, she worked with the RAF throughout the testing phases. Works mainly at some university in Seville. However, she disappeared, either yesterday or the day before. I believe someone naughty got to her, made her an offer she couldn't refuse, and now she's here with the device.'

'Do you think she was involved in the deaths?' Trix had opened up her laptop and was already scrolling through the details. 'Her psych report doesn't give us any indication she's the kind of person who would get off on death. There's every chance she might not even know Mille and Rutter are gone yet; it's only been a week or so, and if she's been off the grid, she probably left the moment the pre-test planning was over.'

She continued scrolling through the details.

'So, what, Garner gets it flown over to her after she leaves? Or she comes up to Scotland without anybody realising, hence her Spain disappearance?' Marlowe asked.

'There's no record of her flying over here, so if she did do that, she probably caught a private jet,' Brad suggested. 'For the money they're going to make off this, a private jet is nothing.'

'So, if it was here, we need to find Doctor Lina Moritz

before she sells the item,' Marlowe concluded, nodding to himself. 'Anybody else? Any friendlies?'

'I've seen your woman, Sonia Shida, walking around,' Brad replied. 'She seemed to be on your side when we were in Vegas.'

Brad's eyes narrowed, and he leant forward.

'St John Steele's here too.'

He grabbed Marlowe's arm before he could move, and Marlowe realised he was halfway out of his seat, Brad's hand holding him back.

'Sacred ground, Highlander,' Brad muttered. 'You might have a problem with him, but all you can do is talk it out.'

'Do you know where he is?' Marlowe asked.

'I do, but it's on the condition I go with you, and you don't take your gun.'

'How about if I just promise I won't shoot him?'

'I think we're gonna need a promise that you won't do anything to him,' Brad forced a smile. 'He's here on behalf of someone else, and I think you're gonna need him on your side, no matter what his problem with you seems to be.'

Marlowe, dumping his suitcase on the sofa, looked over at Trix.

'We'll go check out the location for the auction, and you can get to work checking about—'

'Hell no,' Trix looked up, interrupting him mid-sentence. 'It's mid-afternoon, it's prime suntanning time. I'll be down at the pool until at least six.'

She grinned.

'And then I'm going to start going through the inclusive cocktail menus.'

'With your laptop open?'

'Of course.'

'Then don't die,' Marlowe sighed and glanced back at Brad. 'You know the way?'

'Of course not,' Brad laughed. 'That's what sat nav's for.'

THE OCEAN'S PALACE WAS ANOTHER HOTEL RESORT, HALF-A-mile north along the coast, but unlike the Royal Plaza, which was available to the public, this was very much a private gathering, as Marlowe and Brad pulled up in their rented car.

The "hotel experience" differed from the moment they arrived. For a start, the hotel they were staying at *didn't* have armed guards scowling at them, like this place did.

Interestingly, it was Brad who reached for his weapon, but Marlowe shook his head.

'We leave them here,' he said, placing his CZ in the glove box of the car. 'We don't know what's happening, but as you said, it's sacred ground.'

Reluctantly, Brad passed over his own gun, a SIG Sauer, one of the guns he'd claimed didn't exist on the island which amused Marlowe.

Obviously, Brad had his own favourites too, and didn't play well with others.

Exiting the car, Marlowe and Brad walked towards the main entrance, Marlowe taking the key fob and tossing it to one valet, who passed him a card with a number on it in response.

The two armed guards at the doorway were watching cautiously, and as Marlowe approached, one held up his hand, the other still on the trigger of the assault rifle he had strapped to his neck.

'This is a private building,' he said. 'We don't allow—'

'Do you allow this?' Marlowe asked, pulling out and holding up his Orchid High Council coin.

The guard took the blackened metal coin, checking it carefully. Then, with a nod, he looked at Brad.

'He's with me,' Marlowe said.

'Guests aren't—'

'He's my therapist,' Marlowe continued. 'Do you want me in here without my therapist?'

The guard didn't know what to say, so Marlowe continued for him.

'Are you telling me a member of the High Council can't bring his own therapist into a building? Do you understand the mental distress you're causing me?'

The guard, deciding that this was too much hassle for him, and probably way out of his own pay grade, sighed, waving Marlowe and Brad through into the main building.

'If I'm your therapist,' Brad whispered as they walked in. 'Should I be charging you by the hour?'

'You already did back in Vegas, remember?' Marlowe retorted.

'I never did thank you for that,' Brad grinned, a hint of mischief in his eyes. 'Got myself some nice toys. I appreciate it.'

The building was extravagant in looks but not modern. Marlowe had expected it to be a recent build like the hotel they were staying at, but this seemed more colonial with its grand facade, ornate balconies, and lush, tropical gardens framing the entrance. In addition, there was no reception area to the side where guests could enter. Marlowe got the impression that if you were staying here, you didn't need a reception. People would pick you up and take you directly to your room, no questions asked.

Walking through what seemed to be an open air lobby, they emerged out onto a large patio on top of a set of stairs. Following the stairs down, the wide expanse of white marble gleaming in the sun, they could see a square swimming pool ahead of them, the blue water glinting between cabanas, where beautiful leggy women in almost next to nothing lounged, sunglasses on, either listening to music or audio-books in their headphones, or reading books.

None of them had men with them. Marlowe had to wonder whether they were actually there as guests or whether they were also part of the furniture.

As they were standing at the top of the stairs, a young man, Dominican, walked over to them. He wore a loose, beige polo-shirt with matching trousers, a name badge labelled "Andre", he sported a thin moustache, and his hair was cut short and neat, an iPad in his hand.

'Good afternoon, sir,' he said as he walked over. 'I understand you and your, um, *therapist* have passed our security?'

He looked at Brad with a hint of mockery as he spoke. Marlowe knew Andre didn't believe Brad's true position here, which was fine as far as Marlowe was concerned.

'Are we welcome?' he asked. 'Or is there a problem?'

'Your coin and your position on the High Council of Orchid mean you are welcome,' Andre replied. 'However, Mister Marlowe, your reputation precedes you, and we have to wonder why you're here.'

'Doctor Lina Moritz.' Marlowe wondered how they'd worked his identity out already, and whether they'd been monitoring him since his arrival. If that was the case, then Trix could be in trouble. 'I'm guessing she's staying here. We'd like to speak to her.'

'I'm afraid Doctor Moritz is unavailable to speak to

anybody until the auction,' Andre waved a hand, almost apologetically, while confirming Marlowe's question of whether Moritz was involved somehow. 'I hope you can understand this is not personal, it's simply business. We wouldn't want any of the bidders gaining any kind of advantage over the others. It's simply not cricket.'

Marlowe gave a quick grin at the comment.

'When is the auction?'

'The auction has already started,' Andre started looking through his iPad's pages. 'We have some external bids, but the actual auction itself begins tonight at midnight. I'm assuming your guest and yourself will be here?'

'I'll have a different guest with me,' Marlowe clarified. 'My friend here is bidding on behalf of another conglomerate.'

'Yes,' Andre nodded, looking at Brad. 'I believe Mister Haynes is working with a US bidder.'

Brad raised his eyebrow at this.

'You did your homework,' he said.

'You were biometrically scanned the moment you entered the building,' Andre stated, almost as a matter of fact. 'We do this with everybody we have visit.'

'Good to know,' Marlowe decided to mention this to Trix when he saw her next. If everyone was biometrically checked, there had to be a database somewhere. *That* would be very useful.

'Anyway, enjoy the facilities,' Andre waved dismissively back down at the leggy women by the pool. 'We have a change of clothes if you so require. If you want swimming trunks or anything else, it is available free of charge for all guests and friends. There is also food available on the beach in our Barefoot BBQ. I would suggest trying the burgers. We've been told they're as good as any in the USA.'

'That remains to be seen,' Brad replied.

'I'm sorry we cannot provide you with help regarding Doctor Moritz.'

'That's fine,' Marlowe said. 'We'll be back later.'

He looked around.

'Hey, is St John Steele around?'

He felt Brad tense beside him. But Andre, without breaking stride, nodded and pointed across the swimming pool at a bar beside the edge of the sea.

'You will find Mister Steele there,' he said. 'He is wearing a pale-blue linen shirt and cream chinos. You cannot miss him. He has been waiting for you since you landed.'

Before Marlowe could reply, Andre turned and walked away.

'Gotta admit, I'm impressed,' Brad said. 'That was a hell of a performance.'

Marlowe nodded, already walking towards the bar.

'Are you sure about this?' Brad called out after him.

Marlowe didn't answer for a moment, then paused.

'Do me a favour, Brad,' he eventually replied. 'Have a look around. Scope the place out, yeah? I just need to have a quick chat with Mister Steele.'

'Are you sure you don't need someone beside you?' Brad asked, concerned. 'Maybe to place a reassuring hand on your arm to stop you slashing his throat with a cocktail glass?'

'I won't do anything until the auction's over,' Marlowe said. 'Trust me on that.'

Brad didn't, but let him go anyway, shaking his head as he walked off towards the Barefoot BBQ and the magical burgers they promised.

Marlowe chose not to follow.

Marlowe was on the hunt for bigger game.

10

BEACHFRONT CONFRONTATION

TAKING HIS TIME, MAKING SURE HE WASN'T WALKING INTO A trap, Marlowe strolled as casually as he could over to the bar. He could see Steele sipping at a drink, a Panama hat on his silvered, peppered hair, watching him cautiously as he approached, before relaxing slightly. Marlowe was also in a light, short-sleeved shirt and chinos, and anyone examining him could see there was no telltale bulge of any weapon under his clothing.

Marlowe saw Steele call to the barman, raising a hand as he did so, motioning at one of the bottles on the back counter. The barman then went off and started creating another drink as Marlowe arrived, facing Steele.

St. John Steel was known in both MI6 and MI5 for his skill set, something Marlowe had been warned about when he first heard the name. The man was a ghost, and had proven this by entering and leaving Marlowe's house without any problems on more than one occasion. Added to this, he'd shown himself to be formidable since Marlowe first met him in Paris.

However, he was also the man who killed Marlowe's step-brother Byron in cold blood, leaving Marlowe's own weapon behind to frame him in Las Vegas. Which meant right now, the man couldn't be trusted, and his true intentions were known to nobody.

'Thomas,' Steele said, not rising from the seat he had at the bar, but turning to face the man who now approached.

Marlowe took a deep breath and then finished the trip to the bar, stopping beside the older spy.

'Steele,' he replied.

St John Steele straightened as the barman brought over a strange pale-blue drink.

'I thought I'd order you something,' he said, nodding at his own half-filled duplicate. 'They call them an *Adios*. It's effectively a Long Island Iced Tea, but instead of Coca-Cola, you use Blue Curacao.'

Marlowe nodded, sipped at the drink. It was okay, but he could already tell it was incredibly alcoholic. He didn't believe that St John Steel would be drinking so early in the day if he was going to be around that evening, and was likely trying to lower Marlowe's defences, so he placed it back on the counter, nodding to the barman.

'Its full name is an "Adios Motherf—" Steele started, but was cut off as Marlowe leant past him to call the bartender again.

'Pass me a coconut,' he said, indicating a selection of cut coconuts with straws in the tops. The barman nodded and passed one over.

Marlowe sipped at it as he looked back at St John Steele.

'I appreciate the offer, but it's a bit early in the day for me,' he said. 'I'll be honest, I thought it would be a bit early in the day for you as well. Or is there something I don't know?'

Steele didn't reply, but Marlowe could see that his words had definitely hit their target.

'I didn't think we'd be talking the next time we saw each other,' Steele replied. 'You're a clever man.'

'You guessed I would work out it was you who killed Byron?' Marlowe asked. 'You think I'd have a problem with that?'

'That's not the part I thought you'd have a problem with,' Steele shrugged.

Marlowe smiled darkly.

'Ah, you mean the part where you shot him with my weapon and left it for everyone to see? Yes. It's a shame that the fluorescent drink spillage on your lapel gave you away.'

'Ah!' Steele nodded. 'I wondered how you knew it was me.'

Marlowe paused. Steele had wondered how Marlowe had worked it out, but *knew* that Marlowe had worked it out.

There weren't many people whom Marlowe had told.

'Sounds like you've been chatting to MI5,' he said.

'Marlowe, I've always chatted with MI5,' Steele replied calmly. 'I have friends in the highest of places, and yes, I was told that you'd commented on how I was the one who had killed Byron, and that you could prove it. I had wondered how your proof would come, but now I understand. The uranium glass, ground down and placed in the drinks. Seen by the UV filter, I'm assuming, on the camera?'

Marlowe nodded.

'I don't care that you killed Byron,' he replied. 'The guy was a cancer. He was also a brother I never knew I had, so I don't really want to shed a tear for him. However, I don't appreciate being set up for something I didn't do.'

'Not my suggestion,' Steele nodded. 'I was asked to do it.'

'Really? Marlowe paused, surprised by this. 'You weren't pulling the strings? That does surprise me.'

Steele shrugged as he took a sip of his own drink.

'We all have our paymasters,' he said. 'Some pay more than others.'

He leant back.

'In fact, it's my paymaster who has me here today. I'm guessing you're here for Broad Sword? Bidding for king and country? I'd heard Joanna Karolides was unhappy.'

'Who are *you* bidding for?' Marlowe leant forward. 'There aren't many people in Orchid who are higher than you, the Arbitrator.'

'I've stepped down as the Arbitrator.'

'Yes, but you don't lose the prestige, do you? When a president is no longer a president, he's still called president. He still has the secret service. He still has the sway.'

'I am working for somebody, yes.' Steele shrugged. 'The Orchid High Council is the highest point of the organisation. But Orchid isn't in charge of this little toy anymore, and the new owner is looking at selling to someone else. And that person ...'

He trailed off before returning to his drink, sipping it. Marlowe wondered if he was finding a way to explain who he was working for without giving away the identity.

'Let's just say this one job, when I win the bidding, will set me up for life.'

He waved around the bar, the beach, the ocean.

'Do you know how much this costs?' he asked.

'Honestly, I couldn't give a damn,' Marlowe shrugged.

'That's because you're not living in the life.' Steele leant back on the high chair. 'To live in this world every day for the rest of my life would cost millions. That is my paymaster's promise, Mister Marlowe, and nothing will get in my way.'

'We'll see about that,' Marlowe sipped nonchalantly at the coconut juice. 'You're not the only one bidding.'

'Oh, I know, we've got the CIA, there's a couple of Russians, an oil baron's child. Even the Saudis have sent some people,' Steele shrugged. 'The amount of money that's going to be made is probably the national debt of a small third-world country. This here? It's the bidding to pay for a ticket at the show itself, where the real information gets sold.'

'The ability to overwrite drones.'

'It's not just drones and missiles,' Steele shook his head, almost pitying Marlowe. 'Yes, the device was stuck in a stealth fighter, but Broad Sword is adjustable. It can be placed in anything. It'll take every piece of data sent to it, extrapolate the answers, and give you a response. Imagine Broad Sword in an aircraft carrier. Imagine Broad Sword in a nuclear submarine. Dozens of Broad Swords, all across an army, in every section.'

He leant back lazily, staring at his drink.

'Modern warfare is more nuanced, Thomas. It's no longer just about "kill more of them quicker than they can kill yours" but about social issues - societal responses and pressures to an evolving conflict. "Do not shoot a target in the middle of a school" may be crucial in world opinion - the social dimension to winning a conflict,' he explained. 'But AI today suffers from so-called "Algorithm Bias" and increasingly researchers are trying to find ways to bring social factors into play, as it'll improve the "real world" effectiveness.'

'So what, the war games you put in work differently?'. Do you know how they trained it?'

'Oh indubitably,' Steele smiled. 'Most AI systems gather data and extrapolate actions based on algorithms that detect patterns. You could indeed feed it rules of engagement, war game data, etc, but this remains fairly mechanistic. Broad Sword is trained to think like the enemy, to know what they're about to do before they do it, based on social actions. And, to respond either in kind, or to utterly annihilate. Do you know how they trained it?'

Marlowe shook his head.

'I'm sure you're going to tell me.'

'Of course I am. You'd expect nothing less, after all,' Steele took a sip of his drink. 'The British, the Americans and the French worked together to create it, and placed in war game data and other extrapolated forces information from every scenario they'd considered since the Cold War – which means that whoever gets Broad Sword also gets information on the US army and the British military's tactics, for free.'

'You mentioned the French, too.'

'Yes, but let's face it, that's more a case of "additional content," if you get what I'm saying,' Steele grinned.

Marlowe finally understood. This wasn't just an AI device. This was a backdoor into anyone who wanted to attack the West. And the information on the UK and US battle plans was worth millions on their own, as Broad Sword could use this against the very people who created it, knowing their defences better than they did.

Steele frowned as he noticed Marlowe's attention drifting again.

'I'm sorry, Thomas, am I boring you?'

Marlowe returned his attention to Steele.

'Just looking to see if Doctor Moritz is wandering around,' he replied with a slight smile.

At this, however, Steele started laughing.

'Hoping to have a quiet word, are you?' he asked. 'I'm afraid that won't be happening, Thomas. You see, Doctor Moritz is under lock and key.'

'Really? That's an interesting way to treat a seller.'

At the line, Steele guffawed, a sound Marlowe had never heard him make before.

'You think she's the one selling?' he asked. 'God no, Thomas. Sure, she was involved from the start, and she was working on it, but she's just here for proof of life.'

'Proof of life?'

'Come on, you of all people should know the joys of believing an AI is real when it's nothing but a smokescreen,' Steele winked. 'Doctor Moritz is here to provide proof that Broad Sword does what it says it can.'

Marlowe nodded, and internally he was reassessing the situation. It sounded like Doctor Moritz wasn't quite the willing participant they'd believed she was.

'I see,' he replied. 'Well, it's been pleasant speaking to you. I look forward to seeing you at the auction.'

'Thomas,' Steele spoke as Marlowe walked off. 'Are we going to have a problem at the auction?'

'Not at all,' Marlowe replied, looking back. 'I mean, you took a gun from me, and I liked that gun ...'

He trailed off, staring directly at St John Steele as he finished.

'... But I've promised my friends I won't kill you until afterwards, so you're fine.'

Steele didn't answer, simply watching Marlowe as he gave him a nod and walked away. Marlowe meanwhile was thinking quickly. *So the auction wasn't an actual auction; it was simply a chance to attend the real one?* He had less than six hours before he had to return and there was a lot he needed to do before then. The question was ... *who had Broad Sword now?*

Steele had been quite insistent there were new owners.

Maybe Garner had been more industrious than they'd expected.

———

Trix was in the suite when Marlowe arrived. Brad Haynes had returned to report to whoever was around – Marlowe had got the impression it wasn't Sasha Bordeaux, and found he was a little disappointed at that. He'd hoped Sasha would be here, but it seemed that wasn't to be the case.

'That arrived for you,' Trix said, nodding over at the table. On it was a box. Opening it up, Marlowe was surprised to find what looked to be a tailored tuxedo, most likely perfectly fitting.

'Apparently, you made friends with someone called Andre?' Trix continued. 'The note said he was concerned you might not have the correct attire for tonight.'

She pointed at another box.

'They also sent a dress for me,' she shuddered. 'For shit-hot intelligence gatherers, you would have thought they would have found out I don't like dresses. And their trackers were shit. I burnt them all out with one EMP pass.'

'Well, trackers or not, unfortunately, tonight you're wearing a dress,' Marlowe examined the tuxedo. 'And you *have* to be there, as I'm going to need you as backup.'

'I thought Brad was backup?'

'Brad is here to help, but Brad is also here to buy the

device for the CIA,' Marlowe shook his head. 'And as such, I'm not sure how far we can trust him.'

'You're not sure how far you can trust Brad Haynes?' Trix considered the statement. 'I think we often call that "normal", don't we? As in "normal service has been resumed?" Did you see him? Steele, I mean?'

Marlowe nodded.

'Is he still alive?'

Again, Marlowe nodded, walking over to the minibar fridge and pulling out a bottle of water.

'So, go on then, tell me what happened,' Trix said. 'And don't leave out a single piece of detail. You don't know how important it'll be later.'

'You just want the gossip,' Marlowe said, taking a long, deep mouthful.

Trix shrugged.

'You see, and there you are thinking you don't know me,' she replied. 'Spill, Marlowe. I want to hear it all.'

11

LOT TEN

THE AUCTION STARTED SHORTLY BEFORE MIDNIGHT.

Marlowe hadn't been surprised to find that his tuxedo fitted like a glove. He'd expected nothing less from the level of service so far provided. Trix, however, was more surprised that her dress looked so good on her. She'd repeatedly pointed out that she wasn't one for dresses, preferring trouser suits, but Marlowe had to admit, with this gold strapless dress on and her hair pulled back, Trix Preston looked stunning.

Of course, being told this just irritated her, so Marlowe made a point of repeatedly mentioning it.

They'd returned to the Ocean's Palace resort, Marlowe finding he didn't even need to show his coin to gain entrance. Andre the iPad-wielding organiser had obviously told people that Marlowe was there, and they found themselves unopposed as they walked across to the beach, where the auction was being held.

The night was clear and warm, with barely a breeze in the air, as Marlowe and Trix took champagne glasses from the waiting servers. Across the pool Marlowe could see St John

Steele watching him. Steele raised a glass and, as Marlowe continued scanning the party, he could see across to the side Sonia Shida with a tall blond Japanese man standing beside her, most likely her bodyguard, and Brad Haynes at the bar, pulling at the collar of his tuxedo shirt, looking as out of place as Marlowe felt right now. There were a few other familiar faces. He recognised a West African warlord he'd once upset and decided to stay away from him. There was a Chinese triad owner, and a matriarchal Romanian ruler that Marlowe had once used as an asset. He hoped she'd forgotten who he was, but decided he didn't want to risk it and so kept his face from her.

Many of these people would have known him back in the times before the beard and the hair, and he was relying on this as a kind of disguise.

Of course, they also knew him under other names, Kieran Lachlan, Irish bomb maker being his usual go-to consideration, so it was best he kept to himself for a while. At least until it was too late to keep in the shadows.

The rules of the auction were quite simple; it was a charity art auction with the pieces expected to go for hundreds of thousands of dollars for an orphanage in Punta Cana. Each item, however, represented a different item being sold. If you wanted mercenaries for hire, you picked up a painting by Monet. If you wanted missiles or javelin weapon technology, you picked up a small statue of the Greek goddess Artemis. And if you wanted to be invited to a special secret, exclusive sale for an AI device that could destroy countries, apparently you were bidding on a tiny Russian ballerina in a music box.

Marlowe hadn't been surprised to see that the advance bidding had already been estimated into the hundreds of millions. Even the British government didn't really have that kind of money to throw on such an item, especially one they believed was theirs – although they did pay half a billion pounds once in a quick decision to buy into the failed assets of the OneWeb satellite organisation, so who knew what they'd pay for state secrets. From what he could gather, though, this was more a statement of intent; the top three bidders, once they proved their funding would go elsewhere to have a second, more intimate bidding scenario, likely where the AI was.

After all, nobody was stupid enough to keep a billion-dollar sale on site.

Moritz would likely go with the highest bidder, an additional level of security, perhaps.

Andre could be seen by the side of the stage, talking to a white-haired man with glasses. The hair was thick and lustrous and gave Marlowe the impression that either the man had dyed the hair white deliberately, or this was very much an "old before his time" hairstyle where a young man in his thirties or forties would find his hair going white overnight. It was cut short, left long on top, the glasses were small and rounded, and the tuxedo was a shimmering navy-blue.

As the man walked onto the stage and observed his now awaiting audience, he smiled.

'My name is the Broker, that's all you need to know. We'll begin with lot number one. Bidding starts at five hundred thousand dollars.'

A hand raised. Marlowe didn't recognise the bidder, but he also didn't care. He knew that the item he wanted was several bidding wars down the line, and he probably had a good ten to fifteen minutes before he needed to worry about it. Taking the time to check the beach, he nodded to Trix to go speak to Brad, see if he had any new information, while he walked across towards Sonia Shida, still unsure of whose side she was on.

As he was doing so, he paused.

A harsh-faced, slim woman with short gunmetal grey hair in a pixie cut stood uneasily between two bodyguards. Marlowe recognised her from the photo. Doctor Lina Moritz was as unhappy to be at the party as others were happy, glancing around nervously.

Marlowe decided, mid-stride, to change his tack.

'The auction's that way, sir,' the taller of the two guards said. Wiry and feral looking, his short, black hair was cut close at the sides, with a razor having etched out some kind of tribal design on the left-hand side.

Marlowe looked at him and smiled.

'The item I'm looking to buy tonight was brought here by your companion,' he said, looking at Doctor Moritz. 'I was hoping for a bit of authentication.'

'The authentication will be given during the bidding,' the second guard, similar in looks and clothing to the first but with a more sensible haircut and a moustache, replied. Marlowe guessed from the accents of both and their looks that they were Algerian, maybe French. Marlowe was utterly convinced he'd seen one of them before at a party in Versailles.

So, were they Orchid goons, or ex-Delacroix ones?

'I'd like to hear that from the doctor,' he replied. 'Or are you not allowing her to speak?'

The two men stared coldly at Marlowe. The one with the side cuts held up a hand.

'The doctor will be giving information, but we have been

told not to allow any bidder to gain more intelligence than the others. Surely you'll understand, sir, it's unfair.'

Marlowe nodded, looking around as if bored with the conversation already.

'Are you okay?' he asked Doctor Moritz. 'Are these men bothering you?'

'Sir, we told you—'

'I'm not talking to you,' Marlowe spun to face the first guard, and his voice was so commanding the guard stepped back unconsciously.

'I'm fine,' Doctor Moritz replied, and for the first time Marlowe heard the French Parisian accent of a scared woman. 'I just want this over with.'

Marlowe nodded again.

'We'll speak soon then,' he said, turning to walk away. But as he did so, he saw a man watching him from the side of the bar.

As far as Marlowe could tell, he'd never seen this man before, but the gaze was one of recognition, of familiarity.

Slowly, the man nodded, raised a glass. Then, as the music played and the first winning bid was called at three and a half million, the audience applauding, the man walked over to him.

'Thomas Marlowe?' he asked. 'I have very much wanted to speak with you.'

His voice was soft-spoken and calm, and Marlowe instantly felt threatened.

'I don't think we've met,' he said. 'You are?'

'I have many names,' the man replied. 'But I'm more known by nicknames, affectations, shall we say? You, for example, would know me as the Gravedigger.'

Marlowe kept a smile on his face and outwardly there was

no change to his appearance or emotions, but inwardly his fight-or-flight response was going crazy.

'I believed you were an urban myth,' he said casually.

'Is that why you used my name to steal from a Vegas casino?'

Marlowe grimaced slightly.

'If I caused you any inconvenience, I apologise,' he said. 'I didn't mean to. As I said, I believed the Gravedigger was nothing more than a story—'

'A story that now faces you and is very unhappy. Do you know what happens when someone takes my name in vain?'

'They get a stern telling off?' Marlowe asked, almost hopefully.

This actually made the Gravedigger laugh, and he patted Marlowe on the arm.

'I kill them,' he said. 'They become my next target, no matter what.'

At this, and with a sudden realisation, Marlowe interrupted, holding a finger up.

'Did you shoot up my church?'

The Gravedigger hunched his shoulders in a kind of apologetic shrug.

'It wasn't my best shot,' he said.

'You owe me a pane of glass,' Marlowe replied. 'And it's special leaded stained glass, so I'll be sending you a bill.'

'The only bill that is going to be paid, Mister Marlowe, is the one you'll be paying to me,' the Gravedigger breathed, his voice soft and threatening. Marlowe wrinkled his nose, his mouth shifting to the side slightly, as he took in this rather boastful statement.

'You will understand if I do my best to stop you killing

me,' he stated. 'I kind of like being alive, and being dead would kind of suck.'

The Gravedigger bowed his head slightly, giving a small nod of acceptance.

Marlowe looked around, seeing if anybody was watching him talk to the strange man, but nobody seemed interested in him, which was possibly a good thing.

'Would it matter if I explained I used your name to help take down someone evil,' he continued. 'Someone who had plans that would have made the world a worse place, and I used the Gravedigger as an urban myth, mainly because I needed somebody to be a bogeyman?'

The Gravedigger considered this, staring off over the ocean into the darkness of the night.

'No,' he replied. 'It wouldn't mean anything at all to me. You attacked my professional status, and as such, you need to be punished.'

'But not until the auction's over,' Marlowe added.

'Not until this auction is over,' the Gravedigger nodded. 'As I said, I am a consummate professional, and I would not cause a problem for potential employers down the line.'

'And probable past employers as well,' Marlowe smiled. 'I'm guessing there's a few people here who have used your services.'

The Gravedigger didn't reply.

Marlowe, however, stopped, looking directly at the assassin.

'Were you here because of the auction,' he asked. 'Or were you here because of me?'

'I only have one hit, one target at a time,' the Gravedigger said, using his index finger to tap on Marlowe's chest as, in the background, another bid was won. 'That has been my plan for several days now. I don't need to know about your problems with Silicon Valley, and the chess pieces that have been played by British agents before your mother passed away in London. I care about what's happened in Vegas, not what's happening now.'

Marlowe swallowed, keeping his expression calm. The fact the Gravedigger knew about his mother was mildly disconcerting.

'You should know that whatever happens now could end with the death of thousands,' he replied.

The Gravedigger shrugged.

'The thousands did not pay me to work for them,' he said.

There was a long, uncomfortable moment of silence.

'How did you know it was me?' Marlowe felt a pit of anger rise from his stomach, from his core.

'How did I know it was you, what?'

'Who was using the Gravedigger's name,' Marlowe asked. 'Sure, with hindsight, you know the Gravedigger name was used as part of a heist, but it could have been somebody on their own.'

'I do not know who played the Gravedigger, but believe me, that will be my next charge after I finish you,' the Gravedigger spoke calmly, peacefully, as if this was the most matter-of-fact situation in the world. 'But I was informed of your connection with Orchid, realised the two were obviously connected and I was led to a friend of yours.'

Marlowe felt the ice slide down his spine. Everything seemed to slow down. The surrounding voices became muted as he stared directly at the Gravedigger.

'You killed Monty Barnes,' he stated as fact. He'd known the cartridge had the fingerprint on it, but only now did it feel real.

'Montgomery Barnes died of a heart attack, I heard. Very old man, in his nineties—'

'Who gained a shock when someone blew his door in?' Marlowe's voice was lowering now, as the anger within him built.

The Gravedigger accepted the comment, and shrugged his arms out in a *what-can-I-do* kind of way.

'I was led to Mister Barnes, because Mister Barnes could find you for me,' he said. 'In the end, Mister Barnes didn't lead me to you, but I did find your address in his sat-nav.'

Marlowe said nothing. The chances were that the Gravedigger had been quite fastidious, looking through Monty's old details, probably finding the journey he had taken when he turned up on Marlowe's doorstep, bleeding.

'Raymond Gibson,' Marlowe stated the name calmly. 'He gave you Monty, didn't he?'

The Gravedigger looked as if he didn't want to answer, and Marlowe understood this. He was, after all, asking the Gravedigger to give up a source, but at the same time, the Gravedigger was under the assumption, mistaken or not, that Marlowe wouldn't be lasting very long, and so, as a show of goodwill perhaps, he nodded.

'When I learned that you were the one in Vegas,' he said, 'but had returned to the UK, I looked around for you, asked a few sources, and your name came up in connection with the Mister Gibson you spoke of, although he goes by the more colourful name of Razor. He now works for a busi-nessman, Arun Nadal, who I've worked with in the past, and I was able to gain from Razor the location of Mont-gomery Barnes. From there, I found you. I didn't want to shoot you in your house. I could have taken you out at any moment, whether it was in the nave, in your mezzanine bed area, or in whatever you've placed in the crypt, out of prying eyes.'

He smiled.

'Thermal imaging shows all lies, Mister Marlowe. Once you're dead, perhaps I'll go and have a look. Maybe some of the stock that you have down there will repay the heinous crime you have done to my reputation.'

Marlowe didn't respond. His mouth set tight, his lips thin, slowly, he leant close.

'I got your message, by the way – the cartridge with Monty's fingerprint on it,' he spoke, barely a whisper, but still heard in the busy outdoor area. 'You don't need to worry about hunting me because I'm now hunting you. You killed a friend, and that puts you at the top of my list. When this is done, you don't need to find me, I'll find you, and I'll take my vengeance for everything you did. I gave an apology, and I would have done whatever it took to make things right, but not anymore. I might have damaged your reputation, but you can gain your reputation back. You took something from me that you can't gain back.'

He felt something at his chest, glanced down to see that the Gravedigger had pulled a blade, now aimed at Marlowe, nicking the edge of his tuxedo, the sharp tip already catching a couple of threads. It was a curved Angel Fire G10 Watchdog Karambit knife, vicious in short range fights, and Marlowe was aware that the Gravedigger knew how to use it.

'One quick nick, and you'll bleed out on the floor,' the Gravedigger replied. 'No one will see, no one will care, and you will be quite dead by the time the auction ends and your friends come looking for you.'

Marlowe started to laugh.

'Two things,' he said. 'If I may?'

'Sure.'

Marlowe took his left hand, holding it up and reaching into the breast pocket of the tuxedo. There, with two fingers, he pulled out the blackened orchid coin of the High Council.

'When you looked into me,' he asked, 'did you know this?'

It was obvious that the Gravedigger hadn't, as he stared in an expression that went quite quickly from horror to disinterest.

'This changes nothing,' he replied. 'I could still—'

'If that changes nothing,' Marlowe grinned, 'then you should check my other hand.'

The Gravedigger glanced down and saw in Marlowe's right hand, a razor-sharp Samuel Staniforth Fairbairn-Sykes blade, resting against his groin.

'If it's good enough for the SAS, it's good enough for me,' Marlowe whispered. 'One nick and your femoral artery will go before you can touch me. You want to kill me? Go ahead. Just know that you'll be dying too.'

'Bravo, Mister Marlowe,' the Gravedigger said, stepping back, the Karambit blade disappearing up his sleeve like a magic trick. 'I look forward to seeing you soon.'

There was another round of applause and a cheer from behind Marlowe, and for a second, Marlowe wondered idly if they were cheering his actions. But glancing back at the stage, he saw the Broker had ended yet another auction and was moving along quickly. Now they were on auction number seven. Soon Broad Sword would be up.

He turned back to the Gravedigger and was unsurprised to find the man missing, disappeared into the crowd.

Like a ghost.

12

BIDDING WARRIORS

MARLOWE WANTED TO SPIT TO THE SIDE TO AVERT ANY CURSES placed on him.

The Gravedigger was an urban myth because nobody survived who met him, unless you were high enough on the food chain to pay him extortionate amounts of money to turn the other cheek – and even then you were talking small country national debt levels of money, and Marlowe had now made him an enemy. He'd obviously looked concerned because across the pool he saw Brad and Trix walking across the beach over to him.

'Who was that guy?' Brad asked. 'Looked scary.'

'You have no idea,' Marlowe replied. 'That, guys, was the real Gravedigger, and the man who killed Monty Barnes.'

'So, we kill him next, yeah?' Brad asked.

At this, Marlowe actually found himself chuckling.

'Brad, this guy is the scariest bastard you'll ever meet.'

'That's where you're wrong, Marlowe,' Brad tapped Marlowe on the shoulder in a friendly gesture. 'You keep forgetting that the scariest bastard I'll ever meet is me. So, what's the plan for tonight? I'm guessing you haven't got the budget to buy this item, and looking around, I'm realising that the CIA slush fund I've got to play with isn't gonna go anywhere near it, unless I ignore my restraints and just go for gold. Do we unite?'

'I was thinking more bypass the entire auction, to be honest,' Marlowe nodded at Doctor Moritz, still under guard. 'They've got her under lock and key. And the impression I got when I met her is she's not that happy about it.'

'You intend to steal her?'

'There's one thing that I know about the device,' Marlowe shrugged. 'It's not plug and play. Whoever buys this is going to need an expert to show them how to operate it. And so far, of the three people I know involved in this, two are already dead.'

'So, you think the doc over there is actually part of the sale?'

'Makes sense, get the people to buy for the chance to bid, while introducing the woman who made it, as part of the deal. We'll know in a second,' Marlowe nodded, as the Broker waved aside whatever auction item had been won; some painting by an abstract artist, in reality a box of ground-to-air Javelin missiles which had gone for close to seven million, and made space for a small Russian ballerina in a jewellery box.

'And now,' the Broker grinned, 'it's time for one of our biggest items so far. A Russian ballerina in a jewellery box, clockwork, from the time of Tzar Nicholas himself.'

He looked over at Doctor Moritz, now paling as she stood between the two guards.

'And obviously, for those already having asked, you will receive both the box *and* the ballerina when you win,' he continued. 'We already have advanced bids for this item ... now, who wants to start the bidding at a hundred and fifty million?'

MARLOWE HATED AUCTIONS. HE ALWAYS HAD. PEOPLE TRYING to snipe each other out, rivals driving the prices of items so high that nobody else could get involved, making the price of the item so stupidly extortionate that everything else then became higher priced to match it. He'd seen items at auctions that were worth a hundred dollars end up going for thousands, after two buyers wanted the same item. He was aware this was the point, but it irritated him just as much as he knew this auction was going to irritate him as well.

The moment the Broker said a hundred and fifty, three hands went up.

Within seconds, the bidding had gone to two hundred million dollars.

St John Steele currently had the bid, but then Sonia Shida held up a hand, taking it to two hundred and five million. She blew Steele a kiss, but before she could say anything else, one of the Middle Eastern contingent raised their hand, offering two hundred and ten million.

Marlowe expected this to go on for quite a while. After all, Arab countries would often pay this much just for footballers; it was a "put your money where your mouth is" buy in, to have the chance to get a prototype device that could be reverse engineered and used in anything. An Iranian pushed it to two hundred and twenty million, a Russian oligarch to two hundred and thirty million, likely less than the price of his last super yacht, and the warlord Marlowe had wanted to avoid placed it at two hundred and forty million. By now, people were starting to fade out of this. That was a tall figure just to go to a separate event, and now only the serious players were involved.

Brad looked over at Marlowe.

'This is insane,' he muttered wearily. 'There's no way we can get close to this.'

'We don't need to get close to this,' Marlowe replied. 'Remember, the money isn't changing tonight. This is to get into the top level bidders, so we get to play with the actual bidding later on.'

This said, he turned to the Broker, stepping away from the others.

'Excuse me!' he shouted, looking back at the Broker.

The Broker went to say something else, but then paused as he saw Marlowe standing amid the assembly, hand up.

'I'm sorry, Mister Marlowe, but if you hold your hand up, you'll be bidding for two hundred and forty million.'

'I'm fine about that,' Marlowe said, looking around, smiling at the others. 'I have a question first, though, about authenticity.'

The Broker paused. He wasn't used to this.

'I'm afraid any conversations of this nature would have been done—'

'I only arrived today,' Marlowe replied, interrupting, looking around. 'I'd like to know a little more about the device.'

'Mister Marlowe is ex-MI5,' St John Steele spoke now, his voice raising over the now muttering crowd. 'As such, I doubt the British government has the war chest available to an ex-spook to cover what the bid is currently on, which, by the way, I raise to two hundred and sixty million dollars.'

There was a hush, as everyone looked back at Marlowe.

Marlowe simply reached into his lapel pocket and pulled out once more, the blackened coin of Orchid.

'Mister Steele there is also ex-MI5,' he replied calmly. 'Although if you ask MI5 – and MI6, for that matter, they seem to believe he still works for them. But one thing Mister Steele *is* no longer, is a member of the High Council of Orchid, which I am, having inherited from my *billionaire* father, this coin.'

Marlowe didn't point out that he had inherited only the coin, and not the billions his father owned. He didn't need to. The crowd had already heard what they wanted to hear.

Orchid.

Billionaire father.

'Was this before or after you killed your brother?' Steele snapped.

Marlowe went to snap an answer back, but then paused. This wasn't a crowd that would care about innocence and double-crosses. These were arms dealers, despots, warlords. He decided to change tactics, and let Steele's lies work for him, rather than against him, for a change.

'My billionaire father died, leaving everything to his surviving son,' he spoke up. 'By killing him, *I* became the surviving son. So, why does killing Byron Taylor mean anything bad?'

He saw Steele's eyes widen as he realised that he had just forced his own hand, as Marlowe turned back to the Broker.

'Answer my question,' he said. 'And if I'm happy with it, I'll raise the bidding to three hundred million dollars. On the condition ...'

He looked back at Doctor Moritz, staring at him in horror.

'On the condition that I get time, before the second round of bidding, with the ballerina as well.'

'The ballerina is part of the deal, and this can be arranged,' the Broker nodded. 'What is it exactly that you wish to ask, Mister Marlowe?'

Marlowe let the moment of silence extend, the crowd falling into a hush.

'Where's the item?' Marlowe asked. 'I'm aware I'm buying this beautiful music item, but I'm sure there are additional parts that I'd be gaining as well, in another conversation somewhere else, which takes up even more of my time. And this wonderful children's charity would gain such a lot of money, if I knew where I'd be going to bid for those parts. I'm guessing they're not here, that would be crazy.'

'You are correct,' the Broker replied carefully, performing a dance that gave away just enough, while keeping the secret. 'The additional parts of this beautiful antique jewellery box are elsewhere, ready for the top three bidders, once verified, to attend a personal testing display before last bids are given in a closed envelope auction. After all, we wouldn't expect you to actually spend such money without seeing if the music box works. However, this is a risk capital round – if you don't win the music box in its entirety at the second meeting, you lose the buy in.'

'And will the seller be there?'

The Broker nodded.

'They'll be there as the bidding will, like this, be under the guise of another demonstration,' he replied. 'You'll be there as observers, watching the show, and only after this would the full box and ballerina be sold. I would suggest a private jet to the location provided, as I understand the ballerina doesn't travel well on commercial airlines.'

Marlowe gave a small nod. The Broker was subtly explaining that having a hostage doctor was best used with private jets. And anyone paying three hundred million for the device was likely to have their own fleet of them. But it also meant that the device was somewhere that a jet needed to take him, which could be America, Europe, maybe even back to Scotland.

'I'm a very busy man,' Marlowe said. 'I can't spend days travelling for even more parties and demonstrations, and jet lag would kill me. This item had better be within a five hours' flight.'

'Unfortunately not,' the Broker replied sadly. 'However, I'm sure an asset of your choice could go on your behalf and bid on it for you.'

Marlowe nodded.

'No sale.'

There was a sudden hubbub of sound as Marlowe stepped back.

'I'm not paying for an item that has parts I can't see and examine myself,' he explained, almost apologetically. 'I don't know you. I don't know what you do.'

He knew by saying this, he was antagonising the entire audience. The Broker was likely well known in the industry, in the underworld. Also, by saying this, he was effectively saying that he thought the entire thing was fraudulent. If it was him, Marlowe wouldn't have accepted this. He expected the Broker to do the same.

'Bidding stays with St John Steele, then,' sighing, the Broker replied sadly. 'Two hundred and sixty million dollars. Somebody remove this man.'

'I'm sorry,' the Gravedigger now spoke up from the back. 'But I have a prior commitment with Mister Marlowe, and I made a promise. He cannot leave until the bidding is done.'

Obviously recognising the Gravedigger, the Broker swore to himself as he looked around.

'Does anybody else want to place a bid in?'

'Two hundred and sixty-one million,' Brad Haynes shouted out. 'On behalf of the US government.'

Steele glared across the swimming pool.

'Two hundred and seventy million,' he replied.

'Two hundred and seventy-one million.'

'Two hundred and eighty million,' Sonia Shida now entered the bidding.

'Two hundred and eighty-one million.'

'Three hundred,' Steele almost shouted back in anger.

'Three hundred and one million,' Brad folded his arms. 'I could do this all day, you limey prick. You just tell me the number you stop at, and I'll go one million above it.'

The guards had been distracted by this confrontation, and Marlowe had taken the advantage to slip aside. He was aware the Gravedigger was likely watching him, but he was going to use this to his own advantage. Someone like the Gravedigger would have made sure that all the exits were covered, in case something went wrong, making sure he had a couple of exit routes planned. Maybe even set up some traps to make sure that if he needed to escape, he could.

Tapping his earbud, he muttered so nobody heard, 'Trix, are there any rogue signals that you can see, either on radio or Wi-Fi?'

Trix had already wandered over to the bar beside one of the pools, and was checking her phone. Marlowe knew it wasn't just something to make calls on; the chances were the phone she was using was more detailed and accurate than anything else in that room.

'Three radio detonators,' she breathed, the words coming through clear to Marlowe only. 'Quite basic, quickly placed in, probably done for escape.'

'Can you detonate them?'

'Probably, sure, once I nail the command frequency. Why?'

'When I give the command, set them off,' Marlowe replied.

'But we don't know where they are,' Trix hissed. And across the pool, Marlowe could see her hold her hand to her ear.

'Don't look like you're talking to me,' Marlowe snapped softly, hiding his mouth in case anyone was trying to read his lips. 'I know this is dangerous, but if we don't do that, there's a very strong chance we're going to get blown up ourselves.'

Across the pool, he saw Trix straighten, mutter to herself, and then nod.

Brad, meanwhile, was still playing.

'He hasn't got the money,' Steele protested. 'I want to return to my original bet.'

'I think you'll find that I'm ahead of you in the bidding,' Brad said, obviously enjoying this. 'And what do you mean I don't have the money? I've got the bank of the CIA, the US Treasury itself. Who have you got? A Russian oligarch? Maybe somebody from one of the border states? Maybe the ones we class on a watchlist? We'll just throw sanctions on them, freeze an account or two, and then you're up shit creek.'

The Broker had tired of this as well.

'Mister Haynes,' he sighed, 'you were invited as a representative of the US government and as such, you are welcome here. However, if you cannot prove that you have the funds you're risking here, we will return the bid to Mister Steele for the price he had before you started bidding.'

'Ah, hell, you guys are no fun,' Brad shrugged. 'I reject this. Like that Brit did. I'm going to take my bet away, although I'll point out both of us could have paid the money and you damn well know it. This whole goddamned thing is rigged. You can have the win, Mister Steele. We'll still be going through to the second round.'

'Whatever,' St John Steele said, glaring at him. 'When we're done, I'll make sure personally neither of you leave this—'

'Now,' Marlowe whispered the command, and as he spoke, Trix, ready for the order, set off the three radio detonators that she had found. The first was a large explosive device on the beach, buried in the sand, possibly hours earlier. It was loud and violent and sprayed sand high into the air. As for the other two, one was set into the base of the swimming pool, splashing the water out on everybody. And the third, within the topiary tree system to the right of everyone, exploded outwards, taking out at least three people in the blast.

It caused utter chaos.

Marlowe glanced back to see the Gravedigger staring at him. He wasn't surprised. He was actually smiling, and Marlowe knew exactly why. The Gravedigger had placed these for his own escape, and seeing Marlowe use them for his own advantage, had proven to the Gravedigger that Marlowe was a hunt worth having.

The auction, however, was in freefall. The explosions had come out of nowhere, and many of the attendees of the auction weren't established spies or agents used to this kind of drama. They were billionaires or warlords, bored politicians, people who paid others to deal with this kind of stuff. And now finding themselves as targets and believing they were under attack, ran everywhere, drenched, covered in sand, the smoke from the explosions blinding everyone as they stumbled around.

The Broker had been gathered up by his men, quickly being whisked back behind the stage. Marlowe was aware that many of the people who had bid tonight would want their items, the money not having yet passed, and this would cause an issue there. He was likely looking to get the hell out before anyone came looking.

However, Marlowe wasn't looking for the item. It wasn't here. But Doctor Lina Moritz was. Turning and sprinting towards the two guards on either side of her, he drew his CZ and shot the first in the thigh and the second in the shoulder, before either could pull his own gun. Without breaking a stride, Marlowe grabbed Doctor Moritz by the arm, yanking her backward.

'I'm not going to help you,' she shouted. 'I'm nothing to do with this.'

'For God's sake, Doctor Moritz,' Marlowe replied, hissing as they traversed their way through the crowds, who were also trying to find ways out of this estate. 'I'm trying to destroy the bloody thing. I don't want it, I want you to help me get rid of it.'

At this, Doctor Moritz's hawkish, serious face broke into a smile.

'Well, why didn't you say so,' she said. 'Get me the hell out of here!'

MARLOWE KNEW HE HAD PAINTED A TARGET ON HIS BACK, AND every second that passed, it narrowed in to where the back of his head was ready to be shot at any moment. If he was being honest, he had expected someone to try to take him out already. Random, wild gunfire was already breaking out across the grounds, as various warlords shouted at their security to *do something about this.* Trix telling Marlowe which way to run through his earpiece, and Doctor Moritz was keeping pace beside him, keeping her head down as the bullets flew.

Marlowe made it to the main entrance, where Andre stepped out to block him. He wasn't wearing the beige suit he'd worn earlier; now he was in a tuxedo, holding a hand up.

'This is very—' he started, and Marlowe was aware that he was probably going to say something like *unexpected* or *irregular,* but he didn't have the time for the discussion, so simply slammed his fist into Andre's face, sending him to the floor as he stepped over the unconscious body.

'Get back to the hotel,' he said into his earpiece. 'I'm going to lead them away. Grab everything, we're going home.'

'We've only just got here,' Trix's irritated voice came through the system. 'I had literally an hour in the sun.'

'Well, get used to loss because we're about to fly somewhere else,' Marlowe replied. Deciding he'd rather slow his pursuers than kill anyone, he holstered the CZ and drew his Fairbairn-Sykes knife. Ducking as somebody swung at him, he reversed the knife and slammed the steel pommel into the side of a head, dropping his would-be assailant. Killing people would lead to questions, and he already had one gunshot victim back in Vegas over his head.

As they got to the main entrance, however, he realised there was a significant problem. Brad and Trix had just taken the car, which meant that he had nowhere to throw Doctor Moritz.

Salvation came in the guise of Sonia Shida, pulling up in a black Bentley, the door opening as she leant out.

'Get in, you bloody fool,' she said.

Marlowe pushed Doctor Moritz into the car, diving in behind her as the tall, blond man that he'd seen standing beside Shida earlier in the day pressed his foot on the accelerator and the car sped off.

'Do you know what you've just done?' Shida said. 'Orchid will be furious.'

'Why? Last I saw you were the second highest bid, third if Brad's still allowed to play. That's an invite to the special kids room,' Marlowe replied. 'But to be honest, it's pointless without her.'

'Without her, it won't work,' Shida shook her head. Marlowe went to reply, but then paused in horror as Shida pulled out a gun, aimed it at Doctor Moritz's head, and tightened on the trigger.

'Don't,' he shouted. 'What the bloody hell are you doing?'

'If she dies, the weapon is useless.'

'Maybe not,' Marlowe replied. 'Think about it. There might be somebody else, there might be notes. At least if we've got her with us, she can help us destroy it. I'm guessing you want to destroy it, given the fact that you want to kill her.'

Doctor Moritz, meanwhile, stared, horrified, at the woman with the gun in front of her.

'There are others who could gain access to it,' she said. 'The only way to stop the AI is to destroy the AI. Killing me wouldn't do it. There are at least three others with the correct retinal scans still alive.'

Marlowe grabbed onto the side of the car as they took a corner at speed.

'Sorry,' the driver said. 'We're being chased.'

Marlowe glanced behind, but couldn't see anybody.

'Drones,' the driver continued, nodding up through the clear glass roof of the car. 'They're following us. They know you're in our car. They probably want to know what our plans are.'

'I'd like to know what your plans are as well,' Marlowe replied.

'Thomas Marlowe, you have put me in a very dangerous situation,' Shida snarled. 'You've caused me issues with a plan that I had, but more importantly, I must give you help and assistance as you are also a High Council member of Orchid, and made sure that everyone was aware of this when you raised your coin of office.'

'Looks like the coin has its uses,' Marlowe grinned.

'Very much so,' Shida signed with resignation. 'Although I don't think you've realised exactly what you've done.'

Marlowe didn't like the way the conversation was going, and it wasn't the second screeching turn that made his face look sour.

'What do you mean by that?' he asked, glancing up at the drone, seeing it continuing to follow them.

'I can help you get out of this,' Shida explained. 'I can get you asylum and I can make sure that nobody comes after you. But unfortunately, it means one more thing from you.'

'And what's that?'

'No more play-acting, Mister Marlowe,' Shida replied calmly, her voice unwavering, no matter what the car did as it travelled down the Dominican streets. 'It's time for you to take your place on Orchid's council. And this time, you will be a loyal servant.'

'You remove the drone following us, and I'll consider it,' Marlowe replied.

In response, Shida nodded to the driver who pulled to the side and exited the car, walking to the boot and opening it. Marlowe couldn't see what he'd pulled out, but he closed the boot, walked to the side, there was a *whoosh* followed by an explosion, and the driver climbed back into the driver's seat, tossing a rocket launcher to the side.

'The drone's now removed,' Shida smiled. 'Now, where were we?'

13

PLANE FOOD

They were on a freight plane again.

Marlowe had hoped the last time he'd ever used such a way to travel, when he was on the run escaping from San Francisco, he'd never have to do it again. But back then, Sasha Bordeaux had claimed the only way she could get him to safety without the authorities finding him, was to hide out in the back of a courier plane. Today, it seemed the only way to escape from the Dominican Republic without people realising who he or his companions were, was to repeat the process, courtesy of the CIA.

After escaping the chaos at the Ocean's Palace, Marlowe, Doctor Moritz and Trix, with the help of Sonia Shida, had gathered their items already prepared for a quick exit and head towards Punta Cana Airport, where Brad Haynes was waiting for them, a smile on his lips. As Whitehall seemed to now be working with Sasha Bordeaux in some kind of off-the-books CIA / Security Services operation, via Karolides and back channel meetings, it had been decided that Brad would accompany the fugitives as they moved to the next destination.

The next destination, according to Doctor Moritz, was Seville in Spain, where one of the last surviving architects of the device, Nora Eskildsen could be found, and where she'd been taken from, only a day or two earlier. That, and the fact that a dozen different powerful organisations, possibly including the rogue aspects of Orchid were now hunting them, kill orders likely on all of their heads, meant that it was Marlowe, Trix, Brad, and Doctor Moritz now sitting in the cargo bay, waiting to escape.

The plane was a courier jet for one of the large global delivery organisations, but as there were no direct flights from the Dominican Republic to Spain, Sasha had arranged for them to climb into the belly of a service that went to Heathrow, the plan being, once in England, to use a private jet to fly across into the continent. It made sense; once they were on UK soil, they didn't need to worry about people hunting them from the Dominican Republic, but Marlowe was concerned it exposed them at a time they really couldn't afford it.

He also was concerned about being on UK soil, no matter for how little time, just in case Orchid were able to stop him again.

Trix had found a makeshift changing area behind some of the larger boxes and, using her go-bag, had changed back into a large jumper and a pair of sports-type leggings. She'd also passed Doctor Moritz some of her gym gear – comfy joggers, and a loose t-shirt to wear under a jacket they'd picked up in the hangar before entering the plane. The two were equal in size and shape, and so it wasn't too much of a stretch for the haughty academic to change out of the cocktail dress she'd worn for the auction and into something a little more relaxed.

Marlowe, meanwhile, had just returned to his usual jeans, t-shirt, and sweater, sliding the CZ in a Falco paddle holster onto his hip. As for Brad, he seemed to be the only one prepared. He'd arrived with a "backpack filled with goodies", he claimed. Marlowe was interested to see what these goodies would entail, and surprisingly, some of the goodies involved packed lunches for everybody, which Marlowe was actually quite impressed with. He was even more impressed with "courtesy of the CIA", scrawled on each Tupperware box, likely in Brad's own hand, in a Sharpie pen. No doubt Brad's way of reminding them that this was on America's dime, regardless of who Marlowe was currently working for.

Doctor Moritz had sat silent for most of the flight. Marlowe understood why she would be so reluctant to speak. Only hours earlier, she was being given up as part of an auction, a prisoner for trade. She'd probably assumed that her life was over as she'd now been told two of her companions on the AI project were dead, so she herself likely believed she wasn't long for this world, perhaps dead within a week at most, once her usefulness was finally over.

Marlowe felt sorry for her; even though she'd been rescued, her life would never be the same. She couldn't return to the academic life she'd had before. There were too many people hunting her. And even if they had destroyed the AI device, Doctor Lina Moritz could always reverse-engineer something to create a second one.

Maybe Sonia Shida had been right, and things would have been better if Doctor Moritz had been murdered. A mercy killing to save the world, one life to save many.

No, Marlowe couldn't accept that for the moment. This

haughty, grey-haired academic wasn't the sacrifice she thought she was. Marlowe would keep her alive as long as he could. After all, there were others out there with the same information. Doctor Moritz wasn't the only person who could create such a device.

IT WAS FIVE HOURS INTO THE FLIGHT WHEN SHE FINALLY SPOKE.

'We should have a plan,' she said.

'I agree,' Marlowe replied, sitting up from his makeshift hammock. 'What kind of plan are you thinking?'

'I can lead you to a woman,' Doctor Moritz continued. 'We work together in Seville, created Broad Sword together, and she can help us stop it.'

'Sorry,' Trix frowned, looking up. 'But how do we know she's not connected to whatever's going on?'

'Because I was with her when they took me,' Doctor Moritz shrugged, leaning her head back against the hull of the plane. 'I'd assumed we were safe in Spain. I was stupid, though; I hadn't realised I was being watched, and I went out to grab some food, and I was taken. If they'd been watching me, they'd have been watching her as well, and the chances are she was taken at the same time, or they're waiting for me to return. But if she made it out, she'll be watching, and maybe we can get a message to her?'

Marlowe nodded. If he'd been running this operation, he would have let the contact in Seville go free, watching her to see what happened next. It was dangerous. If they took this opportunity, they were walking into a trap, most likely, but they didn't really have many other options.

'Tell us about this contact,' he said, leaning against the packing straps he'd fashioned into a makeshift hammock.

'Doctor Nora Eskildsen,' Moritz replied. 'She wouldn't side with them. If anything, she'll be resisting their efforts to stop her.'

'And how can you be so sure of this?' Marlowe asked.

'Because she's been my partner for almost twenty years,' Doctor Moritz replied.

'Sometimes money can replace business,' Marlowe started, but Trix tapped him on his knee.

'I don't think she means that kind of partner,' she smiled, looking back at Doctor Moritz. 'How did you guys meet?'

At this, Moritz's face softened, the anxiety suddenly disappearing, as she fell into a memory.

'We were both researchers at the Brain and Mind Institute of École Polytechnique Fédérale de Lausanne,' she explained. 'In Switzerland. We were part of the *Blue Brain Project* - a Swiss brain research initiative that aims to create a digital reconstruction of the mouse brain. It was mainly theoretical back then. We found ourselves at a lot of the same meetings and working late into the night, and one thing led to another.'

She rested her head against the bulkhead of the plane, looking up at the ceiling as much as if she was looking up at the roof.

'If they've hurt her, I'll be lost,' she muttered. 'If she's ... if they've done anything to her, I'll ...'

'Don't think about that,' Marlowe interrupted. 'So, how long have you been working on the AI?'

Doctor Moritz turned her attention back to him. 'Years, Mister Marlowe, for many different countries in turn, each one taking us further before they pulled funding, one way or another. In the end, we had two masters, effectively. After we lost French funding, we'd been part of a unit created by Whitehall to take our research and utilise it to work on a new stealth jet. At the time it was an AI to focus on drone control. But as time went on and more people got involved in the project, we realised that some of the people there had different ideas. We'd had military data inserted while in the drone phase, but this was now becoming outdated as the remit expanded. I'd brought in a French billionaire I'd known to help with the funding of other parts while we worked with the French Government – at the time the project was called *Charlemagne*, and he'd stayed after we moved, but he turned out to be less than honest with his plans.'

'You're talking about Lucien Delacroix?'

'Yes. You've heard of him?'

'Oh, we've heard of him,' Brad chuckled. 'Who was your US contact?'

'A woman named Pearson. A Senator.'

Marlowe nodded. He knew the Democrat Senator Alison Pearson, also a High Council member for Orchid, well. If Delacroix had managed to remove Maureen Kyle, Pearson was the Senator expected to replace her in the televised debate. Which, to Marlowe, meant there was a solid chance she was connected to him, even if she'd stepped aside during the Vegas heist so Marlowe could remove Gabriel Rizzo.

The Orchid High Council seemed to change allegiances like the wind, after all.

'So Pearson, Delacroix ... anyone else?'

'There was a contact in Whitehall, but Nora dealt with them,' Moritz shrugged. 'There was a comms expert for the RAF who worked with us, Flight Lieutenant Lisa Rutter. She designed the interface to the avionics and comms packages on the jet, but she had debts. I don't know what they were, but they'd been long term and crippling. Then one day she didn't have debts. It was almost like she'd won the lottery. But when you win the lottery and all your debts are removed, you don't have a face like the one she had, you understand?'

Marlowe did.

'Someone paid her debts off, but then the debt went to them,' he said. 'Did you ever deal with Squadron Leader Mille?'

'Yes, but it was Nora who dealt with him more. He was involved once we started positioning the Broad Sword AI into the stealth jet,' Doctor Moritz nodded. 'It was his job to fly it, you see, so he had to know what was happening from the start.'

'Dovale?'

'Before Mille, yes. He also helped with the wargame dataset and the drone flying when it was in the early phase.'

Doctor Moritz looked away.

'He played golf a lot,' she said, and her voice was harsh once more.

'Dovale?'

'No, Mille.'

Marlowe didn't need to ask the question. He knew what she was stating.

'Let me guess, it's around then that you met Charles Garner?'

'Only a couple of times,' Moritz admitted. 'I wasn't really needed in RAF Lossiemouth. Most of my work could be conducted directly in Seville at our Institute, and a think tank near London. It had a strange name.'

'Caliburn?'

'Yes,' Moritz nodded.

'You dealt with Sir Walter McKellan?'

'As I said, Nora dealt with the Whitehall assets,' Moritz shrugged. 'She also found the new funding when Delacroix died. A Spanish company, Neville Dinámica.'

Brad had been sitting silently for most of this, but now he leant forward.

'So Charles Garner, on behalf of someone else, convinces your RAF guys to steal the device,' he said to Marlowe. 'Pulling it out or something during the flight, claiming it had taken the aircraft over and then what, running away with it?'

'I think the idea was probably for them to give him the device,' Marlowe said. 'But why they thought they could get away with it, I don't know.'

'I think I might.' Doctor Moritz carried on. 'Mister Garner had never explicitly asked for the device itself, but he'd spoken to Mille often. I was there once, overheard a conversation. I got the impression while hearing them talk that Squadron Leader Mille believed all Garner needed to do was get an expert to look at the item and re-engineer the code. With what I heard over the last couple of days, I think the plan was to crash the plane, let Garner see the item, get what he needed from looking at the code, and then have somebody else, somebody connected to the research and rescue team come back with the device, found in the sea.'

'The perfect crime,' Trix said, whistling. 'No one would have known. So what happened?'

Marlowe chuckled at the realisation.

'Garner realised he didn't need to do that,' he said. 'Why worry about all those hours reverse engineering and trying to fix everything, when you could just take the item itself? He didn't care about Mille or Rutter; he'd paid them off, or whoever he worked for had. They were loose ends he could eliminate at leisure. He could probably claim he was nothing to do with it. The only reason he spoke to us when we visited was because we were Orchid.'

At that, Doctor Moritz flinched.

'Sorry,' Marlowe held a hand up. 'Let me correct that. He believed we were Orchid, when technically we're not really Orchid.'

Brad chuckled.

'Marlowe there's an honorary member of the gang,' he explained to Doctor Moritz. 'Daddy issues. Let's just say the people you dealt with in Orchid aren't the people he deals with, yeah? The woman who saved you in the car, who wanted you dead? She's running along the same lines. Stop the device. Only with him, he has all these Brit ideas of chivalry, so you're safe.'

He grinned as he looked back at Marlowe.

'Every organisation has its rotten apples, and its loyal soldiers, after all.'

Marlowe leant back as Trix whistled in surprise. She'd been working on her laptop, using satellites to gain Wi-Fi, in the same way that intercontinental planes did so, and now her screen had lit up.

'Your girlfriend,' she said, 'isn't just a science boffin, is she?'

'I don't know what you mean,' Doctor Moritz raised her eyebrows, obviously expecting some kind of argument.

'Are you sure about that?' Trix turned her computer around to show the laptop screen. On it was a photo of a woman in her late fifties, maybe early sixties, her hair pale-gold and pulled back, her eyes a piercing blue.

She looked almost smiling in the official photo of the MI6 agency file.

'Your girlfriend's been working for MI6 for the last twenty years,' Trix stated. 'And there's a problem we might have.'

Marlowe frowned, looking across, as reading the page, he saw the name.

'Yeah,' he said. 'Your partner, reports directly to Sir Walter McKellan. I thought as much when you mentioned Caliburn.'

Brad started to laugh.

'Wasn't he the guy that Trix shot in the foot?'

'He was indeed,' Marlowe sighed. 'Maybe we need to stop off in England before catching the jet and have a chat in Whitehall before we continue.'

He burrowed back into his makeshift hammock, shaking his head.

'This was supposed to be a simple mission,' he finished. 'Why is it getting more complicated?'

14

LAYOVER

IF THE GROUND CREW OF HEATHROW AIRPORT WERE SURPRISED to see the small selection of black SUVs, their windows tinted dark, pull up beside the freight plane that had just landed, they didn't show it. Marlowe wondered, as he clambered out of the back of the plane, the others following, whether they were used to seeing scenarios like this; strange stowaways emerging from carrier bays to enter such vehicles.

A man in a suit had climbed out of the first car, watching Marlowe, Doctor Moritz, Brad, and Trix step down from the plane.

'Doctor Moritz, Miss Preston, if you could get into the second car,' he said with a smile. 'Mister Haynes, if you could get into the third, or rather catch a bus perhaps? We'd be happy for you to do that.'

Brad grinned.

'It's good to see you too, Mister Saeed,' he replied.

Vikram Saeed, otherwise known as Vic, nodded at the CIA agent as he now turned his attention towards Marlowe, his thick black eyebrows almost knotting together as his face tried to look as serious as it could.

'You're in with us,' he said, indicating the back seat of the SUV. He didn't open the door. The fact he'd even told Marlowe where to go was more than Marlowe expected. Vic Saeed and Marlowe didn't exactly have the greatest of relationships. Vic was an MI5 agent, like Marlowe, and during the Fractal Destiny case had actively given Marlowe his position back within MI5 during Kate Maybury's escape and the surrounding chaos in Whitehall.

But it had also come out in the process that Vic was an agent of Orchid, and when Marlowe then took down billionaire Lucien Delacroix, Vic and his two associates, Peter Lloyd and Lawrence Jackson, assisted him.

Things hadn't been as smooth as he had expected, but Marlowe found that even though Jackson had turned out to be a traitor and Lloyd had been killed in the process, Vic Saeed had turned up to Trix Preston's apartment suite and had risked his life to save her own, working alongside Tessa Kirk.

The official story was Vic was working undercover in Orchid, on behalf of MI5, and although Marlowe didn't trust him as far as he could throw him, he liked the man and he genuinely believed that Vic Saeed would only betray him if there was something seriously worthwhile.

As Marlowe walked to the car, Vic stepped out to stop him.

'I haven't spoken to you since your little gift,' he spoke softly. Marlowe nodded quietly, glancing around to see if anybody was listening. Vic hadn't been in Vegas, hadn't been to Taylor Coleman's wake; the chances were he wasn't deemed high enough on the chain. Marlowe had effectively piggybacked over a lot of people when he was given the hereditary coin of the Taylor Coleman family.

'I'll be honest, it wasn't exactly a gift I wanted,' Marlowe replied.

Vic shrugged noncommittally, and Marlowe felt that he was trying to look casual and relaxed, while actually still quite annoyed at the situation.

'You're no longer MI5,' he said, gently. 'But the Home Secretary has vouched for you and told us you have clearance almost as high as Sir Walter McKellan. So, even though he's MI6 and seconded me for this, I have to follow your orders. And with the coin that you have, I must follow you there as well, it seems.'

'Vic, you don't need to follow anyone,' Marlowe replied, as he walked over to the door. 'And to be perfectly honest, all I'm seeing is chaos and factions fighting against each other. First it was Delacroix, then it was Gabriel Rizzo, now it's Garner and his whatever-the-hell-he's-doing.'

Vic went to reply but paused, staring at Marlowe, almost as if confused by the answer.

'I don't think *you* understand, Marlowe. The Orchid you've played with so far? Well, that's not the real Orchid,' he said, quietly walking back to the front passenger's door. 'There are layers like an onion. The Orchid that you've been playing with are *other* people on the outside, the billionaires who think they're going to take over the world, and the gangster families who think they can create alliances. But Orchid's been around for over a century, was created from the top societies of the world and it has the highest people *in* the world within it. And the coin you were given? That gives you access to everything, Marlowe. Not just the post-nine-eleven kiddies' table that you've been playing with for the last couple of months. I mean access to presidents, to African warlords, multinational conglomerates. Billionaires and industrialists who don't take court from the Prime Minister would kneel before you. Just because the people you've been dealing with are Championship League, doesn't mean that the people you *could* deal with aren't Premiership material.'

Marlowe took the advice, nodding.

'I understand,' he said. 'You know you didn't have to tell me this, you could have just let me muddle my way through and probably gained my spot when I was eventually removed.'

'But where's the fun in that?' Vic laughed as he opened the door to climb into his seat. 'At the end of the day, much of Orchid is "better the devil you know", and as much as we've had our issues in the past, you are a devil that I know. Talking of devils ...'

'Ballsy of you to call the Home Secretary a devil,' Marlowe frowned.

At this, Vic Sage raised an eyebrow.

'Who said the Home Secretary was meeting with you?' he replied, climbing into the front passenger seat.

Confused, Marlowe opened the door and looked in.

Sir Walter McKellan sat glaring at him. Vicious looking, lean and dressed in the tailored, tweed three-piece of an old-school British spy, McKellan was in his sixties, but looked as if he'd been around for centuries.

'Well, get in,' he said. 'It's bloody cold out there, and my foot really feels it these days thanks to your woman.'

Marlowe gave a small, sickly smile and climbed into the back of the car.

'Put your seatbelt on,' McKellan said as the car moved off. 'We have a small drive before we get to your private jet. Long enough for you to tell me what's going on.'

He turned and glanced at Marlowe.

'It's okay, you can tell me. Joanna Karolides has kept me in the loop on everything this time. It seems we're working together, as she can't really be seen buggering around with a burnt asset like you, while real MoD investigators are in the field..'

'I assume congratulations are in order on that,' Marlowe suggested. At this, McKellan gave a visible grimace.

'Or commiserations,' he replied. 'Do you know how many years MI6 hasn't had to worry about the Home Office? How many years we've had an interesting relationship, but always kept our trousers and pants up? Now, thanks to you and Fractal Destiny, MI6 and MI5 bend over and take it whenever they want to give it to us.'

'Thanks for the rather graphic and crude visual imagery,' Marlowe grimaced at the thought. 'I'm assuming you want a report?'

'Well, from what I can work out already, you've managed to kill a pilot and blow up an exclusive resort in the Dominican Republic,' McKellan glanced at his watch. 'And it's not even Thursday yet.'

Marlowe sighed, placing his head against the back of the chair. It was the most comfortable seat he'd sat in for many hours, and he was very much hoping he wouldn't have to sit in the back of another cargo plane for the second part.

'It sounds like you already know what's going on,' he replied. 'Charles Garner was some kind of middleman for a splinter group within Orchid.'

'You know this how?'

'Because I watched other members of Orchid, high-ranking ones, bid against each other for a chance to be considered for a chance to buy Broad Sword,' Marlowe explained. 'Which sounds like Orchid is going back to how it was during the Cold War; smaller splinter cells, each with their own plans.'

McKellan said nothing, simply staring at Marlowe, waiting for more data.

'From what we can work out, Doctor Moritz was taken from her apartment in Seville, where she'd been staying with her ... well, her partner, Nora Eskildsen, who apparently was also involved in the project itself,' he continued. 'So far we have four names connected to it, and two of them are dead. Which means whoever wants the device is cleaning house, making sure that either no one else can use the device's ocular security system once the buyer has all the details, or they're just really clumsy.'

'Let's not assume that someone like Orchid is clumsy,' McKellan raised an eyebrow at Marlowe. 'Although I do hear they've dropped their standards recently when it comes to new admissions.'

Marlowe ignored the jibe.

'I must admit, sir, I'm quite surprised you're not a member,' he suggested.

'I was asked. Turned it down,' McKellan shrugged. 'I'd started working with Caliburn around that time, and although it wasn't the same – more of a think tank than a Secret Society of Middle-Class Idiots – I could see the type of person they were looking to bring in. Any club that takes that cretinous St John Steele in is not a club I want to be in. Isn't that right, Mister Saeed?'

Marlowe couldn't work out if McKellan was subtly

informing them he knew of Saeed's allegiances, or continuing the MI5 lie of undercover work, but Saeed just smiled, looking back.

'No, sir,' he said. 'You wouldn't want to join any society like that.'

'Especially one that had Oliver Casey within it,' Marlowe added, taking the attention away from Saeed. 'But I'm guessing you didn't know at the time, sir.'

McKellan snapped his head around sharply to glare back at Marlowe.

'You're the one who brought an Orchid agent into Whitehall—'

'And *you're* the one who not only allowed the agent to work for him as an analyst but also gave her an Orchid agent to protect her,' Marlowe growled in response. 'We could carry on back and forth; well done, we've both been burned by Orchid. The only difference is, I seem to be in the middle of it, whereas you get to watch from the sidelines.'

He nodded at the car.

'Or is this your way of getting back into the game?'

'I want to talk to you about Nora,' McKellan ignored the jibe in the same way that Marlowe had ignored his. 'She's been an asset for MI6 – of mine – for decades now. She'd been keeping us updated on what was going on with Broad Sword. To hear that she's been taken is a bit concerning.'

'I'll be honest, sir. I wasn't aware she had been taken,' Marlowe said stiffly. 'All we knew is that there was a possibility—'

'She's been taken,' McKellan interrupted. 'Either that, or she's gone deep to ground. We checked the moment we heard that you'd picked up Doctor Moritz. She's not in her apartment, and no one has seen her for several days. When you arrive in Seville, Mister Marlowe, and wherever you go after that, you're tasked with finding and returning the AI device. If you cannot find and return it, your orders are to destroy anything connected to the AI device by any means necessary. That includes *anyone* who could recreate it.'

Marlowe did a double-take at the comment.

'Are you telling me that if I have to, I need to terminate Doctors Lina Moritz and Nora Eskildsen, who you just told me was one of your own?'

'We cannot let this fall into enemy hands,' McKellan replied sadly. 'I've known Nora Eskildsen a long time, but you don't have friends in this business, Marlowe. If they turn out to be problems, you need to remove them. Likewise, anyone else who gets in your way.'

Marlowe considered the order.

'How well did you know her, sir?' he asked.

McKellan shrugged, looking out of the window as he replied, almost as if not wanting to catch Marlowe's eye.

'I was the one who first trained her, worked on a couple of ops together,' he spoke. 'She was good. Quick, clever, clear-headed, you know what I mean?'

'I do, sir,' Marlowe replied. 'I also note that you keep speaking about her in the past tense. She might not be dead.'

'True,' McKellan nodded. 'She could have been turned, tortured. The list goes on, Marlowe.'

He looked back at the airport as they moved across the runway.

'Your woman, Doctor Moritz,' he said. 'She says she was taken from the apartment while grabbing some food, right?'

'Yes, sir,' Marlowe wasn't surprised that McKellan knew. He assumed Trix had sent an update to the Home Secretary, and Joanna Karolides would have made sure that McKellan was up to date on this as well. They might have hated each other, but the enemy of my enemy was my ally, and very much so in this situation.

'How do you know she's trustworthy?'

Marlowe shook his head.

'I don't,' he replied honestly. 'There's every chance she's with us purely because she wants to get the device and steal it back. I think she worked with Delacroix when he got involved with the French military, and she's French too, so they may have another connection we don't know yet. So, currently the jury's out.'

McKellan gave a small smile at this.

'You're not as naïve as I thought you were then,' he muttered. 'Good to see you've still got a little bit of tradecraft inside you.'

Marlowe took it more as a compliment than as an insult, as McKellan nodded at a small jet they were driving towards.

'Ministerial use,' he said. 'Karolides has cleared it for you and your friends. Go to Seville and find this item, Marlowe.'

'I'm not the only one searching,' Marlowe straightened, unclipping the seatbelt. 'We've got a dozen different people, including what looks to be two sides of Orchid.'

'This is what happens when one of your little men goes rogue,' McKellan smirked. 'You know, as dangerous as Orchid could be, while you fill it with people who just look out for themselves, I think we're mildly safe. Don't get Preston killed.'

'Sir?'

'Karolides likes her.' Now the car had stopped, McKellan motioned to Vic to open the door for them. 'Seems she made an impression on her when you were screwing around with Fractal Destiny. Probably didn't hurt that she shot me in the foot. Karolides likely has that CCTV footage on her phone for those special, quiet, alone moments.'

Marlowe said nothing as Vic Saeed opened the door, allowing him to exit. As he did, McKellan leaned out.

'This is on you, Marlowe,' he continued. 'There's nobody else who can get in there, nobody else who can do this. I'm not blowing smoke up your arse or anything like that, I'm stating the facts. Whoever has this device, they're expecting billions. They're going to look after Broad Sword like it's the biggest baby they've ever had. And we can't give you anything, because the moment we start moving towards it, they'll know. Someone will tell them. I can guarantee you they already know you're heading to Seville, and they'll already have their own tickets. The manifest is set for Madrid, but ...'

He trailed off. Marlowe knew what he was saying.

MI6 was as compromised as everybody else was.

'I'll do my best, sir,' he said.

'When you're finished, maybe we can have a chat about re-establishing you in the *correct* Secret Service,' McKellan smiled. 'One with a better name. Six is so much nicer than five, after all.'

Marlowe raised an eyebrow.

'A job offer, sir?' he asked.

'Well, since I last saw you, you've become a lot more interesting,' McKellan shrugged. 'I quite like the idea of having somebody on the Orchid High Council working for me.'

Marlowe didn't reply. He simply touched his finger to his temple in a doffing-the-hat kind of motion and climbed out of the SUV.

'Marlowe,' McKellan grunted, halting him once more. Marlowe was wondering if the older man was always this terrible at goodbyes. 'Garner was Orchid, working for someone else. You mentioned Orchid was also bidding on the item. Do you genuinely think it's a civil war?'

'I don't know, sir.'

McKellan smiled.

'See? You're not so stupid after all,' he said. 'Find the AI.'

Marlowe nodded one last time, and finally left the car, and McKellan behind him.

Vic was waiting as he walked towards the private jet.

'Seville has an Orchid connection,' he muttered softly. 'I don't know where or who, but I know there's a High Council there. Possibly someone who could help.'

'Or, someone who owes Steele, loved Delacroix, and will happily betray us,' Marlowe shook his head.

At this, Vic laughed.

'What's this "us" shit? Marlowe, you never thought it'd be easy, did you?' he asked. 'If it was, we'd send the screw ups.'

He paused, frowned, and then stared at Marlowe with his piercing brown eyes.

'Oh, wait,' he deadpanned. 'We did.'

Marlowe lazily flipped Vic Saeed the middle finger as, chuckling to himself, Vic climbed back into the car before it drove off.

As Marlowe watched it leave, he realised the others were now with him.

'Fun chat with scary granddad?' Trix asked.

'I've had better,' Marlowe turned, heading for the plane. 'Oh, and Karolides says hi. Ordered me not to get you killed.'

'Of course,' Trix replied as if it was the most obvious thing in the world. 'It's because I'm awesome.'

15

TAPAS TIME

THE NARROW STREET IN SEVILLE'S OLD TOWN WAS SHROUDED IN shadows, the weathered stone buildings looming on either side. Wrought-iron balconies clung to the upper storeys, while wooden doors and shuttered windows stood at street level. The cobblestone pavement glistened under the antique street lamps, the recent rain shower making them slippery to walk on, and freshly watered-by-the-rain potted plants perched outside doorways.

The street curved out of sight, its secrets hidden from view as the old-looking man in the moth-eaten coat sat against one of the yellow painted walls, staring across at the building opposite. His hair was bedraggled and long, pushed under a tattered woollen beanie, and the bottle he drank from was half held in a plastic bag, as if the man had a fear of touching the glass with his bare hands, which were swathed in bandages, his jeans dirtied and caked with the grime of years on the street.

If you saw him, you would avoid him, as he mumbled to

himself and sang snippets of unrecognisable songs. And that was exactly how he liked it.

It was late into the evening as the tourists started to trickle out, heading to their tapas bars and nightclubs. Some were even turning into hotels and guest houses to get changed before the evening's festivities.

But the old man didn't care. The old man wasn't here for that.

A young couple, Chinese tourists visiting the old town walked past, and the Chinese man had paused, and passed the old man a ten euro note. The old man had smiled up at him, mumbling something incoherently as the note disappeared into the folds of his coat, and the couple had continued on, most likely forgetting the man even existed within a matter of steps.

As he watched them leave, the old man leant back against the wall once more, tapping his ear.

'So far I've made twenty-five bucks in a couple of hours,' he said. 'Maybe I can do this more often.'

He wrinkled his nose.

'Although the smelling like piss bit isn't great.'

'But at least this time it's someone else's piss and not yours,' Marlowe's voice came through the earpiece. 'Any movement?'

'No,' Brad grumbled, taking a mouthful from his bottle. It was apple juice, not whisky, but he still grimaced as he took it. 'Why did I have to be the tramp again?'

'Because we could stick a beard on you and no one would recognise you,' Trix's voice now came through the earpiece. 'Marlowe's beard, unfortunately, is already there.'

Brad nodded. They had arrived in Seville a few hours earlier and had checked into a small apartment within a hotel on the Plaza de Armas. The hotel was boutique and very much tourist orientated, with a small tapas bar and a functional hotel gym within. The suites had been small, so instead Marlowe had gained three connecting rooms in an apartment style corner of the floor, all linked from one main door to the corridor, using his traditional plan of picking the most expensive rooms in the hotel, while booking three others at a more modest cost on a lower floor, where now an army of cameras and sensors were waiting for anybody to come visit.

It was what Marlowe always did; providing a decoy room to be attacked in a similar way to what he did with his onetime church apartment. After all, who in their right mind would order expensive suites when trying to keep a low profile?

Marlowe, that's who.

Brad found it amusing. The CIA would have fired him if he'd spent resources in such a way. Brad had then gone out into the town, and found an old man doing exactly what he was doing right now. They'd provided him a night in the hotel, using one of the fake rooms, with room service and a change of clothes, all for the cost of the clothing on his back. When Brad had arranged this, he didn't realise Marlowe hadn't agreed to play him. If he'd have known this, he would have likely found somebody who smelled less like urine. But at least he looked the part.

'They're going to notice me more as the night goes on,' he said. 'I don't have the things that a homeless man would have to bed down on.'

'Understood,' Marlowe said. 'Stay there for the moment, see if anything else happens. It's the last known address of Nora Eskildsen, so if anyone's monitoring it, you should see.'

Brad settled back against the wall and started humming a song. As the night was building up and more people were coming down the street, there was a chance he might double his money by the time he'd finished his mission.

BACK AT THE HOTEL APARTMENTS, AFTER CLAIMING A ROOM, Trix had put together her monitor and keyboard setup on the main area's desk. It wasn't that deep, however, and Marlowe could see that already the monitors that she had planned to place beside the laptop would push the laptop too far ahead for her separate keyboard.

Trix had already realised this and was muttering to herself as she started readjusting everything.

'If you want, you can grab a shower,' she said to Doctor Moritz. 'I know you've not had a chance to really freshen up since the party. I've already ordered some clothing to be sent up from reception, they have a small shop down there. I've asked for my size and a variety of items; they'll be here by the time you return.'

'Underwear would be good,' Doctor Moritz spoke almost sheepishly.

'I'll make sure that's sorted as well,' Trix gave a smile and, gratefully, Doctor Moritz walked off to the bathroom. The moment they were alone, Trix glanced back at Marlowe.

'I don't trust Nora Eskildsen,' she said. 'I've been looking into her file, and your line of how she was trained by McKellan and how she brought Spencer Neville the Third into the mix concerns me.'

'What are you saying?' Marlowe asked.

'I'm saying that although Doctor Moritz there seems to

believe that Nora is the love of her life and has been for almost two decades, I don't know if it's reciprocated,' Trix tapped at her screen, trying to get the touch-sensitive parts to work. 'Look, we all know spies who've gone deep cover, we had to fight a lot of them a little while back, but trust me on this, Marlowe. She's been giving McKellan ongoing updates, right? If she truly loved Moritz, she would have kept her out of them, redacted some of the more concerning parts involving Moritz. But she hasn't. Cold and callous, I've read them, and every single piece has been written with the emotional detachment of an active MI6 officer.'

There was a sound in the bathroom, and they paused, both then smiling as they realised that Doctor Moritz was now singing Celine Dion songs gently to herself in the shower.

'I don't want to see this woman hurt,' Trix whispered. 'Unless, of course, it turns out that *she's* the traitor. You were worried there might be a mole in Whitehall. Well, now we don't know if Nora has been turned, or whether she's been this way since the start.'

'I know,' Marlowe replied cautiously. 'I've been considering the same thing myself, and I didn't need the file to work that one out. McKellan likes to play his cards close to his chest, and he's a devious bastard. But he's a really shit judge of character.'

He counted names off on his finger.

'Kate Maybury worked for him, whether or not he agrees with it, and she screwed him over. Likewise Oliver Casey when he worked for McKellan. Both were working for some splinter group of Orchid.'

He sat on the sofa, rubbing his eyes with his hand.

'If Nora Eskildsen is working with Neville – both Nevilles,

even – and Garner, if she was involved in the team's corruption, then there has to be somebody who would have been involved with her. Somebody who could have passed her messages, a handler of some kind,' he muttered. 'Vic said there were people from Orchid living in Seville. Maybe they could tell us more?'

'Marlowe, you have members of Orchid living everywhere,' Trix chuckled to herself as she looked back at him. 'If Vic meant somebody high, let me look into it.'

Marlowe walked to the table, sat, and pulling out his CZ, dropped the magazine, ejected the round from the chamber, then swiftly field stripped the weapon and began carefully inspecting and cleaning it. He was halfway through when Trix looked back at him.

'Eva Gonzalez,' she said.

'You sure?' Marlowe asked, as he reassembled, cycled, and loaded the CZ.

'I'm using a list we gained during Delacroix's party in Versailles,' Trix was now looking back at the screen as she typed. 'Also, when we were in the *Crime City* virtual office, a Spanish IP pinged, so it makes sense she was there.'

'At the same time as Sonia Shida and Alison Pearson? That's promising.'

'It was also the same time as Delacroix came in, though, remember?' Trix admonished. 'Just because she was there doesn't make her a buddy of ours.'

'Still gives us a starting point,' Marlowe smiled, sliding his CZ back into the holster. 'Got an address?'

MARLOWE WAS GLAD HE WASN'T PLAYING THE PART OF THE tramp, but at least Brad was getting paid, even if it was by sympathetic people, as they smelt him from a distance. Trix, although on the same earpiece, was still at the hotel, Doctor Moritz with her. And while Brad had gone to monitor Nora's apartment, Marlowe had started his own search for Eva Gonzalez. Garner had given the impression back in Scotland that Orchid had assisted in some way with the theft. But Sonia Shida's bidding war with Steele had shown that multiple strands of Orchid were desperate to gain the item. For Marlowe, this meant that once more, the left hand of Orchid didn't know what the right hand was doing.

That showed chaos. Whether it was chaos that Marlowe could use to his advantage, he wasn't sure yet.

Marlowe didn't think he'd ever met Eva Gonzalez, outside of that brief virtual meeting in *Crime City,* a few months earlier. But he couldn't help but wonder whether the fact she lived so close to where Nora had been staying was less of a coincidence than he'd first believed. Trix had managed to pull up a physical address for her, and Marlowe had headed down to have a more "real world" word.

However, as he had arrived, he saw a woman matching Eva's description being escorted into a black SUV. Tall, slim, with black curly hair, and in her late forties, but looking ten years younger, she'd left before he had a chance to discuss the scene with any of the onlookers. He didn't really have time to speak to her. One thing Marlowe was sure about though was that whoever was taking her somewhere, she wasn't going willingly. Whether it was authorities or someone else, Marlowe didn't know. What he *did* know was that if she owed him her life, Eva Gonzalez would be an excellent asset to have.

The street parking near the address was chaotic at best, with cars having parked sideways or pointed out at the road, depending on apparently how the driver felt when they parked. Marlowe had hastened down the line, picking a BMW in the middle of the cars as his target. He had a smart ring on his right hand, positioned carefully on his middle finger, and as he walked past the cars, he would place the ring against the door handles. This wasn't just a ceramic health ring to tell him how he'd slept the previous night; Trix had been playing with this for quite a while, and as he reached the BMW, he heard a click as the ring's signal, emulating the Beemer's fob, convinced the car's brain to unlock the doors.

Hurriedly, in case the actual owner saw this, Marlowe slipped into the driver's seat and pressed the start button. As far as the car was concerned, the fob it needed to turn on was onboard, and so Marlowe quickly pulled out of the parking space, following the black SUV.

IF THE MEN WHO HAD TAKEN EVA GONZALEZ KNEW THEY WERE being followed, they did an excellent job of pretending they didn't. As they drove through the streets of Seville, following the road beside the Guadalquivir River eastwards towards the E-803, Marlowe considered his options. There were two men with Eva when she entered the vehicle. Neither had climbed into a driver's seat. That made at least three, with one more perhaps in the passenger seat. There were no cars following, so they believed they were okay to drive without an escort. He could take out the car quickly, bring Eva back.

But there was still the chance she *wasn't* going unwillingly, and he could cause more of a problem than he wanted.

Instead, he pulled up beside the car to get a better view through the windows.

They were slightly tinted but he had noticed, as it drove off, that the interior of the SUV was still visible through them. So, as he pulled up at the set of lights, he could see on a quick glance that Eva Gonzalez was sitting between the two burly men that had taken her, while an equally burly man sat in the front.

Eva scanned over to him, her face still, and Marlowe saw her eyes widen as she recognised him, before darting her head quickly to the windscreen once more before the guards could see the motion. The lights turned green, and the SUV continued forward, Marlowe now sliding back into the traffic behind it.

That hadn't looked cosy. She was being abducted.

Marlowe continued to tail the black SUV at a cautious distance as it sped eastward along the banks of the Guadalquivir, working out what he could do here. Three opponents were tough, but doable, but they also looked well trained, which changed the rules a little. His knuckles whitened on the steering wheel of the "borrowed" BMW, mind racing with strategy after strategy; all of which weren't good enough and ended with him failing.

At some point, however, the driver must have picked up the fact they were being followed, as suddenly, the SUV swerved into the opposing lane, accelerating to overtake a lumbering truck. Marlowe, forced to keep a distance, and making sure the truck didn't obstruct his view, gunned the engine to keep pace.

The driver of the SUV glanced in his rearview mirror, eyes narrowing as he recognised the pursuing sedan; in an instant, the chase was on.

The SUV veered right at the next intersection, tyres squealing as it careened onto Avenida de la Palmera. The grand avenue, lined with towering palm trees and an off-putting blend of historic Andalusian architecture beside modern buildings, was bustling with locals and tourists. Marlowe followed, the BMW's high-performance engine roaring as he wove through the traffic, trying to keep pace with the SUV as angry horns blared in his wake.

A city bus loomed ahead, lumbering out from a stop. The SUV lurched left, barely avoiding a collision, but Marlowe had no choice but to swerve onto the pavement, scattering terrified pedestrians as he did so. The BMW bounced and shuddered on the rougher bricks and cobbles, nearly clipping a lamppost before Marlowe wrestled it back onto the road.

Up ahead, the Puente del Centenario arched over the river, and Marlowe wondered if this was the target location, but at the last second, the SUV cut left, plunging down the off-ramp towards the winding streets of El Porvenir. Marlowe had no choice but to follow. El Porvenir was a historic neighbourhood, its once-grand homes now faded and crumbling, and the streets were a labyrinth, twisting and turning at odd angles, a legacy of the district's haphazard growth over the centuries. This meant the residential lanes were narrow and choked with cars as the SUV bullied its way through, sideswiping vehicles and sending pedestrians diving for cover.

Marlowe struggled to keep up, the BMW's sleek frame ill suited for the tight quarters. Then the arm and upper body of the guard to Eva's left appeared in the SUVs back window. Taking rough aim with a pistol he fired wildly as the SUV swerved and emptied his magazine at Marlowe, several rounds pinging off the BMW's hood and windshield.

Marlowe ducked low, fighting to keep control of the BMW as it careened down the street. The SUV driver swerved hard, trying to shake him off, but Marlowe clung doggedly to its tail.

The chase entered a small market square, shoppers screaming and diving in panic as the duelling vehicles roared through. Even though it was mid evening, the market was still in full swing, and fruit stands exploded, sending a colourful spray of pulped oranges across the BMW's windshield.

Marlowe hit the wipers, barely able to see. He knew Seville was known for oranges, but this was taking the piss a little.

The SUV made a hard right, barrelling down an alley so narrow the side mirrors nearly touched the walls. In a slightly wider car, Marlowe had no choice but to fall back, desperately searching for another route. He spotted a parallel alley, praying it would intersect with the kidnappers' path. Tyres screeching, he threw the BMW into a skidding turn, nearly losing control as he careened down the narrow passage. Then, up ahead, he spied a flash of black in the night – the SUV was emerging from the alley, just yards away.

Marlowe stomped the accelerator, the BMW leaping forward. The two vehicles raced down the street, engines roaring, now locked in a deadly game of chicken. At the last instant, the SUV flinched first, swerving right down a side street.

Marlowe followed, the BMW's bumper nearly kissing the SUV's rear fender as abruptly, the road ended in a tiny plaza, bordered by warehouses, closed for the evening. The SUV skidded to a halt, penned in, but before Marlowe could do anything he saw the two burly men leap out, dragging a struggling Eva with them.

But Marlowe was faster. Tyres smoking, he swung the BMW broadside, allowing it to skid in what he believed from the movies was called a "Tokyo drift", clipping the SUV's rear bumper. The impact was jarring and the SUV jerked sideways, catching both men, sending them stumbling to the ground, the impact slamming the driver into the front airbag with force, and leaving Eva, who'd been pushed ahead and effectively out of the way of the car crash, still standing for the moment.

Marlowe had mere seconds before the kidnappers recovered. He slammed the BMW into reverse, the wheels smoking as he spun the car to face back out of the alleyway, and a grateful Eva leapt into the passenger seat.

'Drive!' she commanded, as the guards scrambled to their feet, realising their vehicle was in no state to follow, and raising their weapons to fire impotently at the disappearing BMW. Marlowe led the stolen vehicle back out of the alley, and onto the Main Street—

Where a dozen police cars, blue lights flashing, were waiting.

'Shit,' he said, reaching for his gun, already trying to consider plans that didn't involve a gunfight, but was stopped when Eva Gonzalez placed a hand on his wrist.

'They're in there,' she shouted out of the window in Spanish to the officers, who baulked as they saw her face. 'You know what to do.'

The nearest officer nodded, and waved for one car to be moved out of the way, so the BMW could leave.

'You forget, Mister Marlowe,' Eva smiled as she motioned for him to move past, out onto the empty street. 'You're in

Seville now, and you're a High Council member. We control everything.'

She relaxed now, sitting back in the seat as the adrenaline left her body.

'They worked for a Baron I'd screwed over quite successfully,' she laughed. 'If they'd got me to him, I think I wouldn't have been found again. Or, rather, I'd have been found in small pieces all over the place. So thank you, Mister Marlowe.'

She turned and grinned wolfishly at him.

'So, why don't you tell me why you were hanging out around out my house, before I have my men hunt you down and kill you,' she continued, amicably.

16

POSH SNEAKERS

IT WAS SHORTLY BEFORE ELEVEN AT NIGHT WHEN THE FIRST SIGN of life appeared from Nora Eskildsen's apartment.

Brad had almost been ready to give up; the evening was drawing on, and the tourists were thinning out. Had he been a homeless man on the streets of Seville, now was likely the time for him to return to wherever he had his bedding rather than sitting against a street wall, standing out even more.

In fact, he had actually prepared to leave, scrabbling to his feet slowly, feeling the blood returning to his legs, stretching, muttering to himself, and reaching down to pick up the blanket he'd been sitting on for the last few hours, when he saw an incredibly expensive-looking Maserati pull up, and a man climb out of the driver's seat and walk over to the door.

Doctor Moritz had informed them the apartment complex housed three different inhabitants: a young Indian couple, an old Spanish man and his wife, and Nora. The man who had climbed out of his car looked unlike any of those. He was young and blond, with piercing blue eyes, wearing a white shirt with his collar open, which in turn was under a navy-blue, tailored suit. Interestingly, he had worn white leather, "Common Projects" sneakers with this ensemble.

The watch on his wrist was slim and incredibly expensive, with a distinct lack of labels. And, seeing the Maserati, Brad could already deduce that this man was either a proponent of the "quiet luxury" style of dressing, or he genuinely came from old money. Brad knew little about tailoring, but he knew sneakers. The white sneakers that the blond man wore, sneakers he didn't seem to care about getting dirty, were easily five hundred dollars' worth.

The man was talking into his phone as he waited by the door; Brad couldn't hear him clearly, but could tell there was an American accent. Possibly Southern, but he wasn't sure.

West Coast, maybe.

The man was ringing the doorbell again, and Brad could see that the button he had pressed was that of Nora Eskildsen and Lina Moritz.

'I'm telling you, she's not come back here,' he spoke into the phone, muttering to himself as he glanced around. 'The creepy French bitch is in the wind, thanks to my father and that screw-up in the Dominican.'

He paused, listening.

'Eskildsen? How do I know what she's doing? You've met the damned woman, she's a law unto herself. If she's clever, she's gone to the mines, and started prepping a rescue team. Moritz will come back somehow, and then we can move on with things.'

Brad had heard enough and staggered over, drunkenly, towards the blond man.

'Por favor, por favor,' he said in his most broken, guttural

Spanish, holding a hand out, as if he was hoping for gold to be showered into it.

'Oh Christ, it's a goddamned tramp,' the man snapped into the phone. 'God, he smells of piss too. Go away.'

'No comprende, no comprende. Por favor.'

'Christ's sake, what's "piss off you smelly tramp" in Spanish?' the man snapped into the phone. He looked back at Brad, waving his hand in a shooing gesture.

'Piss off,' he said, 'before I hurt you.'

'Por favor,' Brad said, still holding one hand out as, with the other, he pressed a button on the phone in his pocket, forcing a pair with the phone in the man's hand, currently too busy waving at the strange tramp, to notice the screen on his phone flicker as it connected.

'Piss off, before I *kill* you,' the man said slowly and carefully, opening the jacket to reveal a gun in a side holster.

At this, Brad simply held his hands up, looking terrified.

'No, no!' he cried, 'no!'

Staggering away, he started stumbling down the street. He didn't know who the man was, but it sounded like he'd wanted to meet with Nora Eskildsen, and Nora Eskildsen had let him down. But if he knew that Doctor Moritz had been taken to the Dominican Republic, then that meant this young blond man was up to date on the local gossip, which meant Eskildsen was *supposed* to be there.

'Trix, did you get that?' he said.

'I'm listening to him right now,' the voice came through. 'Phone was paired and cloned, I've got everything he has. You have a photo?'

'Couldn't take one without being outed, but I can describe him. Young, slim, blond, money. Expensive white sneakers, tailored suits, slim watches, drives a Maserati ... any idea who this is?'

'That I don't know yet,' Trix replied down the line. 'Could be the son, Spencer Neville the Third, or someone who works for him. But you definitely made a hell of an impression. He's talking about finding some kind of spray to take the smell off the clothing that you've given him.'

'It is quite pungent,' Brad shrugged. 'Hey, keep on him, I'm gonna come back and have a shower.'

'Yeah, about that,' Trix's voice came back down the line. 'Use one of the three decoy rooms, yeah? Dump the clothes in a bag and we'll arrange for someone to come and burn them. I've dropped one of your clothing bags in the first of the rooms.'

'Right, so I've been demoted to the backup rooms?' Brad was astonished and rather insulted by this.

'Only for the shower,' Trix chuckled. 'I'm not having anyone smelling like piss around. Once you're clean, and once you no longer smell, then you can come back and hang out with the cool people. Until then, Mister Haynes? Hobo, clean thyself.'

Brad had been unhappy about this, and spent another two minutes protesting down the line before Trix had claimed there was some kind of problem with the signal and disconnected his earpiece.

She knew he'd be angry, but, to be honest, she had more important things on her mind right now. Marlowe had been involved in some kind of car chase that had got the civil police up in arms, but seemed to be safe now with Eva Gonzalez, and Brad Haynes had found her a contact of Eskildsen and Moritz who knew what was going on, apparently.

Even so, it didn't give them much more than a rather irritated young man annoyed that his meeting wasn't happening.

She glanced back at Doctor Moritz, currently sitting watching the news, which in Spanish seemed to explain about a car chase happening through Seville. Probably Marlowe, knowing their luck. Trix didn't know what to say. She could mention that Brad had got a lead, but she didn't want to raise any hope.

Moritz, however, had other plans, turning to look at Trix the moment she'd disconnected the call.

'Did he find her?' she asked.

'A man went to the door but didn't go in,' Trix shook her head. 'We've cloned the phone and we're hoping we can find something.'

'Young man?' Doctor Moritz rose, frowning. 'There's nobody young in that place.'

'That's the point,' Trix said, as her phone beeped. She started scrolling down through the cloned phone files.

'What did he look like?'

'Brad said he was young, blond, was wearing a suit and a pair of white sneakers. Definitely looked like he came from money.'

Doctor Moritz spat to the side.

'Nora's money tree,' she replied bitterly. 'I know who that is. Our donor, Spencer Neville the Third. Rich prick. Drives around in a sports car, thinks he's better than everybody.'

'Why would he donate to you?'

'Because his dad owns a finance tech company and he wants

to take over,' Doctor Moritz rested her head against the back of the chair, looking up at the ceiling. 'I thought he was innocuous, not worth my time – his father's the more important of the two when you look at it on paper and crunch the numbers – so I never dealt with him. And he only ever spoke with Nora.'

Trix was already typing the name into her laptop; immediately social media images from around the world appeared. Spencer Neville the Third was money, and hung around with a ton of influencers.

'Maybe he was just simply knocking on the door to find out where she was?' Moritz suggested. 'He's funding us, so maybe he was concerned?'

'Maybe.' Trix nodded, keeping her cards close to her chest. 'Let's just see what happens once Marlowe's had a chat with Eva.'

Doctor Moritz nodded, watching Trix carefully.

'I'm a scientist,' she said. 'I'm used to staring at things, getting the smallest items out of information. I can drill down into data, and I can tell when someone's lying to me.'

Trix said nothing, simply nodding once more. Moritz, realising that the conversation wasn't going to continue, leant forward, staring at Trix.

'I know you're lying to me, Miss Preston,' she said. 'I'd like to know why.'

'Unfortunately, Doctor Moritz, at the moment, all you're going to get are lies,' Trix replied sadly. 'Because whatever we find out, I don't think it's going to be beneficial for you. And until we know, I don't really want to talk about it.'

Doctor Moritz puffed her cheeks out and released a breath slowly, accepting this.

'In that case, I think I'll go to bed,' she replied, glancing at the clock on the wall, seeing it had gone past eleven. 'I don't have time to play spies.'

Trix, once more, didn't reply, allowing Doctor Moritz to leave, and once alone, returned to the computer, pulling out some ear buds and playing some music through them to relax. Officially, both Doctor Moritz and Doctor Eskildsen were researchers at the Seville Higher Technical School of Engineering, known in Spanish as La Escuela Superior de Ingeniería, or ETSI, working as a small, private research unit. There was an internal website, an intranet that Trix was able to get through quite quickly. Chances were, nobody expected somebody to hack that; particle physics and advanced technology weren't as interesting, without shiny stage shows and billionaires performing PR stunts. Academic research was a lot easier to get into when you knew the right back doors.

But every university had a duty of transparency; donors needed to be named. However, after a while flicking through the internet, she paused, turning off the music, pulling out an earbud. She thought she'd heard something, but the room next door was silent.

There was no way Doctor Moritz would have been that quick to go to sleep.

'How often did you deal with Spencer?' she called out.

There was no answer.

'Doctor Moritz?'

Still no answer.

Feeling a pit of dread appear in her stomach, Trix quickly rose and walked over to the intervening door, opening it.

Doctor Moritz was gone.

The window was open; the curtains fluttering.

Trix ran to the window, staring out. They were on the fourth floor, and there was no way Doctor Moritz could have escaped, and as the room was part of the apartment, there was no door to the outside corridor – to leave, Moritz would literally have had to walk past her.

Trix frowned as she looked back out of the window. But instead of looking down, this time she looked up. And, as she did so, she saw the last thread of a rope being pulled up and over the top of the hotel.

'Shit,' she whispered, realising someone had come down from the roof and taken Doctor Moritz. 'Major shit.'

Brad was still in the urine-stained clothing of the tramp as he entered the hotel. He had expected to get some complaints, or some pushback from the staff at his appearance and pungent smell, but that late in the evening there was nobody at the front desk, and he could walk past quickly.

The squeal of Trix in his ear paused him.

'Brad! She's gone! They've taken her! I think they're on the roof!'

Brad needed nothing else. With Trix' alert ringing in his ears, he hammered the top button of the elevator, then drew his Sig from its 2 o'clock concealment holster and press checked the weapon, confirming a round in the chamber. If he'd been stopped as a tramp by the police, the gun would have been a problem. But watching Eskildsen's door from the street, he hadn't wanted to be unarmed.

Now he was glad he *was* armed, as it sounded like something worse was happening.

The door opened on the sixth floor of the hotel, and Brad ran to the stairs at the other end, slamming through the door and taking the steps up to the roof, two at a time. He could already hear the helicopter, and cursing, he slammed open the door, staring out as the helicopter started up, away from the roof.

Brad could see Doctor Moritz in the cockpit. She looked stressed, but wasn't struggling, like she had been in the Dominican Republic.

And then Brad saw why. Beside her, unclipping a tactical vest, one used by soldiers and law enforcement when abseiling down buildings, was Doctor Nora Eskildsen.

'Shit!' he screamed. 'Doctor Moritz! Stop!'

But there was no point in shouting. The helicopter was already lifting off and rotating away.

Brad turned, sprinting back to the door.

'Trix!' he shouted into his earpiece. 'You've got to follow that helicopter!'

'And how do I do that?' Trix's voice came through, out of breath, probably from running up the stairs herself. There were only two floors between her and the roof, and she probably felt this was quicker. Brad turned to the stairwell to see Trix emerge, staring up at the helicopter in anger.

'Oh, bollocks!' she said.

'Bollocks indeed,' Brad replied. 'We need to get out there after her.'

He went to move past Trix, but she held up a hand, avoiding touching him, but enough to stop him.

'Dude, you need to have a shower,' she said. 'We ain't going anywhere while you look like that.'

'And the helicopter?'

'Don't worry about the helicopter,' Trix replied. 'Moritz has a tracker on her.'

'When did you do that?' Brad was impressed.

Trix shrugged.

'Back in the plane when I gave her the jogging bottoms,' she said. 'She hasn't changed out of them yet, so I'm hoping we still have her signal.'

'And if we don't?'

'Well then, we're shit out of luck, aren't we?' Trix replied, heading back down the stairs. 'Come on, smelly, let's get you in a bath before Marlowe returns with his new friend.'

17

ENEMIES AND ALLIES

AFTER LEAVING THE SCENE OF THE CRIME, MARLOWE AND EVA had travelled to a small tapas bar on the outskirts of Seville. It was enough off the beaten track to give them some privacy, but Marlowe felt incredibly exposed. Eva Gonzalez, on the other hand, was more than happy to sit, eating away at some patatas bravas.

'Don't worry, Mister Marlowe,' she replied, 'this isn't a date, you're not my type.'

Marlowe hadn't even considered this, but nodded, as if agreeing.

'What is your type?' he asked.

'Older, more mature, slightly rugged. I'm afraid to me you're nothing more than a slightly excitable teenager with a beard.'

'You can't be that much older than me,' Marlowe almost pouted at the comment.

'Oh, I'm a good decade older than you,' Eva Gonzalez smiled. 'But I appreciate the flattery. Now why don't you tell me why you were stalking me?'

'To be honest, I wasn't stalking you,' Marlowe leant back in the chair, picking up the white wine Eva had ordered for him, and sipping at it. Eva had been happy to down entire glasses, but Marlowe still wanted to keep his head straight in case anything else happened. 'I was looking for anybody in Seville who could help me with what was going on.'

'Broad Sword.'

'You know of it?'

'Anything that happens in Seville is known by me,' Eva offered a piece of jamón from the board. Marlowe shook his head.

'Doctor Nora Eskildsen and Doctor Lina Moritz have been working on it for about ten years now,' she spoke through mouthfuls of food. 'They've been given a lot of money by a lot of different countries, but every time they do it, it comes up short. The Americans, the Brits, the Germans, French, even the Spanish, though God knows why we'd want it, have tried to get Broad Sword working in one way or the other.'

She dipped a chunk of bread into some extra virgin olive oil, chewing on it as she pondered the statement.

'Before Broad Sword, it was called Charlemagne. Before Charlemagne, it was called ... I don't know, something else. Same project, different names, similar outcomes.'

'The outcome being it doesn't work?' Marlowe watched Eva.

'Don't worry, this isn't another Fractal Destiny,' Eva replied calmly. 'Some Trojan horse made to steal stuff. This is an active AI. The problem is, it doesn't quite do what it's supposed to. Well, that is, it didn't, until you Brits came up with some ideas.'

Marlowe frowned.

'What kind of ideas?'

'How to make it work,' Eva said. 'Doctor Eskildsen's been in with the Brits for quite a while, but I'm sure you already know about that.'

Marlowe said nothing. He had expected Eva to know of Nora Eskildsen's affiliation with MI6, but the last thing he wanted to do was confirm it in case she was fishing.

'And Moritz?'

'Moritz has been tied to Mossad in the past, as well as the Direction Générale de la Sécurité Extérieure.'

'French Intelligence?'

'Of course,' Eva replied. 'She's a loyal asset to the French, from what I've heard. Either way, they worked with the UK government, as long as the funding was there. One of the last Defence Secretaries was working with them on it quite deeply, using tactical data to teach it, but then she passed away.'

She stopped eating, smiling.

'Actually, I think you were there.'

'You mean Harriet Turnbull,' Marlowe nodded. 'I was there when a sniper took her out.'

'A sniper who worked for Orchid,' Eva said, but Marlowe didn't hear a note of pride in the voice.

'You don't approve?' he asked.

'It was before your time, so you wouldn't understand,' Eva popped a potato into her mouth now, and Marlowe bristled. *Before his time* meant a matter of weeks rather than years. It was shortly after that he'd found out about his father's connection.

'Do you know the history of Orchid?' she continued through a half-filled mouth.

'I think so,' Marlowe said. 'Created during the Crimean

War, it was a collection of secret societies built out of the need for national security. Then, for decades, they worked in tandem with each other, compartmentalising when needed—'

'Such as?'

'The British not telling the Germans and Italians what they knew in World War Two,' Marlowe replied. 'Americans not talking to Russians during the Cold War, stuff like that. And then, after the Twin Towers came down in New York, Orchid decided it was best to work together. They'd lost millions, billions maybe, in that attack, and they knew that if they'd known about it, they could have fixed it.'

'They could have stopped the Towers falling?' Eva raised an eyebrow, almost playfully. Marlowe got the impression she was testing him.

'Knowing what I know about Orchid, I'd say probably not,' he snapped back. 'The impression I got is they'd made sure they got their money out before the Towers went down, but wouldn't do a damn thing to stop it.'

'And if you had controlled Orchid back then?'

'I'd have blown those pilots out of the sky.'

'And if the pilots were Orchid agents, performing their wishes of their masters?'

'I wouldn't have allowed the mission to take place.'

Eva nodded, and Marlowe wasn't sure from her expression whether he'd passed the test or not.

'And then?' she asked, returning to the tapas' plates.

'Well, from what I can work out, you guys realised you could have succeeded if you played well together,' Marlowe continued. 'You unified up to combine your resources, but over the last three or four times I've met with Orchid, we've had billionaires using it as their own banking system, rogue agents going off to try to make money, and crime families believing it's their personal playground. Meanwhile, my father gives me a coin that gives me everything I need to get in, but no one's exactly given me a rule book.'

Eva laughed.

'It's more of a "learning on the job" kind of thing,' she said.

'I can tell,' Marlowe replied.

'Again, Mister Marlowe, please explain to me why you're here?' Eva ate another piece of meat, watching him carefully. 'I mean, I'm glad you were, as you saved me from having to face a rather messy future, but ...'

'I'm looking for allies,' Marlowe stated carefully.

'Oh, Mister Marlowe, you don't have allies,' Eva replied calmly. 'Nobody likes you. St John Steele has been telling everybody how you killed your own brother to get your position.'

'It's amazing how someone's word can be taken when the footage might say something else,' Marlowe leant back.

'Show us the footage that proves you didn't do it ...' Eva paused, leaning forward, her eyes sparkling. 'You've got it, haven't you? Who was it? Steele? Someone he sent? Why aren't you showing it?'

'Maybe I want people to think I killed my brother,' Marlowe replied.

'Good idea,' Eva nodded. 'People might think twice before crossing you. And there are enough people out there who can't stand St John Steele that they might actually side with you if they think he doesn't like you. Why doesn't he like you, Mister Marlowe?'

'Probably because I've buggered up several of his plans,'

Marlowe shrugged. 'I know – no, I *think* Sonia Shida's on my side at the moment.'

'Shida?' Eva poked at a potato while muttering to herself. 'She's a backstabbing bitch if you ask me. And if you genuinely think she's on your side, then you're an utter imbécil. A moron.'

'She might not be on my side,' Marlowe said. 'But I know she doesn't want Broad Sword out there.'

'Because she was trying to buy it?'

'Because she was trying to destroy it. When she thought Doctor Moritz was the only person who could help people understand the device, she tried to shoot her in the head,' Marlowe explained.

'But was that to stop the device from being placed in the wrong hands? Or was that to make sure no one else could play with a device she wanted?'

Marlowe didn't have an answer for that.

'I hear you're being hunted,' Eva Gonzalez placed her hands back on the table, no longer eating.

'Depends who you've heard is hunting me,' Marlowe gave a smile in return.

'The Gravedigger.'

'You know him?'

'We've used him several times in the past,' Eva replied coldly. 'You should have been more careful stealing his identity.'

'As I said to him personally, I thought he was an urban legend,' Marlowe admitted, a little sheepishly. 'Knowing what I know now, I totally wouldn't have.'

He frowned and then shook his head.

'Actually, I probably would have,' he continued. 'But either way, he's taken it way too personally.'

Eva shrugged, accepting the comment.

'You're not the first person to piss him off,' she said. 'But you are the first person to still be standing after an encounter. It's a win, no matter how short-lived it is.'

'He killed a friend of mine,' Marlowe growled. 'He made himself the prey. And once this is done, I'll fix my problem, once and for all.'

'I have no doubt,' Eva nodded slowly, watching Marlowe carefully. 'But now? It's time for you to learn the rules of Orchid.'

She smiled.

'After dessert, of course.'

MARLOWE WAS AWARE HE HAD BEEN GONE FOR A WHILE, BUT HE didn't expect such sullen responses to his re-arrival, following his meeting with Eva.

'Is everything OK?' he asked as he arrived back at the suite, glancing around. 'Where's the doctor?'

'She flew away,' Brad said from the sofa, where he was staring, apparently, at the wall. His hair was wet, having recently showered, probably to get rid of the smell of the tramp off him.

'What do you mean, flew away?' Marlowe now turned to Trix as if hoping she would be a more obvious answer.

'Literally that,' Trix looked up from her laptop, where she was still working through pages of data. 'I found information that said that Nora Eskildsen might have been untrustworthy, and I think she picked up I was lying to her when I said everything was fine.'

She looked away.

'It's on me,' she said. 'All of this. I put on some music to calm myself as I worked. Some basic binaural beats, but a minute or two later, there was some noise that broke through, and when I went to see if she was okay, I saw she'd left her room.'

'Impossible,' Marlowe glanced around at the suite. 'You would have seen her leave.'

'Not the way she went, buddy,' Brad grinned, standing up. 'Someone came down to her window from the roof of the hotel. Then they slapped a harness to her and hauled her ass up to a helicopter that whisked her magically away to God knows where.'

'We got there as the helicopter lifted off,' Trix added. 'It was Eskildsen. We saw her taking off the harness as they left.'

Marlowe swore, slamming his hand against the counter.

'And we just let her leave?'

'What the hell did you expect us to do, cowboy? Shoot the damn chopper down?!'

Marlowe nodded, accepting the situation.

'I let you down,' Trix muttered. 'I wasn't paying attention.'

'You had the door in plain sight and didn't expect her to jump out a window,' Marlowe shook his head. 'You couldn't have planned for this. Please tell me there's a tracker, though.'

'There is. It was in her pair of joggers,' Trix nodded. 'But Eskildsen's not stupid. She's trained by McKellan. The first thing they would have done is scan her for anything. And in fact, the tracker disappears about fifteen miles away to the northeast, just south of Brenes. I'm trying to pull the data now.'

'Can we follow the helicopter?'

'That's what I'm working on at the moment,' Trix tapped

at the screen. 'We'll find it, Marlowe. But we have to look at the options.'

'What options?' Brad walked over to the minibar, pulling out a beer.

'The fact that Nora went back to save her girlfriend,' Marlowe replied, knowing where Trix was going with this. 'We know Nora Eskildsen was missing, but it seems from this and the posh boy you saw outside her house that she's not as hunted and on the run as we thought she was.'

'Either that or she's something bigger and we haven't worked that bit out,' Brad nodded. 'Oh, and "posh boy" turned out to be Spencer Neville the Third.'

He stretched, groaning as his back audibly cracked.

'So anyway, how was your conversation with your pretty Orchid member? Saw your chase on TV. Looked very exciting.'

'Apparently I'm not her type,' Marlowe grinned. 'Although I hadn't really realised I was asking. She prefers them older and a bit more battered, so perhaps you've got a chance.'

'I always have a chance,' Brad smiled. 'What did she say?'

Marlowe motioned for a beer to be passed across, and as he opened the bottle, he sat and faced the other two.

'Orchid's at war,' he said. 'And it has been for decades. The days of the uber secret society with tons of cash and plans to destroy the world are long gone. Now it's fractured alliances and billionaires with agendas.'

'So exactly as we thought,' Trix commented.

'Vic was right though,' Marlowe nodded. 'There is a High Council above the high councils. One that doesn't care for the squabbles and petty arguments. They're just there to keep the ship on course. The coin gives me the right to sit on it, but the

High Council isn't a boardroom. The number of people who have a say could fill a cinema.'

'There's that many coins?'

'There's various coins,' Marlowe explained. 'Gold, silver, and the blackened ones that I have here. All are levels of the High Council. All are connected to areas of Orchid, like the petals of a flower, and each one has its own basis. It's apparently a grandfathered-in clause from when each Orchid cell had its own national identity, as each Orchid cell would have had its own High Council.'

He rose from the chair, pacing.

'Lucien Delacroix was part of the onetime French Orchid, from before the twin towers fell and they all decided to play nice with each other,' he explained. 'They were allied with the West, but they had an arrogance that believed that they were better, stronger. Unfortunately for us, Doctor Moritz was also loosely connected to the French Orchid, from what I can work out.'

'That makes sense,' Brad muttered. 'Do we know how?'

'Eva Gonzalez was under the impression that Moritz was a bit more of a rebel than she gave out. She also had the impression that Moritz had a personal relationship with Delacroix. Not sexual, but they knew each other, so possibly through that.'

'Christ,' Trix started looking back on the screen. 'There's none of that here in Nora Eskildsen's reports.'

'There wouldn't be,' Marlowe shook his head. 'When she started working on Broad Sword, a lot of the aspects of her past were removed by Eskildsen. Probably with the help of MI6 and Sir Walter McKellan.'

'The stupid son of a bitch is *yet again* causing us problems,' Trix grimaced.

'In fairness, I think he believed he was helping this time,' Marlowe replied.

'So what, we thought she was a hostage, part of the deal ... but in effect, she was part of the team selling it?' Brad asked now, finishing his beer.

'Yes and no,' Marlowe continued. 'I think she was a hostage when we saw her, because the people she worked with weren't the ones who stole it. Apparently, things changed a few months ago. The plans had altered. There were mumblings around Orchid of a new direction, shortly after Lucien Delacroix's death.'

'Delacroix wanted it,' Brad nodded. 'That makes sense. Using his connections with Lina Moritz would give him a perfect opportunity to convince her to do what he needed.'

'The problem is,' Marlowe continued, 'while Lucien Delacroix was convincing Doctor Moritz to side with him on this, Nora Eskildsen, working for McKellan and MI6, would have been trying to do the same as well, but in a different direction. At some point, Lucien dies—'

'Thanks to you.'

'At some point he dies, and everything they'd planned starts to change. And by then, someone new enters the game.'

'The kid?' Brad suggested. 'Spencer whatshisname?'

'He's definitely funding it, but he doesn't seem to be the seller,' Marlowe shook his head. 'I remember Garner saying, "I was just a middleman, working for somebody else." I didn't get the impression he worked well with people younger than him, though. He was pretty pissed at me for getting ahead through my family connections, after all.'

'The dad, perhaps?'

Marlowe considered this.

'Perhaps,' he nodded. 'McKellan definitely thought so.

Said he was pushing military contract-level drones called the *Peacekeepers*, using AI tech this weekend in the US. So it fits the narrative, especially as Broad Sword had a *Pacifier* protocol which sounds similar, and the Broker insinuated that the winning bidders would be at another smoke and mirrors auction.'

He walked over to the window, staring out.

'Now we just have to work out if he's also connected to Nora Eskildsen and Lina Moritz,' he said. 'Because honestly? I'm not sure who the hell's siding with whom right now.'

He went to continue, but then stopped.

'Ah, hell,' he muttered. 'I know who would.'

He looked over at the others.

'We need to find the Gravedigger.'

18

DIGGING GRAVES

By the time they'd finished discussing everything it had gone past one in the morning, so Marlowe and the others had decided reluctantly that nothing else could be done for the day, and retreated to their beds to try to gain some sleep before the following morning. Trix, however, had stayed on the computer, convinced that she could fix the problem.

Marlowe didn't tell her not to. He understood that she probably blamed herself for their current situation, although there was nothing she could have done, and Marlowe himself had been the victim of several schemes before, where he'd been convinced of something only to learn he had been completely wrong.

The image of Kate Maybury appeared in his head as he considered this. Trix was right to berate herself. In a way, it'd make sure she wouldn't repeat the same mistake twice. But Marlowe knew that also meant that she'd become less trusting, and that was a sacrifice he wasn't happy about her making.

He had gone into his room and had spent the first two

hours simply lying on the bed, staring up at the ceiling, working through everything that he'd heard from Eva Gonzalez. The thought that there was a deeper version of Orchid, one that he hadn't realised he was technically a member of, had surprised him. This was a society that had spent over a century and a half since the Crimean War priding itself on its secrecy, yet Marlowe, a man who had repeatedly gone against them, had been earmarked as somebody worth continuing with.

He didn't understand the full story there, but Eva had promised to explain to him what was happening, and when he'd contacted her in relation to the Gravedigger, asking if there was any way she could arrange some kind of meeting, she'd made a point down the phone that this was a debt he would have to pay. A debt not only to her, but to the High Council of Orchid itself – and by that, Marlowe knew she meant the highest of councils. Adding this to the debt Sonia Shida claimed he owed as well ... he was starting to owe a lot to the bloody place.

Sighing, he decided to stop thinking about it and get some sleep.

It didn't work.

THEY'D DECIDED THE FOLLOWING MORNING THAT, WITH NO additional information on where the helicopter could have gone, and with only a few miles of tracking possible as Brenes was the last known location, Trix was going to have her work cut out. There was no way you could scan the Spanish countryside, especially the multitudes of national parks out there, and find a simple helicopter. It was a case of finding a needle in a field of haystacks. Brad had suggested using *FlightRadar24*, a global flight tracking service that provides real-time information about air traffic around the world through a combination of ADS-B, MLAT, and radar data, but Trix had shot this down; for a start the helicopter would have flown low over the mountains, causing issues, but with this being a stealth attack, and with *FlightRadar24* primarily tracking aircraft through ADS-B transponders, the pilot had likely switched off the transponder to avoid detection.

However, it was also Trix who came up with the plan to fix this after hunting through helicopter registries. She'd recalled the number stencilled to the side of the helicopter, as it flew away, five alphanumeric characters, and had spent the night trying to hunt down the registry, something that proved harder than she thought with the Spanish authorities servers.

Eventually, though, she leant back, punching the sky.

'Halle-bloody-luya,' she muttered.

'You have something?' Marlowe, looking back from the window, where he'd been staring, deep in thought for the last half hour, asked.

'Of course I have something,' Trix pouted. 'Did you ever doubt me? The alpha number comprises five characters. The first two letters are like a country code, so you can tell right away which country the aircraft is registered in.'

She looked at Brad, now entering the room at the sound of voices. He'd showered and dressed, and had the look of a man ready to go somewhere, waiting for an order to point him in some direction.

'It's kind of like how phone numbers have area codes, so you know if you're calling someone in a different city or country.'

'I know how alpha numbers work,' Brad snapped.

Trix shrugged.

'You're old, I wasn't sure,' she said dismissively. 'Anyway, the last three characters in the registration are specific to the company that owns the aircraft. It's like a fingerprint for that particular aircraft, so you can identify it no matter where it goes. So, when you see a aircraft's alpha number, it's basically telling you, "Hey, I'm from this country, and I belong to this company."'

'And the company is?'

'Neville Dinámica, the Spanish subsidiary of NevTech, a Silicon Valley FinTech company.'

'Neville,' Marlowe nodded slowly at the name. 'This is the kid rather than the dad, though, right?'

'It's what he's been working under, as Dad's apparently nothing to do with Orchid, or at least wasn't the last time we checked on him, and runs Neville Financial Technologies on the West Coast,' Brad replied. 'I had a chat with a mutual friend last night, mentioned his name in passing. It seems the Neville family is well known in the tech world. Kid's a dude bro, a nepo baby. His dad made money in the Silicon Valley boom, and his son seems to be doing his best to spend it all with his "NevTech" offshoot. Basically, he's Kendall Roy from "Succession" without the talent or the brains.'

'So, how did he get involved with all this?'

'That, I don't know,' Brad shrugged. 'But going on the fact that his family comes from tech, and your comment yesterday that Moritz and Nora had been trying to build this AI for decades, I'd say there's every chance that Daddy Dearest was probably involved before Sonny Boy turned up.'

Trix pulled up a photo onto the screen.

'This is Spencer Neville Junior, better known as Buck

Neville,' she said, as the image of a middle-aged man appeared. He was in the Oval Office, standing beside the president, shaking hands in some kind of staged meeting photo. It wasn't Anton McKay, the current president, it was Randall Seymore, his predecessor, so at least four, maybe five years old.

And Marlowe recognised him.

'Buck Neville was in Vegas,' he said. 'At Taylor's funeral. I never spoke to him, and I don't remember seeing him at the heist, but he was there when Byron played the video of his dad.'

'You didn't need to be Orchid to go to that,' Brad mused. 'Maybe he worked with your old man? I mean, the biological father you never spoke to?'

Marlowe cocked his head as he considered this.

'Maybe he was trying to get in,' he said. 'If he was involved with Broad Sword at this point, maybe he was looking for a buyer.'

He looked back at the screen to the right.

'We need answers,' he added. 'Maybe we'll find them at Neville Dinámica.'

It wasn't the first time Marlowe had broken into a corporate office, but it was the first time in a while he'd broken into the CEO's penthouse office, and more importantly, broken into one in Spain. The last time he'd tried something similar to this was in Los Angeles, and the way he'd done it was actually by hacking the humans rather than the technology.

He decided to repeat the opportunity.

Marlowe had arrived at the main reception as a courier. Not the usual UPS or FedEx style, with their uniform jacket on and cap on head. Trix had cobbled together an expensive-looking box, and so Marlowe had arrived in suit and tie, claiming to have been sent directly from America with an item purely for Mister Neville that could only be signed for by the man himself.

Of course, Spencer wasn't there. It's what Marlowe had wanted. If Spencer Neville had turned up, then he would have had to have had a very uncomfortable conversation about why he had a pair of gold-painted sneakers in a posh-looking box. With Doctor Moritz in the wind, however, and Nora Eskildsen having taken her, Marlowe was pretty convinced that if Spencer was anywhere, he'd be with them right now. This would not be a time to sit in his corner office and stare out over Seville.

Of course, once the receptionist explained apologetically in broken English that Mister Neville wasn't in his office, Marlowe reluctantly explained how he couldn't drop the item off, as this was a personal gift from a long-term friend. Sighing, and muttering how it'd be a long journey back, he then asked if he could go to the toilet while he was there, and moments later, after doing so, waved goodbye as he exited the building, still with the apparently expensive item in his hand.

What the receptionist hadn't realised is that the moment Marlowe had gone to the washrooms, he had actually found an external door, on which he had placed an A4 sheet of paper that read:

POR FAVOR, NO CIERRE ESTA PUERTA: LA CERRADURA SIGUE ENTRADA

Roughly translated, this asked not to close the door, as the lock kept catching. Marlowe had learnt in the past that people followed rules, and if they saw one, they would use it. A piece of paper inside the building saying that the door needed to be kept open, an innocuous request more than anything else, would be observed, and with the door closed, someone later on would open it.

Therefore, by the time Marlowe had exited the building, followed it around, taken off his jacket and placed on a pair of brown horn-rimmed glasses, then walked over to the door's external side, he found it was already open. In fact, there were already two people standing outside the door, cheekily smoking, using this as an excuse to get outside. Marlowe wondered if he'd even needed to bother with everything that he'd done beforehand. However, he also needed an exit, and this was a good way of doing so. Using passable Spanish, he bummed a cigarette from one of the two men standing there, "for later", in the process managing to steal their pass before entering the building, leaving the two men alone to smoke in peace. Once in, he could use the ID to gain access to the executive elevator.

Of course, he wouldn't have been so lucky to find a corporate board member on the first opportunity, but that didn't matter, because once Marlowe was in the carriage, he could place a small magnetic box, no larger than a Zippo lighter, to the base of the elevator panel, where Trix, waiting wirelessly, could hack the system and send him up to the penthouse office.

All he had to do now was get in and out before the smoker realised his pass was missing. Hopefully, that would be a while.

THE PENTHOUSE OFFICE WAS PAINTED A DEEP-RED — MORE A burgundy, if he was being honest – over basic plaster, and even though it was on a high floor of a chrome and glass building, it had been deliberately made to look like the main office of a Spanish mansion house, with deep, mahogany bookshelves behind the desk. In a way, it looked like the entire room had been positioned and designed around the desk in the middle, an antique wooden writing desk, modelled very much on the Resolute desk in the White House that as a child John F Kennedy was famously photographed sitting under; the desk that the President of the United States would sit behind.

Marlowe almost chuckled to himself. It was pretty obvious this was the reason that this particular style of desk was in this office. Spencer Neville the Third believed he was such a man of worth.

Once in the office, though, Marlowe worked quickly. There were security cameras, but Trix had paused them, using the same AI technology she'd used before, looping a blank template but allowing the system to create occasional birds flying past the window, or wind to waft through the open pane. They were high enough up that nobody could climb in through the window, but the slight movements would at least stop any security guard from worrying that it was just a simple picture.

Deciding not to begin an intense character analysis of Spencer Neville's Daddy issues, Marlowe quickly scanned the room, checking behind every painting or print on the walls for any kind of secret safe. He then pulled out another small device, around the size of a smartphone, turning it in a slow circle, using ground-penetrating radar built inside it to see if anything metal was within those walls, apart from secure studs and beams.

Nothing popped up; there were no safes in the room. Which, considering two of the walls were floor-to-ceiling windows, made sense.

So, where did he keep the secrets?

Marlowe moved back to the ornate desk in the middle of the room. The thing about desks like this was that when they were built they were made to hold secrets, so Marlowe started examining each drawer as he pulled them out, carefully returning each one to how he'd found it, before eventually finding one, holding pens, some twenty-Euro notes and a couple of USB cables, that had a false bottom. Taking a few of the Euro notes out of habit, and opening the bottom, he found a small external drive.

Marlowe held the external drive up as he looked around. He didn't understand why, but he felt this was a plant. False bases in drawers were obvious, maybe not to the average person, but to Marlowe, this felt like the same as the upstairs room in his secret church.

If there was a secret that could change the world, it wouldn't have been held in a drawer.

'I don't know about this, Trix,' he said into his earpiece. 'It could be a trap. I feel the moment we connect it, he'll know someone's been here.'

'I can create a Faraday cage and air-gap it from the system, but you could be right.' Trix's voice came through the earpiece. 'Is there anything else you can see?'

Marlowe glanced around the desk's surface. It was sparse, with a single monitor, a keyboard, and a mouse that looked like they linked to a MacBook of some kind, a personal laptop that would be held within a dock to the side. The dock was currently empty, meaning the MacBook was gone, likely with Spencer. Marlowe could guess that anything important was probably on that, but MacBooks could be lost. You'd still want to make sure things were backed up elsewhere.

On the other side was a green and gold banker's lamp, the style seen in buildings across the world, as well as in a ton of bric-à-brac stores. This one was well made and obviously expensive. In front of it was an ornate silver picture frame with a photo within. Three men on a golf course, somewhere sunny. Marlowe assumed that the bored-looking younger man on the right, keeping a slight distance from the other two, was Spencer Neville the Third. But of the other two men, Marlowe leant in closer, peering closely. Like before, the face of Buck Neville was familiar, but not instantly recognisable. He had been in Vegas, but Marlowe was convinced he wasn't a player. However, beside him was a familiar man; Charles Garner, full of smiles and excitement, with the three men playing together on a green of what looked to be the Moray Hope Golf Course.

Marlowe picked it up to look closer, but something felt off with the frame; it felt heavier than it should be, and as he shook it, there was a slight rattle, as if part of the backing was loose. Turning it and taking off the back card and stand, Marlowe saw that between the photo and the backing card-board was an ultra-slim portable SSD drive.

Bingo.

Marlowe took the drive and, pulling out his phone, he rummaged around in his pocket until he could find a small dongle that could be connected to it. This had been used when he was killing time in the MI5 gun room for months, a chance to put larger video files onto his phone to watch when he was bored. But now, placing the portable SSD into this, he connected it to his phone and whistled as an entire file system appeared on the screen.

'Trix, I'm uploading you some information,' he said into his earpiece. 'I think we have pretty much everything we need.'

This done, he placed the portable SSD drive back, reattached the frame to the photo, positioned it exactly where it had been, using a small line of unmoved dust as the baseline. Then, rising quickly and placing the external drive back into the base of the drawer, deciding to hold back on the obvious decoy, he exited the office.

He'd almost made it out of the door when a guard saw him.

'Hey!' the guard shouted. 'Hey!'

He then started shouting in Spanish at Marlowe, but Marlowe's Spanish was basic at best and, unable to understand him, Marlowe paused, turned, and gave a weak smile.

'American,' he said in his worst West Coast accent. 'Silicon Valley, San Jose. You speak English?'

'Where is your pass?' the guard said. 'You should wear your pass.'

'Oh, shit, sorry,' Marlowe said, pressing the button to the elevator as he rummaged around in his pockets. 'I lost my lanyard.'

'Always wear pass,' the guard insisted, walking up. 'Show me pass.'

He waggled his fingers, indicating that Marlowe should give him the item. Marlowe knew that the moment he did so, the face on the pass, that of a young, fresh-faced Spanish man, wouldn't match, and so he sighed, pulled out the pass, and gave it to the guard.

The moment the guard looked down at it, Marlowe jabbed his hand, held rigid and straight, into the guard's neck.

The guard's eyes rolled upwards, and he slumped to the ground, falling into Marlowe's arms as the elevator doors opened and Marlowe pulled him in. He knew that once he came out of the elevator, it was a short walk to the door that he had left to be opened, but he also knew that anybody walking into the elevator and finding an unconscious guard on the floor would call an alarm.

He didn't want that. He didn't want anybody to know that he'd been around.

So, rummaging quickly, he pulled out the guard's ID, flicking through it, finding an address. Once found, he slapped the guard in the face, waking him up.

The guard opened his eyes wide and went to move, but realised that Marlowe now aimed his CZ75 directly at his face.

'Pablo,' Marlowe said, holding up the wallet. 'We know who you are. We know where you live. Orchid knows everything.'

He'd hoped the word would be familiar to the guard. If this security officer was walking around the upper levels, the chances were he was given more security clearance than most other people. And, as he'd already learnt from the chase, people seemed to know Orchid around here.

Marlowe leant down.

'If you say a thing,' he said, 'Eva Gonzalez will find you. You know the name?'

The guard nodded, terrified, and Marlowe wondered just how much sway Gonzalez actually had in Seville. Deciding this was a question to ask some other time, Marlowe patted him on the shoulder.

'Go look in the office,' he said. 'There is nothing out of place. We have not taken anything. We have not left anything. We were testing your security, and we found it lacking. But you will not tell anybody, understand?'

The guard nodded again, and Marlowe smiled, pulling out the Euro notes he'd taken from Spencer Neville's desk and passing them over to the guard.

'This is payment,' he said, 'for your vigilance. Now stand up, stay here, and once I leave, give it ten minutes before returning to your post. If you leave early, we will know.'

He pointed at the camera in the elevator.

'We will know.'

The guard nodded dumbly and, as the doors opened, Marlowe smiled at him, holstered his CZ and left.

As he exited through his opened door, taking the A4 sheet with him as he did so, he wondered how long it'd take until Eva Gonzalez heard he'd been taking her name in vain.

He hoped it wouldn't hurt as much as it had when he'd done the same to the Gravedigger.

19

MINING TOWNS

IT WAS AROUND TWO IN THE AFTERNOON WHEN TRIX STARTED slamming her fist on the table and yelling out loudly.

Marlowe opened the door to the main area to find her dancing around as if she was in some kind of nightclub, pumping her fist into the air.

'I found them,' she shouted, looking at him, her eyes blazing in triumph. 'I bloody well found them.'

'Okay,' Marlowe rotated his neck to remove some kinks, glancing at his watch and seeing the time. 'Where are they?'

Trix ran over to the laptop, tapping at one of the screens beside it. She'd returned to her usual computer desk style of setup, where there seemed to be more monitors than keys on a keyboard. 'Fifty miles northeast,' she said. 'In the Sienna Morena Mountains. A few miles north of a small town known as Constantina.'

'And you're sure?' Marlowe asked.

Trix nodded.

'I told you I'd tracked Doctor Moritz. Well, it's about here where they obviously found the tracker and tossed it out of the helicopter, around Brenes,' she said, tapping on the map, around fifteen miles northeast of the hotel. 'Now there's one of two options we have here. The first is that Nora Eskildsen knew there was a tracker, and so they flew around in circles until they could find it, or the tracker was a surprise and they removed it before it got too late.'

'So, which was it?' Brad Haynes asked, opening the door sleepily, staring out from his own bedroom. He was wearing a towelled robe and what looked to be nothing else.

Marlowe hoped to God he wasn't going to let the robe open anytime soon.

Brad rubbed sleepily at his eyes.

'Sorry to interrupt,' he said, 'but nobody can bloody sleep while you're talking.'

'It's two in the afternoon,' Marlowe replied.

'I was working until late,' Brad muttered. 'Decided to have a disco nap and a shower. Haven't managed the second part yet as Preston here's making a goddamned racket.'

'Look at the line,' Trix said, ignoring Brad, as she started tapping the screen. 'It's completely straight. You wouldn't fly ten minutes in one direction and then turn immediately after. They probably started checking her the moment she got into the helicopter, and then tossed it out the moment they found it. Which to me says they weren't landing nearby. So, I followed the route northeast.'

She tapped again on the screen and Marlowe wondered if the monitor was about to fall over at the force of her inputs.

'You start hitting the Sierra Norte de Sevilla Natural Park around here, and towns become a little more scarce,' she explained.

'Sierra Norte?' Brad was still wiping sleep from his eyes.

'So, you've got this huge natural park called the Sierra

Norte de Sevilla, right? It's a proper wilderness, with mountains, forests, and all sorts of wildlife,' Trix explained excitedly, sipping at what was probably a cold cup of coffee. Marlowe didn't want to ask how many she'd had so far. 'You wouldn't want to get lost out there, that's for sure.'

'We knew this earlier,' Marlowe frowned. 'The whole needle in a haystack talk you gave us, yeah?'

'Yeah, but we didn't have this before,' Trix tapped the files now scrolling on her laptop screen. 'I'm going through the file structure; a lot of it is bobbins, sales figures and estimations, hidden because Spencer's been downloading files from Daddy's personal servers, but there's one interesting thing.'

She moved her attention back to the map on the screen, scrolling up.

'There's this place called the Cerro del Hierro here, see? It's like something out of a history book, with all these old iron mines and quarries scattered around. Proper eerie if you ask me. But, here's the thing, if you needed to land a helicopter somewhere without anyone noticing, the Cerro del Hierro would be perfect.'

She pulled up an image, showing a beaten track leading to some single-level white-walled buildings.

'It's in the middle of nowhere, and the terrain is so rough that it'd be a nightmare for anyone trying to track you down,' she continued. 'Plus, you've got all these abandoned buildings and tunnels from the old mining days. Plenty of places to hide out if you needed to lie low for a while. And if you wanted to get someone or something in or out of there quickly, you could easily do it from Constantina.'

Marlowe walked over, staring at the image.

'You seem convinced,' he said.

'The thing is, the Sierra Norte is so big, and there are so

few roads, that it'd be impossible to find out if someone was up to no good out there,' Trix nodded. 'It's the perfect spot for anyone looking to stay off the radar, if you know what I mean. And on this micro SD? A land deed. About three months ago, Neville Dinámica leased a ton of scrubland from the Ministry of the Environment of the Junta de Andalucía.'

'Creating a base of some kind, off the grid?' Brad grunted. 'That sounds like super-villain shit.'

Trix nodded.

'So, knowing this, I started checking satellite technology. One of the good things about having the clearance we've got is I can log into Whitehall and see if there's anything come up in the area.'

'Are you telling me that Whitehall is spying on Spain?'

'It wasn't,' Trix smiled. 'I might have pressed some buttons on a coding file and accidentally started a spy satellite down that route, though.'

Marlowe laughed.

'So, what do we have?' he asked.

Trix went to tap on the screen once more, but then thought about it, hovering her finger over the screen instead.

'The area's riddled with economic issues,' she added. 'From what I've gathered, it's a mix of economic downturns and a shift in agricultural practices. Many farmers in Spain have struggled with profitability, leading to abandonment of, well, less productive land. Cerro del Hierro was an active mine until the eighties when it closed. The Ministry of the Environment turned it into an open air museum about twenty years ago, but that didn't really help the miners.'

'Which means any strangers offering money to rent their land are likely to be welcomed,' Brad added from his room's door, now leaning against the frame.

Marlowe waited, and eventually Trix tentatively pressed the touchscreen, opening a satellite image. It was grainy and speckled, but there was the sharpness of something metal and helicopter-shaped there.

'This was at four in the morning,' she explained. 'If you see here, to the right of the houses, that looks like a helicopter.'

She swiped, and a similar image appeared, although this was clearer.

'Nine this morning, and the helicopter's gone,' Trix looked back at Marlowe. 'Whether that means they hid it somewhere, or they went somewhere else, I don't know.'

Marlowe walked over to the laptop and stared down at the screen, where Trix was currently looking at the recent satellite images, as a new thought came to mind.

'She made a deal,' he said.

'What do you mean?' Trix frowned.

'Look at it,' Marlowe pointed down. 'It's literally a small military camp outside of the town. They've pulled in some mercenaries, and someone's given them a Neville family helicopter. We pretty much can guess who that was, based on the land deed. Lina Moritz wasn't the victim we thought she was.'

He looked around, trying to fight the urge to punch a wall.

'She let herself be taken,' he said. 'Somebody took the device, but it was before they could do what they needed to do. She let herself get taken, so they could work out who had it.'

Trix held up a hand.

'Actually, hold that thought,' she said. 'We have something else.'

She tapped on her keyboard.

'You know how we booked some fake rooms downstairs just in case? Well, one of them is directly below Moritz's room. And the window was open.'

'So?' Brad frowned at this.

'So, we placed recorders and cameras in the rooms, to see if anyone came in,' Marlowe was seeing where the conversation was going. 'I'm guessing one near the window picked up the conversation on the floor above?'

Trix nodded.

'It was outside the window when Nora abseiled down,' she said. 'That's why we didn't hear it in here, but the recorder did. Listen to this.'

She pressed a button and sat back as the recording started.

'Nora?' Moritz's voice, stunned.

'I've come to get you out of here,' Marlowe had never heard Nora Eskildsen's voice, but assumed this was it. *'Come on, we don't have much time.'*

'These people are on our side. I can't leave them.'

'You'd side with them over me? Over us?'

'I don't even know what "us" is anymore.' Marlowe could tell Moritz was angry. *'How did they know to take me, Nora?'*

'Shh, keep your voice down. I don't understand.'

'They took me the moment I left. Only you knew I was going out. How did Spencer's father find out?'

'Maybe Spencer told him. Come on! We need to get you out before they hear! You have to stop the launch event in two days! Spencer is arranging a plane.'

'We can't trust him! They cloned his phone, they said he's—'

There was a faint zap, and a thud. More movement and then the sound of a ratchet being strapped.

'Pull me up,' Nora said, louder now she was outside the

building and closer to the downstairs window. *'She'll come to in a minute and I want to be away from here when she starts yelling at me.'*

Trix stopped the recording.

'A moment later I call out to her,' she said. 'You can just about hear it.'

'Harsh,' Brad muttered. 'Sounded like she tasered her, then pulled her out.'

'Either way, it was against her will,' Marlowe mused. 'She didn't escape. She was kidnapped a second time.'

'But why?' Trix folded her arms. 'Why would Nora Eskildsen risk everything?'

'Maybe because she really loves her?'

'It sounded there that Nora was the one who gave her up,' Brad suggested. 'I'd worry more that we have an issue where Moritz was needed for something else. The whole "you have to stop the launch event in two days" bit seems a little worrying. Not "we" but "you" singular.'

'Her eyes, perhaps?' Trix added. 'She and Nora are two of the only people who can enter the AI code, remember? But if Spencer's sorted a plane for her, we can pretty much agree Broad Sword is elsewhere. Maybe Silicon Valley.'

'Can we check his phone? You cloned it, after all.'

Trix shook her head.

'It went dead this morning,' she muttered. 'I didn't know why, but it's probably because Nora told him we'd cloned it. Bitch.'

'So, wait, the device isn't in Seville?' Brad frowned.

'No,' Marlowe shook his head. 'We always knew it was over five hours on a plane, but the Broker never said it was intercontinental.'

He tapped the screen.

'Dominican Republic to San Jose, where Silicon Valley is? That's a ten, eleven hour flight. We flew in the wrong bloody direction.'

'In fairness, we were under the belief we were saving Moritz's life,' Brad muttered.

Trix was about to reply when there was a polite knock on the door and Brad, in his towelling robe, walked over, opening it with a smile.

'Room service?' he asked.

'We have a message for a Thomas Marlowe,' the man at the door said. He was dressed in the uniform of the hotel reception, and had the sneer of a man who really didn't want to be passing the message.

'I'm Marlowe,' walking across, Marlowe held out a hand for the envelope in the messenger's hand.

'We have a message from Miss Gonzalez,' the man continued. 'She has arranged what you need. The details are in this envelope.'

He held it up.

'She said she would prefer not to do this by email, as such things could be compromised.'

'And a letter from Miss Gonzalez, passed via you, couldn't be compromised?' Trix asked, looking up, possibly insulted by the insinuation that her beloved technology could be tampered with.

If Trix had looked angry at the comment, the man's response to this line was five times the level. He stared at her with an indignance that bordered on fury.

'We have provided passcodes and notes for some of the highest levels in Spanish society,' he said icily. 'To open it would be to lose my honour. To lose my honour would be a death sentence.'

'Yeah, I was just making a joke,' Trix said, waving for Marlowe to take the envelope so they could close the door. 'Jog on, buddy.'

Marlowe passed a twenty euro note across as he took the note.

'I appreciate this,' he said. 'If you see Miss Gonzalez ...'

'Nobody will see Miss Gonzalez,' the man said, abruptly turning and walking away from the door.

Marlowe closed the door, looking back to the others.

'Nice guy,' he deadpanned.

'What is it?' Trix asked as Marlowe examined the envelope and the wax seal on the back. It looked as if Eva Gonzalez had used some hot, melted wax and then her own High Council coin to seal it down.

Opening it up, he read the message.

'The Gravedigger's in town,' he said. 'Arrived a few hours ago.'

'I wonder what made him think you were in Seville?' Trix asked, looking over at the turned-off television. 'Oh, I know. Maybe it was a stupid car chase.'

'Doesn't matter,' Marlowe replied. 'I have a location and a time. With luck, he might help us with what's going on here.'

'And how do you work that one out?'

Marlowe looked back at Brad.

'Because we need more information about who's funding this,' he said. He went to continue but paused as a line from the auction, something the Gravedigger said to him returned.

'I don't need to know about your problems with Silicon Valley, and the chess pieces that have been played by British agents before your mother passed away in London. I care about what's happened in Vegas, not what's happening now.'

Marlowe fought back a chuckle of admiration at the line.

Silicon Valley. The Gravedigger knew even then what was truly going on.

And if this *was* the Neville clan of San Jose, California, then Marlowe felt the Gravedigger was the best person to ask right now.

If he didn't kill him, that was.

20

NO WEAPONS

THE LOCATION EVA HAD PICKED FOR THE MEETING WAS THE
Plaza de España in the heart of Seville, a vibrant tableau of
history and culture. Built for the Ibero-American Exposition
of 1929, its purpose was purely to showcase Spain's industry
and technology exhibits, at the time. Now, its expansive semi-
circular complex, edged by a moat and adorned with ornate
bridges, created to represent Spain's ancient provinces, stood
still, kept as a monument to the country's rich past. And it
was here that Marlowe now stood, under the gaze of the tiled
alcoves, each depicting one of the fifty-two provinces in
Spain, with brightly coloured ceramics.

Marlowe had agreed to the rule of no weapons, although
he was unsure whether the Gravedigger would have done the
same. Nevertheless, he had arrived unarmed, and concerned
about what would happen next. Eva might have planned the
meeting, and Marlowe was calling the shots, however, it
might be the Gravedigger *taking* them.

The meeting had been planned for noon, although by a
quarter past, as the midday sun cast its rays over the Plaza,

Marlowe still stood alone, checking his watch for the twentieth time.

He knew he hadn't been stood up. The Gravedigger was in town and had agreed to the meet. One thing Marlowe had learned was that the Gravedigger kept his promises, which was concerning considering the last offer the Gravedigger had made to Marlowe. Therefore, Marlowe knew that this meant he was being watched right now by the Gravedigger, hopefully not through a sniper sight.

He'd deliberately not worn any body armour, knowing that if it had been seen, the Gravedigger would have classed this as some kind of trick, and so stood there in chinos and a pale-blue linen shirt, turning around slowly so that anybody watching him could see that not only was he unarmed, he was unarmoured.

After another five minutes of waiting, the crowd in front, a group of teenagers with what looked to be a very stressed teacher, moved on from one of the tableaus, and Marlowe faced a lone man in a dark-blue linen blazer, white shirt, and tan trousers.

The Gravedigger didn't give any acknowledgement to Marlowe as he started walking towards him. There was no friendly hello or nod of acceptance. Instead, he wore an ice-cold expression of nothingness, as he made his way through the crowds of tourists, over to Marlowe.

'This has been organised by a client I respect,' he said. 'As such, I have fulfilled her part of the bargain. I have not brought weapons and I will not use them to kill you.'

He looked around the plaza and Marlowe couldn't help, even in this busy tourist thoroughfare, feeling a little exposed.

Also, Marlowe noted the fact that the Gravedigger had

said he wouldn't use weapons to kill him here – not that he wouldn't actually *try* to kill him, still.

He shifted his position in case the Gravedigger was about to attack.

'When we were in the Dominican Republic, you said something,' he started. 'You mentioned that the things that were happening weren't your concern, you were there for me and me alone.'

The Gravedigger nodded.

'You also pointed out that the problems were to do with Silicon Valley and that chess games played before my mother died were none of your concern.'

Once more, the Gravedigger nodded.

Marlowe chanced his luck and continued.

'How did you know I was in the Dominican Republic?'

'I have my own ways.'

Marlowe didn't reply, staring at the Gravedigger, trying to work out if there was more going on than he could see.

'You knew about the auction, didn't you?' he asked carefully.

'I know everything,' the Gravedigger replied, and it was spoken matter-of-factly, not stated as any kind of one-upmanship. 'When I knew you were looking for the AI device that was stolen in Scotland, I knew you would come here. The black market had been talking about the device for several days, and I knew it wasn't worth waiting around in London if you were going to be travelling the world, especially after the Home Secretary asked for your personal help. You went to Scotland, and I went to the Dominican Republic and waited.'

Marlowe mentally noted down the Gravedigger's knowledge of the meeting with Karolides, although a backroom in a public house wasn't exactly the most private of locations.

'Do you know who's selling?' he asked.

The Gravedigger cocked his head slightly, as if curious where this conversation was going.

'Why do you care?' he asked. 'You won't live long enough to see it through.'

'I'm aware the chances are that whoever is involved here has probably hired you at some point,' Marlowe ignored the comment. 'If you have a loyalty—'

'I have no loyalties.' The Gravedigger held a finger up to pause Marlowe, as if a teacher halting a naughty schoolboy. 'My clients will hire me for a job, but they know also that the next job I take could involve them. I do not care about politics. I do not care about secrets.'

He leant closer.

'I care about getting the job done. I care about insults to my professionalism.'

Marlowe sighed theatrically.

'Bloody hell, give it a rest, mate,' he said. 'I'm sick to death of you moaning about that.'

He had expected this to gain some kind of rise from the Gravedigger, but instead, the Gravedigger simply laughed.

'You wish to have this fight now,' he said, again, as if this was a simple statement rather than a question. 'As I said, I will not kill you with a ...'

'I know, I know, and I'm bored already,' Marlowe yawned. 'You're going to kill me without a weapon? Well, guess what, mate?'

He nodded down at the Gravedigger's chest, and as the Gravedigger looked down, he saw a red laser dot hovering over his heart.

'I can tell by your clothing that you're not wearing Kevlar as well,' Marlowe continued. 'Whoopsies.'

'You would go against the rules?' The Gravedigger raised an eyebrow.

'No, I said *I* wouldn't kill you,' Marlowe shook his head. 'That there? That's my mate Brad. He doesn't like you either, and he wasn't part of the deal.'

The Gravedigger held a hand up; he understood, and didn't want to waste time.

'Make your pitch,' he said. 'I'm guessing you have one.'

'I don't care if you like me or not,' Marlowe settled down as he waved for the dot to disappear. 'We *will* be having that fight. The fact you killed Monty Barnes was enough to seal your death warrant as far as I was concerned. But we don't have to have that fight right now, because there's a device out there, Broad Sword, an AI tube that when added to any kind of weapon will make it ten, twenty, a hundred times more dangerous than it would normally be.'

'You still haven't explained why this is important to me.'

'You're the Gravedigger,' Marlowe replied, as if it was the most obvious answer in the world. 'You're the bogeyman for hitmen, so much so people think you can't be real. When you take a mission, you finish the job. I thought you were an urban myth because nobody could be as good as you're claimed to be. You could walk into a crowd of people and take out one person with no collateral damage. You could enter a palace and extract one person with nobody realising. Minimal collateral damage over decades of hits. Your target is your target and nothing else matters.'

'So you know my tactics,' the Gravedigger replied. 'You are not yet convincing me to listen to you.'

'Broad Sword will change the game,' Marlowe explained now. 'It was stolen from a stealth fighter, sure, but it can be placed in anything. It can be copied, reproduced. Imagine an army of drones coming in to take out a rebel spy or an insurgent, or what the drone's owner decides is an insurgent. A freedom fighter, perhaps a rival politician. The AI in the drone will decide what the best option is to take. And that could be the death of hundreds.'

He straightened, allowing some space between them.

'Have you heard the problem about automated vehicles?'

At this, the Gravedigger nodded.

'I know there are issues with how they would work.'

'Hypothetical situation,' Marlowe continued. 'Your car is driving you, and everything's fine. However, during the journey, there is a situation where the car realises there's going to be a violent accident on a bridge. The choices are that it veers away and doesn't cause the accident, but in the process crashes off the bridge, killing you, the owner of the vehicle. Or it could continue on towards the accident, and you have a fifty-fifty chance of dying in it, but a woman and a child are guaranteed to die. What does the AI do?'

The Gravedigger considered the question.

'It depends on its parameters.'

'The parameters are to save life at all costs,' Marlowe said. 'Sure, it could allow the accident to happen. There's only a fifty percent chance its driver would die, but they *would* be injured while the mother and child die. The other way would cause the death of the driver, but the mother and the child would be left alive. One way has one death. The other has two. Needs of the many outweighing the needs of the one and all that.'

He looked around the Plaza.

'Broad Sword is the polar opposite. Broad Sword will look at the target and decide how many people need to be killed in order to achieve the target. How many of the people surrounding the target right now aren't important, are nothing more than collateral, and won't amount to anything if they die. Entire buildings, towns, streets will be destroyed.'

He leant in.

'How many people would you kill if it meant that Adolf Hitler never came into power? A hundred? A thousand? A million? Even that would still be a better deal than the millions upon millions that died in World War Two. And the AI would make that decision without any emotion. The only orders it would have would be from its paymasters. And those people would not be working from any sense of justice. They would work from a sense of greed.'

He smiled.

'You know, the people who hire you all the time.'

'Are you actually trying to appeal to my sense of greed?' the Gravedigger asked. 'That if Broad Sword, or at least the AI heart of it, was involved in weapons that could do my job, I would be out of work?'

'No,' Marlowe shook his head. 'I'm aware you could stop tomorrow and probably have enough money to live on your own private island. Added to the fact that nobody knows who you truly are, you could probably quite happily move on with your life. I'm appealing to the man who takes pride in killing who he's been told to kill, and no one else. In your years of action, your actual "collateral" body count is incredibly low. Do you want to spend your retirement years knowing that every day, people will die in collateral damage through AI attacks that you, months, *years* earlier, could have stopped? Would those ghosts stop you from sleeping at night?'

'You want me to join your team?' the Gravedigger raised an eyebrow.

'Christ no,' Marlowe replied tersely. 'I want you dead. As

we said in the Dominican Republic, a reputation can be repaired, but a dead body can't be reanimated.'

He motioned for the Gravedigger to walk with him as they started across the Plaza.

'All I want is a better idea of what's going on,' he said. 'We know there's a rich kid, Spencer Neville the Third. We know his dad, Buck Neville, is a Silicon Valley billionaire. We know that Doctor Moritz had a connection with Lucien Delacroix, who was a rogue aspect of Orchid. Nora Eskildsen? Well, she's MI6, trained and paid for. And somewhere in all that, there's an AI. We think Eskildsen set up Doctor Moritz to be kidnapped, so she could work out where the AI was being held. The item is yet to be sold, which means it's still where it was going to be, waiting for the second bidding round tomorrow.'

He paused, gathering his thoughts momentarily.

'But she's also working with Spencer Neville, which makes me think the son is making a play for the father, and the father has the item. Are we looking at Silicon Valley or do you know something more?'

The Gravedigger stared at Marlowe, weighing his options.

'I have worked for the Nevilles,' he said. 'I have also worked for Walter McKellan before he was a sir. I know the chess pieces that are being played. I know there's a small camp in a mining village fifty miles northeast of here. But I also know that the item you want isn't there. To gain that, you have to return to Silicon Valley.'

Marlowe nodded at this.

'I thought as much,' he said. 'Do you know why Eskildsen is planning something?'

The Gravedigger shook his head.

'It's not important enough for me to know,' he replied. 'All

I know is that in the Dominican Republic, the seller was Buck Neville, head of Neville Financial Technologies.'

'And you know this how?'

The Gravedigger, for the first time in that meeting, suddenly burst into a smile.

'Who do you think told me where the meeting was?' he asked. 'The item you want is in Silicon Valley, Mister Marlowe. I don't understand why Eskildsen and Spencer Neville the Third are playing soldiers outside of the Cerro del Hierro mines. For that, you'll need to ask them.'

Now it was his turn to lean forward.

'And, when we meet next,' he said, 'we will finish this.'

'Silicon Valley?' Marlowe suggested.

'Silicon Valley,' the Gravedigger agreed.

There was a motion to the side, and Marlowe glanced around to see the teenagers had returned, the teacher now trying to control them again, and bring them into some kind of corralled group.

As he turned back to the Gravedigger, he noticed that the man was gone once more.

'He's like sodding Batman,' he muttered to himself.

'That's incorrect,' Brad admonished through Marlowe's earpiece, the first time he'd spoken since the meeting. 'I've read the books. If he's Batman, that makes you Commissioner Gordon in this situation.'

'And why is that a problem?' Marlowe asked.

'Because I like Commissioner Gordon,' Brad laughed down the line. 'Come on back, kid, we've got decisions to make.'

21

INFILTRATION

As dusk enveloped the Cerro del Hierro mines, the fading light from the setting sun casting long shadows across the desolate landscape, Marlowe parked his car at the end of a long and winding dirt track, far enough from the mines to avoid detection, but close enough to observe the goings on from his vantage point.

It was a hire car, a 4x4 built for mountain scrambling, picked up under one of his fake IDs, and bought with a credit card for a man that didn't exist. He knew it was a risk to use it, that if something bad happened this ID could be burnt, but they hadn't expected to move on in such a way when they started only a few days ago, with Whitehall clearance and a smile.

Stepping into the cool embrace of the "golden hour" twilight, Marlowe adjusted his gear as he moved to a better position. The night-vision goggles, currently resting on his brow, had been brought along to cut through the approaching darkness, revealing the world in hues of green and black – although right now, they were nothing more than a novelty forehead warmer in the evening light.

At his side, the tranquilliser gun promised silence and efficiency, especially as he didn't want to kill anyone if he didn't need to. They still didn't know what the hell was going on after all, and it was something Brad had worryingly held in his own equipment bag. To most people, the thought of a "tranquilliser gun" gave images of a one-shot, CO_2 powered tube pistol, firing ketamine darts at wild animals; or, in film and TV, multiple darts into whatever psychotic criminal was charging at them. Of course, there was the other side, in spy movies like *Mission Impossible,* where the gun looked like a modified Glock, or a Ruger Mk II pistol, and fired multiple cartridges that knocked out an enemy combatant instantly.

Marlowe wasn't a fan of them; the maths never seemed to work in relation to dosage. If you shot somebody that was small, a large amount could kill them. However, if you shot the same amount into somebody who was large, muscled, or had drugs in their system, it might not do anything except for piss them off.

Marlowe hated the uncertainty of such a weapon but had to admit the CIA had done well here. The gun was based around the housing of a Hudson H9A handgun, recently returned to mass market by Daniel Defence, and dubbed the DD9 - but only the weapon's frame remained true to the parent model. Inside, the gun had been repurposed, now powered by a battery and a specific magazine created to hold up to six nanite-infused darts; when a dart was fired, it released a potent sedative, incapacitating a target within seconds, leaving them in a harmless slumber. Marlowe didn't know how it worked, just that the nanites could tell in microseconds the weight and body type of the target, and enough sedative would be released to take them out without killing them.

So Brad reckoned, anyway.

The journey from Seville had taken almost two hours; the sat nav had claimed it was a simple ride up the A-4 to the A-457, deep into the Sienna Morena mountain range, and eventually following the single-lane SE-163 north from Constantina, turning right when the signs to the mining village appeared. The problem with this, though, was that Marlowe didn't want people to know he was coming, and this meant turning off earlier and following trail roads and hiking paths until he could go no further, parking beside Los Lavaderos, a local landmark that seemed to be nothing more than a part of the onetime mining complex; tall, rectangular pillars, reaching for the sky and made of weathered, reddish-brown stone or brick. The walls were crumbling and had deteriorated over time, with some sections missing entirely, revealing the hollow interior of ruins standing in a barren, rocky landscape with sparse vegetation, primarily consisting of small shrubs and grass, the ground covered in loose rocks and debris from the decaying structures.

But, from here, Marlowe could see the makeshift encampment Trix had seen on the satellite map. It was about a quarter of a mile from the main buildings of Cerro del Hierro, now most likely residential housing.

He wished Brad had come with him, but there were too many things to do, and too little time to do them. While Marlowe had been meeting with the Gravedigger, Brad had received news from the Broker that thanks to the almost limitless CIA slush fund, he was classed as one of the last three buyers of Broad Sword, and his final bid, that of three hundred and one million, was now classed as the current, winning bid. Which had probably majorly pissed off St John Steele.

Marlowe hadn't received a message. Apparently, he hadn't been deemed as serious.

Brad had decided, however, to take this news to Spencer the Third, to see if anything came of it. Trix had picked up chatter on his cloned phone before they lost the signal, and saw he was back at the offices of Neville Dinámica. It was an opportunity for Brad to get a take on the man, see if anything else could be learnt – for example, whether Lina Moritz was about to be tied up in his passenger seat thanks to Nora Eskildsen, and whether Neville the Third was really working with his father, or against him. Marlowe hadn't been happy about this, but Brad was a grown man, and after all, the CIA didn't have the best of reputations of playing well with others. There was always going to be a point when his orders countered with Marlowe's plan.

Bringing his mind back to the present, Marlowe returned to the scene at hand. There were guards; Marlowe could see them. He didn't intend to spend much time with them, though. So, moving softly through the rough vegetation, he stalked his first target.

The first encounter was swift and silent, a lone guard distracted by the glow of his phone as he scrolled through messages from a friend or loved one, too focused on whatever conversation he was reading, and unaware of the predator in his midst. Marlowe moved with the silence of a shadow, and fired at close range, the tranq dart slamming into the man's neck as he swatted at it, thinking it was a mosquito, before collapsing seconds later to the ground without a single sound.

Impressed at the speed of the pistol, Marlowe quickly

checked over the guard before pulling him behind another weathered red stone; if anything, he was under equipped for the role, which made Marlowe consider either they were woefully under-prepared for attack, or that the more qualified guards had already left.

Which possibly meant whatever they were guarding had already gone.

As Marlowe advanced, he passed by a tent, army-green and created to merge into the landscape, and almost ran into a second pair of mercenaries, their casual patrol walking straight past him as he ducked back into the folds of the canvas opening. He waited, patience as much a weapon as the gun at his side, until the moment to strike was ripe. The first guard fell to a silent shot from the tranq gun, a figure collapsing into the semi-darkness without a sound. The second, alerted by his partner's fall, turned towards Marlowe – only to take a third dart in the throat, futilely slapping at it as he sank to his knees, his eyes glazing over.

Marlowe had noticed that, as the night drew in, only one tent had a light on inside; he assumed this was what the guards were keeping safe, so started towards it.

The guard at the door, however, was waiting. He was larger than the previous ones, his head shaved and tanned, a Shemagh, more commonly known as a "desert scarf" around his neck. He had a Kevlar vest over a tight T-shirt, canvas combats and boots. He looked military trained, more so than the first three, who felt more like local talent to Marlowe.

Marlowe needed to bring him down fast but luck had gone for a coffee break at that point. He'd tried to fire the gun a fourth time, but the dart had jammed in the barrel. Realising he had to go more "old school" here, Marlowe's attempt at diversion, a stone cast into the night, only escalated the situation as the guard, trained and ready, turned – not with curiosity but with a weapon, a Colt M4A1 raised, expecting an easy target.

Instead, he found Marlowe charging towards him, closing the distance fast, hoping to to render the rifle ineffective.

The guard caught on instinctively and swung his rifle like a club, aiming for Marlowe's head. Marlowe ducked and used his momentum to land a couple of head and neck strikes. This guy was indeed experienced, and huge. Marlowe realized instantly that he needed to end this fight fast – If this beast landed a solid punch to his head or torso, he'd be down for the count – permanently.

The guard brushed off Marlowe's assault and launched a counterattack, forcing Marlowe to go defensive. A heavy fist from the larger man barely grazed Marlowe's cheek yet sent him reeling. Marlowe ducked behind a piece of mining equipment, avoiding follow up punches.

Confident in his brute size and strength, the guard stalked Marlowe as he backpedaled around the tent. Marlowe attempted to draw his CZ, but the guard saw the move and redoubled his assault, throwing Marlowe back on the defensive as the fight moved dangerously closer to true hand to hand combat. The guard threw a haymaker at Marlowe's head he was again able to duck. Marlowe swung a blow of his own that the guard stopped cold, grabbing Marlowe's wrist in one massive paw.

Before the guard could do further damage, Marlowe stepped in and delivered a "glasgow kiss" – The vicious headbutt broke the guard's nose, spraying blood and evoking a furious roar from the injured man. Before the bellowing beast could respond, Marlowe slid in to a combative Aikido Sankyo technique - running his free hand down his trapped arm, he grabbed the guard's wrist and circled under the massive arm, spinning his body 180 degrees and breaking the man's grip. He was now slightly behind and facing his opponent, and had the brute's hand trapped in a two hand hold which, when Marlowe wrenched upward, dislocated the man's shoulder.

As the guard screamed in further anguish, Marlow dropped to one knee pulling the trapped arm around in a reverse loop. The guard pitched forward, and Marlowe leaned back and twisted the trapped wrist, shredding muscles and tendons. Releasing his hold, he drew the DD9 pistol, gripped it by the fore end and viciously Butt-stroked the guard, dropping him into instant unconsciousness.

Marlowe pulled a pair of zip ties from a pocket and secured the guard with arms behind him – Given the damage he'd done, this thing wasn't going anywhere fast. He racked the slide on the DD9 tranquiliser gun, cleared the jam, and shot the guard in his backside, just in case, reasonably sure he wouldn't have to fight the beast again.

'Right then,' he muttered to himself as he stared at the lit-up tent about thirty feet away. 'There's no way you didn't hear that. But, as you've not come out to look, let's see who's in there.'

He pulled aside the canvas door of the tent.

The one thing he didn't expect to find was Nora Eskildsen sitting in the middle of the tent, watching the door and aiming a gun at him.

SPENCER NEVILLE THE THIRD HAD FELT THIS WAS PROBABLY ONE of the shittiest days he'd had in a while.

He didn't like Spain, not even as a holiday destination. If he was being brutally honest, as much as he classed himself as a man of all nations, he hadn't enjoyed Spain for quite a while. Granted, the items he'd had brought over from the States for him: his car, his clothes, his distractions – currently still laying in his penthouse apartment's bed as he was fulfilling his duties for the family – were nice, but didn't give him what he needed.

What he needed was to run the whole goddamn company, rather than his idiot father.

Spencer Neville the *First* had come from nothing. He was a self-made man, and by the time he died, he had created an empire worth billions. His son, Spencer Neville Junior, had taken what was given to him and created something larger, moving away from the banking areas of his father's life and shifting more into the financial technology, or "FinTech" industry, seeing the advantages of it as the financial world had a tectonic movement with the introduction of electronic banking and online stock trading. Within five years of shifting gears, the 2008 global financial crisis aided the growth of FinTech across the globe when by increasing customers demanded non-traditional banking and financial services, and Neville Financial Technologies was one of the highest grossing companies in the world.

And Orchid *still* wouldn't let them play.

Well, Spencer thought to himself as he walked towards his Maserati, *that might have changed, but he'd make sure they regretted the offer.*

It should have been him, not his father, who gained the invite. But he was about to change all that. Once he destroyed Silicon Valley, he'd kill Moritz before she could stop the AI, then Orchid would come to him, and he'd run everything, the God-Emperor of North America. Presidents would be put on hold as they jockeyed for his attention. He'd dance with princesses, and hunt with—

He paused as a man peeled away from the wall beside the car. Spencer looked around in concern – *why hadn't his security stopped this intruder?*

'Mister Neville, I'm Brad Haynes of the CIA,' the man said, obviously American. 'I understand you're about to gain Broad Sword back from your father?'

'I don't know what you're talking about,' Spencer mumbled, stopping in his tracks.

The American smiled.

'That's a shame,' he said. 'Because while the other governments are discussing how to stop you, we at the CIA would like to offer you a blank cheque with a ton of zeroes on display, just to have a look at it. The Broker showed his cards in the Dominican Republic, and although I've an invitation to the *Peacekeeper* Launch, where the real bidding begins, I feel, as you do, that the wrong people are bidding.'

Spencer smiled.

'Oh, you're an *investor*,' he said, warmer now. 'Why didn't you say? Let's talk about this somewhere quieter.'

The American paused, looking around.

'I was hoping we could do this here?' he offered, waving a hand around the garage.

Spencer shook his head, pulling his gun from the holster within his jacket.

'I don't think so,' he said. 'Although it's good to see you don't smell of piss anymore, Mister ... Haynes, was it?'

As Brad Haynes groaned, realising he'd been made, two of Spencer's incredibly expensive Spanish security team arrived, the latter jabbing a taser into the man's back, sending Haynes jerking to the ground.

Spencer continued to his Maserati.

'Dump him in the van and bring him to the plane,' he said. 'I could do with some company as we fly to reach my destiny. He said he was invited, after all.'

He paused, looking at the man on the floor.

'But, if he's pissed himself again, hose the bastard down before you secure him,' he ordered.

22

CAPTIVE AUDIENCE

ALTHOUGH HE'D NEVER SPOKEN TO THE WOMAN BEFORE, HE recognised her from the MI6 dossier that Trix had pulled up. And it was obvious from her expression that Eskildsen recognised Marlowe.

She didn't look well, though. She was blotchy; the veins showing through her pale skin, and her eyes were bloodshot, as if she'd been hit in the eyes with something.

'Are you okay?' he asked, out of habit rather than curiosity.

'Sit down and take that stupid device off your head,' she said. 'You don't need it in here, and you'll go blind if you try to use it with the light on.'

Feeling a little admonished, Marlowe held his hands up, showing that he had no weapon within them.

'Miss Eskildsen,' he said calmly, as if entering the tent was the most normal of occurrences, 'I'd hoped to find Doctor Moritz.'

'I'm sure you did, Mister Marlowe,' Nora Eskildsen

replied amicably, shifting in the chair, groaning slightly as she did, revealing she was in a lot of pain. 'You probably have questions after last night.'

'What, after you abseiled down the side of a hotel, tasered her and then stole her out of our room?' Marlowe raised an eyebrow. 'Tell me, did Walter McKellan teach you that trick, or was that learnt elsewhere by you?'

Eskildsen gave a small nod of acknowledgement.

'It's nice to be appreciated,' she said. 'I apologise for what happened. However, I'm afraid you're too late. You will see by looking around that neither my wife nor the device you're hunting are here.'

'I know,' Marlowe replied casually, sitting down on the only other chair in the tent, a rickety camp chair that groaned and creaked under his weight as he faced the secret agent academic. 'I'm guessing the device is in Silicon Valley, but I didn't know what the situation with Doctor Moritz was.'

He leant closer.

'I'm not sure what your situation is either, Doctor Eskildsen,' he continued. 'Pardon my language, but you look like shit.'

'That's the joy of being poisoned,' Eskildsen replied, shifting in her own chair, the gun lowering. 'Of trusting the wrong person.'

'Spencer did this? Or was it Moritz, getting payback for the taser?'

At this comment, Eskildsen chuckled.

'Oh, it was the brat,' she said, a finger aiming at her eye. 'Didn't want me to use the retina scanner. Realised blowing out my eye's blood vessels stopped that. But he also wanted Lina to himself, and I don't play well with others.'

'So Spencer took Lina Moritz,' Marlowe nodded, reaching for his phone. *Brad needed to know fast.*

As he texted a message, Nora Eskildsen smiled at this.

'You're following along quite nicely,' she said. 'I thought you'd be a bit slower.'

'Oh, don't mistake my speed here for any lack of naivety,' Marlowe commented. 'Now, how do we fix you?'

Nora Eskildsen leant forward in the chair, the gun now held in both hands between her legs as she angled it towards the ground.

'You don't,' she replied. 'It's a fatal cocktail. Slow acting, very painful. I should know, I helped create it for MI6 about eight years ago.'

She looked directly at Marlowe now, her breathing becoming more ragged as she spoke.

'Just under twenty years ago, then-just-Walter McKellan aimed me at a research institute,' she began. 'It was a small, scrappy one, funded by a young French industrialist with high dreams of what he could do with it in Switzerland. During the theoretical groundwork, I met a French researcher named Lina Moritz. It was decided by MI6, who by that point I was working for, that I should befriend Moritz, convince her to become an ally, an asset, if you will. This I did. But, over the years, we became closer. We fell in love. And as each nation failed in its attempts to create a device that could stop wars, we grew disillusioned about everyone we met. Sure, I still sent my reports in, played the dutiful agent to MI6, and sure, Doctor Moritz passed her information on to her sponsor and his own organisation—'

'You mean Lucien Delacroix and Orchid?'

Eskildsen's mouth shrugged. It wasn't a denial.

'But then things changed,' she said. 'For twenty years,

we'd been playing a careful game, but then the technology increased. Do you know Moore's Law?'

Marlowe shook his head, resisting the urge to suggest onetime James Bond actor Roger Moore. Eskildsen, seeing this, nodded to herself, her body shifting slowly and painfully to a more comfortable position as she prepared, most likely, to give some kind of last lecture.

'Moore's Law is an observation made by Gordon Moore, co-founder of Intel, in 1965. He noticed that the number of transistors on a microchip doubles approximately every two years, though the cost of computers would be halved,' she explained, her voice now starting to croak. 'He originally posited that this trend would last a decade, but sixty years on, we've reached a point where we're down to atoms now, making it tougher to keep up. Yet, we're finding new ways to push forward; different materials, quantum computers, and this exponential growth gave us the AI boom. Deep learning, neural networks, all of that. Now, it's about being smart, not just powerful. AI is here now, in our photos and writings, our TV, our film ... you can even ask it questions on the internet, where it gives you answers dependent on what it sees in the data.'

She chuckled now, but Marlowe didn't think it was a laugh derived from humour.

'Half the time, it's incorrect,' she continued, the smile now gone. 'They call it "hallucinations" as in "ah, the AI is hallucinating again" as it gives you a wrong answer. But to the AI, it's not a hallucination. The AI believes it's giving you the exact answer you want, the exact answer you need.'

She shook her head sadly.

'The important question is what happens when the AI decides that the answer it's giving is correct, even when everybody else tells it that it's wrong? It will happen, Mister Marlowe. And sooner than you think.'

'So, if you don't believe in it, and you think it's dangerous, why did you help create it?' Marlowe asked.

Eskildsen started to cough at this, and Marlowe noted the blood flecking at her lips.

'You think we created it? No, Mister Marlowe, we've spent almost twenty years trying to stop it. If we'd wanted to, we could have created the artificial intelligence of the level you have now ten years ago. We decided not to, and being where we were, we could find anyone who was creating such a device or who was succeeding in doing such a thing, and we could stop them.'

'Stop them how?'

'I would inform my paymasters at MI6 that someone was going against us, and they would find a way to do it,' Eskildsen shrugged. 'But unfortunately, I grew too arrogant. I thought we could control everything, and I wasn't paying attention to what was going on. People started creating devices that worked without our knowledge, and Lina's sponsor, the man who had been controlling her, killed himself in the middle of an American primary campaign.'

Marlowe didn't reply, staring straight at her. He knew that Doctor Eskildsen would have gained the intelligence from MI6 that showed how Lucien Delacroix, realising he had lost his opportunity to take out a sitting US president, had rather shot himself, than deal with the authorities after faking his own death at a Paris party days earlier.

'With Delacroix gone, we no longer had funding to keep going,' Eskildsen continued. 'Since the beginning, when it was mainly for drones, we'd built two protocols into the device; the *Pacifier* protocol and the *Devastator* protocol. Both could cause major damage, the latter killing thousands, all in the "defence" of the downed pilot. Nobody would tell it what to do, it'd just, well, do it. Added to that, we'd pushed vital battle data into it, given to us by the UK, French and US armed forces, all to show how a battle should be played, time and time again. It decided, after learning, that "play" wasn't a term it liked.'

She frowned, and Marlowe couldn't tell if this was pain, or the memory.

'So, we decided it was best if the device was destroyed – after all, the battle data alone could bring down half of NATO if Broad Sword's Devastator protocol took control of any of their assets.'

'But other people had their own plans?' Marlowe offered.

'We hadn't realised that Orchid still had grips in the device's design. That Broad Sword had been corrupted by Charles Garner, working with Richard Mille, or that *Pacifier* was being repurposed into the *Peacekeeper* Drone tech, piece by piece.'

'And Mille was involved in this?'

Eskildsen looked to the side, nodding, and then rotated her neck, stretched, groaned at a wave of pain, and stared directly at Marlowe.

'We tried to fix the game,' she explained. 'Rutter was in danger of owing everything to Garner. We provided funding that cleared her debts, stopped her owing Garner. This stopped the titbits of data code being leaked.'

'How?'

'A new investor.'

'Spencer Neville the Third?'

Nora nodded slowly.

'He wanted to create something massive, world changing,

to climb out from under his father's shadow, and it meshed with our own plans,' she wheezed. 'But in the end, we didn't recognise him for the monster he was.'

'And Lisa Rutter?'

'She was still removed. Mille had arranged for her to help him. She believed he was also on our side, but in the end, he wasn't. An industrialist from Silicon Valley had his claws in him, and when they realised she wasn't playing anymore, they decided it was time to remove the threat and steal the item, while making it look like an accident.'

'Mille told me it was an accident, before he died.'

'Mille was led to believe it was,' Nora shrugged. 'Or maybe he convinced himself. You're Orchid, aren't you? Like Garner?'

Marlowe shook his head.

'I'm learning that I'm really not,' he replied.

Eskildsen shrugged.

'Either way, at the time I had this new Spanish investor – well, at least he was working through a Spanish subsidiary - who claimed to be on my side. His family had always been barred from joining Orchid. Something to do with them not being the "right type of people". Probably something else down the line, but this had always been a bee in his bonnet.'

'Spencer Neville the Third?'

Eskildsen nodded.

'He believed Garner and his team should be stopped, but their investor was someone we weren't expecting, but who he'd known about all along.'

'Let me guess. His dad.'

Eskildsen smiled weakly.

'Apparently, Buck Neville finally gained a shiny coin, and

was outed as the Silicon Valley industrialist,' she said. 'You understand the reference to a "shiny coin," right?'

'So, let me see if I got this right,' Marlowe ignored the comment. 'Spencer the Third wants to take down his dad, so that he can take over the company. Dad, meanwhile, has finally joined Orchid, and probably got in by offering Broad Sword as a bribe.'

'Correct, in part.'

'What part am I missing?'

Nora Eskildsen started coughing, heavy, wracking waves of pain that left her gasping, holding onto the chair.

'He doesn't want to take over his father's Silicon Valley company,' she whispered. 'He wants to take over *all* the companies. He's going to use Lina's retina scan to hack into Broad Sword and turn it into an angel of destruction.'

'When you say hack, you mean it's already in something?'

Nora Eskildsen laughed weakly at this.

'Broad Sword doesn't need to be in a stealth fighter to control it. That was just so Mille could take the device. Originally it was a drone protocol, able to override coding of other such drones, taking control of them. So, imagine it using the almost-forgotten part of the code, and controlling two hundred drones, each one with enough firepower to take out a building.'

Marlowe stared in horror at the Norwegian Doctor. This was the exact horror scenario he'd used to sway the Gravedigger.

'He intends to hack into the brain, and decimate Silicon Valley with his father's creation, the *Peacekeeper* Drone, after reawakening the *Devastator* protocol,' she said. 'Leave it as nothing but ash, and then detonate the AI itself, leaving the blame in his father's lap.'

Marlowe rose. He could see immediately how this would play out. Spencer would turn the test into an apocalypse. The people wouldn't stand a chance. It would destroy Neville Financial Technologies, and not only would Buck Neville be charged with the crimes, but the off-books auction for the AI would fall apart the moment the AI detonated its brain.

Then Spencer would come in, having created enough of a buffer between his father and NevTech, Spencer's company, buy out the shares, clean up the company, become the hero of Silicon Valley ... all while wiping out his rivals. And Marlowe knew damn well that the real Broad Sword would still be somewhere, waiting to be used again, already planned to be sold for billions to terrorists and warlords, all looking to control tech that could stop, or even reprogramme drone attacks forever.

Regardless of his father's dreams, Spencer Neville the Third had worked out the greatest middle finger to his father in history, at the cost of thousands of lives. And that was just the first wave.

'We need to get you to a hospital,' he said.

Doctor Nora Eskildsen didn't reply. Instead, she raised her gun until it rested under her chin.

'Unfortunately, I'm past that stage,' she said. 'I can't fight this; I need to accept that.'

'You need—'

'What I need, Mister Marlowe, is for you to stop Spencer, save Lina, and avenge me.'

She took a deep breath and sighed it out.

'I can help you,' Marlowe pleaded. 'You don't need to do this.'

'I'm afraid I do, Mister Marlowe,' she said calmly. 'I'm one of the five people whose eyes were linked to the AI. Only

Moritz and Dovale are left. While I live, I'm a threat, and believe me, right now, living is incredibly painful and long-winded.'

She raised her shirt, and Marlowe could see a monitor strapped to her ribs.

'I remove this, he poisons Lina with the same biotoxin he gave me. If I live or get better, he poisons Lina with the same biotoxin. Either way, the same painful death I'm facing goes to her, too. I can't do that. The only way she lives is if I die, Mister Marlowe. He wants me to kill myself, and I can't refuse, or the woman I love suffers the same fate. I can't be allowed to stay alive to stop him, you see.'

She stared Marlowe directly in the eye.

'I know you're considering stopping me, but know the moment you move a muscle, I will pull the trigger,' she said. 'I waited for you. I knew you'd come, and I wanted to prepare you, and also to give a message. You're here on Walter McKellen's orders, aren't you?'

'Well, it's the Home Secretary—'

'But she works with McKellan,' Eskildsen interrupted. 'You need to let him know that everything that happens, it's all his fault. If he hadn't started this, hadn't placed me in with Lina ...'

She smiled wistfully.

'Actually, thank him for that,' she said. 'A good, last memory. Remember these numbers, Marlowe. 1-7-7-6.'

With this said, Doctor Nora Eskildsen pulled the trigger.

The gunshot echoed around the tent as her dead body fell to the ground, and Marlowe stared down for a long, quiet moment.

She'd committed suicide to save the woman she loved –

and to pass a message. Killed by a bored nepo baby who wanted to burn the world down.

It was petty. It was grotesque.

And Marlowe was going to make Spencer Neville the sodding Third pay for it with his life.

Slowly, and without taking his eyes off the body, Marlowe pulled out his phone, dialling Trix.

They needed to find Brad – and fast.

23

WELCOME TO THE VALLEY

THIS WAS THE GREATEST DAY OF SPENCER "BUCK" NEVILLE JR'S life.

All his life, he'd waited for when the secret society known as Orchid would accept his family into their ranks. His father, who built his way up from nothing, had never felt worthy enough to be involved. But now, with the creation of the *Peacekeeper*, an AI drone that could solve all problems with the simple inclusion of high-level weaponry and an attitude to match, all of that changed.

His entire *world* had changed.

In one day's time, he was going to show the world what Neville Financial Technologies could be. No longer just about financial technology or stock market data, Neville Financial Technologies had pivoted, moving itself into the military acquisitions and weaponry domain – an area of profitability that made financial technology systems profits look like beer money in comparison.

That the device was a *lie* didn't matter to Buck Neville. That the device was stolen technology was even further down his list of cares. By the time people realised that the AI device known as Broad Sword was deep within the control system, hidden behind walls upon walls of dominant coding, the machines would be gone, taken by less scrupulous countries and powers.

Your nation has sanctions put upon it? You're on the list.

The West isn't happy with you? Join the club. We have badges.

The *Peacekeeper* was going to be a device that, on the outside, performed incredible tasks, but only used a percentage of what Broad Sword could do, deliberately so, ensuring that although seen as masterful, revolutionary technology, it was still not close enough to raise eyebrows. The real protocol, the *Devastator*, all the killing power of Broad Sword with the emotionless fury of a righteous force with added societal context, was what was going to make him the *true* money. And tomorrow, on the San Jose Hills, he was going to show the three highest bidders, as well as a couple of warlords who bid high and late, exactly why he was worthy of the Orchid coin he'd been promised, with a weapon test display using only two of the two hundred drones he'd already built. The Broker had a deal of three hundred million already on the table, and he knew the onetime Arbitrator of Orchid, as well as a current High Council member were both turning up with blank cheque books to counter this. Added to this, the other warlords he'd invited along could join the waiting list for a fee, likely hundreds of millions each, providing them with their own pet AIs.

Life was good. And soon Buck Neville could buy out his son's fledgling startup, NevTech, and use it to build on Buck's technology.

The snot-nosed little shit could work for him for a change. Get his hands dirty, rather than partying with whores.

Buck had first been placed onto this path by another entrepreneur, a weapons dealer by the name of Taylor Coleman. A newly minted billionaire on paper, he was a small fish compared to the Neville family's legacy, but Taylor Coleman had something that Buck Neville never had. Something that had burned away at Buck's soul as he watched this *nobody* parade around within Orchid's inner circle. He hadn't understood why his father, Spencer the First didn't care about this membership. Orchid had their fingers in every pie in the world, and if they wanted, they could take each pie for themselves. The Neville family had even had their occasional tussles with Orchid members over the decades, and every time they'd come out bloodied and battered.

Buck had become sick of this. He had decided he needed to find an edge.

Weirdly enough, the edge had come through his son, Spencer the Third. The boy had been exiled to Spain to learn the business techniques of the industry, but in actuality, he'd been sent to Spain to keep him from screwing around in the Hamptons. His penchant for high-class escorts, and drug-filled binges where he apparently did his best to fulfil every wish-list item left by Emperor Caligula, had been alienating him with a lot of the West Coast elite. By sending him to Spain, Buck had ensured he couldn't affect anything that happened.

What he hadn't realised was that Neville Dinámica, the Spanish franchise in Seville that Spencer had been exiled to and given to own, had been sniffing around next-gen research after the French Industrialist Lucien Delacroix had committed suicide. After that, and after the rumours of

Delacroix trying to sabotage the US elections had surfaced, people moved away from his companies, and Spencer, seeing an opportunity in Spain had pounced, and succeeded more than he could ever have expected, allying with some dogshit university research campus, and a couple of nobody lesbians who reckoned they knew the future.

Amazingly, though, both they and his son had been right.

Buck Neville, dead set in the middle of his family line, spat to the side. It was a dry spit. He had been too nervous to drink anything all morning. The opportunity of gaining membership into Orchid was so close he was terrified he would somehow fail, screw it up, but it looked instead like his son was going to do that for him.

Turning from the window where he stared out at the buildings of Silicon Valley beneath him, Buck clenched his hands behind his back and started walking back towards the boardroom. It was time to inform the board what was *really* going to happen tomorrow. Some would complain. Others would see the logic. Some would have to be removed. Buck hoped that many of them would understand the moment they saw the dollar signs and zeros added to the figure estimates they were about to make.

The ones that didn't … well, they would have their relationships with Neville Financial Technologies terminated with prejudice – not in the way his son would have wanted, with two bullets placed into the back of their skulls, deep in some Arizona desert, but by cast-iron NDAs and handshake deals that'd kill them in other ways if they ever spoke out. It wasn't a thought he wanted to entertain. It wasn't a decision he wanted to make. But if he wanted to be part of Orchid, he had to think like Orchid. And with his son breathing down his neck and his father's legacy at stake, Spencer "Buck"

Neville Jr. was determined to do everything it would take to become the man he aspired to be.

His phone buzzed.

Walking over to his desk, he pressed the intercom button.

'What?' he snapped. 'I told you I didn't want to be disturbed.'

'Charles Garner is on the line,' his secretary's voice spoke through the speaker. 'He sounds quite irate.'

Buck sighed, telling his secretary to put the man through, and then, a moment later, clicking the now flashing red button on the keypad.

'Garner,' he said. 'What do you want?'

'Your son's screwing everything up, Buck,' Charles Garner's voice replied. 'I did everything you needed. Gained you the item. Found you the people who could help.'

'What you did, Mister Garner,' Buck replied calmly, 'was broker an agreement. You provided me with an item that I needed. Now, that contract has been closed. I have the item, and you have the money I promised you. There is nothing more to be done here.'

'I'm hearing nasty things,' Garner continued down the line. 'You know the pilot, the Squadron Leader killed himself, right? Shot himself on the parade ground after admitting he offed the Flight Lieutenant. Well, now the Wing Commander's gone missing on the base. Do you know anything about that?'

Buck did. In fact, Thomas Dovale was in an office down the hallway, keeping out of sight until the demonstration. And as such, he knew best to keep his mouth shut.

'Nope. I don't know anything about your mad paranoia fantasies, Mister Garner.'

'What about the doctors from the Spanish university?

Nora Eskildsen and Lina Moritz?' Garner continued. 'They've disappeared from their Seville apartment. Would your son know anything about that?'

'Do you have a point?' Buck sighed audibly, while hoping privately that Garner didn't have one, and was just fishing for more money; he was dangerously close to working out Buck's plans, and that wouldn't be good.

'My point is you have a psycho for a kid, and he's coming for you,' Garner snapped back down the line, and Buck almost interrupted, to demand *how dare he speak to his betters like that*. But before he could, Garner had continued. 'He's been killing off assets, working his own agenda, seeing who came out of the woodwork. You know who did? Coleman's kid. The one who killed Delacroix.'

Now Buck's interest was piqued.

'And I care because?'

'Because your son thinks you stole from him,' Garner replied testily. 'You made him look weak. And he'll kill everyone to make sure they know he's stronger than you.'

'I think I know my son better than some Brit banker who's hidden away in some nowhere golf club,' Buck, now tiring of the conversation again, replied icily. 'The only reason you're involved in this, Charlie, is because you were in the right place at the right time.'

'I spent years planning this!' Garner spluttered. 'How dare you, I'll—'

Buck Neville never heard what Charles Garner was going to do because he disconnected the call.

After a moment, he buzzed his secretary.

'Where's my son?' he asked.

There was a clacking of keys on the keyboard, and then the secretary replied.

'He's on one of the private jets,' she said. 'He's expected to land in San Jose in about five hours.'

Without answering, Buck Neville disconnected the call as he considered this. If his son was about to take a shot at the father, this would be the time to do it.

Unfortunately for him, this time, the father had the firepower.

———

BRAD HAYNES HAD BEEN CAPTURED MANY TIMES OVER HIS lengthy career, from the forests of the Amazon to homesteads in Iraq. His Seal training had made sure he always knew how not only to avoid giving away state secrets but also how to find the aspects in each situation that gave him scope for escape.

This one, however, was different.

He'd woken in a Lear Jet's plush leather seat, a new pair of jogging bottoms on, and a table in front of him. He was also locked into the seatbelt, a combination lock held over the latch, keeping him secure. He could check his pockets, but found everything he'd had with him was gone: the phone, his folding knife, even the utility blade he kept inside his boot, all missing, likely taken when his trousers were swapped.

Christ, I hope I didn't piss myself when they tasered me. Marlowe would never let me hear the end of it.

That said, this was also the first time he was tasered, captured, and then fed marinated Canadian lobster, with crushed avocado on a tarragon Marie Rose sauce.

It was some of the best food he'd ever eaten, definitely the best he'd ever had on a plane, although he would have preferred it if they'd provided him with a juicy ribeye, medium to rare. But beggars couldn't be choosers, especially when you were strapped to a chair heading to God knows where.

He'd spent the first half an hour, after realising his items were gone, examining every inch of the plane. He couldn't reach much but he could see. It was small, maybe a twelve-seater at best, and split into two compartments; the first four seats were in front of a curtain, while the remaining eight were behind, nestled into the rear of the plane. Behind him, it looked like there was a small galley where two stewardesses worked, and beside them were two small bathrooms. Brad had hoped this wasn't a long flight; being strapped to a chair would make it very difficult when he needed a bathroom break.

Across the aisle from him, and currently asleep, was Doctor Lina Moritz. Initially, he'd assumed that she too had been tasered, but after an hour of sitting around, waiting for her to wake up, he'd realised that she was most likely drugged, probably before she was carried onto the flight.

Straining and reaching across the aisle, Brad eventually used his fingertips to prod her repeatedly until she shook herself awake, blearily and groggily staring at him.

'Morning,' he said with a smile as she rubbed her eyes, glancing across the aisle at him. She too was apparently secured into her seatbelt, and Moritz startled as she realised who was talking to her, but then softened when she saw that Brad too was secured.

He pointed at his straps, shrugging in a *what-could-I-do* kind of way, mainly to ease the situation.

'When did they get you?' he asked.

'Nora,' Moritz muttered, almost angrily. 'I didn't want to leave you. She turned up at my window.'

'We know,' Brad nodded. 'We heard.'

'You had my room bugged?'

'No, we had the room downstairs bugged, and it heard the conversation you had with Nora through the window,' Brad shrugged. 'Blame Preston, she just loves her technology. Either way, we know Nora took you against your will. I'm guessing that she gave you up.'

At this, however, Moritz shook her head vigorously.

'She was betrayed,' she said, her French accent coming through as her anger built. 'The rich boy screwed her over. I told her not to trust him, but she wouldn't believe me.'

Brad nodded at this. It was new information, and he hoped that whatever had happened hadn't affected Marlowe and his trip to Cerro del Hierro.

'I'm guessing they took you from the mines,' he said.

Moritz nodded, frowning.

'You knew?'

'We're very good at what we do,' Brad replied. 'We knew the helicopter had landed at Cerro del Hierro. It was more a case of working out how willing you were in the process. Marlowe had gone to pick you up, but it sounds like there wasn't much of an option.'

Moritz sadly shook her head.

'Unfortunately not,' she replied, as she rested her head back against the seat, shuddering at a memory.

'When I was dragged away from her, he let me watch,' she whispered. 'They injected her with something. I didn't see what it was, but Spencer said she would never see me again.'

She looked away out of the window, and Brad could see that she was trying hard not to cry.

'He killed her,' she said. 'He killed her, and there was nothing I could do about it.'

There was a rustling where the curtains were, and Spencer Neville the Third walked through with a smile on his face.

'Aha, I thought I heard talking,' he said, almost as if he was having a conversation with friends, as he looked down at his watch. 'It seems you're both awake, and we've still got four hours of flying left before we land.'

Brad glanced out of the window and could see that underneath the clouds there was ground. They weren't over the ocean, which meant they were flying across a large land-mass, West Coast then, likely Silicon Valley.

Spencer sat opposite Brad, reaching over and taking a piece of lobster from the plate, placing it into his mouth and chewing on it. It was very much a "what's-yours-is-mine" gesture, and Brad almost felt impressed. Spencer was quite arrogant and at the moment was on top, loving the moment.

He'd remember this when he eventually killed the smug little prick.

Finishing the morsel, Spencer turned and looked directly at Brad.

'I've been told I can't kill you,' he said. 'Apparently, the CIA has made mutterings you are their legal representative in this matter, and your money will be used in the bidding of Broad Sword.'

'Why do you care?' Brad asked. 'It's your pops who's got it, not you.'

'True,' Spencer nodded. 'But, after I finish, I'll need people to buy the technology. Somali warlords, religious extremists, people like the CIA. The last thing I want to do is kill a prospective buyer, especially when the starting price is three hundred million dollars, and we expect to triple that.'

He leant forward, patting Brad on the arm.

'So buck up, Braddy boy. Looks like you're gonna be staying alive until the bidding ends. You'll get to see everything that happens, front-row seat.'

Brad slowly raised his middle finger.

'I ain't giving a single red cent to you,' he said. 'Our arrangement was with the Broker—'

'And the Broker will work for me once my father is removed.'

'You genuinely think your father will go?'

'When his drones go wild and kill thousands of people, I expect him to sit down in his office and blow his fucking brains out,' Spencer shrugged.

Brad ignored the crude language, glancing over at Doctor Moritz, who was still waking up from whatever drugs she'd been filled with.

'And her?'

'She's my way in,' Spencer continued. 'You see, my father has Broad Sword, and he's placed a basic form of it into his Peacekeeper drones. But Broad Sword has multiple levels of destruction, all linked through an AI hive mind. There's another protocol, a partitioned drive known as the *Devastator*. And when that is opened and actioned by Miss Moritz's retinal scan, then every single drone, all using bastardised code from the source and therefore still linked, will change their basic settings. All I have to do is connect to the original Broad Sword, flick the switch, and light everything up.'

He relaxed into the seat, staring at Brad.

'Two hundred drones, armed with the greatest weapons money can buy. All done to show militaries and countries that my father has balls.'

He chuckled to himself.

'I'm gonna remove them with AGM-114R9X Hellfire

Missiles. They have kinetic warheads with pop-out blades designed to minimise collateral damage, but they'll slice them off happily. And then I'll play with the AIM-9X Sidewinders and the GBU-12 Paveways. I'll have a bigger body count than every *John Wick* movie combined with anything Schwarzenegger and Stallone did, and I don't even need to be there when it happens.'

He stretched his neck, yawning.

'He'll have kept Broad Sword nearby. It'll likely be in his offices. They, by the way, won't be attacked during my vengeance against my father. They will be left, partly to cement the fact that my father is a genocidal maniac who killed thousands of people, but also so I have somewhere to sit when I take over the firm.'

'You're insane,' Brad said.

'I would like some food,' Moritz spoke softly, before Spencer could reply, or add to his grandiose scheme.

'Of course,' Spencer picked up Brad's plate, half-eaten, and passed it across. 'Here, have this.'

'I need cutlery.'

Spencer clicked his fingers twice, and a flight attendant arrived from the galley with a knife, fork, and napkin in hand. The knife and fork were either solid silver or near as damn it, and Moritz took them, staring down at the plate.

Then, before anyone could stop her, she rammed the fork into her right eye.

The cabin turned into chaos.

Spencer leapt across the aisle, screaming 'No!' and grabbing the fork before she could continue, tossing it away. Moritz, her right eye now destroyed, blood streaming from the socket, was laughing, trying desperately to take the knife from the table to pierce her other eye. Brad knew what she was trying to do, and so did Spencer, punching her hard in the face, sending her rocking back, as one of his security guards came running from the front, staunching the blood with a napkin from the table.

'Get the medic,' Spencer said. 'She knew what she was trying to do. She needs to be ready before we get off this plane.'

'Sir, her eye ...'

'I don't give a shit about her right eye,' Spencer glared at the guard. 'She only needs one. Strap her down so she can't move, and fix the goddamned thing.'

He glanced back at Brad.

'You try something stupid like that, and I'll kill you.'

'You don't need my eyes,' Brad shrugged. 'Why the hell would I do that?'

There was another rustle through the curtains, and a new arrival came running through, wearing the white-shirted uniform of a pilot.

'The co-pilot's the medic,' the guard said as a man ran over, examining Moritz.

'We need to staunch the wound,' the co-pilot said. 'The napkin won't work. She'll need to go to a hospital as soon as we arrive.'

'She's not going to any hospital,' Spencer said, looking up at him and then frowning. 'I don't know you.'

'We've flown several times, sir,' the co-pilot said. 'You've actually said the same thing to me on three occasions last year. I rarely have to come into the cabin, as we don't usually have women losing their eyeballs.'

'Are you criticising?'

'No, sir, just stating a fact.' The co-pilot knelt down. 'I can

stem the wound, and I can make sure it's packed up, but she'll
need to be looked at some time when we land.'

'She will,' Spencer said. 'But it'll be on my schedule, not
yours.'

He rose, walking back to the curtain.

'Fix her up, tranquillise her, and then fly the goddamn
plane.'

He glanced back at Brad.

'As for you, you'd better make sure that you're ready to bid
high, Mister Haynes. Or else we'll be having a long conversation, possibly with another fork.'

Brad sat back, allowing Spencer to leave, turning from the
curtain and now watching the co-pilot whispering to Moritz,
soothing her as he injected her with what looked to be some
kind of sedative. Then, as the guards stepped back, allowing
him space to move, the co-pilot turned and winked at Brad.

It was a subtle movement, but it confirmed what Brad had
believed to be some kind of hallucination from his recent
unconscious state.

It seemed, from the wink, that *Vikram Saeed* was the co-
pilot.

24

BUSINESS CLASS

Marlowe knew there would be a jet waiting for him. He hadn't realised Walter McKellan would be joining them.

Brad had gone missing. His rental car was near the offices of Neville Dinámica, but nobody seemed to know where he was, and his phone had been kindly left in the glove compartment. Marlowe hoped this didn't mean he was in a landfill somewhere. If anything, the fact the CIA were claiming to have hundreds of millions at his disposal was enough to at least consider a ransom for him, rather than a funeral.

The chances were that Spencer Neville the Third had taken him to San Jose with him, either by choice, or against his wishes. Either way, Marlowe would find out when he reached America, too. Maybe Brad was even sitting in "cattle class", next to Lina Moritz.

God, Marlowe hoped so.

The jet, stationed at a small airfield north of Seville, had been arranged by Trix the moment Marlowe had called with the details of what happened at the mining camp, and by the time he arrived back at the hotel, she was packed and ready to go. Interestingly, Eva Gonzalez had provided a police escort to get them there in good time, but Marlowe couldn't work out whether this was to help him, or to get him out of her country as quick as possible. Either way, the plane was fuelled and ready to go the moment they climbed on. It was a Falcon 2000EX, a business jet developed by Dassault Aviation, with two Pratt & Whitney Canada PW308C engines, allowing it to cover up to four thousand nautical miles at almost Mach one. Inside was a ten-passenger cabin, although it only had two on this leg. Marlowe had hoped to go the whole way, but the pilot, citing a need to refuel before the longer journey to Silicon Valley, landed the jet at Biggin Hill, just south of London. It took half an hour to prepare for the next leg of their trip, during which Walter McKellan arrived, glaring at Marlowe and Trix.

'I want to hear everything,' he said, settling opposite Marlowe and buckling his seatbelt.

'She'd been poisoned,' Marlowe replied, ignoring any pleasantries. 'He left her there as a message. He knew we'd find her. He wanted us to know what was going on.'

'Why in God's name would he warn us?' McKellan asked.

'Because he's mad,' Trix said from across the cabin.

'He doesn't think we can stop him,' Marlowe shrugged. 'He has Lina Moritz, which means he can use her retinal scan to access the AI. He doesn't want us stopping him, so he killed Nora Eskilden, ensuring her eyes couldn't be used, dead or alive.'

Marlowe leant forward, resting his elbows on a desk now between him and Walter McKellan.

'This plane will take just over eight hours to get to San Jose,' he said. 'We'll be arriving two, maybe three hours, tops, before Buck Neville unveils his new items. We should be mobilising the army, the navy, the military, anyone.'

'And say what?' McKellan asked. 'The British government contacts America and says, "Hey, by the way, we happen to have lost this really important AI device, which is now going to wreak havoc on all of your people, oh, and they also have your battle data, sorry about that." How do you think that's going to affect our relationship? As it is, Anton McKay and Charles Baker can't stand each other. The only person he seems to like or trust is you.'

Marlowe accepted the compliment.

'That's only because I've saved his life a couple of times,' he said. 'The fact is, the CIA already know about it, and are looking to buy it back. We, meanwhile are chasing our tails, and we're not equipped for this.'

'Well, we have to be,' McKellan replied. 'Maybe it's time for you to call in some favours of your own. All I've got are me, you, Miss Preston here, and Vic Saeed.'

Marlowe frowned.

'Where does he come into this?'

'He's on a jet crossing the Atlantic right now,' McKellan smiled. 'He arrived in Seville yesterday afternoon and has been masquerading as the co-pilot of Spencer Neville's aircraft.'

Marlowe glanced back at Trix.

'We think Spencer has kidnapped a CIA agent named Brad Haynes,' he said. 'We couldn't get hold of him when we came back, and the last thing he was doing was scouting the situation.'

'He was negotiating on behalf of the CIA,' McKellan replied. 'We intercepted the directive. Someone in Langley ordered him to make an offer to acquire the device. As you said, the CIA were offering hundreds of millions. It seems Mister Haynes was kept on as the bidder.'

Marlowe leant back against his chair.

'Oh, that bloody fool,' he muttered. 'He was only supposed to assess the situation.'

'Don't be too harsh on him,' McKellan said, a rare note of sympathy in his voice. 'He's a good soldier; he follows orders. Unlike some people.'

Marlowe raised an eyebrow.

'I'm sure you're a fine soldier in your own right, following orders,' McKellan shrugged. 'The problem is the people giving those orders shouldn't be trusted, either.'

'Orchid?'

'No, you bloody fool,' McKellan actually laughed. 'I'm referring to Emilia Wintergreen or Alexander Curtis.'

Marlowe dismissed the comment. Walter McKellan's disdain for MI5 was well known, complaining whenever their agents were involved in operations he considered solely MI6's domain. Marlowe was actually stunned he'd allowed Vic Saeed into the field.

'So, if we can't use agents, why are you here?' Marlowe asked.

'Do you doubt my field capabilities?' McKellan raised an eyebrow. 'Son, I was conducting field ops for MI6 when you were still nursing milk from your mum's teats. And I'm referring to your infancy, not your teenage years.'

Trying to restrain himself, Marlowe forgot about the seatbelt, a reminder of his current constraints, falling back into the chair as he jerked briefly upwards before falling back.

McKellan chuckled.

'If you can't handle the insults, you shouldn't be in this business,' he said.

'For your information, I never wanted to be in this mess in the first place,' Marlowe retorted. 'This was a favour to Karolides, nothing more.'

McKellan, reflective for a moment, and conceded.

'Also, I should acknowledge much of this mess stems from our obsession with spy tradecraft secrecy regarding Nora Eskildsen, and attempting to conceal our collaboration with the French government, which led to isolating her and Moritz in a Spanish lab,' he reluctantly admitted. 'Could we have conducted our operations in London? Sure, but unfortunately, Brexit complicated things further, introducing an insurmountable amount of bureaucratic red tape and complicating academic research grants. Moreover, Lucien Delacroix became involved, necessitating discretion.'

'And how did you plan to maintain such secrecy about British involvement?' Marlowe interjected. 'Of the five individuals involved, three were RAF officers.'

'True,' McKellan acknowledged. 'But that was confidential. To outsiders, this was merely an emerging adaptive technology. Eskildsen and Moritz worked independently in an EU university, hence the private funding.'

He sighed, leaning back as the engines hummed, signalling the plane's imminent departure.

'Look, lad,' he said. 'Lucien Delacroix was a trusted former member of the French Security Services. We didn't foresee his drastic change in ideology. But you're the one who ultimately stopped him.'

Marlowe remained silent, unsure if this was a jab or not.

'While we had external funding for Broad Sword, we could argue it wasn't a governmental project,' McKellan continued. 'It sounds absurd, but it was effective. We were aware of his affiliation with Orchid, but he was also a member of Caliburn, a think tank focused on advancing the human spirit. We genuinely believed he was benevolent.'

'Until he wasn't,' Marlowe echoed.

McKellan nodded in agreement.

'Until he wasn't.'

'How the hell did the Neville family get involved?' Trix said.

'His dad,' McKellan nodded at Marlowe, who grimaced.

'Of course it bloody was,' he said. 'What did my dad do?'

'Taylor Coleman had got interested in AI,' McKellan explained. 'You might not have liked the man; he might have been a massive pain in the arse for anyone who met him, but at the end of the day, he understood how weapons were going to progress in the future. He knew that the advancement of weaponry would involve an AI, and he'd started looking into it.'

Trix now turned her attention back to Marlowe and McKellan.

'We know that Lucien and Taylor had worked together in the past and were close; after all, it was Taylor who faked Lucien's death, knowing that he would soon die himself,' she added. 'No one would punish him; it was the act of a dying man, Lucien would be left to do what he needed to do.'

'But Lucien had wanted to keep a level of distance here,' McKellan, annoyed at being interrupted, continued. 'He was probably expecting to cause distrust and disservice in the world, when he attacked McKay on live TV, but he wanted the AI in his pocket as a backup, and so he started bringing in other people to take on small amounts of funding. Buck Neville was one of them.'

Marlowe nodded at this.

'Let me guess,' he replied. 'Buck Neville thought this was his opportunity to get in with Orchid.'

'Taylor probably led him along, convinced him it was a good idea,' Trix replied. 'But then Taylor died. From what I can work out through the micro SD card you found—'

'SD card?' McKellan frowned.

'Basically, Spencer had a folder that held every dodgy dealing by his dad, and hid it on a drive we found,' Trix was back on her laptop as she spoke. 'By this point, Buck Neville was in up to his knees in shit. Somebody got involved and suggested he started moving things around, maybe pointed out that the deal that had been made by Lucien wasn't that good, the French military weren't going to pay that much, *we* weren't going to pay that much, but terrorists and extremists, that was a far more lucrative market.'

'I'm guessing Buck Neville wasn't a patriot,' McKellan griped, looking back at Trix, who simply shrugged.

'We'll probably never know,' she said. 'The problem came when Spencer Neville the Third appeared on the scene. You see, artificial intelligence and futuristic technology were his area. Daddy Dearest was actually the FinTech guy. Spencer was annoyed that Buck was trying to muscle in on his scheme, and decided he would take Lucien's project and finance the larger part through a separate company, NevTech.'

'So, father and son were both working on the same project without knowing?'

'Oh no,' Trix shook her head. 'From the files on the drive and messages I found on the cloned phone before it disconnected, they both knew. The problem for Buck was he couldn't stop his son, and the problem for Spencer was he couldn't remove his dad. The only way that they could move on to what they each needed to do was if the item was stolen.'

'So, Buck Neville deals with Charles Garner,' McKellan stroked his chin. 'One thing we know is that Charles Garner was part of Taylor Coleman's Orchid crew. There's every chance that Taylor Coleman would have been working with Garner to sway Buck Neville to their cause.'

'Jesus,' Marlowe shook his head. 'Garner said he'd stepped away from Orchid because of what they did. We thought he meant Orchid had made a move, but he's on about the fact that they let me stay.'

The plane had increased in speed and Marlowe felt the pressure of gravity hit him as it took off, flying up into the early morning sky.

'You'd better get yourself some sleep,' McKellan replied. 'When we hit the ground, you'll be running. Buck Neville has two hundred fully armed drones.'

'And you know this for sure because ...'

'I know this because we sold them to him.'

Marlowe shook his head again.

'No wonder nobody in the bloody government wants us involved in this. The shit that'll come out if we don't stop it ...'

'The drones are armed and dangerous,' McKellan admitted. 'And from what we can work out, Buck Neville has used somebody to open the AI and reverse engineer the data. They can't get all of it, but they've got enough to create a basic AI device that can do what they need it to do: run, jump, climb trees, all that shit. It's effectively no cleverer than a dog, but he'll make out it's the next big thing. Probably set up some pre-arranged stunts to make things look better.'

Marlowe felt a sudden cold sliver of ice slide down his back.

'Who did they get to open it up?' he asked. 'Eskildsen, Rutter and Mille are dead, and Moritz is held by Spencer the Third.'

'We're not sure,' McKellan replied. 'But from what Preston there has been passing on, the only person it could have been is Wing Commander Thomas Dovale, who went missing yesterday after visiting the Moray Hope Golf Club.'

Marlowe nodded at this. *That made sense.*

'Charles Garner's still working with Daddy then,' he said.

'It looks so,' McKellan replied. 'But here's the problem. Buck Neville has placed Broad Sword, or at least a very basic copy of every Broad Sword, into each of his Peacekeeper drones, without removing the fail-safes.'

Marlowe thought back to what Nora Eskildsen had said.

'The Pacifiers will become the Devastators. That's why Spencer's taking Moritz with him,' he replied. 'She's the only other one who can get into the system. They're a hive-mind system, all linked, right? He's going to hack into the network, and he's going to upgrade the level of threat.'

He glanced over at Trix.

'*Devastator* protocol.'

Trix nodded, her face pale.

'If he does this,' she said, 'there's no stopping him. Two hundred of these drones with the weapons they've each got. They might only use one or two for the test, but he could launch every single one of them in one go. They wouldn't be prepared. These drones could take out all of Silicon Valley in less than an hour.'

'That's his plan,' Marlowe thumped his fist against the table. 'He doesn't want money. He wants to destroy everything with ruthless aggression, and then invite the world's terrorists to a yard sale. We need to get the National Guard in.'

'As I said, the relationship—'

'Damn our special relationship!' Marlowe shouted. 'We need to keep those drones out of the sky!'

'I agree, but, keeping the histrionics aside, we simply need to stop him before he can activate the protocol,' McKellan said.

'And how do we do that?'

'We kill Moritz before she can scan her retina.'

'No,' Marlowe shook his head. 'I refuse to believe that's the only option we have.'

'What other options are there?' McKellan snapped.

'I don't know yet,' Marlowe gave a weak smile. 'But I have just over eight hours to think of some.'

Trix made a strange yelping noise.

'For once, I think I know what to do,' she said excitedly. 'The numbers Nora Eskildsen gave you, I think that's the Broad Sword override.'

'We still need to be *connected* to override, though,' Marlowe frowned.

'Yeah, and I can sort that, too. Is there any chance of finding a 3D printer that I can specially calibrate once we land?'

'Preston, it's Silicon Valley,' McKellan frowned. 'They probably give you one when you land.'

'Then we're off to the races,' Trix smiled. 'And, for once, I'm riding the horse.'

25

SHOWTIME

OVER THE NEXT TWO HOURS, THE "CO-PILOT" HAD RETURNED twice to check on Moritz. Her eye had been packed and bandaged, and Vic had claimed to Spencer, who had checked only once during the rest of the flight, that she was good enough to travel once they landed. It was given as a suggestion that the travelling would be to a hospital, but Brad knew that as far as Spencer was concerned, the travelling was going to be straight to Silicon Valley, where her remaining eye would destroy the west coast of America and destabilise the technical side of the country for a hundred years.

During that time, Vic had briefly spoken to Brad, but not much, and mainly in the aspect of a medic, checking Brad was feeling okay, stuff like that. On the third time, however, the guards had relaxed. He was familiar to them now. He wasn't a threat. He was the pilot of the plane, after all. As he finished checking on Moritz's wounds, he glanced over at Brad and frowned.

'The man looks pale,' he said. 'Has he been to the toilet?'

'He can hold it.'

'You've given him seafood,' Vic leaned forwards now, checking Brad, who, realising this was some kind of plan, played along, groaning a little. 'Did you check if he could eat that?'

The two guards glanced at each other nervously, and the taller of them decided he wasn't needed after all, and left behind the curtain, probably to get away from whatever was about to happen.

'Sir, do you have any allergies?' the other guard reluctantly asked.

'Seafood,' Brad smiled weakly at the guard. 'I couldn't really say no to the meal though, it looked delicious.'

'Do you feel sick?'

Brad nodded. Vic looked back at the guard.

'You need to take him to the toilet,' he said.

'He's locked down for a reason.'

'If he doesn't get there soon, he's going to throw up all over this fancy leather furniture,' Vic snapped. 'And I don't know about you, but I'm not cleaning this up. Here, I'll come with you. There's two of us and one of him. I'll even sedate him.'

He pulled a pill from a pillbox in the medical kit, passing one to Brad's mouth – although he'd palmed it back the moment he'd done this, slipping it into his pocket.

'Here,' he said, as Brad pretended to swallow the tablet. 'Take this, it'll make you drowsy in about three minutes.'

Vic then leant closer, checking his eyes, looking at the pupils, shining a torch at them, and nodding to himself, as if deciding the mythical tablet was working.

The guard moved in, demanding Brad now open his mouth to show that there was no tablet within sight. Brad did so without any problems – after all, there was no tablet in his mouth – and then pretended he was feeling drowsier.

'He won't be asleep, but he'll be more susceptible to suggestion,' Vic said to the guard. 'Come on, let's get him to the toilet before he passes out or shits himself.'

Slowly, the guard unclipped Brad, lifting him to his feet, and with Vic to the side, he walked Brad into the bathroom at the back. It was the same style and design as any airplane bathroom: a small sink to the side of an airplane toilet.

Brad was able to shut the concertina door and, finally alone, rested back against the bulkhead for a moment. Even though he hadn't taken the sedative, he still felt woozy from the shock the taser had given him a few hours earlier. Reaching into his jacket pocket, he pulled out the item he'd felt Vic Saeed secrete into it as they lifted him up.

It was a Kershaw Ken Onion 1840 shallot, a viciously sharp assisted opening folding knife with a lethal three and a half-inch blade - a small note wrapped around it. Brad opened it up, skimming it. It read

To be used in the utmost of emergencies. You need to be where the action happens, so stay with Spencer as long as you can.

Brad nodded to himself, threw the paper into the toilet and pressed the flush, watching the paper as it disappeared forever. He knew what Vic was saying. He needed to stay near Moritz, and if anybody tried to kill her, or do something terrible, he was to use the knife. Either to save her, to save himself, or – and this was the one he didn't really want _ to remove her last remaining eye before she could do anything.

Secreting the blade back into his boot, knowing that it had already been searched and wouldn't be looked at again, he exited the toilet and, with the guard and Vic leading him back, walked to his seat, sitting down and holding his hands up, allowing the guard to secure him back into it, while Vic, claiming he had to return to the cockpit, left once more.

'How long till we land?' he asked.

'Matter of hours now,' the guard shrugged.

Brad nodded.

'Military trained?'

'Special Forces.'

'I was a SEAL,' Brad smiled. 'We ate pricks like you for breakfast.'

The onetime Special Forces guard grinned and then punched Brad squarely on the nose. It wasn't enough to bring blood, but it hurt like hell, and Brad chuckled to himself as the guard walked off, back past the curtain.

Alone again, he glanced over at the unconscious Doctor Moritz.

He was impressed. It was a ballsy move to try to take out her eyes.

He just hoped he'd be there to save her before she lost the other.

AROUND EIGHT IN THE MORNING THE JET CONTAINING Marlowe, Trix, and McKellan landed on the south runway of Minetá International Airport, north of San Jose and beside "PayPal Park", a strangely unreal football pitch – or soccer, as it was America – that seemed wildly out of place for the area.

The flight itself had taken just under nine hours, but with the time difference, it almost felt like they landed at the same time they'd left. McKellan had arranged for some CIA attention once they arrived, so as Marlowe exited the plane, the large black SUV that waited for him opened its rear passenger door, and a familiar person climbed out.

She was tall, attractive and had red shoulder-length hair. She also had a face of fury as she faced the arrivals.

'I understand you've got my man captured,' Sasha Bordeaux said angrily.

'Don't blame me for this,' Marlowe shook his head. 'I wasn't the one who told him to try to make some kind of offer.'

Sasha grimaced at the comment, taking the admonishment.

'Yeah, fine,' she said. 'I know, that's on me.'

'You're damn right that's on you,' Marlowe snapped. 'If he hadn't done that, he'd be here right now. Instead, we don't know where he is, and—'

'He's in Silicon Valley,' Sasha interrupted him. 'Spencer Neville the Third's plane landed three hours ago. We had a chat with the co-pilot.'

Marlowe nodded to this. Sasha and Vic Saeed had met before, although it wasn't the friendliest of conversations at the time. Vic had even spent time on her own personal jet, or at least the CIA's jet. Thinking back, Marlowe had spent more time learning how to play the game of *Crime City* than discussing the plane itself, but he recalled Vic had spent some time in the cockpit talking to the pilots.

Once a pilot, always a pilot.

McKellan had explained on the flight that Vic Saeed had a history of flight training, having worked with domestic commercial jets in the UK before he joined MI5, and having been a member of the RAF cadets as a child, learning to fly Cessna aircrafts as part of the training.

'Moritz has been injured, lost an eye during the flight,' Sasha continued as McKellan walked down the steps from the plane.

'That was careless,' McKellan muttered.

'She tried to take her eyes out with a fork,' Sasha said, snapping back. 'So I'd really like it if you would stop with your dry British humour and leave it at the plane door.'

McKellan glared at the younger woman, and Marlowe realised that neither of them had ever met before.

This would be an experience.

'So, what's the plan?' he asked, deciding to change the subject, divert attention and defuse the situation.

'From what Vic could work out on the flight, Buck Neville is going to be providing a show in a couple of hours,' Sasha looked at her watch. 'The show is for the Peacekeeper drones, of which he has two hundred. He'll be launching two of them, and showing what they can do over the hills to the east of San Jose, just off Mount Hamilton. It's a party trick show. He'll have them do some preset routines, show what they can do, and work with the most basic of AI systems.'

'How has he managed to start it?'

'He has Thomas Dovale in his office,' Sasha replied. 'I believe you've met. Apparently, he paid him a significant amount of money to take an unplanned sabbatical from the RAF.'

'That makes sense, as Dovale was involved in this from the start, from when they were trialling drones,' Trix now added, walking down the steps, lugging her tech-filled bags with her. 'He later worked with Mille and Rutter, and the two of *them* were definitely involved in something. And there was the fact they were shagging.'

Sasha paused, glancing back at her.

'They were what?'

'Mille, Rutter, and Dovale. Doing the dirty.'

'It was a bit of a love triangle, from what I hear,' Marlowe clarified. 'One of the fellow officers had said Dovale and Rutter had had a Christmas fling, which had stopped because he was married. But there was some kind of jealousy between him, Rutter, and Mille.'

'If they were that close, it makes sense they all knew what was going on,' Sasha nodded. 'Either way, Dovale has opened up whatever Buck Neville has, but he doesn't have access to the internals in the same way that Doctors Moritz and Eskildsen did.'

'It's why Moritz was taken and Eskildsen was left to die.'

Sasha acknowledged Marlowe's comment.

'We believe the plan, from what Vic Saeed told us, is for Spencer Neville the Third to take Moritz, and use her to hack into the Broad Sword brain itself, which is somewhere secure within Neville Financial Technologies. Once Moritz is in, they can use her expertise, or at least use people with a similar expertise if she refuses, to work through the main data, something that Dovale could never do, and trigger the Devastator protocol, while activating every single drone in the process.'

'So we stop them first, right?'

'Sure, old man. We hadn't considered that,' Sasha snapped back sarcastically. 'The problem we have is the moment we take this down, we have to acknowledge we know about it. Better to quietly close it down in the background.'

'And how do we manage that?' Marlowe asked.

Sasha Bordeaux turned and grinned a winning smile at him.

'Why *you*, of course.'

———

Buck Neville stared out at the scene in front of him. The vistas of Mount Hamilton and the Arizona Valley were truly panoramic and beautiful, and later that morning, he was going to set explosions off all over the place.

It hadn't gone down well when he'd suggested what he wanted to do. The park rangers of the surrounding Joseph D. Grant County Park had contested this and complained bitterly, but military power was more important in this world of change and uncertainty, and the US Government shut them down with a single word that was whispered in their ear, and a briefcase of concessions. Buck Neville had also made a solid argument for a quick weapons display with minimal collateral or environmental damage, and they reluctantly stepped back.

He stood in what was called the nerve centre of Neville Financial Technologies, a tall, chrome and glass estate that on one side looked over San Jose from the top of the Mount Pleasant foothills, and the other looked up at Mount Hamilton itself. Wide panoramic windows looked out onto the vista in front, while within, it was almost like some kind of skybox, with food being positioned to the side by caterers, comfortable seats, and televisions everywhere. At the front was a single computer with what looked to be some kind of gaming console on it. This was the *pièce de résistance*, as far as Buck Neville was concerned. He intended to use this control cockpit to show how the drones could be both piloted, and also allowed to perform their own tasks. It also gave the added bonus of a visual spectacle that the audience could actively get involved in, a more tangible situation than just watching two drones fight through a window.

But that wasn't all they could see through the window. Beneath them, they could look out into what was usually a car park, but today a holding area for two hundred Peace-keeper drones, most of which were turned off, purely there for shock and awe value. Only two would be used in this presentation; one piloted by RAF Wing Commander Dovale, although Buck wasn't sure if he was still technically a Wing Commander, since he'd gone AWOL off his base, and the second controlled by the Peacekeeper AI brain itself.

A perfect mixture of man versus machine. More than one man, actually – the drone would also be targeting another human asset in the second part of the test, one of his security team, proving that, as the man ran through crowds, got in and out of vehicles, everything a rogue agent or enemy combatant might do, the drone could still follow them.

It was exciting, and he was about to make a lot of money - because while he demonstrated this, he would also run a separate auction, using this eye candy to convince other warlords and terrorists, and probably people from the CIA as well, all the sneaky types working from the shadows, that this drone was definitely something that you wanted to at least have a couple of. The winners of the Dominican Republic auction would now be even more desperate to win, and Buck hoped to at least triple the initial bid of three hundred million dollars, and that was just for the AI.

The drones themselves would push this well into the billions.

On the subject of that, though, something felt wrong.

He'd been told that Brad Haynes, the CIA's spokesperson in this auction, had flown over with his son, but as of yet, he had heard nothing from either Brad or Spencer. Buck knew the plane had landed a few hours earlier – he paid people a lot of money to inform him of these things – and he knew that the plane itself had had some kind of accident on board, as medics had been called in to take somebody from it.

But, apart from that, he knew nothing.

Clicking his tongue against the top of his mouth, he turned to his assistant, Jorge.

'Have we heard anything from my son?' he asked.

'I'm sorry, sir,' Jorge looked up from his pad and shook his head. 'It looks like your son has sent his apologies. He will not be attending your performance.'

'My what?'

'The magnificent display that you have organised,' Jorge quickly adjusted his comment.

Buck didn't mind. This was a performance. Smoke and mirrors to make the investors think they were buying something incredible, when to be perfectly honest, it was mainly done purely to sell the bigger, more secret weaponry.

'Major Dovale—'

'Wing Commander Dovale, sir,' Jorge corrected, 'is preparing the drones.'

Buck nodded at this, glad that Dovale was finally earning his keep. Since he'd arrived, he'd sat in his plush, expensive hotel suite, ordering takeout and muttering to himself. Sure, people had died on his base and his career was probably over, but the money he'd make today for one demonstration was more than he'd probably make in the rest of his entire military career.

The man should be bloody grateful, not miserable.

Still, he needed his expertise to fly the drone, but any monkey could fly a drone. What he really needed was

Dovale's retina scan, and that had been provided as soon as he arrived.

Sighing, he looked back out of the window at the vista in front of him.

So, his son didn't want to turn up. That meant his son was playing a different game.

'Sir, so you are aware, Sonia Shida from Orchid and St John Steele have both arrived,' Jorge commented, looking up from the pad.

'Shida?'

'She was the third-highest bidder after the Broker removed Thomas Marlowe from the bidding.'

Buck nodded, raising an eyebrow. He'd known that Taylor Coleman's son had been at the auction, but he hadn't realised that he'd been removed. That was a shame. He'd heard so much about Thomas Marlowe he wanted to meet the man.

'Fine,' he said. 'My son's not turning up, the CIA hasn't arrived, but we've got people who want to buy, and the others will be here within an hour.'

He looked out of the window one last time, staring down at the army of drones beneath him, wondering what game his son was playing.

'It's showtime,' he said.

26

DEMONSTRATION

Marlowe tapped his fingers against the desk as he stared at the map on the screen.

'This is going to take several fronts,' he said, leaning closer so he could peer at the map. 'The first front is here.'

He tapped the screen; an industrial complex looking eastward out onto the vista of the park leading to Mount Hamilton.

'This is where the presentation will be, where Buck Neville, Dovale, and the drones are,' he leant back, considering this. 'The drones need to be taken out. Do we know how they're going to be showing them?'

'One drone is AI-based, the other will be piloted by a human,' Sasha said. 'If he's there, it's probably going to be Wing Commander Dovale. The drones were provided by the British military, after all.'

'Thank you for reminding me of that,' McKellan grumbled. 'So, Dovale will be in the building controlling one device.'

'His retina scan will have accessed the Pacifier protocol,

and the other drone will probably be using that as well,' Sasha replied.

'It's not the two drones I'm worried about,' Marlowe tapped the map on the other side of San Jose, in Cupertino, on the west side of the valley. 'That's the head office of NevTech. This is where Lina Moritz and Brad Haynes are being held, according to Vic. Do we know if they've moved?'

'Vic's currently staking out the building. He hasn't seen anybody leave yet. But that doesn't necessarily mean they're actually still there,' Trix replied from her computer, looking over at them. 'Broad Sword's a hive system, so once they use Lina Moritz's remaining eye to connect through the Neville infrastructure and access the Devastator protocol, they can make sure it uploads to every drone there. Dovale might have control of one, but he'll have one hundred and ninety-nine fighters wanting to take him out.'

Marlowe whistled.

'When they named it, they named it right,' he nodded to himself. 'Do we know if Brad is ready to go?'

'From what Vic said, he's armed with a knife, and the element of surprise,' Trix shrugged. 'Whether or not that means he has an opportunity ...'

'Brad Haynes is a good agent,' Sasha added, leaning against the door to the office they currently used, as if about to leave. 'He'll do what needs to be done.'

Marlowe nodded at the comment. He'd worked with Brad enough times to know that Sasha was telling the truth.

'Right then,' he said, 'Spencer Neville the Third is in his office over there, while his dad is over here preparing to start his event. Trix, where do you need to be?'

Trix opened up a small case she'd been fiddling around with, removing a 3D printed ball. It was a replica of an eyeball, even down to the iris. She turned it in her hand, letting it shine in the light. Marlowe knew it wasn't one of her usual acrylic ones, but it looked damn close.

'I need to be where Dovale is,' she said. 'They'd have provided him with a link into the network. I can piggyback that.'

'And you're sure it'll work?' Sasha asked, frowning.

'Dovale was given access when he first worked on the project, before being promoted,' Trix nodded. 'It was early days, lower levels only. Sure, he can probably get into where Pacifier is, and there's a few upper-level file systems he knows what to do with, but the real stuff, that's beyond his pay grade, and where Devastator would have been.'

'Nora said that only her and Moritz had access,' McKellan said.

'Exactly, but the pilot, Mille – and Rutter? Even their lower-level access was enough to connect and disable from the stealth jet. It's why they were used to steal it, and probably why both were killed,' Marlowe added. 'Mille, killing Rutter, accidentally or not, before faking her hanging, convincing her he was on her side until he wasn't, and then taking his own life.'

He looked to the side, unable to fully comprehend what had happened in order for this one moment to occur.

'Trix took a photo, an in-depth scan of Mille's eye before he died. That scan is now in three-dimensional form, and we'll be able to use it to convince Broad Sword that Mille is there. It'll access far deeper sub-layers than Dovale's access would give him.'

'It'll still be lower levels, though.'

'Yeah, but Mille wasn't a hacker genius like Trix,' Marlowe replied. 'Once she's in, she'll be able to get access to the higher levels. Just like the levels that Karolides gave me and Trix. Swanky ID cards that give us abilities far beyond our usual ranking.'

'Don't get too used to those,' McKellan replied.

'Of course not,' Marlowe smiled politely. 'That would be crazy.'

He tapped on the screen once more.

'We'll have to rely on Vic and Brad getting Moritz out of the main building,' he said. 'Once it all goes wrong, Spencer will probably try to make his way over to Dad, get to the source before everything goes to hell. Therefore, I think it's best if we upset the main event.'

He leant back, looking around the office as he considered this.

'If we can stop the Devastator drones from launching, then we can stop a lot of the problems. Sure, we might still have one or two to remove, but I'm pretty convinced that the American military is good enough to remove a couple of rogue drones. Who knows, we might even convince Dovale to blow them out of the sky for us, with the one he'll likely control for the demonstration.'

'Are you sure about this?'

'Not really, but what options do we have? Brad can be the hero for a change, save Moritz. Vic and McKellan can go in and make sure he doesn't take the device for the American government,' this was said while looking at Sasha. 'While me, Trix, and Sasha will go have a chat with Daddy, and see if he'll let us tap that four-digit code into Broad Sword.'

'I'm not overjoyed by the number,' McKellan grumbled.

'What, 1776? The start of the War of Independence. I wonder why?' Sasha smiled before looking at Marlowe.

'I think I should go with McKellan,' she continued cooly. 'I want to make sure my man is okay.'

Marlowe glanced at McKellan, who shrugged.

'You're aware this could be a lot harder than you're making it sound,' Trix replied. 'St John Steele will be there, as will representatives of a dozen militaries, most of whom don't like you. Also, don't forget, the Gravedigger's probably turned up by now.'

At the name, McKellan, who had heard nothing about this, glanced up.

'Peter's here?' he asked.

Marlowe stopped everything, turning back to face the older man.

'Peter?'

'Peter Jericho.' McKellan replied. 'The Gravedigger.'

'How the hell do you know the first name of the Gravedigger?'

'Because I trained with him back in the day,' McKellan shrugged. 'One of the youngest recruits we ever had. If you've got him annoyed at you, you might as well fill out your will documents right now, Mister Marlowe. I've rescinded my offer of looking to employ you. We don't employ ghosts.'

'That's not what I heard,' Trix muttered.

'Don't worry about the Gravedigger,' Marlowe shook his head. 'He became my target the moment he killed Monty Barnes.'

McKellan hadn't been part of this conversation either, and his eyes narrowed.

'Are you sure?'

'Sure as a heart attack,' Marlowe nodded. 'He even tried to shoot me, leaving a rifle cartridge with Monty's fingerprint on it. The guy's a prick, but he's got style.'

McKellan nodded slowly.

'Then you have the Secret Service's permission to execute him.'

Marlowe raised an eyebrow.

'I didn't think I needed it in the first place,' he said.

'If you'd killed the Gravedigger without informing us ...' McKellan shook his head sadly. 'You would have been made a traitor. You see, the Gravedigger has done many things for many people, but ... some of the deepest, darkest things were for Her Majesty's government back in the day. The guy is a literal war hero.'

'Well, we can give him a nice funeral when I've finished with him,' Marlowe growled. 'Shall we get ready?'

'LADIES AND GENTLEMEN,' BUCK NEVILLE BEAMED, STANDING IN front of his floor-to-ceiling windows, the vista of the Arizona Valley behind him. 'Thank you for coming today to see the future of military engineering.'

There was a mumbling of discontent at this. Several of the invited guests had connections to the American military, and Buck knew that this multiple-continental viewing would have ruffled some feathers. American heads of military had their favourites, and Neville Financial Technologies was not one of them. Even the name didn't scream out a military contractor.

Buck Neville didn't mind. By the end of the day, he'd have made enough money to buy out his idiot son and take NevTech as the new arm of his industry.

Immediately after he sold Broad Sword to Orchid for billions and gained his place on the High Council, that was.

St John Steele and Sonia Shida, both high-ranking Orchid members, were also standing in the group. Both had been given an opportunity to bid for Broad Sword, and were ready to spend, and spend large.

'Today, you will see the future of aerial combat,' Buck continued, pointing down to the drones in the car park beneath them. 'Of the two hundred Peacekeeper drones we already have, two will be released into the wild to fly in a remote-controlled dogfight. The first will be fully AI, utilising our Pacifier protocol technology.'

He lowered his voice, moving slightly closer as if about to give a major secret.

'This has been designed from the ground up by Neville Financial Technology engineers and is, we believe, the most advanced form of artificial intelligence out there. You will be safe with this technology looking out for you.'

He glanced at the others in the room. Warlords, mercenaries, and people who didn't care about protecting people.

They knew what he was saying.

This was a weapon that could protect but also destroy.

'What about the Devastator protocol?' one of them asked. 'I'd heard your drones came with this.'

'The Devastator protocol is still in beta testing,' Buck replied apologetically. 'As such, it will not be for sale today. Of course, people who purchase these will have the opportunity to discuss this in future upgrades.'

'This isn't a smartphone or a Tesla,' Sonia Shida snapped. 'We're not expecting patches on what we buy, Mister Neville. We expect the finished product.'

'Unfortunately, in the world of artificial intelligence, there is never a finished product,' Buck shrugged. 'There will always be updates, and the joy of the Peacekeeper drones is that once you purchase, you will receive all access, all updates, firmware, and software.'

There was a muttering in the crowd where Buck knew what needed to be said had been expressed.

Now it was time to take away the stick and offer the carrot.

He nodded to the door where a guard to the side tapped twice on it and then opened the door, allowing ex-Wing Commander Thomas Dovale to enter the main viewing room.

Buck Neville was impressed. Dovale had gone all out on this. He was wearing his actual RAF flight suit, showing his rank, his unit, and half a dozen other various medals for gallantry and suchlike. This was the flight suit of a combat pilot, and everybody who saw him knew this was not a man who would take things lightly. Dovale nodded to the audience, shook hands with Buck, and then walked over to a small computer system wired to what looked to be a camera at the side.

'Wing Commander Dovale of the RAF has been working on this for a while,' Buck explained to the audience. 'In fact, it's got its origins in an RAF device known as Broad Sword, although our device is nothing like that.'

He looked back at the crowd, the slightest of smiles on his lips.

'My lawyers told me to say that,' he winked. 'Either way, Wing Commander Dovale is the only person in this room who can activate the Peacekeeper drones – until you purchase one for yourself. His retinal scan will begin the test.'

Dovale nodded, leant close to the camera, and the audience watched as a small green line of laser light moved up and down his eye, scanning it, placing it into the system, and then beeping with acceptance. As this happened, the cockpit area burst into life with lights flashing, screens starting, and the computer that controlled the drone finally waking up.

Dovale said nothing as he continued over to it, climbing into the chair – it was designed like a gamer's chair but with the slightest of differences, allowing more comfort and a seating system more akin to the fighter jets he flew – and prepared to "fly". There were three screens laid out next to each other, the ones on both sides angled in slightly to give the impression of a windowed cockpit, and the screens themselves showed that of the car park below.

'This is the camera at the front of one of the Pacifier protocol Peacekeeper drones,' Buck explained. 'This will be the one that Wing Commander Dovale will be flying. The other ...'

He waved out of the window as another drone rose into the air.

'This will be his target.'

He pointed at a television screen, which now turned on, showing the footage from that AI-controlled drone.

'You will see in real time the fight that happens. We have been given permission to use minor armaments for the display, but each drone is equipped with AGM-114R9X Hellfire Missiles with kinetic warheads with pop-out blades, AIM-9X Sidewinders, GBU-38 Joint Direct Attack Munition for ground assaults, and GBU-12 Paveways. As you can imagine, if someone was to take hold of even one of these drones and use it against America, the death toll would be catastrophic.'

Again, it was a comment mainly for the *anti*-Americans in the room.

Dovale smiled as he pulled on the yoke in his control

section centre, and on the screen, the drone was seen to rise into the air.

'Whenever you'd like to start the demonstration, Wing Commander,' Buck smiled. 'It is, as they say, in your hands.'

As the crowd gathered closer around the control cockpit area, Buck took the opportunity to slip to the back, turning to Jorge, his face finally showing his true anger.

'Get my son on the phone,' he hissed. 'I want to know where the son of a bitch is.'

27

SATELLITE OFFICE

When Brad Haynes was a young man, he had joined the Navy SEALs.

It had been tough, but over the years, he had built up a reputation as someone who was quick to action, never scared to enter a scene, no matter what might happen. When he moved across to the CIA, it was a different matter. Here, you were supposed to pause, wait, and check every angle before moving. It had been a learning experience for Brad, but over time, just like in the SEALs, over decades of service, he'd made it work for him. However, there was something about the waiting, knowing that at some point you would spur into action, but until that point, you were forced to do nothing, that frustrated him beyond anything else.

And this was how he felt right now.

He had been placed in a back office at NevTech in Cupertino, on the western side of Silicon Valley. Spencer Neville the Third and his goons had taken Doctor Moritz into the next office, which from the limited view Brad had seen, looked to be some kind of ornate corner office with chrome and glass, and a slightly rustic, more traditional back wall, where the glass table containing the phone, computer, and desk pad of Spencer's daytime job rested. This was obviously Spencer's office, and the entire building had been emptied for the day, probably some kind of connection to the launch happening across the town. But, with the lack of people around, it was very easy to make their way from the underground car park all the way to the penthouse offices of the upper floor, where only the board and the high-level managers were allowed to breathe the rarified air.

Vic Saeed had stayed as well, claiming that as a medic, he should keep constant attention on Doctor Moritz. Spencer hadn't wanted to bring a doctor into the situation; he didn't really seem to care what happened to her after the day ended. Therefore, with a visit to the hospital out of the question and with Spencer not needing Moritz past whatever happened soon, and not giving a damn about her long-term health and fitness, he'd decided that Vic Saeed would be the acceptable, more discreet option. He even offered Vic a bigger payout in cash for performing this off-the-books service. Vic, however, had claimed magnanimously that he did it for the company - and for Spencer Neville the Third.

It was laying it on a little much, but Brad appreciated the gesture. Vic was doing his best to sound just like the very lackeys that Spencer didn't like; someone to be ignored once everything had been fixed, someone to stay in the corner and say nothing.

The guards hadn't noticed, but Brad had spotted that Vic was carrying a concealed pistol in the 4 o'clock position on his waist. Brad didn't know what it was - probably a Glock or a SIG Sauer - MI5 loved those. Whatever it was, it was far better than the folding knife that constituted his entire personal armoury. While checking Brad for the alleged seafood allergy he had received on the plane, Vic had whispered to "wait for his signal before starting anything". Currently, Brad Haynes was still important because of his connection to the CIA and Washington, but with no opportunity to pay for the device, and with Buck Neville and the Broker being elsewhere, Brad wondered exactly *how* he would be assisting Spencer the Third.

Brad had spent half an hour checking the office for potential weapons, but there was nothing - even the table was screwed together in such a way that he couldn't pull a leg off. He had his knife and an armed ally in Vic, and he just needed to make sure that whatever happened, occurred before Moritz was forced to use her remaining eye to turn on the retina display of the Devastator protocol, after which she'd likely end up dying of a bullet to the brain.

Brad knew the moment that happened, he was likely to suffer the same fate - it was apparently quite a common malady.

After an hour of waiting, the Special Forces guard, the one who'd punched him in the face, had appeared, grabbed and dragged him in to the main office. There Spencer was sitting behind his desk working on his laptop, two or three suited aides behind him, checking their own iPads busily.

Brad was shoved onto a couch beside Moritz, heavily bandaged and looking like she'd been drugged. Vic Saeed stood beside Moritz, looking nervous. The other two burly security guards that had been on the plane stood across from them, scowling.

On the other side of the office, away from the beautiful view of Cupertino, sat a device - Brad didn't know for certain what it was - it looked like a computer. One component he did recognise was an optical scanner, meaning this had to be the device that would link them to Broad Sword once Moritz placed her eye against the retina scanner.

That was what he had to stop.

'You're alive for one reason,' Spencer said without looking up. 'We need you to pass a message to the CIA; it's about my father.'

'And what message would you like me to pass?' Brad asked. But before he could gain a reply, one of the aides leant across to Spencer as his iPad beeped. After a whisper, Spencer spat out an expletive, rose, and walked over to a television against the wall. Brad could see the television had a webcam set underneath it, and grumbling to himself, Spencer pressed a button, turning it on.

It was some kind of intercom system in the same way that Microsoft Teams or Zoom would be used, and this showed the entire room through the web camera, a tiny image in the corner as the main part of the screen was filled with the furious life-sized face of Buck Neville.

'What in God's name are you playing at, boy?' Buck snapped. 'You were supposed to be here with our CIA asset.'

'I'm sorry, Father, plans have changed,' Spencer sighed, a little more theatrically than he probably should have. 'I can't make it, which is probably a good idea because things are about to go quite bad for you.'

At this, Buck went to reply, spluttered, and then leant closer to his screen, where he could see in the larger picture that Doctor Moritz was sitting in the background.

'Is that Doctor Lina Moritz?'

'Yes,' Spencer replied. 'I brought her from Spain just for this. We'll come and visit you real soon, Father, but I'm a little busy.'

He paused and grinned.

'Have you started yet? Have Orchid made their pitch? Or are you still sucking their cocks like the cuck that you are?'

'Now you listen here, you little shit—'

The screen flashed black as Spencer, bored, cut the feed. He glanced to an aide who nodded.

'They started the demonstration five minutes ago, sir.'

'Then I think it's time to start,' Spencer grinned, glancing over at Doctor Moritz. 'I think it's time for us to log into Pop's little playtime date and absolutely screw it over.'

At the statement, Brad Haynes realised he had only seconds to act; if Moritz used her eye to enter Broad Sword, she wouldn't be needed anymore. Turning, he saw Vic discretely draw a Glock from his concealed holster and secret it next to his leg. Brad knew it was go time, so he the drew the Kershaw folding blade and quietly flicked it open as he stepped forward...

Only to stop as Vic Saeed raised his Glock and aimed at the centre of his chest.

'I wouldn't do that, Mister Haynes,' Vic stated calmly. 'As Mister Neville said, your job is very simple now. You're to contact the CIA and tell them that Buck Neville has become a traitor.'

Brad stared in utter disbelief at Vic.

'You're working with him?'

'No,' Vic grinned. 'I work for Orchid, and Orchid is working with him.'

At this, he turned and bowed to Spencer.

'Welcome to Orchid, Mister Neville,' he said. 'First of your family.'

Brad had spent so much time staring in horror at the situation, he hadn't noticed that Moritz's eye had been placed in front of the scanner and had been accepted into the system. As the computer beeped, and Spencer yelped with delight, returning to his laptop, Vic kept his gun aimed, trained on Brad.

'You might as well drop the tiny blade,' Vic said. 'You were never going to get any further. I only gave you it so you could feel powerful. People who feel powerful are often slow to react.'

'I never trusted you,' Brad said. 'I should have kept to what I said to you the first time we met. Do you remember that?'

'You said "Now get back onto your little Ryanair flight, piss off back across the Irish Sea, and go tell Mummy and Daddy in Whitehall you're not needed, as the CIA have pulled the big toys out of the box, and you're too small to play with them."' Vic replied. 'But as you can see, I'm the one with the big toys now.'

'All that time, Marlowe thought you were on his side,' Brad spat. 'Even McKellan thought you were still working for King and Country.'

Vic moved closer, the muzzle of the Glock gun now imprinting on Brad's forehead.

'I've spent years working for Orchid,' he hissed. 'And in that time, I have done what was needed to be done to move up the ranks. For someone like Thomas Marlowe to walk in, taking his father's greasy, money-damaged nepotism coin, and overstep me? Balls to that. The Orchid I work for isn't the Orchid that *he* wants. The Orchid I work for is the Orchid that will do whatever they need to do to take over the world.'

He glanced back at Spencer Neville, sitting at his desk.

'And NevTech will be our sword,' he said. 'NevTech will strike down our foes.'

Brad wanted to scream, to attack, but he was impotent, unable to do anything, held back by a Glock he knew would blow his head off if he so much as twitched.

'It's done,' Spencer laughed, looking up from the screen as he sat back. 'Call your CIA friends, Mister Haynes, and tell them that my father has just accessed the Devastator protocol on his incredibly peaceful Peacemaker drones.'

He sniffed and smiled.

'I think things are going to get very exciting soon. I'm really glad you're here to see it.'

He looked back at Vic now, nodding his head towards Doctor Moritz.

'We don't need her anymore. You know what to do.'

'No! Wait—' Brad shouted, but it was too late. Vic Saeed spun and fired, and the scanner burst into flames, sparks flying as it began to burn.

'What? Do you think I'm some kind of monster?' Spencer chuckled. 'I wouldn't kill her for that. I don't need to. No one else will ever be able to turn this off. Dovale doesn't have the level to do it, and Eskildsen, Rutter and Mille are dead. Marlowe has lost, and Silicon Valley is about to be decimated.'

He rested his arms on the desk.

'Again, I suggest you make the call before we deem the CIA to be just as much an enemy as anyone else.'

Defeated, Brad nodded.

'It seems like you've won,' he said. 'For the moment.'

'SIR, YOU NEED TO COME QUICK.'

Jorge opened the door, calling to Buck Neville, his face a

pale mask of horror. Buck, still gritting his teeth over the argument he'd had with his son, glanced back at his aide and was about to snap a response until he saw the expression.

Something's gone wrong.

'What's happened?'

'Sir, you need to see.'

Storming out of the small office to the side, Buck returned to the viewing area.

It was chaos. Everybody had moved to the windows, staring out, and Wing Commander Dovale glanced back at him.

'This wasn't me,' he said. 'I swear this wasn't me.'

'What wasn't you?' Buck said as he walked over to the window, checking the notes on his aide's iPad. 'What's that bloody noise?'

'That's the sound of one hundred and ninety-eight more drones taking off,' St John Steele said as he turned to face the billionaire. 'Your Peacekeeper drones have now activated the Devastator protocol. Which means that apart from the one drone flown by Wing Commander Dovale there, you have one hundred and ninety-eight drones armed and ready to destroy the West Coast of America.'

At this, and realising the display was effectively over, Sonia Shida folded her arms.

'In that case, we rescind our offer,' she said simply. 'But we do appreciate the fact that you're about to show us exactly what these high-powered weapons can do when they're really, *really* effective.'

Buck stared in horror. He'd wanted to bring in the dark side of the arms industry. That's where the money was. But this was not part of the plan.

This was his son.

He turned back to Dovale.

'Turn it off,' he begged. 'Use your eye, the retina scanner thing.'

'This is a higher level than I have,' Dovale shook his head, staring out of the window. 'I can't stop this.'

Buck Neville turned and faced the army of drones as they swarmed into the sky. Each one of them could level a playing field without trying, and almost two hundred of them were now about to take out the hundred biggest buildings in Silicon Valley.

Not only would it be a massacre, but it would also set the tech sector back decades.

'They'll blame me,' he whispered. 'They'll claim I did it. That's why he's got the CIA guy with him—'

He stopped as the first explosion was heard.

'What do I do?' he whispered. 'What do I do?'

MARLOWE HAD EXPECTED IT TO BE HARDER TO BREAK INTO Neville Financial Technologies, but as it was, the front reception was empty. It was almost as if the entire business had been given the day off, even security.

Marlowe could understand that. With the amount of high-level dignitaries and probable foreign warlords that would be upstairs in the main area, the last thing they wanted was any members of the staff to see these faces, maybe post them on social media.

This was a very private and exclusive demonstration.

Marlowe chuckled. That two drones were trying to blow the living shit out of each other, high above the Arizona

Valley, didn't make it that private, but the people watching from within these walls would be unknown.

That was why the building had been emptied, most likely.

It made it easier for Marlowe, however, because although they'd locked the doors to ensure civilians couldn't get in, Marlowe wasn't a civilian and had enough devices and lock pick experience to get through pretty much every single lock in front of him. It also helped that once getting through into the main lobby, a quick check behind the security counter found a spare pass that had been left behind, one that got him through the first level of doors without breaking a sweat.

It was only once he got to the point of penetrating the upper levels did he find himself having a problem.

It was also here when the first explosions started.

Marlowe had assumed that this was part of the display, that Dovale, in one of his drones, would have some kind of aerial dogfight, showing how well they could attack and defend from each other, while firing weapons that made a loud noise and a pretty explosion, but didn't destroy the millions of dollars' worth of drone technology that was currently being used. It was only when a more intense wave of explosions echoed through the building, that Marlowe turned and ran over to one window, glancing out.

He could see San Jose in front of him, and in the air, he could see a swarm of drones making their way across the town.

Oh shit, it's already started.

Marlowe didn't have time for niceties now, and instead went for brute force. The executive elevator needed a key to get through, but Marlowe didn't have one. However, Trix

Preston did, and as Marlowe ran back to the elevator, huffing and puffing, Trix finally made it to the floor where he was.

'You could have bloody waited for me,' she grumbled, gathering her breath.

'We're in a rush,' Marlowe replied, pointing at the window. 'It's already started.'

'Yeah, and you've just noticed that,' Trix snapped back. 'Don't make out that's the reason you're running. You're running because you're an idiot.'

'Well, you're here now,' Marlowe replied, banging on the keypad, waiting for the elevator to turn up. 'Make yourself useful and open this bloody thing.'

'Make yourself useful,' Trix mocked as she attached a device to the panel, hacking into the system wirelessly. 'You know, it's a real shock that you've never settled down with a woman. You're such a keeper.'

She stepped back as there was a beep, and then the light appeared on the display, showing the elevator was on its way.

'There you go, sir,' she said. 'Making myself useful just for you.'

Marlowe winced; he hadn't meant to snap, but all thoughts disappeared from his mind as the elevator doors opened to reveal a man facing them, with a Desert Eagle .50AE pistol aimed directly at Marlowe.

'Mister Marlowe,' the Gravedigger said, 'I'm afraid your journey stops here.'

Marlowe, glancing at a pistol muzzle big enough to park a car in, instinctively pulled Trix behind him.

'She's not part of this,' he said.

'And I'm fine with that.' The Gravedigger stepped out of the elevator now, walking forward, Marlowe moving backwards. 'You see, I have a new contract.'

'I thought you only took one at a time, Peter?' Marlowe asked.

The Gravedigger, hearing his real name, flinched a little, and Marlowe felt a small, internal shout of triumph.

He was fallible. He could be beaten.

'I've been hired to kill you,' he said. 'I was going to do it anyway, so why not make some money?'

'Fine by me,' Marlowe said. 'I was looking for a moment to kill you, anyway.'

The Gravedigger looked at Trix, thought for a moment, and then stepped aside, allowing the doorway of the elevator to be clear.

'I have no issue with you, Miss Preston,' he said. 'And if you feel you can find a way to stop whatever's going on, I have no problem with you doing so. Godspeed.'

Trix looked at Marlowe, and he gave her a small nod.

'Fix this,' he said. 'I'll meet you later.'

'Much later,' the Gravedigger replied. 'When you die of old age and find him waiting at the pearly gates later.'

Trix said nothing, weakly nodding, and ran into the elevator, hammering on the penthouse suite button. As the doors slid shut, the Gravedigger smiled at Marlowe.

'This has been a receipt long waiting,' he said. 'How would you like to die?'

'In bed, surrounded by women, and when I'm ninety years old,' Marlowe replied. 'But I'm guessing that's not an option?'

The Gravedigger chuckled. For the first time, Marlowe felt it was a genuine emotion.

And then the Gravedigger opened fire.

28

TURNAROUND

BY THE TIME TRIX ARRIVED ON THE PENTHOUSE LEVEL OF
Neville Financial Technologies, many of the attendees and
invited guests had already found ways to leave the demonstration, realising that soon they would be arrested by the
imminent authorities who were probably arriving at speed.
And, considering that many of them were likely there ille-
gally, there was probably a queue somewhere for the freight
elevator, with warlords who'd hated each other for years
reluctantly sharing carriages with each other, as long as they
got out quickly.

Even Sonia Shida was leaving as Trix entered, nodding
behind, where, standing in the middle of an almost empty
room now, Buck Neville looked over at her in utter confusion
as she arrived.

'Good luck with whatever you and Thomas are planning,'
she said.

'You could stay and help.'

'Not my fight,' Shida gave a slight bow. 'But I won't fight
you.'

'Could you at least help Marlowe with the Gravedigger? They're downstairs, killing each other.'

At this, Shida frowned.

'That's Steele,' she said. 'If I see a way to help, I will.'

This stated, she left on the now-returned elevator. Trix held little hope in the offer; Shida was likely heading straight for the car park.

She looked back at Buck Neville.

'Who the hell are you?' he asked.

'I'm the woman who's going to save your arse,' Trix replied, walking in and looking at Dovale.

'Afternoon, Wing Commander. I understand you guys have shit the bed quite badly this time.'

Dovale was still in his cockpit, although he didn't seem to be doing anything.

'There's no point continuing,' he said, his voice forlorn and broken. 'It's over.'

'It's over when I say it's over,' Trix retorted, walking over to the device with the scanner attached and leaning down. 'Let me guess, you can't stop the drones because you can't get into the system?'

One technician looked up from his tablet and nodded.

'Exactly,' he confirmed. 'Spencer Neville the Third—'

'Has hacked your system while you all high-fived your-selves over this great presentation, using stolen British mili-tary technology,' Trix replied coldly. 'Your name is?'

'Jorge.'

'Well, Jorge, you'd better monitor your data connection to the AI,' Trix grinned, 'because I'm about to save your life.'

She pulled a white plastic ball out of her pocket, wiped it carefully against her sweater, and then presented it into the scanner. Jorge stared, stunned, as it beeped twice, and then lines of data scrolled down the screen of his iPad.

'How?' Dovale whispered.

'Squadron Leader Mille,' Trix replied as he stared at her in utter amazement. 'I took a deep scan of his eye when we were at RAF Lossiemouth. I thought it might come in handy down the line.'

There were some outraged beeps from the system, as a protocol that had been let out of the box earlier was now being pushed back in.

'We're in.' Jorge was overjoyed as he looked back at the others.

'Quick, before they realise we're in, terminate the project,' Dovale, suddenly animated, ordered. 'We might have a lifeline here.'

'Won't that involve lots of drones collapsing from the sky?' Trix enquired. 'You know, with all those terrible, explosive missiles strapped to them?'

'They'll return into their failsafe mode,' Jorge reassured her, looking back at Buck Neville, who stared at them, dumbfounded. 'The only problem we've got is the one we set up for the test.'

'Why?'

'Because it was upgraded to the Devastator protocol as well, when the system was hacked,' Dovale replied. 'But it had been set off beforehand, which means it's not currently connected to the hive anymore, and it won't return to base.'

'Well then, Wing Commander,' Trix said, 'I'm afraid you're going to have to take it out. I'm guessing you know how to use the controls?'

Wing Commander Dovale stared at Trix for a long,

drawn-out moment, and then, looking back at the cockpit, he nodded.

'It's what they trained me for, after all,' he acknowledged.

'Good,' Trix nodded. 'Because while you're doing that, I need to hack an armed and pissed off AI.'

IF WALTER MCKELLAN WAS ANNOYED THAT HE HAD TO WORK with Sasha Bordeaux, within five minutes of seeing her work, he'd changed his opinion.

The woman might have been CIA and she might have been some kind of mysterious enigma who played on the fact that nobody knew who she was, but she was good. Within ten minutes of arriving at NevTech's strangely empty offices in Cupertino, she'd already bypassed three system locks and made her way to the upper levels. They'd found one guard, and before he'd even realised they were there, Bordeaux had taken him out quietly, efficiently, with some kind of move involving three fingers to his throat that even McKellan wasn't sure he could have replicated.

'You'll have to teach me that at some point,' he said.

Sasha smiled as they pulled the body to the side.

'No offence, old man, but your fingers are too brittle and they'll break the moment you try it,' she replied.

'I think you'll find I'm not as brittle as you think,' McKellan raised an eyebrow.

'Flirting with me, gramps?' Sasha shrugged. 'You're not my type.'

'Younger and bearded, perhaps?'

'I couldn't possibly say,' Sasha grinned.

The elevator was locked down, but the building was only

five storeys high. Reluctantly, McKellan nodded as Sasha opened the fire door, and the two of them made their way as quickly and as quietly as they could up the staircase.

———

BRAD HADN'T FELT SO LOW IN YEARS. HE HATED FAILURE. THE last time he'd been this bad was when his friends had started to die, when the Rubicon sleepers had taken them out and he'd been forced to run for his life, hiding out in a sleepy village in the middle of England. It was Marlowe who found him, brought him out of hiding, and in a way, it was Marlowe who returned him to the CIA, although in a weird, indentured servant version, with Sasha Bordeaux and her merry band of CIA miscreants.

But in all that time, he hadn't failed.

Sure, he'd stretched the rules a lot, but as he watched Spencer Neville punching the sky as the drones soared in the air above San Jose, small black dots that Brad knew to be almost two hundred fully armed and dangerous drones travelling to take thousands of lives, he wanted nothing more than to leap across the desk and strangle the bastard.

However, Vic Saeed, gun in hand, was making sure that would never happen.

Doctor Moritz sat back on the sofa, and Brad wasn't sure she'd even realised what had happened. The amount of painkillers and medication pumping through her system had turned her into an effective zombie. All he could do was sit and wait for his inevitable death. He still had his blade, but in a room full of guns, the blade was the weakest weapon.

Spencer was checking his phone now, laughing as he did so.

'It seems that Orchid is now contacting me to buy the item,' he said. 'The damned thing's still at my pop's, and they think I'm the one that owns it. And they don't even realise I've already been invited to join them.'

'In a way, you do own it,' Vic replied. 'The data that's come down after the Doctor there donated her retina scan must be able to be reverse-engineered. You don't actually need Broad Sword anymore. You can create your own version.'

'Which you can then pass on to Vic's Dollar Store brand of Orchid,' Brad snapped.

'Are you annoyed because we're not allowing your friends to play with us?' Vic laughed. 'You should be lucky you're still alive to watch the end of everything.'

He waved out of the window.

'This isn't really the end, you know. These drones, these are small fry. We've been preparing for this. What you're watching now is a demonstration, but not the one people were expecting. We have thousands of drones ready to go, armed, armoured and very capable indeed. Once we reverse engineer Broad Sword, the Devastator protocol will be in every single one of them.'

Spencer nodded at this.

'We will rain a level of terror upon this planet that no one has seen in generations,' he proclaimed.

'Jesus, who pissed on your chips?' Brad shook his head. 'You know what I don't like about people like you?'

He didn't continue, his head rocking back as Vic moved forward and pistol-whipped him across the face. Brad chuckled, wiping the blood from his lip, glancing to the side and pausing for a second as he saw the shadow the other side of the door.

He couldn't be sure, but it very much looked like his boss and the old guy, McKellan, moving through the other office.

'Go on then, what?' Vic asked, wiping the blood from his gun.

'No imagination,' Brad sat back with a smile.

Maybe he wasn't about to die, after all.

As Trix watched Wing Commander Dovale flying the drone from his remote-controlled cockpit, she realised just how high the stakes were here. Broad Sword had been created as the next-gen AI device that would enhance pilots' abilities. Not only that, the AI would ensure that if the pilot was indisposed, it'd be able to do the job for them, and likely better. Trix wasn't a fan of AI. She understood it was a necessary evil, but there were always points where AI itself would be the problem in the room.

Today, such a problem was happening with Dovale.

With the one hundred and ninety-eight Peacemaker drones already returning to base, Dovale only had to worry about one – a Devastator protocol drone that at one point was going to be his rival, dogfighting above the hills of Mount Hamilton, but now was already on a mission to take out what looked to be the Apple campus, further southwest, in Cupertino.

Dovale was probably quite good at being a Wing Commander, and he had hours of experience flying state-of-the-art fighters for the RAF, but he wasn't *this* good. Trix realised with a sudden, terrified realisation that the AI was too fast. It would control the situation, making the adjustments – that would take seconds for Dovale to make – in milliseconds.

It was a losing battle. The only way he could possibly win would be to sacrifice his own drone into the Devastator AI-controlled one. But the problem was, currently, he wouldn't reach it in time.

Before anybody could say anything, she rushed forward, grabbing the tablet from Jorge.

'Show me that,' she said.

'Hey,' Jorge replied, 'I don't think ...'

Trix spun and glared at him.

'I've examined this coding since before Spain,' she said. 'I looked at it in Lossiemouth. I looked at it on the way to Lossiemouth, on the way *from* Lossiemouth. I know more about this coding than probably anybody in this room, and *you're* the guys who stole it. So unless you really want to blow up one of your biggest rivals and all get arrested for the imminent act of terrorism your drone is about to perform, I'd suggest you shut the hell up and let me work.'

Jorge said nothing, and Trix quickly placed the iPad down onto the table, using the stand to place it upright, pulling out a Bluetooth keyboard from her bag and connecting it. Now she could start typing faster, working into the source code, finding what was once Broad Sword, and bringing it to the surface.

She knew she couldn't beat Broad Sword. It was AI.

She knew she couldn't stop Broad Sword. Once it had begun, it would continue until it was destroyed.

What she could do, however, was slow it down, distract it, overload the data travelling through, find it new problems to extrapolate, things that would help in some small way in making the device a little easier to take out if you were human.

Easier said than done, she thought to herself, as she started typing long lines of code into the system, uploading it as soon as she could, purely to gain an advantage.

'What's your plan, Preston?' Dovale asked from the cockpit, already sweating.

'I'm going to give Broad Sword a classic case of resource exhaustion,' she replied, glancing at Jorge's confused expression. 'It's just tech speak for making the AI brain run a marathon in flip-flops. We'll send it on a wild goose chase, calculating Fibonacci numbers to the moon and back.'

'Fibonacci numbers?'

Trix carried on working as she spoke, her fingers playing over the keyboard faster than she'd ever typed before.

'Yeah, they're like a sequence where each number is the sum of the two before it,' she explained. 'Sounds simple, but it gets mental pretty quick. This'll have Broad Sword so tied up trying to crunch these insane numbers, it'll barely notice as we sneak up and knock that drone right out of the sky.'

'She looked back at Jorge with a smile.

'It's all about distraction, mate. Keep it busy with one hand, land the knockout with the other. Pure magic.'

'And if that doesn't work?'

'We'll access a memory leak I saw when we were examining the code,' Trix replied almost casually. 'It's not when you forget to remember something. It's tech wizardry at its finest. We're gonna convince Broad Sword it's got endless space to think, but really, we're tying its shoelaces together.'

She looked up at one of the other technicians in the room, staring in shock at her.

'You need to feed it a bunch of tasks, okay?' she shouted

across the room. 'Sounds simple, barely an inconvenience to Broad Sword, but here's the kicker. Each one's like a black hole, sucking up memory and not giving it back. It's like lending cash to that mate who always "forgets" to pay you back. Before you know it, the AI's scraping the bottom of the barrel, trying to remember its own name, let alone fly a drone. We're talking serious brain fog. With that and the resource exhaustion, we should give Dovale enough of an edge here, until Marlowe can get to the device and enter the kill code.'

'Amazing,' Jorge was genuinely impressed. 'Mister Neville, you should hire this woman.'

'No offence, Jorge, but Buck Neville disappeared two minutes ago,' Trix replied, eyes locked on the screen. 'I think you should start looking for a new job yourself soon.'

29

RETRIBUTION

A GUNSHOT SHATTERED THE SILENCE OF THE NOONDAY OFFICE as Marlowe, having expected danger since the Gravedigger appeared, had just enough foresight to dive for cover behind a desk as a 300 grain jacketed hollow point .50AE round slammed into a two drawer steel filing cabinet and left it a twisted heap of scrap metal. The smell of gunpowder briefly overpowered the stale office air as the Gravedigger, a mere ghost against the thick haze of gunsmoke, advanced with calculated steps.

'A gun?' Marlowe shouted out as, his back against the cold floor, he quickly gauged his surroundings. The office layout was unknown to him, yet the generic design was all too familiar. Desks, chairs, computers – all had the possibility to be potential tools in this unexpected duel. 'A bloody Desert Eagle, too? I thought this was personal. Hell, mate, trained monkeys could kill with that cannon! So much for your sodding rep!'

The Gravedigger paused at the jibe, considering this.

'You have a suggestion?'

'No guns!' Marlowe shouted back. 'You want me dead? Fight with knives and earn it.'

There was a silence, and Marlowe almost risked popping his head over the edge of the desk he was currently hiding behind, to see if the Gravedigger had taken the bait, but knew that if the Gravedigger hadn't, he'd catch a round so big it'd tear his entire head off of his body the moment he did so. He knew Trix would be upstairs doing her job so he needed to get past this, and find the device itself. Though, if this fight was decided with gunshots, he could lose everything in a second, and the device would never receive the code.

At least with knives, he had a chance.

'Fine,' the Gravedigger's voice spoke out across the office. 'No guns.'

It was a welcome statement, but Marlowe frowned; the voice had come from somewhere else in the office area. Which meant the Gravedigger hadn't paused to consider the offer, he'd carried on flanking his target.

He could be anywhere. Marlowe needed a momentary advantage, and right now the daytime sun, complete with the fluorescent lighting strips above, didn't really help him.

Beside the desk was an extension cord, a heavy double-plug on one end, and a single plug on the other, with about six feet of cord between them. Marlowe quickly unplugged the cable, wondering if he could use it as some kind of whip or rope weapon.

'To fight with knives, I have to see you,' the Gravedigger's voice echoed around the office. 'Come out and fight me, Mister Marlowe.'

There. His first mistake. To the right, about two desks away. A movement that matched the direction of the voice.

Got you, you bastard.

Grabbing a metal pen tray from the drawers beside the desk, and with a surprisingly practiced ease, Marlowe launched it in the area where the Gravedigger was, but not at his opponent - instead, he threw it at the overhead fluorescent light. There was an explosion of light and sparks as the metal missile broke the bulb, and a semi-darkness engulfed the room, as silently, Marlowe relocated, his movements a whisper among the shadows.

He didn't want to move too far away; he needed to finish this fast, and so he navigated the makeshift battlefield, utilising desks and filing cabinets as shields from potential attacks. The semi-darkness was his ally, but at the same time, it was also his enemy, masking both hunter and prey.

Which was which Marlowe wasn't sure.

At a workstation, he paused as he found a heavy stapler, its weight promising.

'This is boring, Thomas,' the Gravedigger's voice echoed. 'If I don't see you by the count of three, I'll start shooting again.'

As the Gravedigger neared, now with the gun back in his grip, Marlowe picked up the stapler and hurled it hard at him. The throw was precise; the solid chunk of steel struck the assassin's gun hand, eliciting a loud curse and a louder roar of another massive 300 grain .50 AE round that bored its way into the ceiling.

The Gravedigger, surprised, retaliated instinctively, brushing the contents on a desk off the top, sending a keyboard towards Marlowe as he rose from his hiding position. It was a lucky shot, and struck Marlowe's temple, a sharp pain briefly clouding his vision.

The moment of distraction was all the Gravedigger needed to close the distance.

Seizing a moment, as he stumbled back against the wall, Marlowe hit the fire alarm with his elbow, the shrill sound slicing through the air, adding chaos to confusion.

'Had enough, yet, Peter?' Marlowe shouted over the din, deciding now that leveraging the psychological angle was a good way to build more irrational anger in his opponent, his voice calm and mocking. 'Did you really think you were hunting me—'

He didn't finish. His psychological angle hadn't worked, and the Gravedigger charged into him at speed, taking him off his feet. They collided in a clash of desperation and skill; Marlowe, using the environment to his advantage, manoeuvred the Gravedigger against a desk, momentarily winding him. But the Gravedigger's response was swift, a brutal elbow strike to Marlowe's ribcage, sending shockwaves of pain through his body.

In retaliation, Marlowe now used the extension cable as a whip, swinging it viciously at the assassin, the double socket connecting hard against the Gravedigger's left eye socket, sending him staggering back with a scream. Marlowe went for a second attack, but the Gravedigger caught the cable first, yanking it out of Marlowe's hand.

The duel narrowed to the sharpness of blades now; Marlowe with his familiar Samuel Staniforth Fairburn-Sykes, and the Gravedigger with his Angel Fire G10 Watchdog Karambit, their movements more cautious now, their shadows almost dancing in the dim light that filtered in from outside.

The Gravedigger was furious to be schooled in the way he had, and slashed viciously with the curved blade, while Marlowe, focused and patient, awaited his moment. It came when the Gravedigger, perhaps too eager, overextended a thrust, the blade nicking Marlowe's jacket as it passed. Seizing the opportunity, Marlowe executed a calculated kick to the Gravedigger's knee, destabilising him, while a targeted strike to the arm forced the Gravedigger to relinquish his blade.

Cornered and overpowered, the Gravedigger found himself pinned against the wall by Marlowe, the latter's arm a bar across his throat; not to kill, but to assert undeniable dominance.

'For someone who claims to be a Gravedigger,' Marlowe hissed, close to his adversary's ear, 'you're nothing more than another name on a headstone.'

Without warning, Marlowe buried the blade of his Fairbairn-Sykes into the Gravedigger's stomach, their eyes locked. Withdrawing the blood soaked blade, he wiped it casually on the Gravedigger's pant leg.

'You won't die immediately from that,' Marlowe continued. 'Although you'll need immediate medical attention. Your choice now is whether you'd rather continue this pointless fight against me and die, or save your own life.'

The fight left the Gravedigger's eyes, replaced by a grudging respect, a realisation that he had underestimated his opponent from the start.

'You said you wanted to kill me,' he croaked.

'I do, but life's too short, and I don't need the hassle,' Marlowe nodded. 'But before I forget ...'

He rammed the knife back into the shoulder of the Gravedigger's knife arm.

'That's for Monty, you wanker,' he hissed as he stepped back, again cleaning the blade on his opponent's clothing.

Marlowe stepped back and sheathed his knife, now drawing his CZ, aiming it at the Gravedigger's head.

'Tell your client you've cancelled the hit. You owe me a life, after all.'

The Gravedigger didn't say anything, instead he turned, gripping his side, now bleeding from two wounds as he limped out of the open-plan office.

Marlowe rested back against the wall and let out a breath. He really hadn't expected that to work.

But now he had another fight to continue. Taking a pencil from a desk to his side, he walked over to the Gravedigger's discarded pistol, picked it up by placing the pencil through the trigger guard, and dumped it into a manilla envelope on top of a desk, folding the end of the envelope over. He had plans for this, after all, and didn't want any prints to be smudged.

Now, looking at the elevator, seeing it'd continued down to the underground basement, he knew where he needed to be.

FOR ALL OF HIS TALK ABOUT HANGING OUT WITH WARLORDS AND terrorists, Buck Neville had never really classed himself as a criminal.

Sure, he'd skirted the line a few times, but when you were the CEO of a company that was basically financial technology, the most you would deal with was white-collar crimes.

The theft of Broad Sword, and working with Orchid, had turned out to be a massive failure. Not only had Orchid moved away from providing him with his own admission into their ranks, instead apparently passing it on to his son, they had also disappeared the moment the drones were taken over, with both Shida and Steele deserting like rats once there was a chance to make it to the elevators.

The least they could have done was help me remove the link, he thought to himself, as he exited the elevator into the car park, looking around for his chauffeur-driven limo. He needed to get to Cupertino as quickly as possible, find his son and slap some sense into his head.

Maybe I shouldn't have given him my name.

Still, things weren't as bad as they could have been. The two hundred fully armed Peacemaker drones, amped up on amphetamines and acting like meth heads on coke, were now stopped, or at least were stopping. Sure, Dovale would have to stop the last one, but one drone going wild wasn't as bad as an entire army. He had a legal team who could argue with that one.

Under his arm, he carried a plastic tube, the kind that designers would place papers into. It was about the size of an A2 document holder with a screw-top lid. It was heavier than a tube containing papers, however. This was Broad Sword, currently linked to the network, but as soon as Buck got it away from the building's Wi-Fi system, and found some kind of makeshift Faraday cage for it, with luck, he'd be able to walk away unscathed.

That was, until he saw St John Steele standing by his car, waiting for him.

St John Steele looked furious; Buck understood that. Steele had obviously assumed he'd be gaining something important today, but instead all he had was the mess that Neville's son had left.

'This isn't my fault,' Buck said quickly, holding his hands up. 'You can't hang this on me.'

'We worked for months to get this,' Steele replied coldly. 'I spent weeks convincing people to push that price up so that we would gain the best money we possibly could. Three hundred million from the CIA was nothing compared to what we were going to get. We were looking at billions upon billions here, and you screwed it up by letting your son come and play.'

'I didn't realise he was playing the game as well.'

'No,' Steele shook his head. 'You didn't realise he was playing the game *so well*.'

He walked over to Buck now, holding his hand out expectantly.

'Give me Broad Sword.'

'Wait, no,' Buck shook his head now, backing away, glancing around to see if somebody around would assist him in this. 'I spent money getting this. We've spent millions making sure that the drones—'

'You've still got the drones. And once you've removed Broad Sword's AI from them, you'll still be able to make your money back in some kind of yard sale.' Steele matched Buck; for every step he took back, Steele took a step forward, keeping the space between them the same. 'Orchid is unhappy with you.'

'Orchid's unhappy with me? I'm unhappy with goddamn Orchid! This was supposed to be my way in!' Buck grimaced, angrily kicking at the ground. 'Goddamn Delacroix shouldn't have died. This was going to be sorted, we were going to run the world.'

'And instead, you let your son try to destroy it,' Steele shook his head. 'It's over. At least if we have the Broad Sword AI, we can do something with it.'

Buck nodded reluctantly. But then his eyes glittered as he raised his head, glaring at St John Steele.

'Three hundred and one million,' he said. 'That was the price the CIA offered. You give me that, you can have this.'

'Don't be a fool,' Steele shook his head sadly. 'You know that's not going to happen now.'

'Then give me a seat at the table,' Buck pleaded. 'You owe me. I've got nothing. The moment it comes out what happened, I'm going to be destroyed.'

'That's not our problem. You had your opportunity to get where you wanted to be. Your son took it. And now, from what I can work out, he has your place within the ranks of Orchid. Will you give me Broad Sword?'

'No,' Buck's voice wasn't defiant. It was pleading, begging, hoping that Steele would reconsider and allow him to keep the toy in his hands.

St John Steele wasn't listening, though, and he certainly wasn't reconsidering any time soon. With a sigh, he drew a Sig Sauer P365 and aimed it at Buck's chest

'Such a shame,' he said, as he went to pull the trigger.

The gunshot echoed around the car park.

And then Steele dropped the gun in pain, staring at his now bleeding hand.

The round had struck the gun's barrel, shattering the weapon. And as he clutched at his bleeding fingers, Steele looked over at the elevator doors where, standing beside them, having used the staircase, was Marlowe, his CZ in hand.

'We still haven't discussed the receipt I owe you for my half-brother,' Marlowe said. 'I suggest you leave the billionaire alone.'

'I thought the Gravedigger was sorting you out,' Steele muttered. 'God knows we offered him enough.'

'Yeah, I think you'll find that contract is now void,' Marlowe smiled, walking towards them both, his CZ leading the way. 'Mister Neville, you'll be leaving Broad Sword here.'

'Or what?' Buck straightened, suddenly filled with bravado, now somebody was apparently helping him stop Steele.

'Or else I'll shoot you with Steele's other gun,' Marlowe smiled, nodding downwards at Steele's ankle. 'Yeah, I know you've got a little Sig P938 down there, and if you think I'm stupid enough to let you go for it, then by all means, give it a try.'

He turned back to Buck Neville.

'Mister Steele here killed my half-brother and tried to pin it on me,' he said. 'It's only fair I return the favour. So you have a choice, you can either give me Broad Sword, or you can die where you stand, and I frame him for it. Trust me, I won't lose a night's sleep over what you've done.'

'I've done nothing,' Buck protested.

'Richard Mille. Lisa Rutter. Nora Eskildsen. Lina Moritz,' The names came easily as Marlowe stepped closer to Buck, taking a step each time he stated a name. 'I know you worked with Charles Garner. I know you allied with Orchid to get this sorted ... but now it's over. My partner upstairs has stopped your missiles. If anything, you might be able to claim some kind of terrorist cyber-attack. What the hell, you could even throw your son under a bus. He's been trying to do that to you for the last couple of days.'

'My son—'

'Is probably right now being taken into custody by the

CIA,' Marlowe interrupted. 'If anything, he'll want what's in your hands. Do you seriously think he won't kill you to get it?'

'If you give it to Marlowe, you damn us all,' Steele said quickly. 'He's not Orchid.'

'Are you going to listen to the man who, a minute ago, was going to shoot you?' Marlowe shrugged. 'Your call, Buck. What would your dad do?'

'My father was a banker,' Buck frowned.

'I know,' Marlowe replied calmly. 'He would have been the biggest villain in the room. What would your dad have done?'

Buck looked from Steele to Marlowe, and then back to Steele again.

He sighed and then passed the tube over to Marlowe.

'He would have stayed alive to fight another day,' he said. 'And that's what I'm going to do, Mister Marlowe.'

'Good answer,' Marlowe said, turning back to Steele. 'And you? You need to go to a hospital. You can catch the same Uber as the Gravedigger.'

Before anybody could say anything, he raised his CZ and shot Steele in the thigh, staring dispassionately as the man fell to his knees, screaming in pain as he gripped at the wound.

'And that's for my brother,' he finished as, with one last disgusted look at Buck, he turned to walk away.

'Wait!' Buck shouted. 'What about my son? He still has one rogue drone! With the firepower he has, he could still take out a chunk of Apple's campus!'

Marlowe paused and looked back.

'What makes you think he's aiming at Apple?'

'Cupertino!' Buck replied. 'He's heading straight for it!'

Marlowe thought about this, and then nodded.

'True,' he said. 'He's heading towards Cupertino. But that's not the only building there.'

He winked.

'It'd be a damned shame if someone with the Broad Sword code convinced the drone the Apple campus was, in fact, another Cupertino building ... say that of NevTech?'

'But you'd need Broad Sword itself to do such a thing ...' Buck trailed off as Marlowe opened the tube, pulled out the metal brain of Broad Sword and tapped in a four-number code.

1-7-7-6

It was the year of the American War of Independence, numbers given to him by Nora Eskildsen before she died.

Her final "screw you" to the Nevilles.

'We'll say hi to your son for you,' he said as he watched the light click green, meaning access was now redirected to Trix. He closed the tube again, and walked off towards the elevator. 'You'll be able to go pick him up soon. He'll be all over the car park.'

MANY FLOORS ABOVE THE CAR PARK, TRIX RECEIVED A MESSAGE on the screen, and pumped her fist into the air.

'Wing Commander, stand down,' she said, entering code into the system. 'You've kept it busy long enough, and I now have full access.'

'But if I stop attacking, the drone will get away!' Dovale looked around in horror. 'It'll carry on with its target!'

'I know,' Trix grinned. 'But that's been prepared for. Marlowe just regained Broad Sword itself, and we have full control once more.'

As Dovale reluctantly turned his drone away from the confrontation, Trix tapped a number on her phone, holding it to her ear as she watched the data on the screen shift and swirl, as the lone Devastator protocol drone continued on its new trajectory.

'McKellan, it's Preston,' she said. 'If you're going to do something, I'd suggest doing it now, because you've got about three minutes before all hell breaks loose there.'

30

ENDGAME

In NevTech's Cupertino offices, everything was chaos.

Spencer Neville the Third, seeing his dreams collapsing to nothing, was furious, blaming his father's lack of ambition, spitting out angrily how "he'd buckled under the strain, while Spencer would never have done this", while forcing his two loyal technicians to do what they could to regain any semblance of control over the drones.

Doctor Moritz, meanwhile, had apparently awoken from her stupor and sat on the sofa, chuckling to herself.

'I could have done this for you,' she replied mockingly. 'I could have fixed this in an instant if you hadn't shot up the scanner system.'

'Shut your mouth!' Spencer screamed at her. 'Shut your whore mouth!'

Brad had risen from his chair while the chaos was happening and, with Vic's gun still trained on him, had been allowed to walk over to the window, where he stared out over Cupertino and San Jose.

'We've got a drone coming towards us,' he said.

'It's not coming towards us,' Spencer snapped back. 'It's going to take out the Apple Campus. At least we'll get something out of this.'

One of the technicians, looking up, paled.

'Sir,' he whispered, 'Mister Haynes is right, it's not going to Apple, it's coming straight for us.'

As he looked around and saw the terrified expressions across the office, Brad started to laugh.

'Looks like when they took over the drones, they worked out the controls,' he said. 'I wonder if they've allowed the Wing Commander to fly that one personally at us.'

Spencer turned around to scream expletives at him, but Vic Saeed had already decided he'd had enough and stormed over to Brad.

'Time for you to end,' he hissed, raising the weapon, aiming it directly at Brad's face.

But Brad had been waiting for this.

He'd known, having seen them a couple of times out of the corner of his eye now, that both McKellan and Sasha were outside the office, waiting for a moment to strike. Knowing they'd come through the main office door on the right, he'd deliberately moved to the left, constantly monitoring the layout of the office.

Spencer was by the window to his right, Doctor Moritz was on a sofa at the back. There were two technicians who wouldn't be any problem at all and two guards who looked just as terrified as the technicians did, but were now distracted by what was going on with Vic and Brad on the other side. By moving left across the office and allowing Vic to aim the gun at him, Brad had effectively diverted all attention away from the right-hand side entrance where, as Vic raised his gun to aim at Brad's face, McKellan and Sasha, guns in hand, now burst into the office.

'Guns down!' Sasha shouted. 'Guns down on the floor!'

The two guards turned at this sudden change in situation. The Special Forces guy who had punched Brad on the plane was the first to react, but he wasn't quick enough, and caught a round in the throat from Sasha, then fell to the floor, grabbing at his neck as he bled out on the carpet. McKellan, meanwhile, fired at the other guard and caught him in the shoulder, spinning him around and relieving him of his weapon. McKellan's sudden appearance had clearly spooked Vic, who hadn't expected to see his, technically ex-boss, appear out of nowhere.

It was instant pandemonium, and that was all Brad needed. He flicked the big Kershaw folding knife open and spun on Vic, who'd lost his focus as all hell had broken loose. He swept a devastating cut across the wrist of Vic's gun hand and a second to the shoulder, causing him to lose the weapon. Reversing his grip on the knife, he stepped inside Vic's guard and delivered a vicious butt strike to the man's temple. Blood fountained from both wounds as Vic collapsed, out cold and bleeding.

'As I said,' Brad muttered down at him now. 'You're too small to play with the big boy toys.'

McKellan, meanwhile, had rounded up the two technicians and the lone surviving guard, the Special Forces guard having already bled out on the floor, pulling them towards the door of the office.

'We need to get out now,' he said, pointing with the gun in hand at the drone approaching the building. 'That drone is turning up with God knows what ammunition attached to blow the shit out of us and there's no way it's going to stop.'

'It was supposed to destroy Apple,' Spencer whined to himself, reluctantly turning to walk away from the window. Ignored in all the confusion, Doctor Moritz had quietly risen, walked over to where Vic Saeed had fallen and picked up his discarded Glock. She turned and aimed the pistol in a firm grip, squarely at the billionaire's son.

'You're not going anywhere,' she said coldly. 'You're going to stay right here with a perfect view of everything that happens.'

'Doctor Moritz—' McKellan started, but paused as Doctor Moritz spun on him, gun raised.

'He took my eye,' she said. 'He killed my wife, he destroyed my career. I'll never be able to live my life again. I'll have to go into protection, change my name, change my job, always looking over my shoulder, in case someone's looking to force me to build another Broad Sword. The one-eyed scientist who can never teach again, who's lost her entire world because of this arrogant bastard.'

She shook her head.

'I'm not leaving, but I suggest you go quickly,' she repeated as she looked out of the window, and following her gaze, Brad saw the drone was getting closer. 'I'd say you have a minute and a half before this entire building floor turns into ash.'

'I get what you're saying, and I respect your choice,' McKellan replied, looking over at Sasha. 'You have a problem with this?'

'Not one that means we have to stay up here,' Sasha was already herding the technicians out of the door. 'Tick tock, old man.'

Chuckling, McKellan eventually nodded at Brad.

'Would you like to bring my rogue agent with you, please?'

Brad looked down at Vic, clutching at his side, groaning, and sighed reluctantly.

'Do I have to?' he asked. 'I'd really like this guy to blow up, too.'

'I'm afraid he needs to come back to London,' McKellan replied. 'Trust me, it won't be a happy ending for him.'

Brad muttered to himself as he pulled the groaning Vic Saeed up to his feet. He knew things weren't going to go well for the turncoat. He'd had his opportunity to create his own future, failed miserably, and now it looked like Vic Saeed's time had run out. Brad almost felt sorry for the man. It would have been an easier ending for him to blow up with his new boss. However, that wasn't to be the end of his story, so with McKellan pulling the injured guard through the door, and Sasha corralling the technicians, Brad pulled the groaning Vic to the door. Before he left, he paused and looked back at Lina Moritz, gun aimed directly at Spencer.

'Are you sure about this?' he asked.

'Go,' Moritz replied, nodding. 'You have less than a minute to get down a few floors before the upper levels get utterly destroyed.'

At this, Brad went to leave, stopped, and then turned and saluted her.

He didn't know what else to do.

Then, dragging the bleeding Vic Saeed with him, Brad Haynes ran for the stairs.

Spencer Neville the Third started to chuckle.

'I don't know what your plan is, but it's failed,' he said arrogantly. 'They're not going to let the missiles strike the building. They'll stop it. It's over, nothing more's gonna happen.'

He turned to face Doctor Moritz now, and his face turned into a sneer.

'And then when they *do* stop it? You'll have to decide if you're going to kill me yourself or not. I don't think you've got it in you, you're too much of an academic. So, then? I'll take that gun off you, shoot out your remaining eye and make you eat one last bull—'

Her eyes cold and emotionless, Doctor Lina Moritz pulled the trigger of Vic Saeed's gun, still aimed at Spencer. He felt the bullet punch him in his shoulder, spinning him around and sending him down to his knees.

'That's better,' Moritz said calmly, lowering the weapon. 'I enjoy seeing you on your knees as you wait for your death.'

Spencer muttered something likely insulting and equally arrogant as usual, but so soft she didn't hear. Instead of asking what it was, she walked over, grabbed the groaning man roughly by the shoulders, ignoring his yelps of pain as her nails crept into where the bullet had gone, and spun him to face the window and the approaching drone.

'Open your eyes and see what you have reaped,' she said. 'This is for Nora, you son of a bitch.'

Spencer went to reply, probably to say some witty and insulting response, but he didn't get his chance, as before the words could leave his mouth, the Peacekeeper drone running the Devastator protocol and armed to the teeth with AGM-114R9X Hellfire Missiles with kinetic warheads with pop-out blades, AIM-9X Sidewinders, GBU-38 Joint Direct Attack Munition for ground assaults, and GBU-12 Paveways, fired the entirety of its arsenal in one go at the NevTech building's management level.

The explosion was heard across town.

Strangely though, apart from anybody trapped on that floor, of which nothing would ever be found, there were no casualties.

Spencer Neville the Third and Doctor Lina Moritz were vaporised immediately.

BRAD, MCKELLAN, SASHA AND THEIR CAPTIVES WERE ALREADY three storeys lower as the building shook and the sprinklers popped open, soaking them as they continued to the basement level. Brad paused, glancing back upwards. He wasn't annoyed that Spencer Neville the Third was dead, but that Lina Moritz had stayed to finish the job had caught him by surprise, and once more he had the feeling that somehow, he'd failed her.

'Come on,' Sasha shouted. 'If we're any slower, the building's probably gonna collapse on us.'

Brad gave a weak smile and continued down the stairs, pushing Vic in front of him.

'You always give me the best scenarios,' he said.

31

EPILOGUE

AND, JUST LIKE THAT, IT WAS OVER.

With the destruction of NevTech in Cupertino, the recent disappearance of Buck Neville, believed to be on the run for the murder of his son at the Cupertino offices, the mounting costs of the federal case against him, and the return of one hundred and ninety-nine Peacekeeper drones at the car park outside of the Neville Financial Technologies office, chaos ensued.

As the authorities arrived in force, mainly composed of local police, FBI, NSA, and CIA agents, all claiming complete and utter dominion over the situation, Marlowe and Trix decided it was time to disappear. Dovale, although in the end a hero, who had helped delay the drone long enough for Trix to change its direction was still part of the group that'd created this whole mess in the first place, and was arrested and taken into custody by terrifying-looking suited men. He wouldn't be returning to the RAF anytime soon, although Marlowe later heard that McKellan had asked for his extradition to the UK so he could be tried for his part in the deaths of Lisa Rutter and Richard Mille, alongside the recently arrested Charles Garner.

Marlowe had felt sorry for Dovale for about ten seconds, before he remembered all the other bad shit the man had done, and how he had sold out his country for money. And then he felt better about seeing the bastard hung out to dry.

St John Steele and the Gravedigger had never arrived at the hospital, and if Marlowe was being brutally honest with himself, he hadn't expected them to. He knew that there would be a dozen off-book surgeons within a stone's throw of the building who could have patched them up, either coming to each of them, or to be travelled to. Marlowe wasn't even sure if the two men would have gone together, although if they did, Marlowe would have loved to have been a fly on the way for *that* tense conversation. Still, against all odds, and in a way against Marlowe's hopes and wishes, they were both alive, for the moment.

Marlowe didn't know when he would see either of them again, but he knew the meetings would be inevitable, which was fine, as far as he was concerned. Both men had gone against him, and both men had come up short. The Gravedigger would think twice before deciding that Marlowe was still worth his time, aware he now owed Marlowe a life debt, perhaps deciding to focus instead on rebuilding a reputation that he could, after all, be proud of.

Whereas Marlowe still had a debt he owed the Gravedigger. And that debt would be made good eventually, as would all debts owed over Monty Barnes.

They had returned to London on McKellan's jet, this time just the three passengers: Marlowe, Trix, and McKellan. Both Dovale and Vic Saeed would be brought on a different transport, one that had far fewer plush seats, and way more guns aimed at them. On landing, Marlowe had given his excuses and disappeared before the briefing with Karolides. He knew he'd have to give her a briefing at some point, but McKellan had Broad Sword now, and would pass it back to her later that day so he could give the bloody debriefing instead. And, as far as Karolides was concerned, she'd be holding all of this over Robertson, the new Defence Secretary, and definitely making sure that Charles Baker knew she was the one who saved his arse. Karolides' career was once more on the up.

What they didn't know was that Marlowe had kept his promise to Nora Eskildsen and Lina Moritz; the data inside Broad Sword had been corrupted by Trix on his request, the legacy protocols no longer able to function in any way. It was nothing more than a very pretty tube of tech, and no amount of reverse engineering would fix it.

Which was for the best, as far as he was concerned.

Marlowe's return to his onetime church apartment saw him spending the next week decompressing from the events that had unfolded in Spain, Scotland, and California, while replacing both the small pane of leaded glass the Gravedigger had shot out, and more security on the roof of the building next door. One thing the Gravedigger had done was expose a potential chink in the defence armour, and Marlowe was grateful for that, as he also made sure the clear lines of sight the window gave into his main living area were now blocked with tall items or lamps, deliberately positioned to break up the view.

Unless they had a thermal sniper, that was. And if they did, he'd be screwed, anyway.

He also remembered a line the Gravedigger had spoken in the Dominican Republic about the apartment.

'I could have taken you out at any moment, whether it was in the nave, in your mezzanine bed area, or in whatever you've placed in the crypt, out of prying eyes. Thermal imaging shows all lies, Mister Marlowe. Once you're dead, perhaps I'll go and have a look. Maybe some of the stock that you have down there will repay the heinous crime you have done to my reputation.'

The Gravedigger was alive and knew about the crypt.

Maybe it hadn't been the brightest of ideas, leaving him alive, but Marlowe had been in a hurry, and the Gravedigger, for all his flaws, seemed to be an honourable man. That said, Marlowe decided to upgrade the door into the crypt room, spending a good few days with thick metal sheeting and high-end welding equipment, as he beefed up both doors to that reminiscent of a survival shelter, with far better locks to get through.

Oddly, this more than anything reminded him of his mother's own vault, one she'd had in the back garden that'd been destroyed when he was on the run during the Rubicon case. There was a case to be made that this meant he was as crazy paranoid as she was, but you were only paranoid if they weren't out to get you, so Marlowe felt he was all right on this.

For the moment, anyway.

On the sixth day, Alexander Curtis visited him.

'I'm taking over the London desk next week,' he said by

introduction as Marlowe opened the large church door, walking past him into the apartment. 'I'd like you to return.'

'Wow, Thomas, I love what you've done with the place,' Marlowe replied mockingly as he closed the door. 'You don't need me. You have enough loyal drones.'

'Not all so loyal, it seems,' Curtis walked over to the kitchen area, rummaging through the cupboards. 'Where do you keep your vodka? Surely you've not gone bloody teetotal on me.'

Marlowe didn't want to mention the good stuff was downstairs, so found a bottle and two glasses, passing a glass of neat vodka over to his onetime boss.

Curtis toasted him.

'You heard about Saeed?'

'That he's a treasonous piece of shit? I knew that already.'

'No, he's been let off,' Curtis shook his head. 'Claims he was sent in by Robertson himself, as a sleeper agent against Neville, and that he would never have actively killed a CIA agent.'

Marlowe almost choked on the vodka.

'So, he's an undercover Orchid spy, and he's an undercover Neville ally?' He shook his head. 'Brad should have killed him when he had a chance. Or McKellan should have demanded he come with us, and we could have tossed him out over the Atlantic.'

'Either way, he's out of the Security Service,' Curtis sipped at the vodka. 'We'll have him on admin leave while he recovers, and then there'll be a shakeup. Robertson's already asked for him to work in Whitehall while recuperating.'

'Robertson sounds like Orchid, and the wrong kind of Orchid,' Marlowe muttered darkly.

'I thought you might have been able to confirm or deny

that,' Curtis said apologetically. 'It's come out that some of the London deals that Garner made, the ones that gave him the cash to open the clubs in Scotland, were done through Russell Robertson's pre-Westminster companies. He was likely Orchid well before he became an MP.'

'And as the new Minister for Defence, he could have had hands-on access to Broad Sword,' Marlowe nodded to himself. 'Do we know his plan?'

'No, and he's too big right now to take down,' Curtis said. 'Of course, off the books …'

Marlowe chuckled.

'You want me to take him out,' he answered. 'I'll look into him. But I'm not coming back.'

'I heard McKellan offered you a transfer and a promotion if you went over the wall to MI6?'

'I turned him down, too,' Marlowe smiled. 'I don't play well with others.'

Curtis finished the glass and placed it on the counter, rising from the breakfast bar stool as he did so.

'When you're bored with the vigilante crap and want to come back, call me,' he said with a nod. 'After all, you owe us now.'

'And how do you see that?' Marlowe asked after him, but Curtis was already at the door.

'One last thing, it seems Broad Sword doesn't work anymore,' he smiled as he turned back to Marlowe. 'Robertson's spitting bullets. Good work.'

And with that Curtis left, closing it behind him.

Marlowe shook his head and went to place Curtis's glass in the sink, but paused as he noticed the folded piece of paper under it, obviously secreted there by Curtis before he left.

Opening it up, he read the note.

Thought you'd want this.

Under the line of text was an address, a phone number and a name.

Raymond "Razor" Gibson.

Marlowe looked back to the door with a smile.

'Now that's a hell of a good recruitment technique,' he muttered to himself as, note in hand, he adjourned to his downstairs apartment.

After all, there was work to do.

RAZOR GIBSON HAD GONE UP IN THE WORLD NOW FAR FROM HIS Loughton address. Since agreeing to bring his talents to Arun Nadal's team, he now lived in a three-bedroom townhouse off Olympic Park in Stratford. It was a high tech, burglar-proof address, which he used mainly to rest his head, usually after he finished partying each night into the early morning.

It took Marlowe less than a minute to break the locks and disconnect the security system. So, when Razor arrived alone around four-thirty in the morning, the sight of Marlowe sitting there, gun in hand in his favourite armchair, was not what he'd expected.

Marlowe smiled coldly.

'Morning, Razor,' he said. 'Take a seat.'

He motioned to the sofa with the gun. It wasn't his CZ, instead it was an absolutely huge Desert Eagle. Picked up in

Silicon Valley, licensed to a Peter Jericho, the Gravedigger, and to make sure there wasn't any DNA or fingerprint evidence on it, Marlowe had worn latex gloves while holding the weapon.

Within seconds of noting Marlowe, Raymond knew how this was likely to go, and to his credit, he didn't step back, puffing out his chest and straightening his shoulders.

'I know why you're here,' he said. 'It was the old man, wasn't it?'

'The guy who took him out,' Marlowe nodded. 'He told me you were the one who aimed him at Monty Barnes. You're aware Monty died because of that?'

'Yeah,' Razor shrugged. 'Couldn't give a shit.'

'You know what? I believe you,' Marlowe said. 'And I respect that. Which is why I'm making this quick.'

'Making what qui—'

Razor stopped talking as soon as Marlowe fired, the massive 300 grain round hitting Raymond "Razor" Gibson in the chest, dead centre. Marlowe had considered shooting him in the face, but he knew the sadness one could have when unable to recognise the person you were burying. And he knew from their last meeting that Raymond Gibson would have a grieving mother and sister.

His eyes dead and glassy, the slightest of surprised expressions on his face, the corpse of Razor Gibson crumpled to the floor as if his strings had been cut.

Marlowe rose from the chair and stared down at the body, nodded to himself, and then tossed the Desert Eagle to the floor. As far as anybody would be concerned, the Gravedigger had returned to tie up a loose end, and that was exactly how Marlowe wanted it.

There you go, Monty.

Pulling off his latex gloves, Marlowe stuffed them in his pocket as he exited the townhouse and walked the two streets to his burgundy Jaguar XS, deep in thought.

Broad Sword might have been over, and Razor Gibson might now be dead, but Marlowe had the sinking feeling that things were only just beginning.

But that was fine.

Because he was ready to get started.

Tom Marlowe will return in his next thriller

ROGUE SIGNAL

Order Now at Amazon:

Mybook.to/roguesignal

Released 14th October, 2024

Gain up-to-the-moment information on the release by signing up to the Jack Gatland VIP Reader's Club!

Join at http://bit.ly/jackgatlandVIP

ACKNOWLEDGEMENTS

When you write a series of books, you find that there are a ton of people out there who help you, sometimes without even realising, and so I wanted to say thanks.

There are people I need to thank, and they know who they are, including my brother Chris Lee, Jacqueline Beard MBE, who has copyedited all my books since the very beginning, editor Sian Phillips and weapon specialist Eben Atwater, all of whom have made my books way better than they have every right to be.

Also, I couldn't have done this without my growing army of ARC and beta readers, who not only show me where I falter, but also raise awareness of me in the social media world, ensuring that other people learn of my books.

But mainly, I tip my hat and thank you. *The reader.* Who once took a chance on an unknown author in a pile of Kindle books, and thought you'd give them a go, and who has carried on this far with them, as well as the spin off books I now release.

I write these books for you. And with luck, he'll keep on solving them for a very long time.

Jack Gatland / Tony Lee,
   London, May, 2024

ABOUT THE AUTHOR

Jack Gatland is the pen name of *#1 New York Times Bestselling Author* Tony Lee, who has been writing in all media for thirty-five years, including comics, graphic novels, middle grade books, audio drama, TV and film for *DC Comics, Marvel, BBC, ITV, Random House, Penguin USA, Hachette* and a ton of other publishers and broadcasters.

These have included licenses such as *Doctor Who, Spider Man, X-Men, Star Trek, Battlestar Galactica, MacGyver,* BBC's *Doctors, Wallace and Gromit* and *Shrek,* as well as work created with musicians such as *Iron Maiden, Bruce Dickinson, Ozzy Osbourne, Joe Satriani* and *Megadeth.*

As Tony, he's toured the world talking to reluctant readers with his 'Change The Channel' school tours, and lectures on screenwriting and comic scripting for *Raindance* in London.

As Jack, he's written several book series now - a police procedural featuring *DI Declan Walsh and the officers of the Temple Inn Crime Unit,* a spinoff featuring "cop for criminals" *Ellie Reckless and her team,* a third espionage spinoff series featuring burnt MI5 agent *Tom Marlowe,* an action adventure series featuring conman-turned-treasure hunter *Damian Lucas,* and a standalone novel set in a New York boardroom.

An introvert West Londoner by heart, he lives with his wife Tracy and dog Fosco, just outside London.

Feel free to follow Jack on all his social media by clicking on the links below. Over time these can be places where we can engage, discuss Declan, Ellie, Tom and others, and put the world to rights.

Want more books by Jack Gatland? Turn the page...

LETTER FROM THE DEAD

"BY THE TIME YOU READ THIS, I WILL BE DEAD..."

A TWENTY YEAR OLD MURDER...
A PRIME MINISTER LEADERSHIP BATTLE...
A PARANOID, HOMELESS EX-MINISTER...
AN EVANGELICAL PREACHER WITH A SECRET...

DI DECLAN WALSH HAS HAD BETTER FIRST DAYS...

AVAILABLE ON AMAZON / KINDLEUNLIMITED

THE THEFT OF A **PRICELESS** PAINTING...
A GANGSTER WITH A **CRIPPLING DEBT**...
A **BODY COUNT** RISING BY THE HOUR...

AND ELLIE RECKLESS IS CAUGHT IN THE MIDDLE.

JACK GATLAND

PAINT
— THE —
DEAD

A 'COP FOR CRIMINALS' ELLIE RECKLESS NOVEL

A NEW PROCEDURAL CRIME SERIES WITH
A TWIST - FROM THE CREATOR OF THE
BESTSELLING 'DI DECLAN WALSH' SERIES

AVAILABLE ON AMAZON / KINDLE UNLIMITED

Made in United States
North Haven, CT
01 June 2024

53185124R00233